DELTA OF CASSIOPEIA

Also by Ted Morrissey

Fiction
The Artist Spoke
Mrs Saville
First Kings and Other Stories
The Curvatures of Hurt
Crowsong for the Stricken
Weeping with an Ancient God
An Untimely Frost
Figures in Blue
Men of Winter

Scholarship
A Concise Summary and Analysis of The Mueller Report
Trauma Theory as a Method for Understanding Literary Texts
The 'Beowulf' Poet and His Real Monsters

DELTA OF CASSIOPEIA

COLLECTED STORIES AND SONNETS

TED MORRISSEY

TWELVE WINTERS

a literary project

Delta of Cassiopeia Copyright © 2023 Ted Morrissey

This is a work of fiction. Names, characters, places, and incidents either are the product of the author's imagination or are used fictitiously. Any resemblance to actual persons, living or dead, events, or locales is entirely coincidental. All rights reserved. No part of this book may be used or reproduced in any manner whatsoever without written permission except in the case of brief quotations embodied in critical articles and reviews.

Published by Twelve Winters, a literary project.

P. O. Box 414 • Sherman, Illinois 62684-0414 • twelvewinters.com

Delta of Cassiopeia: Collected Stories and Sonnets was first published by Twelve Winters in 2023. It is also available in other editions.

Cover and interior page design by the author.

Cover art copyright © 2023 Ted Morrissey. All rights reserved.

ISBN
978-1-7331949-9-0

Printed in the United States of America

*For Melissa, always.
And for my students,
past, present and future.*

One sentence, divinely composed, goes on and on
like the biblical proverbs, the couplets of Pope, or
the witticisms of Wilde.

— WILLIAM H. GASS

CONTENTS

Introduction

Delta of Cassiopeia

I'VE BEEN WANTING to publish a collection like this for a long while, and nearly did so in 2012. The plans with my publisher at the time fell through, which, in retrospect, was for the best. It was the proverbial spark that ignited what had been a long-standing urge to start my own press. The difficulty that I'd had finding outlets for my fiction, especially novels, and the frustrations that I encountered once such outlets were found prompted me to undertake Twelve Winters Press. I based the concept and the mission of Twelve Winters on that of the legendary Hogarth Press, created by Leonard and Virginia Woolf to not only publish her avant-garde fiction but the forward-thinking work of other writers who would become known as modernists.

In the decade since I began Twelve Winters, I have published several of my books in addition to novels, story collections, poetry collections and children's books by other authors who encountered many of the same obstacles and disappointments that I did. None of us, to be sure, have become household names. In fact, Twelve Winters loses money every year, and I have kept it afloat by underwriting it with the money I've made as a teacher and librarian. Twelve Winters is not uniquely unsuccessful, from a financial standpoint (there are, thankfully, other ways to measure success). Book publishing has been an increasingly difficult business in, let's say, the last thirty years or so. With the rise in popularity of television, then the internet, then the combining of them via streaming services (like Netflix and Hulu etc., etc., etc.), the number of people who are avid readers has declined at a steeper and steeper angle.

The writers and publishers of serious (or challenging, experimental, avant-garde, artful—choose your adjective) fiction have always attracted a small share of the reading audience, and now it's a small share of what itself is a small share of the entertainment audience. The critic Steven Moore writes eloquently about the challenges facing what he calls "innovative" fiction in the introduction to volume I of his brilliant *The Novel: An Alternative History*. He quotes the Yugoslav writer Dubravka Ugrešić: "Nowadays, writers who cannot adapt to commercial demands end up in their own personal ghetto of anonymity and poverty."

In this introduction I will expound, from time to time, on this topic (a writer's personal ghetto of anonymity and poverty), but I also direct you to my blog for related papers I've delivered, specifically "Writing Too Good to Publish" and "The Loss of the Literary Voice and Its Consequences." These papers speak more to the state of *book* publishing, and not so much to *story* publishing, which is my focus here.

For now let me return to the business at hand: this collection of stories and sonnets, which I've titled by borrowing from James Joyce (more regarding this in a bit). The stories here began appearing in the early 1990s, and the lion's share were written and published in the early 2000s. Others have been written much more recently, within the last few years. Some appeared in well-known (or at least well-respected) journals (like *Glimmer Train Stories*, *Paris Transcontinental* and *The Chariton Review*), while others found homes in more obscure venues. Well-known or not, nearly all of them have ceased publication (and perhaps have been defunct for many years)—such is the way with literary journals. Therefore, without my collecting them and publishing the pieces as a book, they would, in essence, disappear, as if they had never been written. They may still.

It is perhaps doubly fortuitous that my first attempt at publishing a collection fell through. In addition to spurring me to found Twelve Winters, it also allowed the collection to grow, to mature, and (I believe) to become more meaningful (to me, if no one else). The situation is not unlike Joyce's collection *Dubliners*, in that when originally accepted for publication it consisted of fewer stories than the version that eventually came out in 1914. The years of close calls and publishing disappointments allowed *Dubliners* to grow by three stories, including the masterpiece "The Dead."

Similarly, had I managed to publish a collection in 2012, it would be missing several of the stories that are included here and all of the sonnets—and thus it would be absent, in my view, my best work to date.

I realize I've already compared myself, at least indirectly, to Virginia Woolf and James Joyce and that I risk being seen as arrogant. It's not a label I would aspire to, but all art requires an element of self-confidence, of ego. Artists must believe they have something worth saying, some perspective that is worthwhile, if they're going to share their art with the public. I suppose the writer who has no desire to publish, or the painter no desire to show and so on, could be said to be creating art without an element of ego. But most artists create with the idea that they will share their art with someone, somehow, sometime, somewhere. And if the sharing is an act of ego, it is also an act of courage. To share one's art is to make oneself vulnerable.

Perhaps the writer who self-publishes is the most vulnerable (and therefore the most courageous?). Unlike other art forms, there remains a stigma attached to self-publication, the idea being the writer who self-publishes is lesser somehow than one whose work is brought out by someone else. Meanwhile, the band that establishes its own record label, the artist who opens their own gallery, the fashion designer who establishes their own line, the architect who creates their own firm, the entrepreneur who begins their own business . . . they are all brave, forward-looking, independent, risk-taking rebels. But the writer who puts out their own work, as they want it presented to the world, is an amateurish hack in many eyes.

Yet there is a long and proud tradition of self- and self-funded publication. I've already mentioned Virginia Woolf's Hogarth Press (a classic example), and I've alluded to Joyce's *Dubliners*, whose eventual publisher only agreed to bring out the controversial collection if Joyce purchased enough copies himself to guarantee that the house would at least break even. A much-abridged list of other self-publishers (in some form or another) includes Edgar Allan Poe, Emily Brontë, Anne Brontë, Charles Dickens, Herman Melville, Walt Whitman, Samuel Clemens, Emily Dickinson and Anaïs Nin.

Profoundly aware of the stigma attached to self-publication, I deliberately attempted to make the first few books of my own that I published via Twelve Winters appear to be published by someone else. That is, I didn't assert credit as the book designer and cover designer. However, with *Crowsong for the Stricken* (2017) I began stepping from behind the curtain, and with 2018's *Mrs Saville* I fully embraced my books as wholly my own creative efforts. The advantage of being my own publisher (as well as design department, not to mention marketing department) is that I can integrate every aspect of the book into a single artistic vision. When working with other publishers, one must compromise with editors, graphic designers, and illustrators. The book becomes a group effort, for better or (not infrequently) for worse.

I prefer to have control over every element. This independence has allowed me to develop book designs that likely would not have been embraced by publishers of a more traditional bent. With *Crowsong*, for example, I printed each episode's epigraph in mirror-image, and included the page number only on every fifth page (as one might number every fifth line of a poem). With *Mrs Saville*, a sequel to *Frankenstein*, I designed it in the epistolary motif of Mary Shelley's original. I included in *The Artist Spoke* my own photography that only indirectly connects to the plot of the novel; in essence, the photos communicate a narrative of their own. In the hardcover edition of *The Artist Spoke*, the photographs are reproduced in color, an expense that practically no other publisher would have approved (probably prudently).

While writing a new work I begin to think about the eventual design, including the cover image. It's not uncommon for me to have those elements largely worked out before the writing is done, sometimes years before. Of course, I'm open to revising those design plans as the book evolves.

For this collection, I've opted to keep the design simple. As you'll see, I view the contents as four distinct parts; and only a plainspoken design harmonizes with all four sections. For the cover image, I scrolled through thousands of my photos until I found one that I think captures the mood of the collection as a whole, including its title, which was a late choice. I had been considering an "and Other Stories" sort of title. Then I was re-reading *Ulysses* (I reread it often, in part because I teach a course in *Ulysses*), and a scene in "Proteus" seemed especially apropos to the spirit of this thing I was creating.

In the episode, Stephen Dedalus is strolling along Sandy-mount Strand (actually at the moment he is seated on a rock) when he is suddenly inspired to write a poem, which he scribbles on a piece of paper torn from a letter he is carrying. He thinks, "Who ever anywhere will read these written words? Signs on a white field. Somewhere to someone in your flutiest voice." The passage seems to capture the writer's need to write without knowing who, if anyone, will read their work. Ultimately, it is not the reading of it that matters; it is the writing itself. I also like Joyce's phrase "in your flutiest voice," that is, your most poetic, your most musical, your most artistic voice. (I'll return to this idea.)

Earlier in this same paragraph, Stephen, considering the image of his shadow on the beach, thinks, "Darkly they are there behind this light, darkness shining in the brightness, delta of Cassiopeia, worlds." Joyce refers to the constellation Cassiopeia and its delta four times in *Ulysses*, and in typical Joycean fashion the image carries a complex of multiple and multiplying meanings. For me, though, in this moment on Sandymount Strand, "delta of Cassiopeia" evokes the idea of the worlds created through fictive imagination, and the fact that these worlds—no matter how expertly drawn by the writer—will always come (only come) to their fullest fruition via the participation of the reader. Behind every meaning deliberately constructed by the writer, there will be shadow meanings awaiting each individual reader. In fact, there are shadow meanings unknown, consciously, to writers themselves.

By titling this collection *Delta of Cassiopeia*, I want to emphasize these key aspects of the writing/reading process: that meaning-making is a joint enterprise of the writer and reader; and that there are meanings in the text not even the writer is aware of. As my literary idol William H. Gass expressed it, "You hope that the amount of meaning that you can pack into a book will always be more than you are capable of consciously understanding. Otherwise, the book is likely to be as thin as you are. You have to trick your medium into doing far better than you, as a conscious and clearheaded person, might manage." One of my pleasures in bringing together this collection has been reading pieces that I haven't looked at since the near-miss of the 2012 collection, which was more than a decade ago—and *then* I hadn't read some of the stories in a decade or more. With the benefit of temporal distance, I see meanings and impetuses that were hidden from me when I was writing them originally. Oftentimes it is truly like reading the work of another writer; and, in a very genuine sense, I *was* another writer, another person.

I also like the phrase "delta of Cassiopeia" for the book's title because in the paragraph in which it first appears Stephen Dedalus is compelled to write as if a slave to his creative process, to his Muse, if you will. This is a phenomenon, a feeling, a compulsion that most writers understand. I certainly do. That is, I've written these stories and sonnets because I *must*; in essence I had no choice in the matter. William Gass spoke to this aspect of the writing process as well, saying, "The contemporary American writer is in no way a part of the social and political scene. . . . Whatever work he does must proceed from a reckless inner need. The world does not beckon, nor does it greatly reward. . . . Serious writing must nowadays be written for the sake of the art." I must underscore that Gass's "nowadays" was 1976. The situation as he describes it has only grown more acute since then.

Indeed, Gass famously quipped (well, famous in certain circles) that he hoped the novel he was writing, *The Tunnel*, "will be such a good book no one will want to publish it." Already, in 1971, Gass saw the handwriting on the wall: There was an inverse correlation between the quality of writing and the odds of finding a publisher; and that, of course, was due to the dearth of readers wanting truly well-written material. In the last half century, the situation has only gotten worse for writers of serious, challenging, experimental, avant-garde, artful, innovative books.

Thus I offer *Delta of Cassiopeia* to the world with the full understanding that in all likelihood practically no one will read these stories and sonnets, at least not now. I will be upfront and acknowledge that one of my motivations for bringing out this work, as well as every other, is the hope that one day they will find an appreciative audience of more than a handful of readers. It may take decades or centuries or millennia; or it may never happen. Regardless, like Stephen Dedalus on the strand, I'm compelled to keep writing, to proceed from my reckless inner need, as Gass phrased it.

Recently I had the realization that my attitude regarding for whom I write has shifted. I used to imagine idealized readers who would be drawn to my fiction because they wanted a book with more meat on the bone than the typical page-turning bestseller. Slowly I've come to understand that about the only people who will read my books are paid reviewers and contest judges. I feel like the farm kids who devotedly raise a piglet or calf or lamb from infancy for the sole purpose of having it judged at the fair and hopefully winning a blue ribbon. I have all but given up on book launches and signings, considering that the last two I planned (even before the pandemic) attracted precisely two people total, and they both came to the same sad launch (an interested wife who dragged along her accommodating husband). Accomplished mathematicians can determine how many attended the other launch.

I state for the record, historical and biographical, over a four-year period I spent in the neighborhood of $25,000 on promotion of my books—including advertisements in *The New York Review of Books*, *Booklist* (a journal of the American Library Association), Spotify, book club promotions, and various social media platforms—which led to a mere handful of book sales, probably less than $20 in revenue. I maintained a personal website (as well as the Twelve Winters website), and was active on Facebook, Twitter and Instagram. Meanwhile, my books had done well in independent press competitions and garnered many generous reviews. Nevertheless, establishing a readership has seemed all but impossible.

AS I MENTIONED EARLIER, I see this collection as divided into four distinct parts, with the short stories falling into three of those divisions, and the sonnets constituting the fourth part. The reason for these distinctions has to do with two events in my life that reshaped my sense of myself as a writer of fiction, which I consider my primary creative focus. These events were encountering two writers who basically remade me—or, rather, who inspired me to remake myself in images that their aesthetic philosophies inspired.

I was born in 1962 and graduated from high school in 1980, consequently I was raised in the era of Ernest Hemingway. That is to say, Hemingway's writing persona and his work were integral parts of my education and of my sense of what a writer should be. My high school and my undergraduate English teachers were, by and large, Hemingway devotees, so his stories and novels were omnipresent on course reading lists. My introduction to writing and publishing was in the context of journalism, which fit hand-in-glove with the image that Hemingway presented as a writer. He was a journalist first, before transitioning into becoming a short-story writer and novelist. I saw myself on a kindred trajectory.

As such, I emulated the journalistic style that Hemingway brought to his fictional prose: short, straightforward sentences whose clarity was paramount. When I began taking creative writing classes in college, I followed those Hemingway-inspired dicta, and I was still following them when I began working on my M.A. in English with an emphasis in fiction writing in 1992. There are pieces in this collection that were written for my master's courses.

It was during this time that my first art-altering event occurred. Namely, I took a class with the poet Juan Felipe Herrera (who would much later become Poet Laureate of the United States). In addition to being a gifted poet, Juan Felipe was an amazing teacher. With Juan Felipe's encouragement and guidance, I began to cast off the example of Hemingway as a model for my writing, and in particular his reliance on personal experience for fictive material. I had always followed the (cliché) advice of "write what you know," as Hemingway had done—but, let's face it, Papa lived an exceedingly colorful life, while my life had been the epitome of mundane, of monochrome.

Juan Felipe forced me outside the bubble of autobiography by having us write something (a poem, a story, a script—Juan Felipe didn't care) based on the text we were studying at the time: *I, Rigoberta Menchu: An Indian Woman in Guatemala*. In response to the assignment, I fictionalized an episode from Menchu's book by writing a first-person story in the persona of a made-up Indian character named Chinkó. When Juan Felipe returned the short story to me his only comment was written on the top of the first page: "Ready for pub.," meaning it was ready for publication (without a single revision), which was a stark contrast to what I was experiencing in my fiction workshopping courses, where every story was torn asunder and ground beneath my classmates' bootheels. Autopsied to death.

To that point, I hadn't been able to get any of my short stories published, but with the encouragement of Juan Felipe's lone comment, I found a little journal at Indiana University, *Chiricú*, that published stories and poems in English, Spanish and Portuguese. I sent it to them (and only them). A few months later the miracle happened for which all unpublished writers yearn: I received my first acceptance letter. The experience taught me two invaluable lessons. First, I didn't have to rely on personal experience ("what I know") to write effective stories; in fact, writing in the guise of a totally unfamiliar persona can be quite liberating and allow writers to tell stories well beyond their usual frame of reference. Moreover, I could build a believable fictional world solely through the use of secondary-source material. Unlike Hemingway, I didn't have to experience firsthand war or bullfighting or infidelity or big-game hunting to write about it convincingly. My imagination was up to the challenge of writing outside my own life story.

The second invaluable lesson was that I was capable of writing a publishable story without any assistance or intervention from anyone. During this time I was mainly working with the novelist Kent Haruf, and he helped me to understand this concept as well. Frequently it was Kent who was leading the workshopping classes I was taking, yet his advice to me was to largely ignore the critiques I was receiving from my classmates (and even the critiques I was receiving from my instructors). Kent's point was that writers can't possibly integrate every suggestion that they receive in workshop. Trying to incorporate them all into a revision leads to a disastrous mishmash of styles, combined with incongruent plots and characters who are conflicted but not in a good way. Instead, said Kent, when writers submit stories for critique they probably have a suspicion or two already regarding this or that element that may not be working as well as it might. So during the critique session, just listen for comments about those specific things. Essentially, disregard everything else.

It took some time for Juan Felipe's lessons to fully take hold, so I continued to write autobiographically rooted material, much of which found publication, and those pieces are included here in the section titled "Early Stories." The stories that I wrote that were not overtly autobiographical, including "Chinkó," are in the section titled "Transitional Stories." I might also call them "Post-Juan Felipe" stories.

I graduated with my master's in 1995. I was determined to become a novelist, and not *just* a short-story writer. Still under the sway of Hemingway, I wrote a novel based on my undergraduate days at Southern Illinois University, Carbondale, titled "Recalling Susanna" (to date unpublished). Then with the lessons learned from Juan Felipe I wrote a novella titled *Weeping with an Ancient God* (a fictionalized version of author Herman Melville's real-life experience of living among cannibals on the Marquesas Islands), and a novel titled *Men of Winter* (a sequel, of sorts, to Homer's *Odyssey* set in early-twentieth-century Siberia).

The next art-altering event happened in 2009, while preparing to write my doctoral dissertation on postmodern literature: my discovery of William H. Gass, whose influence on my writing, my teaching, my thinking, my *life* has been absolutely profound. Gass's prose style was antithetical to Hemingway's. His sentences are elaborate, rife with poetic flourishes—what he refers to as "jingling" in his essay "Retrospection" in which he identifies seven "quirks" that dominated his writing style (he wrote the essay when he was 87). In short, Gass taught me not to be afraid of language. Or said differently, he gave me license to use my linguistic gifts, and not hide them like a self-conscious teenage girl who tries to disguise her sudden development in folds of loose-fitting fabric.

I love language, and I let that love-light shine into every corner of the composition, no matter how remote from the load-bearing claim: William Gass gave me that.

So, the twenty stories in this collection appear in three categories: "Early Stories" (my Hemingway days, so to speak), "Transitional Stories" (the kinds of stories I wrote after my fortunate encounter with Juan Felipe Herrera), and "Crowsong Stories" (my after-Gass work). I present them in reverse chronology, perhaps in the spirit of putting my favorite foot forward.

The term "Crowsong" derives from my 2017 novel *Crowsong for the Stricken*, an experimental narrative comprising twelve episodes that work as both chapters of the novel and stand-alone short stories. After the novel's publication I continued to be interested in the characters and their world, so I kept writing chapters/stories, thinking that I may release a revised edition of the novel that includes the new material. I wrote two such pieces—"Vox Humana" and "The Cold Dark March to Winter" —and a third, "Weird Soliloquies," grew out of the second. That is, what became "Weird Soliloquies" was originally intended to be a section of "The Cold Dark March to Winter." However, I decided that it wasn't working as part of the story and took it out. Nevertheless, I liked the piece, so I developed it further and ended up publishing it as a stand-alone . . . *thing* (it strikes me as perhaps a prose poem more than a short story). For the collection, I considered reintegrating it into "The Cold Dark March" but ultimately my previous assessments still seem sound.

(I'll mention that I wrote a fourth story, "First Kings," while still thinking about releasing a new edition of *Crowsong* with the added material. Instead, "First Kings" propelled me in a revised direction, and it has become the beginning of a new novel, titled, I think, *The Strophes of Job*—how and when it will be published remain uncertain. Even though the three "Crowsong Stories" offered here make sense as stand-alone pieces, there is greater sense to be made of them if read in the context of the novel *Crowsong for the Stricken*, and more so still with the coming novel, *The Strophes of Job*, a prequel. Several of the *Strophes* have been published independently, including in some online journals—I mention in case anyone would like a preview.)

Also included in this section is "Retribution," which is not a *Crowsong* story. It is a translation of the Grendel's mother episode in the Old English poem *Beowulf*. I assert that it *fits* because it was written in the midst of the *Crowsong* pieces (in the summer and fall of 2019), and it shares with them several attributes (which I'll leave the reader to judge). In recent months I've returned to work on the poem and hope to eventually publish a complete translation of *Beowulf*. As demonstrated in "Retribution," mine is a noncanonical reading that is still firmly rooted in the poet's original language. I've discussed my approach in academic articles that can be found online: "*Abreat* v. *Abræd*: Reconsidering the Grendel's Mother Episode in *Beowulf*" and "The Abduction of Aeschere: A Few Words Regarding a Few Words in My Translation of the Grendel's Mother Episode."

I FIND I WANT to say a few words about the early stories for posterity's sake. I've already mentioned the situation that led to

"Chinkó," my first published story. As grateful as I was to *Chiricú* for taking the story, it felt a bit like a freakish occurrence that was unlikely to be repeated. That is, my sense of myself as a writer was still in that realistic, Hemingway-esque mode. I wasn't going to be writing a series of stories—leave be a novel—in the persona of an indigenous person in Guatemala. So, in a way, I still felt that my true writer-self was unpublished. That soon changed when *Paris Transcontinental* accepted "Mix," the story that prompted Kent Haruf to tell me to disregard nearly all of the suggestions I was getting in workshop. My classmates had destroyed "Mix" when I shared it with them, so I totally rewrote it, trying to incorporate as many of their suggestions as possible. The resulting monstrosity is what led Kent to tell me to trust my own writing instincts over the well-meaning but often wrong-headed advice of my classmates. So I went back to the original draft, except with one significant change that was completely my idea. I had written the story in first-person, and I decided to give the narrator some distance from the story by revising it into close third-person. I didn't change anything about the story other than to turn "I" into "he," "my" into "his," and so on. It was the same story but with a distinctly different feel.

So when the envelope arrived from Paris informing me the editor had accepted "Mix," it felt like my first acceptance all over again. It is, then, in my personal history as a writer, quite significant. Nevertheless, I feel some uneasiness including it here. It is a story about race, and it includes the n-word (twice). It is an honest story: *true* in the way Hemingway encouraged *truth*. The year 2023, however, is very different from the early 1990s (I reference the 1992 Los Angeles riots in the beginning of the story —the riots that were sparked by the acquittal of the police officers who had mercilessly beaten Rodney King), and it's trickier now for white, male, heterosexual writers to write about certain issues, like race, or women, or sexual orientation. I've felt more and more boxed in as a writer—like many of the most important and engaging issues of the day are off limits to me. I get it; I understand. And I'd never write "Mix" or a story like it today. I just wouldn't risk the potential backlash, and I'm wary to include it here. Yet I have . . . in part because I think of this collection as a message in a bottle to future readers, and there's no way to predict what the climate will be like then when it comes to such matters. Perhaps, if nothing else, it will provide a useful snapshot into the historical and cultural record of the time of its writing and publication.

Another noteworthy early short story is "Fische Stories," which appeared in *Glimmer Train Stories*. It's noteworthy for at least two reasons. *Glimmer Train* was one of those magazines practically every short-story writer wanted to be in. Sisters Linda Davies and Susan Burmeister began the journal in 1990, ceasing publication in 2019. According to the journal's website, they would receive about 40,000 submissions a year. Besides the prestige, *Glimmer Train* actually paid its contributors for their work. For "Fische Stories," which was in issue number 43, summer 2002, I was paid $500 (an amount approaching $900 today).

Because of the publication in *Glimmer Train*, I was contacted by a New York literary agent (keep in mind that for a born-and-raised Midwestern writer, New York City seems as distant and as magical as Xanadu). At the time I was as adjunct instructor at Springfield College in Illinois, and I vividly recall going to my faculty mailbox and finding a letter from the agent. It was thrilling. Things were finally unfolding as they were meant to, I thought. There'd been a standard path to book publication for writers of fiction throughout the twentieth century (and the nineteenth, perhaps even rooted in the eighteenth). Writers would begin by placing stories in literary magazines with small circulations. As they continued to hone their craft, they'd start placing stories in nationally distributed magazines (like *Atlantic Monthly*, *Collier's*, *Esquire*, *Redbook*, *Cosmopolitan*, *Playboy*, etc.), which would allow them to build an audience of readers and get the attention of an agent or publisher who would champion their first novel.

There had been a Golden Age of magazine publication for much of the twentieth century, when fiction writers could make a good living selling stories to magazines. In the 1920s, F. Scott Fitzgerald and Zelda lived their legendary highlife almost solely from Fitz's short stories, which could fetch as much as $4,000 each (nearly $60,000 in 2023 money). It's estimated that during the 1920s and 30s Fitzgerald made almost a quarter of a million dollars from 164 magazine stories (more than $3.25 million today). A generation later, in the 1950s, Kurt Vonnegut Jr. sold four stories to magazines in the course of about eighteen months, allowing him to quit his job in the marketing department at General Electric and devote himself fully to writing. At the time, Vonnegut was supporting a wife and six children.

By the 1960s, however, television had begun turning the Golden Age into lead. And by the time I started to write effectively enough to publish, the Golden Age was a rapidly receding memory. In sum, television had superseded book reading as a popular pastime, and nationally distributed magazines had either severely cut back or eliminated space for short stories altogether, thus closing a crucial avenue for new writers to build an audience—let alone make a living.

With the *Glimmer Train* publication, I had at last attracted the attention of a New York-based agent. I replied immediately of course, letting her know I didn't have a novel yet (I said I was writing one—if I was, I had a draft of a chapter or something like that), but I had a novella: a 36,000-word fictionalized biography of Herman Melville's experience in the Marquesas Islands when he was a young sailor. She wasn't especially excited about a novella but agreed to look at it. Not surprisingly, she wasn't interested in representing it. When my novel was finished, she'd be happy to take a look.

I'd barely begun writing what would become *Men of Winter*,

a sequel of sorts to Homer's *Odyssey*. It took another three years to complete the manuscript. The ink was barely dry when I began looking for the agent. She'd moved to a different agency in New York. I contacted her. She remembered me and was willing to read the manuscript. I eagerly watched the mailbox for weeks, and she eventually replied . . . in the negative. She wouldn't be taking on *Men of Winter*. To say I was disappointed barely begins to describe what I was feeling.

Over time I found two other agents who would try to get *Men of Winter* published. Neither was successful. After years and years of searching for a publisher, I found a new small press to bring it out. The experience was underwhelming, and we ultimately fell out over the collection I was hoping they'd bring out next (the collection that evolved into this collection).

Let me go back to the *Glimmer Train* publication because it was significant in another way. When the journal's editor (either Susan or Linda—I can't recall) contacted me, the acceptance was provisional. She thought I'd used the main character's name too frequently, and that I should change some of the *Fische* and *Fische's* to *he* and *him* and *his*. Not a problem. It's hard to imagine now, but we were in a technological transition period. I'd contacted *Glimmer Train* the old-fashioned way, via a physical manuscript sent in a brown envelope, accompanied by a cover letter and an SASE (self-addressed, stamped envelope). However, Susan (let's say) contacted me via email. This was, I think, the year 2000 (or 1999 . . . Christmas Eve).

Email was a new-fangled thing, but attaching files to email *wasn't* yet. I made the revisions to "Fische Stories" promptly and sent the revised story to *Glimmer Train*. I'm sure I included a cover letter, but I didn't bother sending an SASE because I knew I'd hear back via email (fancy). I waited a couple of weeks before emailing Susan to see if she'd received the revised manuscript. No, but they received so many submissions, it may take awhile to unearth it. She said we should wait a bit longer, and if it didn't show up, I should resend it and write "MS REQUESTED BY SUSAN" in huge letters on the envelope. It didn't show, so I sent the story again, labeled as directed. In a few days, Susan emailed to say she'd read it and it was what they had in mind; she'd be mailing me a contract. Hooray.

(Fear not, whoever may still be with me: We're getting to the point of this anecdote.) It was the first Monday in March, what used to be Casimir Pulaski Day here in Illinois, when I went to my mailbox and found *two* envelopes from *Glimmer Train*: a large FedEx envelope, and a business-size envelope. A little surprised, I opened the business-size envelope first, and it contained a rejection of "Fische Stories" along with a mild admonishment for not including a self-addressed, stamped envelope. In the FedEx envelope was the contract to publish it.

I knew immediately what had happened. The first revised story was received by some assistant or junior editor who didn't bother reading the cover letter to know that it was a requested manuscript. The reader didn't care for it, and rejected it.

So, in the long history of writing and publishing, I'm surely the only writer to simultaneously receive an acceptance and rejection for the same story from the same magazine side by side in the mailbox. The unique experience underscored, for me, the subjectivity of publication. In one reader's eyes, the story beat out literally tens of thousands of other submissions to win a place in one of the most prestigious journals of the day; meanwhile, for another reader, it was easily rejected out of hand. The *Glimmer Train Stories* episode (along with many others that speak to this subjectivity) has softened the blow of rejection through the years.

Subjectivity is one wild-card factor when it comes to publishing. Another is timing. Included in this volume is the early story "Unnatural Deeds," which caught the eye of the fiction editor at *Esquire* magazine. Publishing in *Esquire* would've been another opportunity to attract the attention of an agent and have my work read by a larger audience. Unfortunately, wrote the editor, they had either just published or just accepted for publication (I don't recall) a story by T. C. Boyle (at the time, T. Coraghessan Boyle) that was very similar to "Unnatural Deeds" so he was going to pass. Otherwise. . . .

And then of course there's dumb luck, including dumb bad luck. I don't remember the year exactly (maybe around 2008 or 2009), and I don't remember which story I was shopping around (then and now I have multiple pieces in circulation looking for a publisher). I'd sent something to *Harvard Review*, and a few months later I received an email from a young woman named Rachel (M. R.) Branwen who identified herself as a reader for *Harvard Review*. She said she liked whatever story I'd sent them, and she'd recommended it up the editorial food chain. Her reason for contacting me, though, was that she was founding her own literary journal, *Slush Pile Magazine*, and she wondered if I had anything I'd like to contribute to the inaugural issue.

I appreciated her interest in my writing, so I sent her two chapters from *Men of Winter* (still unpublished at the time). Meanwhile, I waited for word from *Harvard Review*, mildly optimistic (or a shade less pessimistic than usual). And waited, and waited, until I forgot about it altogether. Truly. Then one day, some two years later, I received an email from the (an) editor at the *Review*. It wasn't an acceptance or rejection, but an apology. They'd been rearranging the furniture in the editorial office, and when they moved a filing cabinet they discovered a folder of submissions (all earmarked for further consideration) that had somehow fallen behind the cabinet and gone missing.

My submission was among the lost-and-found. Whatever story I'd sent them, it had been published elsewhere. It didn't matter—the editor wasn't offering publication. Rather, to make amends, *Harvard Review* was offering to look at something else and give it a prioritized reading and response. I sent them another piece, and true to their word they read it—and rejected it—with impressive celerity.

To be clear, I don't record these anecdotes as evidence of my unusually ill-fated efforts. Poor, poor me. On the contrary, I record them because I suspect they are similar to the disappointments and near-misses of practically every writer. As I tell my MFA students: It's a jungle out there. Writers must develop a skin as thick as an elephant's to survive the vicissitudes of the writing life. For every acceptance, for every modest award, for every publishing pittance, there are a hundred rejections and setbacks and unkind criticisms. But mostly there is no response whatsoever. To be published is *not* to be read. Most things, whether a haiku or an epic novel, seem to be born into a black void completely vacant of readers. They are elsewhere, binging on Netflix, betting on sports, and blasting virtual enemies.

THE FINAL SECTION of this collection is my "Laertes Sonnet Sequence," twelve poems written in apostrophe to my father, Vince, who passed away suddenly in 2012. I've always been interested in poetry, especially the sonnet form, but rarely had I written poetry in my own name. I mean that I've frequently included characters in my fiction who are poets, and I've written poems or parts of poems in their names (see, for example, *Men of Winter* and, especially, *An Untimely Frost*). Perhaps I lacked confidence in my abilities as a poet, so I preferred to hide behind my fictional characters. If readers found the poetry wanting, it was *their* poetry, not mine.

As I said, my father died in 2012, and I was having difficulty processing the loss. It occurred to me in late 2015 or early 2016 that I may be able to use my interest in sonnets to help with the grief by writing some sonnets to my father. We spoke every Sunday morning by telephone for an hour or two, and I was missing those conversations especially. Over the next few years, I would write a sonnet every so often, and I had some success in placing them and in their receiving some modest accolades. They are Petrarchan sonnets, with strong narrative threads. That is, each tells a story in miniature, and together they create an almost novelistic impression. At least, I believe they do.

Laertes, by the way, is Odysseus' beloved father, and they are reunited when the lost wanderer at last returns to Ithaca.

IT IS APPROPRIATE to acknowledge where these stories and sonnets were first published, so I'll (nearly) end this introduction with an expression of appreciation to the editors who found value in them and shared them with readers for the first time.

CROWSONG STORIES: "Vox Humana" (*Blue Lake Review*), and "Weird Soliloquies" (*briars lit*). "The Cold Dark March to Winter" is slated for publication via The International Conference on the Short Story in English, to be held in Singapore in 2023, after years of postponements due to the Covid pandemic. The *Beowulf* translation, "Retribution," appeared in *EKL Review*.

TRANSITIONAL STORIES: "Chinkó" (*Chiricú*), "A Wintering Place" (*Eleven Eleven*; also reprinted as an appendix to the paperback edition of *Mrs Saville*), and "Communion with the Dead" (*The Chariton Review*; note that the original title of this story was "Nekuia"). I'm also including two pieces that aren't quite like the others in that they *have* been published in book form: the long story "Figures in Blue" (originally published as an e-book novelette by Battered Suitcase Press), and "Melvill in the Marquesas" (published by *The Final Draft*; it is the first section of *Weeping with an Ancient God*, which I brought out via Twelve Winters Press; incidentally, "Melvill" is not a typo, but rather the way the author's family spelled their name originally).

EARLY STORIES: "The Composure of Death" (*Pisgah Review*), "Walkin' the Dog" (*Spilling Ink Review*), "Unnatural Deeds" (*Leaf Garden*), "Missing the Earth" (*Oakbend Review*), "An Alabaster Moon" (*PANK*), "In a Strange City" (*Eureka Literary*

Magazine), "Fische Stories" (*Glimmer Train Stories*), "When the Night Is New" (self-published in *A Summer's Reading*, a literary journal I edited and published from 1997 to 2004), "Mix" (*Paris Transcontinental*), and "Cougars in the Hills" and "Watching Close" (both in *The Sleepy Weasel*). These last two pieces were written for Kent Haruf's workshop courses. Kent would challenge us to write a single-page story with a beginning, middle and end. I suppose they qualify as "flash" fiction, my only such examples.

Laertes Sonnet Sequence: "Shroud" (*Bellevue Literary Review*), "Pilgrim" (*the tiny journal*), "Ingots" (Haunted Waters Press), "Obsolescence" (*Prime Number Magazine*), "Galaxie" (*Fare Forward*), and "Mass" (*Grand Little Things*). "Awakening" and "Dignity" were accepted for publication, but, alas, the editors held onto the poems for two years before acknowledging that they would be unable to continue publishing their journal. I understand, and appreciate their intentions nevertheless; thus, the sonnets appear here for the first time in print, as do "Acts," "Argonaut," "Seedlings," and "Symmetry." Their first public airing was for the Facebook program *C.A.M.P.* in which I read the complete sequence.

I began writing this introduction in Honolulu, where my wife and I were vacationing. We were only there, in Waikiki, a few days, but I immediately established a routine of waking before sunrise, going to the balcony of our hotel room (on the fourteenth floor), and drinking Kona coffee while I waited for my friend the ocean to materialize, little by little, out of the black of night. It was a near-religious experience each morning. Once the sun was fully up, I'd turn to my laptop and this introduction. It occurred to me that the slowly appearing Pacific was like the creative process. At first, the writer knows there is something there in the psyche—a story, a novel, a poem, something. Maybe they have a vague sense of it (some of what is out there is black sky, some is black ocean, but where one begins and the other ends is undefinable). There may be distant lights that lisp some sense of the seascape. Whether the lights are a cruise ship or a fishing boat or a tanker, it's difficult to say. As the writer begins to work through the process—putting words on paper or screen—contours emerge. Sky, ocean, clouds, waves . . . all become clear with the dawning daylight. It's a story; it's a novel; it's this; it's that. And the thing becomes more and more populated with characters and circumstances and nuances of color, just as charter boats and surfers and particolored parasailers begin their day in the brilliant tropical sun.

The tableau, over time, achieves its form.

I hope that you, dear reader, will find a tableau or two to taste within this delta, *Delta of Cassiopeia*.

T. M.

Honolulu, Hawaii

Sherman, Illinois

Nov.-Dec. 2022/Jan. 2023

Where not specifically noted, my sources are (in order): Gass's Preface to *In the Heart of the Heart of the Country*; *Conversations with William H. Gass*; Gass's *Life Sentences*; Fitzgerald-related websites and the film *The Great Gatsby in Connecticut*; and introductory material for *Kurt Vonnegut Complete Stories*.

Crowsong Stories

Vox Humana

You sailed like Ulysses through the border-void—
fiery atmosphere below, black oblivion beyond—
your own Scylla and Charybdis. A distant dream: Ithaca.
            — A. E. Wilson, from "Yuri Gagarin" (1962)

HER BROTHER HARRY hadn't written from Korea for more than a year, or at least none of his letters got through. Then out of the blue he called, said he was in South Carolina, he was taking a train, then a bus and he'd be in Crawford at the Trailways terminal in three days: Could Annette or Tim pick him up? Tim and the car had been gone for three weeks and two days at that point. It was too complicated to explain over the phone, especially long distance, so Annette said she would see her brother in Crawford. It required her taking a day off from school and borrowing Carl Reynolds's Ford, but she managed it.

She arrived at the bus terminal a few minutes late but suspected the bus would be even later. However, she'd only stepped from the car when she spotted Harry on a bench in front of the station, which also sat vacant and lonely. Harry was lost in his own thoughts and didn't notice her right away, which gave Annette a few moments to look at her brother and truly see him, almost the way a stranger might take him in. He was thin, perhaps even wiry beneath clothes that looked like hand-me-downs from an older and somewhat larger brother, nonexistent. His hair was brown with—was it possible?—the beginning streaks of white at his temples. It'd been cut short but that was weeks ago and the neat haircut had been growing of its own accord. Trousers of summer-weight wool, soon to be unquestionably out of season; a cotton shirt with a button-down collar, unbuttoned, and zippered jacket, unzipped, also soon to be too light for the time of year. His shoes may have been new but definitely in need of an energetic polishing. Harry was smoking, something he must've picked up in the service. More accurately, he was watching the lit cigarette between his fingers, as if a complicated thing which warranted careful study.

Annette was reluctant to interrupt his seemingly peaceful contemplation, but Harry must've sensed her presence, or someone's, and he looked up. Sis, he said, not so much in greeting as in practicing. He hadn't seen his sister in nearly five years, and perhaps with all that had transpired in the intervening years he needed a sort of rehearsal to reprise his role as kid brother.

Look at you, said Annette kissing him on the cheek, rough with stubble. You're so skinny. The scent of his cigarette elicited a recollection of Tim, who would smoke after dinner, and the memory was unpleasant and unwelcome.

The Army isn't known for its haute cuisine. Quite the opposite. He exhaled a final breath of smoke and stepped on the butt with the toe of his shoe.

The car's just over here.

He slung an army-green duffel over his shoulder and picked up a medium-size suitcase, old-fashioned, with leather straps—his only possessions it would seem.

On the drive back Annette tried to make small talk, which in itself felt strange, to speak to her brother as she would a virtual stranger, but Harry's responses were perfunctory at best. Annette wondered if he was upset to be in the passenger seat. Maybe he'd become one of those men who felt it was a fact of biology that the male of the species should always take the wheel. Tim believed it. After a while, Annette decided her brother's taciturnity was more a matter of his preferring quiet. So she left him to his own thoughts, and he seemed content to watch the old familiar countryside, rushing past in its early orange hues, the fields dotted here and there with farm animals.

You can smoke if you like—probably best to roll down the window.

Harry took out his pack of Chesterfields.

ANNETTE HAD ONLY BEGUN to use the spare bedroom as a what-not room—she'd set up her ironing-board, for example—so it was easy enough to prepare for Harry's arrival when he called. He hadn't asked to stay but she assumed, and apparently correctly. He didn't inquire about Tim, either, or about anything for that matter. Annette imagined Tim's absence from her life was abundantly clear. Harry put away his few things almost as soon as they got back, and easy as that they were roommates.

Annette wondered if she should have a welcome-home party for Harry, but growing up he'd had few close friends, and fewer still remained in the village. Zane Robbins's bone spurs kept him out of the service, as did Herbert Green's vertigo. Zane worked the family farm. Herb lived at home, taking correspondence courses. There was Beth Ann Ferguson, too, the school librarian. Harry and Beth Ann had gone to a dance or two together, nothing serious. As far as Annette knew, Beth Ann wasn't seeing anyone—nor had she ever indicated that she wanted to be.

Harry had been a quiet, bookish boy, yet he didn't find school especially interesting. He would have preferred to stay home, reading and studying whatever he pleased. It wasn't surprising when the Army attached him to a unit specializing in linguistics, not as a translator but as a transcriber. Harry lugged his portable typewriter and folding table and chair from one encampment to another, usually near the front line. His typewriter's steel case saved him from injury twice, once deflecting a wildly off-target bullet, another time a piece of shrapnel as long as his thumb. The case bore the scars of those close calls, along with the innumerable hard knocks from time in-country, each leaving its mark on the Army-issue Olympia that he returned to the quartermaster before his discharge. The carriage-return arm was bent, the carriage itself tended to slip when underlining, and the ribbon had been worn so thin it was opaque in spots, well past being re-inked. Harry had managed his final transcript and submitted it along with its carbons to the lieutenant who was his immediate superior.

For months it seemed that his only words were those that belonged to the North and South Koreans who had been interrogated or interviewed, respectively. Their stories, whether mostly true or mostly false, had been his stories, their lives his life. He felt as if he only existed when he was transcribing, and the brief interval between scripts was a time of silent incompleteness and waiting to be reanimated by the story of the next bearer of words. Meanwhile, the horrors of the conflict multiplied around him like an earthquake's suffocating rubble. The only relief was immersing himself in the transcribed lives of others. The night-colored letters on the paper, hammered there by the Olympia's solid strokes, formed a fortress against the bodies torn asunder, friend and foe alike, combatant and collateral kill, men and women, children. Even the images of slain animals haunted him, family pets, and livestock slaughtered in fields and left to rot.

By the time Annette met him at the bus station in Crawford Harry hadn't completed a transcript in nearly two months, weeks exposed to the world without periodic relief inside the sanctuary of others' words. Their stories, no matter how horrific the images they related, were like invocations that protected his fragile sanity. Harry could slip behind the walls of words and breathe more easily for a few blessed minutes.

* * *

ANNETTE HAD LEFT HARRY alone to go to school. She probably thought he was sleeping in on his first morning back home, but in fact he'd been awake for hours listening to the cricket chirp of night transform to the birdsong of morning. Then Annette was up rushing through her routine. He loved his sister and appreciated her giving him a place to stay, truly, but the idea of speaking to her—to anyone—was overwhelming. Conversation was exhausting. Sometimes the exhaustion came from trying to think of something to say, and sometimes it came from holding back the torrent of words wanting to break forth. For months Harry had found himself at one extreme or the other. When he was transcribing, the words of others were enough and he didn't feel the crippling pressure to unearth or embank his own.

At last Annette left for school, and the house was quiet. Harry dressed then went to the kitchen. He checked the icebox and breadbox. He might eat something eventually but he needed coffee and a smoke. He prepared the coffeepot and lit the burner with a kitchen match. While he waited for the water to boil, he went to the bookcase in his sister's small dining room and perused the selection of hardcovers and paperbacks. Several of the latter were Armed Services Editions, leftovers from the previous war still circulating a decade later. Harry ran his finger along the spines, listening for the coffeepot's boil. One title in particular arrested his attention: Carl Sandburg's *Chicago Poems*. He took the well-worn paperback from the shelf and in a few minutes was seated on the back porch with the Sandburg, his coffee, and cigarettes.

It was a cool morning; leaves from an elm lay on the steps, a scarlet harbinger of winter's slow approach. The book of poetry was divided into sections, and the one titled 'War Poems (1914-1915)' stood out. Obviously they were inspired by the Great War, but he suspected the Great War was as terrible as his own, or any other. He lit a cigarette and began reading. Later, one image especially would stay with him—*Red drips from my chin where I have been eating. Not all the blood, nowhere near all, is wiped off my mouth.*

He sat on the porch for a long while with the poems and the thoughts they conjured. Mrs. Holcomb next door had come out and spent some time cleaning fallen leaves from her flowerbeds and primping the mums and asters. She pretended not to see Harry, not wanting to disturb his privacy perhaps; or maybe she truly didn't see him, half hidden by the porch itself.

ON HER WAY HOME from school, Annette stopped at the grocery for a piece of sirloin and some new potatoes. Normally her main meal was the hot one prepared by the school cooks; then at night she would nibble on cold cuts and crackers or some fruit. When Tim left she wondered if it was because of her inadequate dinners, at least in part. But, no, he seemed generally unhappy with everything and everyone, inside and outside their home. It wasn't as simple as poorly prepared meals. Still, it sometimes nagged her. Maybe because so many of the wives took such pride in their ability to cook, and several were associated with a particularly popular dish: Mrs. Reynolds's rabbit stew, Mrs. Abernathy's quail in white gravy, Mrs. Johnston's minted lambchops, Mrs. Phillips's fried chicken and cornbread, Mrs. Whittle's chicken and dumplings, Mrs. Smythe's morel soufflé, Mrs. Moreland's honey-glazed pork roast. . . .

On one level Annette knew Tim's happiness was beyond her influence—no effort great or small seemed capable of achieving it for long—yet his discontent picked at her peace of mind. She would think of the eagle that tortured bound Prometheus, little by little without interruption. Tim's leaving triggered a tide of complex emotions, some sharp, some subtle, but the most immediate and most profound was simple relief: The harpy had suddenly ceased plucking at her liver, and it was, in a word, glorious.

These thoughts and feelings returned to her as she was preparing the meal for Harry and her, and she examined them like exhibits in a museum, or, better, like specimens in a zoo—for they were safely sealed off but still very much alive, and their quickness lent them an element of danger, should one or two of the more predatory types get loose.

Annette scraped cubed potatoes from the cutting-board into the pan of salted boiling water. Harry was in the living room. The evening news was on, the picture more snowy than usual. It didn't seem to matter: He sipped at his can of Falstaff and stared at the fuzzy newsman, the Zenith's sound all but off. She considered attempting a conversation—about something, anything—but her brother appeared content so she elected to let him be and focus on making their dinner.

While she stirred the roiling potatoes she thought of all the times she wanted to talk with Tim—always in an attempt to make things better, it seemed in retrospect, either via a conversation that dealt with a problem or one that deflected from it—eventually, however, the futility of talk, of any kind, became clear, and it was simpler to keep within her own thoughts. Even though this felt different, Annette resolved that she wouldn't let avoiding conversations with her brother become a pattern.

They ate at the dining-room table. Harry turned off the television, and he poured his beer into a glass. Drinking from the can at the table must've seemed poor etiquette.

Everything smells great, Netta.

It was the first time he'd used her nickname since coming home, but rather than a sign of normality it felt a forced attempt to mimic it.

Thank you, she said. I'm afraid I'm out of practice in the kitchen. She thought that Harry must be wondering about Tim's absence, but he hadn't said a word. Did he wonder, did he assume, or did he not even notice?

Some of Tim's things remained. Old clothes in the closet of the spare room (now, Harry's room), odds and ends of tools in the shed, along with various shovels and spades and the mower, an item or two in the back of this drawer or that. To Annette these stray remainders were reminders of Tim's absence, but perhaps to others, to Harry, they were as unworthy of note as a burned out bulb, or the unraked leaves in the corner of the yard.

She wondered at times if there was something wrong with her. Shouldn't she be devastated Tim had left and their marriage of six years was through? Shouldn't she become weepy at the thought of it? Shouldn't she be lonely, and desperate to fill some vacuous void?

Everything told her she should be all of these things and more. In truth, though, she felt only serenity and the strange stirrings of contentment. Now her life could have meaning which she herself ascribed to it. She was just beginning to understand Tim's abandonment and what it may mean for her when Harry called about his discharge and his needing a ride. As they sat across the table from one another, eating the sirloin and mashed potatoes, Annette found herself wondering how long her brother would be staying with her. It was an uncharitable line of thought and she tried to dismiss it altogether. The click and scrape of Harry's fork as he scooped up tinefuls of potato punctuated her selfish speculations.

You're almost out. Would you like another Falstaff?

Harry looked at the finger of yellow liquid in his glass. Sure, sis, thanks.

Annette pushed herself away from the table and her unkind thoughts. She retrieved a can from the icebox, punctured its top twice, big and small; then returned to the table and poured some of the beer into her brother's glass. Her water glass was empty so she poured the rest of the beer for herself. Annette took her seat:

I was thinking, we should have a welcome-home party for

you, give everyone a chance to say hello all at once. I'm sure we could use the basement of the church. I'll speak with Pastor Phillips. She didn't say: Letting everyone know you're back may prompt someone to offer you a job. She tried to imagine what Harry would've done if he hadn't gone off to Korea. It was difficult to imagine. He'd always been a bookish, quiet sort of child, though not much interested in school unless it was a subject he especially liked. Mythology, for example, and the Trojan War. Homer's *Iliad* was a favorite and of course Odysseus' great wanderings. She recalled his making a cyclops out of papier-mâché. It was nearly three feet tall and required most of their immediate neighbors' old newspapers, torn into strips.

PLANS WERE MADE for a potluck in the church's basement. Pastor Phillips insisted that the Methodist Ladies Auxiliary would supply the main course and cake. Guests could bring salads and sides. The pastor imagined that the whole village would turn out to welcome Harry home. The returns of World War Two boys, less than a decade earlier, were still fresh in most folks' minds. Those were some bona fide parties, said Pastor Phillips, grinning a bit mischievously beneath his thick glasses. He would have Mrs. Holcomb put a notice about Harry's party in the bulletin. Between that and word-of-mouth, the whole village will be in the know in no time. The pastor enjoyed his turn of phrase.

Annette thanked him before hurrying from his office to get to school on time.

HARRY HAD SPENT the morning reading, thinking, smoking, drinking coffee. The sky was gray and mildly threatening as he considered it from his sister's back porch. They were nearly out of coffee, and he was down to his last two cigarettes. They were low on bread also, and cornflakes. All the time sitting, relaxing, had given way to a goading restlessness, so he decided to walk to the grocery to restock essentials. He was already feeling a trifle guilty about staying with Annette and not pulling his own weight, especially since Tim seemed to be out of the picture. He felt that he should say something about his absent brother-in-law but he didn't want to pry—that was one excuse he allowed himself. Really, though, it had more to do with his belief that if he broached the subject, it may lead to his sister confessing a cascade of heavy, complicated emotions, and it would be more than he could bear. There was so much heaviness and complication inside of him already, he sensed that another straw more may be his undoing. He may collapse beneath it all. Besides, he never cared much for Tim Wilson, and it was a pleasant surprise not having him around.

Annette kept a sturdy wicker basket with long handles on a hook next to the backdoor for the express purpose of carrying items home from the grocery store. Harry knew, in part, because she'd had the same basket for years. He removed it from its hook and began walking to Wilson's Grocery (the owner was a cousin, once or twice removed, of Annette's husband). It was a short walk along Willow Street to Main, made shorter by Harry's hurrying: the skies looked more threatening than they had from the porch. Large, icy drops were beginning to pelt him as he reached the store. He regretted his timing as he didn't know how long he'd be pinned down by the rain.

There was a young woman working the counter whom he didn't recognize. How could that be? It was a place where everyone knew everyone. He was Wilson's only customer at the moment. Harry nodded hello to the blond-haired girl; she was working a crossword puzzle. He began surveying the small store's slim inventory.

Outside, the rain intensified. Harry could hear it monsooning against the roof, raindrops mixed with pellets of hail. It was warm inside the store. He felt sweat on his neck. The girl seemed unconcerned about the weather as she filled in letters of her puzzle with a yellow pencil. Light glinted off canisters of soup. Harry blinked at the shards of white. He heard the first grumble of thunder. The girl looked up too. She smiled briefly—perhaps reassuringly—then returned to her crossword.

Harry's mouth was dry. He wanted a long drink of beer. A flash of lightning broke across the gray, instantly followed by the thunder's crash. Harry dropped the basket and unbuttoned the top button of his shirt: He was suffocating. His t-shirt was soaked under his arms and along his ribs and spine. He was near a bin of vegetables. He fought an instinct to squat behind it, shielding himself from the flashing windows.

Another bolt then bellow of thunder. He put his hand on the wooden bin for support. A head of purple cabbage shifted and fell to the floor. As he watched it topple, the bin's wet scent of boggy earth rose around him like a closing bag. Another head fell. He may have kicked it as he lurched forward, or it may have been that his legs felt as stiff as crutches—but he lost his balance and groped for a handhold. He found a rack of sealed jars. One or two fell and glass shrapneled across the floor as the briny smell of pickles rippled over him. He couldn't breathe. Harry fumbled his way out of the store, which felt as claustrophobic as a coffin. More items may have fallen and burst in his wake.

Down the streets rain running in streams, calling his name, someone. Red umbrella, porch, Annette's, blanket on his shoulders, Annette's. Smoking.

DONALD AND RITA GALE (née Hopkins) were both only-children of parents who had them later in life. Thus Annette Elizabeth and Harrison Scott Gale grew up with no extended family to speak of. Their father had a distant cousin, a nun, whom they met once at the funeral of a still more distant cousin, a salesman of some sort, door-to-door. Don Gale passed (coronary) when

Annette and Harry were in their early teens; Rita five years later (cancer). They'd been dutiful parents but not doting. Annette, who was a voracious reader starting in childhood with the works of Lewis Carroll, soon advancing to Jane Austen then the Brontës and beyond, came to think of her parents, especially her father, as affectionate in a British sort of way—though he was as Midwestern American as a boy and then a man could be. Her mother wasn't quite as aloof as her father, but she seemed to prefer her husband's company to her children's, and she was devastated nearly to the point of petrification at his sudden passing. In Annette's recollection her mother had died shortly after her father. She would have to remind herself there was a five-year interval, during which her mother seemed morbidly intent on joining her spouse in death. Rita showed the preoccupation of a commuter who'd missed her train but was determined to catch the next.

SOMETIMES HARRY SAW the Koreans who were the subjects of the translations he typed into transcripts, in triplicate. Seeing them was more likely if they were South Koreans. But it usually took several days or even weeks for the translated interviews to reach him for transcription. So he rarely had any idea whose words he was reading. Over time, his mind began selecting one of a small collection of Korean faces as the subject. While working on a transcript, Harry would automatically assign a face to the voice he heard in the words. He thought of them almost as masks stored in a theatrical cabinet, except of course real, living faces. The mask—thickset or thin, bright-eyed or beady, saintly or sinister—spoke the words he read on the pages, the Koreans' comments and confessions, rendered into English by the translators, most of whom broadcast an air of superiority. They delivered the words Mosaically, as if Jehovah's own, not to be doubted, leave be amended. One could almost smell the acrid scent of a burned bush upon the pages.

After a time the Korean faces began appearing in his dreams, whispering to him in English with their distinct accents. They floated in an ethereal sea, a space all their own, a sort of in-between but with no sense of what lay before or beyond. In the beginning, they whispered snippets of the transcripts he'd typed on the portable Olympia. One night, though, they started murmuring of other things, barely audible in the rush of ether, only partly formed, mostly pieces of images, a helter-skelter of tiles from incomplete mosaics. Harry woke in the dark tent knowing something was different—knowing *he* was different.

More and more the faces spoke to him when he was awake, in the background of his consciousness, like distant voices in a crowded theater before the opening curtain. He'd catch a word or phrase, not enough to constitute a whole thought, just enough to remain frustratingly at the edge of intelligibility. He thought of the cast who occupied the fringes of his psyche as his own Greek chorus, a joke meant to lessen his fears about their worrisome presence, but it had little effect.

ANNETTE HAD INFORMED her teaching colleagues about the welcome-home party while they were in the faculty dining-room. She communicated the details over the noise of scraping forks and slicing knives. Two teachers immediately gave their regrets. The remaining dozen or so implied they would attend by not saying they couldn't. Annette wanted to be sure about Beth Ann Ferguson's attendance.

When the end-of-the-day bell had rung and the students had rushed away as if the school was sinking, Annette went to the room which served as the library. Bookcases, tall and short, cut the space into narrow aisles. Beth Ann's desk, constructed of some ancient wood, dark and dense, stood sentinel near one wall. Beth Ann was so diminutive, when she sat at her mammoth desk, she could at first look like one of the children. She was not at her desk, however, and Annette believed for a moment that she'd already left; then she heard a sound among the tall stacks, and she found the little librarian in the 800s.

Annette startled her. Sorry, Beth Ann—I thought you probably heard me come in.

It's o.k. She peered up, above her half reading glasses, which she wore on a cord around her neck.

For a second Annette doubted what she knew to be true, that Beth Ann and Harry were the same age. With her hair pinned back, and her reading glasses, and her blue dress with the lace collar, Miss Ferguson projected the image of an older woman. Earrings of pearl, like grandmotherly types in the village wore for special occasions, looked almost too weighty for Beth Ann's delicate ears. Annette wondered if she, too, presented a similarly dowdy persona. She hoped not.

I couldn't recall if you were at lunch when I mentioned Harry's party, Annette fibbed.

Yes, it sounds like a nice thing for Harry. She replaced a book to its spot on the shelf. Euripides. Annette knew the collection, and sometimes shared an excerpt from *The Trojan Women* with her class as further context for Homer. The stacks were pleasantly heavy with the musty scent of old books; there was also a floral trace of Beth Ann's powder—subtle but it stood out because of its strangeness among the rows and rows of rarely read books.

Do you think you can make it? To Harry's party?

I'm not sure . . . I may have plans. The lie lingered in the air between them. Beth Ann added, I may have a friend coming in from out of town. The lie maintained its buoyancy in spite of the added weight.

Your friend would be welcome, of course. I'm sure it would mean the world to Harry to have you there.

I'll see. I'll try to make it. She pulled a book from the shelf. Aeschylus. Thank you. . . .

Thank you. Annette manufactured a smile of warmth. As she was leaving the library she thought of *The Libation Bearers*.

DURING THE THIRTY-SIX-HOUR cross-country trip Harry discovered that reading helped to calm the chorus—not quiet their voices completely, nor drown them out, but at least the author's voice could distract his attention from the chorus' multilayered murmuring. On the bus Harry was reading a collection of New England ghost stories, and he found that some authorial voices were better at distracting from the Korean chorus than others. The more complex the sentence structure, the more obscure the vocabulary—the further the narrative distanced the incoherent choir. The ghost stories were sweet relief.

At Annette's home, Harry doubted that the collection of Sandburg poems would have much effect, but the poet's voice could more than distract Harry; in fact, some of the poems seemed to get the choral voices to stop altogether, for a few minutes at least. It was something about their rhythm, perhaps interwoven with particularly vivid images, that provoked the chorus' silence, ceased their steady whispering, like a wind that is harbinger to storm.

> *I cannot tell you now;*
> *When the wind's drive and whirl*
> *Blow me along no longer*

The poem was titled 'The Great Hunt,' but it seemed to be more about seeking than hunting, thought Harry, because he associated hunting with killing, and the poem was about seeking someone with a great soul, or searching for that great soul beyond death. In any event, the words froze him in the realization of his solitariness, in understanding the lonely state of his own soul. He wondered if his soul was great, or could be great.

Harry savored the moment's utter silence as if rays of golden light temporarily tore through a stubborn gray cover.

MOST OF THE TRANSLATIONS Harry typed were the quintessence of banality—subjects' mundane descriptions of daily routines, uninspired details of local topographical features not included on the Army Corps' survey maps, and rambling acknowledgments of connections between family members and friends. One day, however, a translation landed in Harry's assignment box that was out of the ordinary: A South Korean, from Taejon, identified only as Im, was interviewed and claimed his profession as master storyteller. As substantiation Im told a tale that was so ancient no one knew its attribution, he said. Its title was translated as 'The Tale of the Old Man with No Legs.' It turned out to be a frame narrative (Harry recalled when he first learned the term in English class—*Arabian Nights*, Chaucer's *Tales*, *The Ancient Mariner*). The unnamed narrator meets an old man with no legs on the wharf and inquires as to how he lost them. The old man recounts,

In my youth I was a sailor, one among a crew of twenty whose ship was battered by a terrible storm and driven many leagues from our course. We came to an island unknown to us. A strange-looking keep stood on the headland overlooking the sea. We were hungry and thirsty and exhausted from our ordeal in the storm. We had no choice but to ask for assistance. We climbed to the keep and called at the tall, queerly arched door. No one responded so we pushed the door ajar and entered the barely illumined interior. The smell of animals was strong and at a distance we heard the bleating of sheep and other pasture creatures. We were relieved, for surely the master of the keep had plenty of food and could spare some for lost, woebegone travelers in need. Our relief was fleeting, however. Just then a giant, terrible to behold, came into dim view from the dark edges of the vast room. We made our plea to the giant, who loomed above us as a very large man does tiny children. He made no reply, but went to the door and secured it with a ponderous timber. We were trapped. He disappeared into the dark only to return momentarily with a pile of wood and start a blazing bonfire. Still without a word he snatched one of our number and proceeded to roast him alive; then eat him to every last morsel. Meanwhile all that we could do was watch in horror.

When the giant finished his meal, he drank greedily from an earthen vessel, which must have held strong spirits for soon the giant lay on his back snoring, a sound like felled trees tumbling together. We rushed to the door and tried to budge the timber which held it fast but it was too massive. One of our number had a small knife used mainly for carving figures. We resolved to blind the giant and slash his throat. We managed the first order of business, but the terrible injury woke him to sudden rage and frantically he grasped for us. We scrambled to the far side of the room, where we found the giant's sheep and pigs. He followed us but every time he reached down he clutched an animal instead of a man. We each picked up a sheep and carried it on our back. The giant went to the door and opened it so that his stock could go to pasture, which allowed us to escape the keep. We ran for our lives to the beach and our waiting ship.

The giant heard our clamoring down the rocks and called to his brethren for assistance. We boarded our ship but before we could reach open water the giants held us fast. We beat their hands with oars and clubs and stabbed them with fishing lances until they released us, and the tide carried us away. Weary from our escape, however, we soon ran upon treacherous shoals, which tore the ship asunder. All of my mates drowned. I clung to a piece of the timber, a rib of the splintered ship, and was the sole survivor. As I floated in the sea, a frightful fish bit off my legs. I washed upon a lonely island, where I remained marooned for many years—surviving against all odds.

Harry recognized the Korean tale from Odysseus's great wanderings as well as from Sinbad's voyages—all the ancient authors drawing from some still more ancient source, a common human headwater.

AS THE DAY of his welcome-home party approached, Harry felt more and more uneasy. Perhaps it was the very idea of it: The village no longer felt like home. No place did. It seemed, then, that the idea was to welcome him to a strange place, one that offered no hope of becoming familiar.

The village had donned a disquieting mask

The line came to him—alone in the house, brewing coffee—as if spoken (whispered) by someone else. It took him a moment to attribute it to the chorus, which was whispering other words: a flood of images. As soon as the coffee was done he took a cup to the back porch, along with a notepad he found in a drawer and a pen. It was a chilly morning but Harry was warm enough in a heavy sweater, with a scarf knotted around his neck—in addition to the words burning inside of him. He scribbled the line about the disquieting mask, then the next:

as dramatic a change as from Drama to Comedy, from Dionysus to Apollo, from Discord to Calm

He sat for a long while writing the words, working them, before he accepted that he was making a poem. He wrought images into lines and lines into stanzas. Harry discovered that the chaos of his chorus had become a more tamable torrent, one that could be checked with dikes and causeways and dams, by controlling diction, syntax and punctuation—even blank spaces provided some buffer for the rising tide of words.

In the corner of the spare room there was a small desk on which sat an Underwood typewriter. Harry took the pages of handwritten poetry—with their crossouts and insertions, arrows and asterisks—and sat in front of the machine. Even his juxtaposition to the typewriter calmed his mind further. He found clean sheets of onionskin in one of the desk drawers and rolled a sheet into the carriage. He worked to bring meaning to the disordered ideas and images. After a time he had a draft with which he felt some level of satisfaction. He unrolled it from the carriage, folded the newborn poem in thirds, and placed it inside Sandburg's *Chicago Poems*. He'd titled it 'The Human Voice.'

THE LADIES AUXILIARY prepared most of the food, including their signature hamloaf, and decorated the church basement. Annette's students made a banner out of an old sheet and purple fabric paint: Welcome Home, Harry!! There was some debate as to whether 'Harry' should be 'Mr. Gale' or 'Cpl. Gale,' but Annette decided the simplest approach best. The banner hung on the basement wall above the refreshments table. Mrs. Holcomb had made a cake, white icing with purple script repeating the message, and color scheme, of the banner.

Pastor Phillips had placed a notice about the welcome-home in the bulletin, prominently anchoring the front page; and he made special mention of it during both services. Other notices were posted here and there: the windows of Owens' Café and Reynolds' Barber Shop, on the bulletin-board in the library, and on the wall at the Farm Service office.

HARRY: (*To the Audience.*) I hold no animosity for my neighbors—but neither do they hold a special place in my heart. They strike me as ghosts, a part of my past that has returned to me unwanted and unbidden, even though it is I who has returned to them. They dully occupy a space which should be my future, as yet unformed. Are there seeds beneath the soil that shall claw their way to the surface and the enlivening light? Or have they lain dormant too long and forgotten their purpose, and will merely rot in the damp earth? Food for another's dream.

Annette: Are you ready? The guest of honor shouldn't be late, not even fashionably so.

Harry: (*To the Audience still.*) I cannot of course count my sister a ghost. That would be unkind, for one, and she has always been kind to me; even when we were children. Also, there is life and living in her more so than most of her (our) neighbors. She is a seed whose brave shoot may yet break into the light—perhaps only to whither in the inhospitable climate. She may be brave enough to try, but am I brave enough to let her?

Chorus: Harry has not broached the subject but Annette has obviously been abandoned by her husband. Tim loaded the car with what he wanted—leaving enough behind to tell the tale of his departure—and he drove toward some other future. Though this place is rife with spirits, a new Asphodel, how could Harry abandon his sister too? It could be the last bit that breaks her.

Annette: Look. They've made you a banner: Welcome Home, Harry!!

Pastor Phillips: Here's our war hero. Let us shake your hand.

Jim Goodpath: Welcome home!

Carl Reynolds: It's good to see you!

Harry: Thank you, Pastor, for lending us use of the basement, and for arranging the food.

Pastor: You're welcome. The ladies were delighted to have a project. It's been a slow year in the wedding and funeral departments, sadly and gladly, respectively.

Chorus: A funeral, that's what this feels like to Harry: The village turning out to pay their respects, then have a free meal and eat a piece of white cake. He manufactures a smile for new arrivals and shakes hands and responds to the same few questions again and again. When did he get back? What's he going to do? Implied: Will he be staying? A couple of weeks ago . . . ? . . . ? The too-sweet smell of the hamloaf reminds him of his parents' funerals.

Pastor Phillips: (*Confidentially.*) Your arrival home was quite fortuitous—the timing we mean.

Harry: Timing?

Jim Goodpath: Just when she needed a man.

Chorus: It's a well-established fact that a woman needs a man. The several women in the village and in its history who appear to have successfully ignored the fact are mere exceptions: Outliers, often nearly as literal of a term as figurative. Harry looks across the basement at his sister, whom he would describe as thoughtful, but not unhappy. It makes sense: There is much to consider, given her change of circumstance.

Pastor: I have been saying an extra little prayer for Annette— and here you are . . . and for your safe return to us, too, of course.

Carl Reynolds: Let's get your picture.

Pastor: I see you have a new toy.

Carl: Picked up the new flash in Crawford yesterday. Been chomping at the bit to try it out.

Chorus: Harry has brought the ragged copy of *Chicago Poems* with him, in his side pocket—the weight of the book against his hip, slight as it is, gives him a sense of security. He takes the Sandburg from his pocket to pose for Carl Reynolds, amateur but avid photographer.

Carl: That's great. Chin up a bit, smile, on three. . . .

Chorus: The exploding bulb dazzles Harry for a second. As his vision clears he sees Beth Ann Ferguson standing next to Carl, as if she has materialized with the burst of light. At first, before his vision returns completely, he thinks she is a child at Mr. Reynolds's side. When he recognizes Beth Ann, he recalls that her childhood nickname was Polly, something to do with a story about a parrot in one of their primers. Harry must be imagining it, but a faint residue of the blinding light seems to linger in the space around Beth Ann, like an aura.

Harry: Hi. I didn't notice you come in.

Chorus: His extended hand holds the book of poetry still, as if an offering. Beth Ann takes the accidental gift and looks at the spine before returning it.

Beth Ann: Sandburg.

Chorus: Eruption of laughter, if you please. . . . Thank you. It is because Mr. Abernathy has gotten into the basement storage-room where the church's theatrical properties are kept and emerged wearing a goat mask. Mayor Whittle and Doc Higgins join in, and they are a cow and a pig. The trio begin to make the appropriate noises, much to the group's general delight.

Pastor Phillips: What do you think, Harry? Bet you didn't know this would be a masquerade.

High noon inside the playhouse large cool fishes glisten singing of life in the sun: Chorus.

Harry: I need a smoke.

Beth Ann: I could use some air.

A grinning skull waves of sound beat the sidewalk a new way: Chorus.

Harry: The night is clear. The stars are like comets. They should all have tails of stardust.

Beth Ann: You always noticed the oddest things, Harry Gale.

Harry: Did I? I'd nearly forgotten.

Cars whir by when high waves come closer into the hoofs on a winter night: Chorus.

Beth Ann: Is something wrong?

Harry: No. . . .

Soft echoes on a bronze pony in the cold and lonely snow and into dawn: Chorus.

Harry: Do you have a car?

Beth Ann: I can use my dad's Mercury.

Harry: Would you drive me to Crawford? To the bus terminal?

Beth Ann: What? Now?—Do you want to let Annette know?

Harry: I can call. She can send me my things.

Alone with a picture after the dead beat their hands outside of what poets leave their skulls in the sun for: Chorus.

The Cold Dark March to Winter

WHEN SHALL WE FOUR meet again? asked Rebecca.

That's my line, sort of. Shirley smacked her on the arm with a copy of the play.

After school tomorrow? suggested Miss Ferguson.

We could bring our lunches to the library, said Frankie. Go over some ideas.

Beth Ann normally ate in the teachers' lounge but it always required an effort to be gregarious, plus a break from the cigarette smoke was welcome. All right, at lunch then.

ThankThaThanks, Miss Ferguson! chimed the three girls as they gathered their books and coats.

You'd better put those on. There's definitely a nip in the air. Apparently the Almanac is calling for an early snow, said Beth Ann, realizing how old-fashioned it made her sound, how out-of-touch. She wasn't much older than her novice thespians, who would be graduating after spring term. Graduating to what? Their options were the same as when she'd graduated, five years earlier: marriage and motherhood, or business school in Crawford to study typing, filing and shorthand, or some truly mindless work and wage earning. Beth Ann Ferguson, who'd always preferred books to people, charted a different path by taking a correspondence course in library science and being available when the former school librarian retired, after more than forty years among the musty stacks. Beth Ann couldn't imagine herself doing this, or anything, for forty years.

She lived across the street from the school with her mother in the only home Beth Ann had ever known, so the turn in the weather was of little consequence to her. From the library's window she watched the girls depart for their homes and shortly they were lost from view. A pickup truck turned onto the street, Mr. Abernathy's she knew without even thinking about it, and in its headlamp beams she saw a cyclonic swirl of leaves stirred up by a gust of wind and the truck's accelerating wheels.

Her mother would be keeping dinner for her, soup and a sandwich, but Beth Ann decided to linger a bit. There were books she could reshelve, and perhaps there were resources that could assist her contribution to the winter play. Mrs. Wilson, the upper-grades English teacher, had decided to do what she called 'Scenes from Shakespeare'—Hamlet's poor Yorick speech, Romeo and Juliet's garden scene, Henry V's once more unto the breach rallying cry, Lady Macbeth's distressed sleepwalking, and so on—and she'd asked Beth Ann to help with the Weird Sisters' incantation scene. Annette Wilson had been directing the school's student productions for years, but this was by far the most ambitious. It would have been surprising except that something had been changing in Mrs. Wilson, something difficult to define, a greater confidence combined with a more pacific calm. Her husband had left her, according to village gossip, but instead of being devastated she was chrysalizing into a new person.

Beth Ann envied Annette's dawning independence. She felt trapped in the shell of her personality, tied to being the person she'd always been, held back from becoming someone else: someone she didn't even know yet, of whom, in fact, she could barely detect an indistinct silhouette, like a shadow fallen across the walk behind her.

She went to the stack of books on her desk, about a dozen titles to be replaced to the shelves. The desk was an enormous hardwood sentinel by the door, and when Beth Ann sat at it she knew it added to the impression of her being a child still. Just shy of five-feet when standing barefoot, Beth Ann dressed like the dowdiest grandmother in the village, always in dark dresses or a white blouse with a dark skirt while at school, even a ubiquitous string of fauxpearls—all to project the image, and authority, of someone older. She sometimes wondered if the style of dress only gave the suggestion of a child playing at dress-up.

By the time she finished reshelving the books rain had begun streaking the library's windows. Her mother would be listening for her at the kitchen door. She felt a pang of guilt at keeping her mother waiting, and a simultaneous twinge of irritation at her mother's fretful attention. Beth Ann opened the door to the small office, directly behind the desk. She shut the door and locked it before switching on the light. There were no windows. There was a rolling chair little taller than a milking stool, shelving on one wall, and a trio of metal filing cabinets, all locked. Beth Ann wore a wire bracelet on her wrist that held a dozen keys, like charms.

She slipped the bracelet from her hand and used one of its smallest keys to unlock the middle filing cabinet, whose drawers were labeled *Requisitions 1948-50*, *1951-53*, and *1954-56*. She pulled out the top drawer, extending it as far as it would go. In the back of the heavy drawer, under an old leatherbound ledger, was a metal cashbox. Beth sat and placed the cashbox on her lap, then used another key to unlock it.

On top of the box's contents was a stack of yellowed ledger sheets. Beneath the sheets was a small black book, another kind of ledger, and on its cover was written *Discretionary Funds, 1898-1901*.

Between the pages of the old book was a photograph of a woman that Beth Ann hid there. Her pale skin glowed like sun-drenched petals, her hair was as dark as night dropped down a well—but it was her patch of black which most magnetized Beth

Ann. When she was twelve Beth Ann and her parents visited an ancient relative who lived in a town halfway to Danville. The old man sat in a chair the entire visit, buried in hand-knitted rugs, coughing and wheezing and dying. Bored, Beth Ann snooped in the upstairs bedrooms. In the bottom drawer of an antique bureau she found the set of startling photographs. Her first impulse was to turn away but they had instantly bewitched her. She'd never stolen anything before yet she couldn't completely part with these hypnotizingly sordid images, so she slipped one of the sepia prints out of her dying relative's house. Over the years, she lived with the fear of having the picture discovered by her parents. When she was hired as the school librarian, a position which came with locking doors and cabinets and cashboxes, she decided the safest thing was to keep the picture here, where, if discovered, a long-ago predecessor could be implied—adding another mark of deceitfulness to the array of sins the pictured woman had caused her to commit over the years.

Beth Ann was compelled to dig out the old photograph because of the girl, Frankie. Being around her set off the same kinds of feelings as the photo did, sparked the same sorts of thoughts. The compulsion was amplified by the bond that obviously existed between Frankie and Rebecca, a bond Shirley sensed too, and one which provoked a jealousy in Shirley that filled the space around the three girls like a seeping gas.

Beth Ann gazed at the photograph until the woman's white flesh and black patch were freshly imprinted on her mind's eye. Then she shut off the light, hoping to keep what came next, and the shame of it, a secret from even herself. She tried to will it otherwise, but the woman's face, the woman's flesh became Frankie's. The woman's black patch.

WHEN BETH ANN ARRIVED at school Frankie was waiting in the hall outside the library door. Good morning, said Beth Ann trying not to sound self-conscious as she slipped off the wire of keys to unlock the door.

Good morning. Sorry to be lying in wait but I finished *Silas Marner* and want to check out *The Mill on the Floss.*

You've developed a taste for George Eliot. Beth Ann opened the door and had Frankie go in first.

I have. I was up too late finishing it, but I couldn't help myself. Frankie set *Silas Marner* on Miss Ferguson's desk. I'm afraid I may be falling asleep in Mr. Henderson's class, she said confidentially.

Not a fan of proofs and theorems? Beth Ann turned on the light switch.

They're o.k.—Frankie was making her way toward *The Mill on the Floss*—but it's right before lunch, and Mr. H's teaching manner is very . . . calming.

That's a good word. Beth Ann placed her sack lunch in the bottom drawer of the desk. She thought of the woman in the picture, perched on the edge of an elegant drawing-room settee. She thought of Frankie perching on the settee, which she always imagined was crimson, with gold tassels dangling from its upholstered arms.

I usually have time to read in Mrs. Wilson's class, and Mrs. Mesmore's sometimes. I want to be prepared just in case. Frankie set the heavy book on Beth Ann's desk.

Beth Ann pulled out her chair. A thick cushion raised her to a workable height. She advanced the date on the stamper while Frankie wrote her name on the book's card. It hasn't been checked out for more than five years, she said. I always feel a bit sad for books if no one has read them for a while. Frankie's dark hair was shorter than most girls' and swept over to one side, rather boyishly. It often hung down and obscured one eye, which somehow intensified the pristine green of the one in view, the one which had a way of both demanding Beth Ann's attention and diverting it away. No other student, no other person, had ever provoked such a confusion of feelings in her.

Beth Ann stamped the card and the due-date slip in the book. I know what you mean. Two weeks, she said, like always.

Frankie blew on the wet ink a moment before closing the cover. Two weeks, she repeated. Thanks, Miss Ferguson.

The door opened. There you are, said Rebecca. We're going to be late. She smiled hello at Miss Ferguson and took Frankie by the arm. Bookworm, she said to the librarian.

There are worse things, said Beth Ann. Have a good day, ladies.

The pair shut the door as they hurried off. The noise of children rushing and chattering in the hallway spiked for a moment as Rebecca came and went.

Beth Ann touched the cover of *Silas Marner* where many fingers had worn the cloth shiny.

MOM, I'M GOING for a walk, Beth Ann said toward the sewing-room where her mother spent her evenings, even though there was little sewing to do. She would listen to the radio, read from her Bible, drink a cup of tea.

A walk, replied her mother as she turned down the Sylvania's volume. Be sure to wear your coat and hat, the brown knit one, maybe mittens too.

Be back in a bit. Beth Ann took the coat from the peg by the kitchen door. The hat was in the sleeve. She didn't bother with mittens.

Fall was her favorite season, especially late fall, when the temperature at night would come close to freezing and in the morning everything would be lightly glazed with frost, leaving a fairy-tale luster on the colorful mums and asters which grew in three-season beds, and grass which had gone dormant for the season, and the carpets of leaves that collected in ditches and various corners here and there. For a brief time the village looked like somewhere else, and Beth Ann often ached for anywhere but the village.

It was just such a night, with leaves skittering along the ground, more heard than seen, and an amber moon, no longer quite full, brushing the edges of the ambulating clouds. All Hallows' Eve was past, and they were on the cold dark march to winter.

Frankie's father had bought the old O'Brien place, probably without knowing its history. The O'Briens had been gone for more than a generation yet the village still called it the O'Brien place. The entire family died within its walls except the daughter, Elizabeth, who moved away as soon as she was well enough. She was seen around the village from time to time—not an aging Elizabeth O'Brien, but the teenage girl who was said to have survived the ordeal, a beautiful emerald-eyed ghost whose blond ponytail was tied with a ribbon of black silk. Sometimes she spoke to people, it was said, especially people who had just lost a loved one, or were about to. No one knew what happened to her after she left the village, or why her spirit seemed to haunt it still.

Beth Ann had never encountered Elizabeth O'Brien, but her father claimed to have spoken with her on the night of Beth Ann's birth, which was also the night of her sister's death, the baby who was to be Ann: Beth and Ann, identical girls, named for their grandmothers, but Ann's cord took her life before it had begun. Beth's parents added the Ann to her name so that she could be both girls, the living one and the dead one. They didn't think of it in that way probably, but the effect had been the same on Beth Ann, who felt forever conjoined to her absent sister, and forever guilty that she was the one to survive. Her parents should have felt equal parts joy and grief at the birth and death of their girls, but grief must be the more powerful emotion, Beth Ann reasoned, for it had won the day and all the days thereafter.

When her father died, Beth Ann wondered if she'd be visited by Elizabeth O'Brien. When she was not, she concluded, The ghost girl only comes at the loss of a loved one.

These were among her thoughts as she walked the village's windy streets, pretending not to be going to Frankie's house. What, after all, would be the purpose?

When Frankie and her father moved to the village the previous summer, people were critical behind her back, though barely. Besides her short, boyish hairstyle, they criticized her clothing. She wore skirts and dresses like the other girls, but they appeared chosen with little thought and every article could stand an enthusiastic ironing. And why the nickname Frankie? What was wrong with Francine? Nevertheless, Frankie had a magnetic quality. There was a confidence in the way she carried herself, again almost boyish in its naturalness, but it was her eyes and the set of her gaze which Beth Ann found most mesmerizing: she always looked to be challenging you, or at least ready to. Beth Ann couldn't imagine anyone taking advantage of Frankie, and that innate authority was perhaps her most compelling quality.

Beth Ann knew she was not alone in her attraction to Frankie. The boys took note of her, as well as grown men in the village. Even Rebecca's father, Pastor Phillips, who'd soon become like a second father, focused an attentive eye on Frankie as she returned up the aisle to her pew during Sunday service. Beth Ann observed surreptitiously from the final row, also keen to watch Frankie's every move. Frankie was a temptress and didn't seem to know it, a Drusilla whose divinely gifted beauty drove men and women alike toward their darker impulses.

The old O'Brien place was two and a half stories with a wide porch, like most of the houses in the village. It was painted white with dark-colored shutters (the precise shade of which one couldn't see at night). There was a light in an upstairs room, likely a bedroom. The curtains were partially pulled back yet

Beth Ann couldn't really see into the room. The leafless limbs of an ancient tree in the front yard also obscured her view.

She stood on the walk across the street. If the wind stopped for a moment, she might hear music, faintly, maybe coming from the lighted room, possibly Frankie's room. There may have been movement, just then, a body crossing in then out of view ever so briefly. Or it may have been shadows of the stripped limbs falling across the muntined panes.

The moon washed the house in a saffron-amber bath.

Hands in her coat pockets, Beth Ann stared up at the window for several minutes, picking up and considering her feelings like items in a curiosity shop, each one unnamable and possibly no longer of use.

Beth Ann hadn't heard the approach of the girl who stood on the walk in front of Frankie's house, also peering upward but at a more severe angle. The impression was that she suddenly materialized there. Her back was to Beth Ann, whose first thought was of Elizabeth O'Brien's ghost, revisiting her old home. The girl wore a wool coat and cap, and the hair that spilled beneath it was too dark for her to be the ghost of the golden-headed girl. Then Beth Ann had the odd idea the feminine figure was the spirit of her dead sister, grown up and Beth Ann's exact age.

A spike of wind threatened to blow off the wool cap, and the girl reached up to secure it. Her movements made the truth plain: it was Shirley Donaldson who stood alone, a solitary apparition, in front of Frankie's house. The breeze carried a voice to Beth Ann. Shirley was speaking to herself, perhaps debating whether or not she should knock on her nemesis's door. Shirley turned her head and said, I know, I know. She was agitated. Perhaps there was someone else there. Beth Ann searched the moonlit space but found not a soul.

Shirley's soliloquy ceased when the upstairs light went out. Momentarily the front door began to open, and Shirley ducked into the shadows of the yard, behind a thick evergreen bush next to the porch.

Frankie and Rebecca came from the house. They bounded down the porch steps as lithe and as lighthearted as fawns. Frankie said something that made Rebecca laugh.

They reached the brick walk and turned to their left; Shirley was in no danger of being discovered. After a few moments she emerged from her hiding place and began to follow her classmates.

Beth Ann then started following Shirley, still on the opposite side of the street. Beth Ann wasn't sure why she wanted to trail after the girls, maybe simple curiosity. She thought Shirley might catch up with Frankie and Rebecca, call out to them. Some part of her must have wanted to, but Shirley hung back and stayed in the street's wavering shadows.

The wind was such that now and again Beth Ann could hear Frankie and Rebecca's chirpy banter, merry and light. She thought she also detected Shirley's morosely accented monologue. No meaning, however, accompanied the words which rode the rising and falling wind.

The girls turned onto Main Street, and Shirley hesitated at the corner. Beth Ann too. She carefully worked her way to Main, parallel to Shirley, by cutting through the Reynolds' yard, concealing herself behind their swaying willow tree. Standing at the edge of the yard, Beth Ann again watched the three girls. She had the sense that she was some sort of fulcrum: ahead of her were Rebecca, Frankie and Shirley, and behind, all in a row, her dead sister, Elizabeth O'Brien and the woman from the old photograph. She turned but of course found no one, leave be any spectral figures, any watchful phantoms.

Shirley had moved to the corner of the hardware store, long closed for the evening, where she could observe her two classmates. Beth Ann was farther away but had a mostly unfettered view of the square and gazebo, washed in the moon's amber light.

Frankie and Rebecca scampered around the gazebo, and up and down its steps, taking turns chasing and being chased. Laughing, almost squealing at times. Beth Ann had never seen this side of the girls. Rebecca didn't surprise her but she never imagined Frankie in this way—Frankie who seemed too worldly, even at seventeen, to be so carefree, so happy in such a childlike way.

Meanwhile Shirley was whispering fiercely to someone who seemed to be just at her shoulder. Beth Ann heard, I know, I will! before Shirley stepped out of the shadow of the hardware store.

At the same instant a pickup truck, Bobby Anthony's, rumbled up from Maple Street and stopped on the opposite side of the square. The driver, Bobby presumably, honked twice as the passenger window rolled down. It was difficult to hear clearly, above the wind and the Ford's engine, but Beth Ann caught . . . you two . . . crazy . . . here, before the girls walked up to the truck to talk.

Shirley retreated into the shadows.

After a minute the passenger door opened with a rusty wince and it was Egg Bishop who got out. Even at a distance there was no mistaking his body's angular, athletic confidence, and, besides, Egg and Bobby were good friends. Frankie and Rebecca climbed into the truck's cab while Egg deftly hopped into the bed of the Ford. The four teenagers pulled away from the square, onto Pine Street and out of view.

Beth Ann thought of saying something to Shirley, whose loneliness and hurt filled the night air like smoke from an unwholesome fire, but how could she account for her own spying on the scene from the dark of Carl Reynolds's yard? Shirley's shape was barely discernible as she stood whispering to something in the dark. Beth Ann turned and walked the opposite way.

* * *

WE HAVE AN IDEA for our costumes, said Rebecca. She didn't say it but Beth Ann knew we meant her and Frankie. Shirley was no longer animated, as she had been when they met the previous day. She was the most excited of the girls to be cast as the Weird Sisters. Today, as they had their sack lunches in the library, Shirley was quiet and withdrawn. Beth Ann couldn't help wondering if she might be a more natural Lady Macbeth.

All right, said Beth Ann. Let's hear it.

We were inspired by Greek mythology as much as the play itself. What if we have the bodies of crows? Black feathers and wings, and maybe black leotards.

Bird bodies, said Beth Ann, like the Sirens.

Exactly, said Frankie, toying with the crust of her ham sandwich.

I like it. It's original, as far as I know. What are your thoughts, Shirley?

It's fine, it's good.

Shirley's great at costumes, said Rebecca. I bet you can make them really creepy. Remember the headless horseman you made freshman year? That was great.

Shirley offered a thin smile. Sure, sounds terrific. She sipped some milk through her straw.

We really want to get this boil and bubble scene just right, make it terrifying if we can, said Rebecca. She'd pulled the rind from her bologna and was fingering the thin strip of casing. We know the perfect place to rehearse, just to get the feel right. Then we can transfer it to the stage. She seemed reluctant to reveal the spot. Lucifer's Cave.

Shirley set her milk down, and the bottle's glass bottom hit the table hard. Are you crazy?

Beth Ann didn't say anything. Rebecca couldn't be serious.

Frankie said, I know what you're thinking but it's not what

everybody believes. Lucifer doesn't really live in the cave. That's a myth, a ridiculous myth.

Shirley spoke to Rebecca: You're fine with this? It doesn't sound like you. She was angry.

Beth Ann said, Relax. I don't think that's a good idea, girls. I applaud your ambition but that may be getting carried away with your roles. It happens.

Frankie and Rebecca exchanged looks. Frankie appeared irritated now. Tell them, she said.

Rebecca had rolled her bologna rind into a ball, which she placed in a crumpled sheet of wax paper. She said, We've been there, Frankie and me, to Lucifer's Cave. Last summer. It's fine. There's nothing dangerous. Certainly the devil doesn't live there. Like Frankie said, it's just an old myth, a wives' tale.

I can't believe you, said Shirley, barely able to contain herself. I *don't* believe you. This is just a story. You didn't used to be a liar. She was speaking to Rebecca but daggered a look at Frankie. She pushed back the heavy library chair, nearly knocking it over, and left like a tearful and petulant thunderhead.

After she had gone: Don't tell, Frankie said to Beth Ann. Please.

I . . . began Beth Ann, not sure what would follow. I won't. Her head was filled with Frankie, trying to comprehend her. She seemed to be not just from another town but another world, an alien place not governed by the same rules, the same codes of conduct, not even the same laws of physics.

Thank you, Miss Ferguson, said Frankie.

Shirley will be o.k., said Rebecca. She'll come around.

They hurried through their lunches to finish before the bell. When the girls had gone, Beth Ann disposed of the remnants of Shirley's lunch. She'd only managed a bite of her peanut butter sandwich. Beth Ann hoped she wouldn't be hungry, but she knew hunger, hunger for food, was the least of her worries. She was starving for Rebecca's friendship, for her love, for the way things were before Frankie and her father moved to the village. She may starve nearly to death from that hunger, thought Beth Ann, who felt her own gnawing need, ill-defined but ever-present.

THE INTERLIBRARY LOAN TRUCK had visited and brought two titles for Beth Ann: *Sonnets from the Portuguese* and *Ethan Frome*, Elizabeth Barret Browning and Edith Wharton. Throughout the day Beth Ann tried to distract herself from unpleasant thoughts associated with Shirley's loneliness and her own sense of isolation by looking forward to being alone with the books, secure in the sphere created by their words. She recognized the irony of seeking solace from loneliness in isolation, yet she longed for her time alone within the books' insular worlds.

After school Rebecca and Frankie came to the library to work on their lines but Shirley had gone straight home, saying she didn't feel well. She'll be fine, repeated Rebecca. Beth Ann read Shirley's lines, but it wasn't the same as having all of the Sisters together, so the session ended early.

Beth Ann was on her way shortly, after spending a few minutes in her office. In just the brief walk across the street to her house, the feeling of being followed returned to her. Before entering the kitchen, Beth Ann glanced behind her: of course there was no one. She quickly ate the stew her mother had left for her on the stove and prepared to go out.

Leaving again? her mother asked from her sewing-room. She'd turned down the volume on the Sylvania to hear her daughter's reply.

Just going for a walk. She would have preferred to slip out unnoticed but her mother knew the sound of every activity in the house, which she'd occupied since her wedding day thirty-seven years before, a teenage bride the age of Rebecca, Frankie and Shirley now. With its hardwood floors, worn rugs, aged hinges, gravity toilets, creaking stairs and venerable pipes, Beth Ann's mother knew all, seated in her sewing-room like a Sybil. Even with the ubiquitous radio she was able to infer everything with an uncanny arachnid precision.

Wear your scarf and hat, said her mother. Winter is in the air. The Almanac says there'll be a hard frost before All Souls. The radio's volume rose to its former level.

All right, Mother. Beth Ann resisted the urge to walk into her lair, take up the Sylvania and smash it against the wall so hard that the plaster may crack, the radio's voice suddenly silenced, mid hymn or some aborted report.

Beth Ann knotted the scarf around her neck, pulled on her hat and coat and left the kitchen, which still smelled heavily of beef stew.

The temperature was chillier tonight, the darkness more leaden. She thought of the Greek myth of the siblings Night and Darkness, children of Chaos, and it seemed that tonight Darkness had the upper hand in their ancient, never-ending rivalry. She needn't pretend she was simply out for a walk; she acknowledged her purpose and set out for Frankie's house, the old O'Brien place. She may not be home. She may be at Rebecca's. It was a cold night but she didn't mind whatever effort it required to track down Frankie, though she had no intention of speaking with her. Beth Ann only wanted to see her through a window, or just know Frankie was at home and relatively near to her. It was a cold night and she didn't mind acknowledging that Frankie was the object of her desire, as she seemed to be so many others'.

Frankie was off limits to her in more ways than Beth Ann could name, but she could gaze upon her, and be near her, and project her into the world of the old photo, to displace the woman of the luminous skin, a kind of down-to-earth Diana in some mystical intimate space, an object of so many desires herself. The picture was so old the woman and her admirers were likely dead—all that remained was her image and the feelings she could still inflame.

Were those the feelings of her father, the night he came to Beth Ann's bed, to comfort her—I heard your nightmare—but she recalled no nightmare, nothing as strange or as unsettling as her father at that moment. He crawled beneath the covers to comfort her further—There's a good girl. She was twelve. Her mother had been having one of her terrible headaches for a day or two and had taken the blue pills that make her sleep dead to the world. Her father was hurting her in a way she'd never been hurt—There's a good girl, Annie. Maybe this was the nightmare he'd heard her having. She tried to wake—Daddy loves you. Cigarette smoke, shaving lotion, beer.

She'd only had the nightmare once, but the world afterward was forever altered. He died when she was nineteen, a stroke. He'd been shoveling snow. It was March, a day or two before spring. 'Bewitched' was on her mother's radio *Couldn't sleep, wouldn't sleep, Love came and told me, Shouldn't sleep* when she glanced out the window and saw him lying in the snow. Why would he lie in the snow? That's an odd thing to do. His shovel lay diagonally across the cleared walk.

All was quiet at Frankie's house, and at Rebecca's. Beth Ann saw Pastor Phillips pass a window, perhaps holding a book, perhaps it was a Bible—however, there was no sign of the pastor's daughter and Frankie.

Beth Ann decided to go to Shirley Donaldson's even though it seemed unlikely the girls would be there, unless Rebecca was trying to smooth things over between her two antagonistic friends. Behind her, Beth Ann felt the Argos eyes of the three specters: her sister, Elizabeth O'Brien and the photograph woman, who more and more resembled Frankie.

The streets of the village were quiet. Beth Ann had seen the tail lights of a truck at a distance, like the enraged eyes of a dragon, but otherwise no one was out on this cold, damp night. November, soon to be winter's December. Why was *she*? Beth

Ann felt a restlessness, some close kin of anger, and only physical activity kept it from crossing over into something uglier, an emotion she would likely release at her mother for lack of a more deserving recipient.

When Beth Ann reached the Donaldsons', the house was mostly dark, save for a light shining dimly and perhaps candescently in an upstairs window. As she walked beyond the house, however, she saw a brighter light in the large garage. The harsh bulb beaconed through the panes and fell in yellow parallelograms on the lawn. The garage's door was ajar, and Beth Ann could hear rummaging.

She went to the side of the garage opposite the house to peek in a window there. She had no fear of being caught snooping, she realized. She felt as insubstantial as one of the apparitions which trailed behind her, like a being only half-formed in a space it was meant to occupy fully.

Something inside the garage was propped against the window, making it difficult to gain a good view. Plus Beth Ann was so small she had to stand on tiptoe to see in the window at all. Nevertheless, it was definitely Shirley who was picking through a metal toolbox, open on her father's worktable in the back of the garage. There were tools arranged in orderly rows on the pegboard in front of Shirley but apparently none of those would do.

As Beth Ann became more accustomed to peering through the glass, she saw that Shirley had a knapsack which she was filling with whatever items she located, until it had a bulky heft. Shirley was turned in a way that prevented Beth Ann from seeing the items she placed inside.

Shirley lifted the knapsack onto one shoulder, switched off the worktable light, and exited the garage. Beth Ann paid out some distance then began to follow her on the winter-dark street.

Shirley walked with determination, urgency even; so much

so Beth Ann had nearly to run to keep her in sight. It was hardly the first time she wished her legs were longer, her gait greater.

Shirley turned onto Main Street, passed the hardware store, the library, Owens' Café. The gazebo in the square, absent of moonlight, crouched as a dark structure, a touch menacing and even mechanical, a collector and container of sorrowful souls.

Beth Ann clung to the edge of the square, both wary of and grateful for the darkness. She was beginning to perspire with the exertion of keeping pace with Shirley, who seemed so focused on her course Beth Ann speculated that keeping her distance was probably unnecessary as Shirley wouldn't notice her if she was at her heel. Then she had the odd thought that she too was a ghostly figure, like the three who haunted her.

Beth Ann quickened her already quick stride and closed the distance. She listened for the sound of her own footfalls and was relieved to detect their echoing off the brick walk. Shirley turned the corner onto Park Street, and there was no question she was headed toward Hollis Woods, which rested on the shoulder of the village. The woods were considered off limits after dark, their unlighted footpaths too treacherous. Still, the more rebellious teenagers were rumored to sneak into the woods from time to time, their fathers' filched liquor in hand. Or there were whispers of other goings-on. Beth Ann had never entered the woods at night.

Just before reaching the woods' boundary Shirley switched on a flashlight—Beth Ann saw its beam bounce along the ground. It must have come from Shirley's bulky knapsack.

Beth Ann followed the dancing bead of light because Shirley had become all but invisible on the path through Hollis Woods. Her light wasn't slowing at all. If anything, she'd increased her pace. For a brief moment Beth Ann thought about the possibility of losing track of Shirley and being there in the woods on the darkest of nights, a place which had always bore the brushstrokes of menace, especially after nightfall—and she was surprised to discover she wasn't afraid. The presences she sensed at her back were a comfort, familiar companions who posed no threat at all. Also, Beth Ann knew where Shirley was going, and that they would find Frankie and Rebecca already there.

In fact, Shirley had reached the departure in the main path which led to Lucifer's Cave. In Shirley's light Beth Ann saw the simple barricade which barred entrance to the overgrown way. The sawhorse of faded diagonal stripes had been moved aside, and Shirley stepped past it. Beth Ann had never considered how inadequate the barrier was for keeping people from wandering into such a dangerous place: the cave's reputation—the myth itself—was the real obstruction.

Though still several yards behind, Beth Ann's vision was fully adjusted to the dark and she saw Shirley's shape silhouetted against a soft glow of sallow light that must have marked the cave's entrance.

Shirley's flashlight went out as her shadow slipped inside.

Beth Ann tried to control her breathing. Her heart was racing from the exertion but she tried not to make a sound. She could tell it was candlelight that washed the contours of the cave's opening. An echo of singsong voices escaped the interior of the den. She too went inside. A scent like black, overturned earth.

Shirley was just a few feet in front of her, stock still and apparently unnoticed by Frankie and Rebecca, who were holding hands in the center of the small cave, where they'd placed a stockpot, substitute for the Sisters' cauldron. They were incanting the lines from the play, Scale of dragon, tooth of wolf. . . . Dozens of candles were aglow throughout the cave, especially along the far wall where an alien shape was set in the rock, a creature with sharp claws and a head equine in form, a creature carved or captured in the stone. The dozens of candle flames wriggling in the drafty cave cast their weird light on the thing and gave it animation.

Finger of birth-strangled babe—the girls looked at each other and giggled just as Beth Ann noticed the hammer, just as she noticed Shirley raise it. Beth Ann tried to step forward to stop her or at least to call out, but hands seemed to restrain her and cold fingers stifled her words as she watched Shirley rush forward, claw-hammer overhead, hell-bent on smashing the beast.

Weird Soliloquies

***FIRST*. WHEN SHALL WE** three meet again, in thunder, lightning or in rain? We six really, for we carry too the fate of our phantasmal familiars, messengers from those murdering ministers. The dark shape of his shadow sits at my shoulder whispering, murmuring, urging just out of view. He sows fear of Fife, warns of Fife's unmothered machinations, flashes and rumbles revelations, forecasting the past we've always known: the look, the tone, the posture projecting peril. Paterfamilias. Which turn of time is worse? The untimely death of a youthful father, or his longevity and the lengthening of the long black nights of menace which stretch into morning, into months—where the brightness of day is only associated with black bunting and mourning dress. Clothes the color of the bruise around mother's eye and the one ringing brother's arm. Arm, arm and out. But there is no out. No one knows. Perhaps some suspect, Rebecca's father, Dr. Higgins, Mr. Reynolds. Mr. Reynolds, who watches mother with a careful, lupine keenness, on the street, in church, almost piercing the pew where we sit, father and mother on either side, brother and I in between, the smell of sacred wax, sweat, and secrets all around. Rebecca's father's words fall upon us, his sermon soaking us steadily, pressing my hair against my neck, plastering my skirt against my thighs. (Like this storm, whose contours are seen solely in revelatory flashes.) I look three pews ahead at the back of Rebecca's blond head as she sits with the usurper, Frankie, a friendship at first forced by her father, but now embraced and feverishly felt. More than usurper: thief, bedlamite, whore. She should be sent out, banished, but instead is held dear in spite of her insolence—she has no love of this place, this church, this faith—only of Rebecca and the anticipation of her corruption, her downfall, her destruction. It is as plain as the past, if only they would open their eyes to it, see the fate which frolics before them, like naked satyrs and nymphs, carousing and copulating in the ritual spring rain. But we shall reclaim Rebecca, the only one who quiets the chaos of our darkness, who calms our storm-surged sea. Rebecca, our past must stretch into a future without the usurper, the thief, the whore. She must return to my bed and forsake the bedlamite. The shadowed head at my shoulder whispers it is so, his chafed lips brush my ear, his charnel-house breath clouds my cheek, his pestilent presence pricks the sides of my vaulting purpose. But Frankie mustn't know our feelings: our false face must be a fair mask, our foul design a marvelous mystery.

Second. When the hurly-burly's done, when the battle's lost and won. Whose bloody babe be this? Surely not mine. Yet he laments to my milkless breast, dissatisfied with my denials of motherhood. Just as Shirley has tried to deny me Frankie. Why can we not all three be friends, as bound as sisters? Fate after all has delivered us here, to this desert place, where Blight has stood his baneful watch upon our battlements since this forsaken place was settled. But we must acknowledge, the babe and I, the blight was brightened when Frankie came. Frankie who wore her pain as a challenge, who seemed to neither need nor want friendship, indeed affection, when really the bottom of her need had fallen so far she'd lost touch with its terminus. Perhaps the bloody babe who mouths a maternal warning is the dead brother that took Frankie's mother too, both untimely ripped from Frankie's life, and her father's: his wound remains open and bloody for anyone to see. The seller of seed harbors a barren soul. Frankie's hurt lay deeper, in some dark, sealed-off corner, a hidden space where scar tissue could be probed only if one searched persistently enough. Over time she shared the burden of her scarification, which in the night would ache with the pain of the old wound. (Lightning breaks a corner of the sky as wind-driven drops prick like icy shrapnel.) Perhaps the bloody babe is Frankie's, or Frankie herself, or both—akin to God's being the Father and Son—a twist Frankie would riotously reject. The bloody babe's whispered words carry the motherless warning, as well as an interjection to be bold and well-resolved: single-minded, vicious even, in our determination. If so I must hold it dearer still, for fear that Shirley and her phantom familiar will wrest Frankie from me, and Frankie's love, for she must feel the same burning star, a new and bewildering combustion in my breast—something a boy was to evoke, yet it flares at the heated touch of Frankie's hand, the defiant focus of her eyes, the lilt of longing in her tongue. We must deny our denial, the babe and I. We must embrace that amorous ember, even if we are burned beyond recognition.

Third. That will be ere the set of sun. Darkness has been descending on Rebecca and Shirley's friendship, an unlikely thing from the start, due only to geography, as improbable as the forest uprooting itself. Instead of Birnam, here it is Hollis Woods, where Rebecca and I clasped hands and hearts for the first time, in the dank cave where legend alleges Lucifer lives. Shirley holds onto her old friend with a breathless anxiety. I understand: the fearful foreboding of loss, the acidic anticipation of isolation. Just as this child clings to me, with his needled bough and crown of thorns promising what appears a bright future but the flash is only the foretaste of doom. He is the age my brother would be, should be. There was a name chosen but father will not bring it to his lips, as if a poisoned chalice, as if the poor child's name were a malediction—yet the silence and secrecy are their own kind of curse, their own sort of sentence in our house, where emptiness is an unfailing reminder of loss, a deafening herald of death—as absent of life as abandoned Dunsinane. Indeed, a museum to grief whose central exhibits dominate due to their absence, like an elaborate frame whose canvas has been slashed and stolen to reveal the cracked plaster behind, the stained paper beyond. Rebecca, however, has begun to fill that space, especially when she sleeps beside me, her shoulder and hip and thigh kissing my shoulder, hip, thigh beneath the blanket. Sometimes I fight sleep to prolong the thought of her presence, the awareness of her arrival in my life. An unlikely slice of luck, of happiness (as unexpected as that flash of lightning now, as surprising as the pricking drops of wind-driven rain).

Retribution

Excerpt from a prose poetry translation
of *Beowulf* (ll. 1321-1590)

Beowulf, a visiting Geat, has rid King Hrothgar's hall of Grendel, the menacing creature who has been murdering the Danes for twelve long years, but the next night Grendel's mother attacks the hall in retribution for her son's death. And Beowulf is called on again.

[20]

HROTHGAR, HELMET OF THE SCYLDINGS, replied [to Beowulf]: Ask not after our happiness—for sorrow again lurks in our luckless land. Aeschere, Yrmenlaf's elder brother, is lost, my keeper of secrets and wellspring of wisdom. We stood shoulder-to-shoulder striking as one when clashing footsoldiers tried to remove our boar-crested heads. However bathed in bravery a man should be, demonstrating a nobility from olden times, that was princely Aeshere. But now a wandering blood-thirsty wight has snatched him from Hereot hoping for a rich reward. The bold terror has fled somewhere, perhaps to devour her hapless victim, I cannot say. She has avenged the crushing grip by which you caught Grendel on his last night, payment for my people's pernicious annihilation. Something terrible has now befallen Aeschere in this feud, his future likely forfeited, as a new threat, a vicious visitant, has come to continue the deadly quarrel after a death among her clan. Many a thane knows the weight of a heart's bitter weeping following the loss of a beloved brother-in-arms, a generous bearer of gifts. Now that hand which would have given you—all of you!—your heart's desire is hidden from us.

It has been reported by those who work the land, and confirmed by my councilors, that two powerful prowlers have been spotted among the marshes, queer characters who rule over the waste-lands. One, according to the most reliable reports, has a feminine form, while the other misshapen outcast seems male, but larger and more powerful than any other . . . man at least: Grendel, or so he was named by the workers of the earth in days long gone. No father for the pair is known, nor whether any other fear-some creatures came before them. They live in a place shrouded in secrecy, a treacherous track thick with wolves, where windy cliffs loom above the waste-land and dark waters cascade into a tumult that races toward the nether-world. Marked off in miles, it is not far, their hoarfrosted fen, where firmly rooted woods darken the wretched water. There, kinsmen claim, flames flicker ominously upon the flood, night after night. No man lives, no matter how old or how wise, who can surmise the mere's malig-nant depths. The hard-horned hart, high-stepper of the heath, pushed there by hounds, would rather surrender to the savage pack than hide—it is such an unholy place. Black waves blast to-ward the heavens when hostile storms further disturb the surge, salting the air as if the sky were weeping. Now you alone can save us, even though you know not this perilous place. You may find her there, this sinister creature. Dare to seek her, and if you survive the fight, I shall again reward you with the worthiest treasure of wound gold.

[21]

BEOWULF, SON OF ECGTHEOW, replied: Your wisdom must in-form you it is better to punish those who pile sorrow at our door than to be forlorn over a friend's sad fate. We must all bear knowing our life in this world will end. Allow whoever is able to achieve their glory before death. For afterward, it will be their most enduring memorial. Take heart, wisest watchman of the realm—we shall swiftly take to the track of Grendel's dam, and on this threat I will make good: She has no chance to lose herself, not in the earth's embrace, not among the mountain's forest, not on the sea's sandy floor—flee where she will. Patience can be excruciating, but I know you will practice it today. The ancient one's spirit was lifted by this bold speech, and he gave thanks to God, praised the All-Powerful.

Then Hrothgar's mount was duly dressed, a haughty warhorse with a mane of intricate braids. The wise old king set off in a magnificent manner, leading a fine troop of linden-bearing footsoldiers. The tracks were easily seen where she had borne the best of thanes along the forest floor and directly to her dark domain. The lifeless captive had always helped Hrothgar watch over his home. The king and his company worked their way along the unwelcoming path, at times so narrow they were compelled to squeeze through one by one, then edge along a high seawall where myriad monsters made their home. He went first, with some seasoned soldiers, to spy out the land. Quickly they came to a forbidding forest where mountain trees angled above gray rock. Below, the water was grim with gore. Misery dealt a murderous blow to the Danes on that sea-cliff—to every last warrior, including the friends of the Scyldings—when they came upon Aeschere's severed head. The bloody sea-surge boiled with gore, upon which all were drawn to gaze. Then battle-horns sounded, singing their readiness for war—and the waiting soldiers stole a moment's rest.

The water churned with many strange creatures of the sea, while kindred monsters lay upon the rocks, the sorts of sea-serpents and wild beasts that menace mariners as they navigate early-morning channels. The creatures sank away, furious and fulminating, the second they heard the battle-horns' sharp song. A Geat, their chief archer, used his bow to bury a war-hardened shaft in one such water-beast, cutting short its struggles. It swam slowly in the surf toward the realm of death. A barbed javelin designed for hunting boars hooked the desperate wave-roamer and hauled it onto the rocks. All gaped at the gruesome guest.

Beowulf dressed for battle, not in the least mindful of his mortality. The well-made mail, ample and artfully adorned, must safeguard his body as he searched the sea, shielding his breast when caught in the grip of war, in the malicious grasp of a murderous foe. A rare helmet—refulgent and complete with a curtain of rings covering the neck, created by a master smith of the olden days—would protect the hero's head; and when the sandy seafloor was churned into a cloud of chaos, a boar-crest amulet would prove impenetrable to any war-sword or battleax. At this critical moment Hrothgar's humbled advisor, Unferth, lent Beowulf a powerful aid: the specially hilted sword known as Hrunting, a nightmare of a weapon, highly treasured in times of strife. Its ferric edge was festooned with terrible tendrils, poison-laced thorns hard-varnished with the blood of the vanquished. It had proved worthy of every warrior who had wielded it in the stronghold of his enemies. Indeed, this was hardly the first time it would be relied upon to carry out an act of courage. It seemed certain that Unferth, son of Ecglaf, wanted to forget the drunken insults he had hurled at the superior swordsman, skilled in feats of strength, when he lent him the weapon. He would not dare risk his life beneath that turbulent tide—in his failure to seek fame he lost his good name forever. Not so for the other, the man wardrobed in war-gear.

[22]

BEOWULF, SON OF ECGTHEOW, said: I am eager to set off, son of Healfdene, wisest of kings and gold-friend to your men. Bear in mind our arrangement, of which we spoke before, that should I fall in fulfilling my promise, you will embrace the role of my father. Likewise, grant your guardianship to my young comrades, closest of companions, if this battle carries me off. Furthermore, beloved Hrothgar, forward to Hygelac the spectacular gifts you have showered upon me. Thus the great leader of the Geats, Hrethel's son, when he is struck by the magnificence of the treasure, will realize that I have made the most of my time here and was richly rewarded by a gracious ring-giver. And you, Unferth, man widely known, have this revered heirloom—this hard-edged sword with its perfect blade expertly patterned after the sea. I shall bear Hrunting in my hunt for fame, or be borne away by death.

After these bold words, the much-loved leader of the Weather-Geats rushed away without awaiting reply, and the swirling sea accepted the impetuous warrior. Then daylight helped him discover the dim bottom.

Soon the grim and greedy one who had ruled that watery realm with a ravenous ferocity for some fifty years sensed that a man from above was penetrating her unwelcoming place. She clutched the warrior in her wicked claws, hoping to pierce the woven rings of his shirt, but it saved his body and his life from her searching, sickening fingers. Coming to the bottom, the mere-wolf managed the ring-clad prince toward her warren, and, in spite of his resolve, he was restrained from freeing his weapon. All the while a bevy of mysterious sea-beasts beat at his battle-mail and tore at it with their tusks as they pursued the tangled pair. Then the hero discovered he had entered some kind of hostile hall, cut off from the water and the current's cruel grip, due to the hall's high roof. He saw the white light of a fire, its flames flickering brightly.

The valiant visitor also saw the sickening lake-wife, duchess of this lepers' den. He swung the ring-embellished war-sword, saving nothing back, and its aria was a hideous battle-song against her head. But the guest found that the gleaming blade would not bite, let alone prove baneful, its edge failing the imperiled prince. That precious treasure had prevailed countless times in hand-to-hand conflict, cutting helmets, hewing harnesses, delivering enemies to their doom—this was its debut failure.

Recalling his fame and retaining his courage, the determination of Hyglac's kinsman was intact. The enraged warrior tossed to the ground the artfully adorned sword, though rigid and razor-edged. He must trust in his own tireless grip. Such is required of a man if his reputation in battle is to become legendary. He must be willing to forfeit his life.

The War-Geats' great prince grasped Grendel's mother by her hair, harboring no remorse for the move. Many a hard battle helped him to keep his head, and he used his swelling rage to force his lethal lover to the floor. She instantly retaliated with the grasp of her terrible talons, clawing at him. The relentless onslaught wearied the strongest of warriors, the surest of foot, so that he stumbled and fell. She put her full weight upon the visitor to her hall and brandished a short sword, its blade broad and biting, meaning to avenge her only son, her sole offspring. Across his shoulder and breast lay the braided mail, and it protected his body from being pierced or hacked. The Geats' guardian, Ecgtheow's son, would have perished there, beneath the wide earth, if not for his battle-tested gear, true to its purpose in helping holy God determine the contest's victor. The Ruler of the heavens easily foresaw the right result when Beowulf again was upright.

[23]

THEN HE SPOTTED among the scattered war-gear a blade imbued with countless victories in battle, an ancient sword, strong-edged and worthy of the finest fighters. It was a choice weapon but far more than most men could wield in combat—only the hardiest of heroes could harness its special might, manufactured, as it was, by giants. The Scyldings' bold savior drew the ring-marked blade and struck with fury, breaking the bone-rings of her neck, the ancient blade slicing straight through, her body doomed. Lifeless, it crumpled to the floor. The sword-blade glinted with gore—the swordsman with satisfaction.

A light flared, illuminating the interior, as if heaven's own candle had pierced the pall. He surveyed the chamber, quickly turning to the wall. Hygelac's thane, still furiously focused, took up his weapon by its heavy hilt. The blade would prove its worth once more as the warrior wished to repay Grendel for the vicious work he performed on the West-Danes. Hrothgar's hearth-friends, fifteen dozing Danes, were devoured during a recent attack, and as many carried off as a loathsome prize for later. The fierce champion had rewarded him for that, as was evident when he found Grendel, battle-worn, in his final resting-place. He lay dead, obviously drained of life, fatally injured as he was in Heorot. His shattered corpse split wide open, suffering a sort of second brutal death upon Beowulf's merciless sword-stroke, severing completely his head.

Transitional Stories

Chinkó

I AM WRETCHED. I am a disgrace, he thinks, on the verge of tears as he half stumbles along the dark path from the cantina. The warm, humid air makes his knuckles sting. It is too dark to see, but Chinkó imagines his hands to be bloody messes; perhaps a finger or two are broken. His injuries are the least of his problems. After two long, back-breaking months at the *finca* picking coffee beans he has been thrown out, penniless. Back home, in the *Altiplano*, his wife is expecting him to bring home enough money to plant a larger field—to provide more food for his growing family, who so often seem ill and malnourished. But now . . . all is lost.

Chinkó slips and tumbles into a patch of high grass. The dry blades scratch his face and arms. He lies there as if dead, wishing he were.

Inside his head, he curses the *ladinos* and their rotten tequila. It poisoned his mind; he couldn't think. Why else would he start a fight with another Indian worker? Why else would he smash up the cantina, breaking bottles and chairs? Why else would he fight the *ladinos* who came to stop him, calling him "loco" as they beat him with sticks?

Chinkó sees the ugly white face of the overseer as he spits on him and tells him to leave before he is killed.

Lying in the dark patch of grass, invisible, Chinkó's despair is absolute. He must decide: Do I walk the many miles up the mountain roads to my village, where my wife will find me too loathsome to argue with? Or do I wade into the sea until the salt water fills my lungs? Even the fish will have no appetite for his moldering corpse, he believes.

Chinkó listens to the night sounds, which are so different from his mountain home. He misses the mournful shrieks of the monkeys in the rain forest canopy, and the clatter of the giant locust. Chinkó listens hard, wishing that by some miracle the sounds of the *Altiplano* will drift down to him. But, again, he is without hope.

There is a sound, though, that seems familiar, yet strange. It is the noise of the Indian workers in the *galera*, at the other end of the path. But the Indians are louder, more agitated than usual. Have they already heard of his disgrace? No, that could not be it. The Indians have no common language, so they cannot be gossiping about pitiful Chinkó. Only a few in the *galera* are from his village.

Curiosity forces him to his feet, and he continues down the path. In a minute Chinkó sees the glow of the small fires around the open *galera*, which is simply supporting posts and a roof of waxy banana leaves. No walls. The fires are not for warmth; the Guatemalan night is oppressive. The smoke helps to ward off mosquitoes, but its effects are limited.

There are hundreds of Indians, plus their dogs, cats and other animals, in the *galera*. Immediately, Chinkó sees that at the center of the agitation is the Menchú woman from his village. She is speaking to the *caporal*, a young *ladino*, no more than twenty. A machete hangs from his belt, its wide blade weakly reflecting the firelight. Near the woman are two of her children, a girl of about ten and a little boy who is just a baby. They are alone; her husband and older children were taken to another *finca*. The mother is frustrated, desperate. She cannot speak the *ladino*'s Spanish, and the overseer knows little of her village's dialect.

Chinkó understands what she is saying: "My child is dying.

He needs medicine." It is true; in the weak light of the fires, the boy is soaked in perspiration and his breathing is labored. His tiny, starving body trembles.

"No more medicine," says the *caporal* sternly. "Owe too much already."

"What is my child dies?"

"We are not responsible." He walks away and stands by another overseer.

The mother does not understand, but Chinkó is there now and he explains: "The *caporal* says that the *ladinos* will not help you bury your child. You must figure out something yourself."

She stares into Chinkó's face, too full of despair to speak.

"Momma." It is the little girl; she gestures toward her brother.

The Menchú woman kneels by her child and places her ear over his chest, then she caresses his face. She does not need to say it: the little boy is dead.

The *caporal* approaches her. "You have half a day. You may rent a place in the owner's field. Half a day. No more."

The mother has not looked at the *caporal*. Maybe she has not heard. Chinkó says, "They will let you take a half day away from work to bury your child, but you must pay the owner for a burial plot."

The mother's voice is far away. "We have no money; we owe for medicine. I am already two days behind in my work quotas. I will not be able to make up an additional half day; they will kick us out."

News has somehow spread through the *galera* about the boy's death. It is clear that the other workers are sorry for the mother, but they do not want the body left there. In the warm, moist air disease will be quick to come.

An old woman from a nearby villages approaches the Menchú woman. She is holding a small wooden box with a lid, which must have carried supplies for her family. Inside the box is a piece of soiled cloth and some *yuru* plants. The juice from the mountain plants is used for many things by the Indians. When rubbed on the skin of the dead, it slows the decomposition.

The *caporal* is impatient for a response. Chinkó understands that for the mother it is not the debt or the loss of work that adds to her sorrow. The idea that her baby will be buried at the *finca* and will not return to the *Altiplano* is crushing her.

An Indian man comes forward and in his hands is a wad of paper money and coins that he has collected from the other workers. He does not speak the language of Chinkó's village, but it is clear he is offering the money for transportation—so that the Menchú woman can take her children, one of whom is alive and one of whom is dead, and leave.

But if she does not work, what's left of her family will suffer.

Chinkó leans close to the woman: "Prepare you child, and I will take him home for you. Please."

She does not understand the reason for Chinkó's offer (perhaps simple generosity), but the mother has no choice. Without words, she strips the clothes from her dead child, and begins the process of anointing him with the *yuru*. After, she uses a wooden needle and thread to sew him into the cloth. The *caporal* brings a hammer and nails, and Chinkó uses them to seal the boy in the box.

For an hour, the Menchú woman is left alone with her son in his makeshift coffin. She quietly says her prayers, the ancient Indian ones and the ones taught by the Catholic missionaries.

Before dawn, which comes early out of the sea, the box is tied to Chinkó's back with a *pita* rope and he begins the walk to the bus station. It will be a long hot ride up the mountain, but his terrible task will make it bearable.

A Wintering Place

for M. W. S.

THE NOMADS OF THE STEPPES call me a name which loosely translates to 'Black Giant.' Giant is understandable, but the other. . . . Perhaps it is because of my hair, which has grown long down my back. I keep it tied with a leather thong. Perhaps it is because of my cloak—once a dark, rich leather which has been continually exposed to the elements and soaked in seawater several times. Then again, perhaps the nomads have the ability to see into my heart, for it too must be as black as midnight, as black as a vulture's wing, as black as the earth where my victims lie—their bodies strewn across three continents: Europe, Asia, and finally the Arctic. A zigzag trail of blood as crooked as the scars that cover my body like a taut snare. I have not killed—Man anyway—for a long time. Yet the blood seems fresh on my hands. The nomads must sense it too. They keep clear of me. When I have been spotted, they post triple the usual number of sentries for a few nights. No matter. I pass quietly through their encampment, a virtual city of tents, taking what I need. Only what I need—this is important—and only when I need it. Food usually, occasionally ammunition or matches. And I try to pay for what I take. Twice I left them bearskins, another time a leather pouch of herbs. Often I leave toys for their children—figures carved of wood or rock or bone. Animal shapes—bear, deer, squirrel, owl—and figures resembling their nomadic parents. Men with long mustaches and wide shoulders. Women with large eyes, full breasts and long straight hair. Once I carved a likeness of myself but I destroyed the hideous chunk of wood in the fire. I trust the elders give these trinkets to the children. I don't think they associate this covert form of barter with me. Surely they believe one such as I could not possibly slip into their camp, past their vigilant sentries, past their skittish blue-eyed dogs, past the wakeful mothers who fear for their babes. They fear sickness, they fear hunger, and they fear that the Black Giant will snatch them for his stew. Sometimes I hear them muttering about me in the night. I often linger in their camp, listening to their sounds, the walls of their felt tents doing little to insulate them from me. The whimperings of a feverish child, the gibberish of a delusional old man. Couples whispering long into the dark night about their hopes and troubles. Or sometimes I hear their lovemaking—such a foreign sound to my ears. Though I am in a sense a virgin, I somehow recollect the dance of it, and the smell and the taste of it. All of these things come flooding back to me—flooding back from the nameless void which is my past. There is no word, no phrase in any language for my origin. There was a married couple whose trouble *was* lovemaking. I would hear them fumble in their tent, then silence and sighing, then they would speak in voices below hearing. I could only detect the tone. The woman coos as if to an infant. His voice becomes increasingly agitated. Finally he walks in quiet fury from the tent and pisses in the dark. I see his steam rising in the light of a recently full moon. He is bare-chested in spite of the cold. I stay cloaked in shadow, as silent as a tree. The woman begins crying. I wanted to help them. I carved a phallus from ashwood. It took me days to shape and smooth the phallus. Often I was overcome with grief and loneliness and a painful sense of irony. Here I am, healthy and vital, full of love, and I have no one. When I was finished, feeling exhausted and empty, I crept into their tent city. I easily found the home of the troubled couple—I have the senses of a wolf—and I left the phallus outside their tent's opening. I wrapped it in a piece of my finest leather, so that they would know it was a gift and not a cruel joke. I have not been back to eavesdrop on their tent. I could not take another act of kindness being misunderstood and dismissed. It would plunge me into suicidal despair, yet I do not have the courage for suicide. I attempted it once, just after my father died. I stood at the northern rim of the world and set myself on fire. I writhed like a serpent. Then the ice must have cracked and I dropped into the frigid sea. I gulped in the salty water, trying to drown myself. I lost consciousness but awoke on a jagged raft of ice. Involuntarily resurrected once again. I recall little of the weeks that followed. Animal instinct for survival. I made my way south, back toward Man. Man, my cousin at least if not my brother. I have a sense that I made most of the journey on my hands and knees. I ate leaves and grass, much of which I vomited. I ate birds' eggs from their nests. The birds had no sense of how to defend their young against a predator such as I. At one point, my nadir, I found the droppings of a bear and chewed on the bits of undigested bone in its feces. Then one morning, before first light, I woke to the sound of human voices and the smell of horses. I thought I was hallucinating. It was a tribe of nomads en route to their wintering place. That night I had my first taste of bread in many months. I trailed them for days, and gradually, thanks to my thieving, my strength returned. One night I stole a rifle and a knife. The next day the nomads found a field-dressed buck in their path. They paused just long enough to prepare the venison for travel. The nomads finally reached their winter camp in a narrow valley between lavender mountains. I do not know the names of the peaks but they remind me of my father's beloved Mont Blanc. Living in the shadows of these mountains I have an odd feeling of reassurance. It was the day I decided to partially ascend one of the mountains that the nomads first saw me. I was on an exposed face of rock when a small hunting party spotted me. I heard their excited voices far below. Their word for *bear* drifted up to me but they must have quickly dismissed the notion. I was awkwardly making my way toward some cover when a bullet struck an outcropping of rock an arm's length away. It was a shot of experimentation, I am convinced: They wanted to see if I would react like Man or Beast. The nomads are expert marksmen. Even at that distance and odd angle, they could have shot me through the heart. I suspect their experiment proved inconclusive, and they had not a clue if I were Man or Beast. That night I heard the name 'Black Giant' for the first time. Already the tale had been elaborated. It seemed I was transporting the carcass of a bear cub up the mountain, and that when fired upon, I returned a volley of stones. Later I heard that I rolled a huge boulder down at them, narrowly missing their leader, whom I appeared to know instinctively. There was even talk that I was a winged creature and was in fact flying up the mountain. I have been more careful since, and they have only seen me at a great distance—which must exaggerate my size. To them I must truly appear eight feet tall, a height my father ascribed to me, but even though he was a man of science, a physician in fact, my father was prone to hyperbole. Unfortunately he was also prone to destruction, a trait I unfortunately inherited. Since my most recent resurrection, I have tried very hard not to succumb to that side of my nature. I have taken up lodging in an inconspicuous cave at the base of the southern mountain. I store my possessions here; I can cook my food in a small fire pit I have dug. To my astonishment I discovered a pool of fresh water in the back of the cave, where no light can penetrate. The water is so bracing it must be fed from high up on the mountain. I inspected the cave for a bear or puma or some other wild animal but there was none. Of course, bats reside in the cave, thousands of them. Their cacophonous squeaking just before dark was annoying at first. Otherwise they are tolerable fellow lodgers. This species of bat has enormous ears and no snout whatsoever, and it has a slightly sour taste, like that of rat. I was forced to eat rats when stowing away on a freighter bound for Arkhangelsk. The cats on the ship were more adept at catching rats than I, so I ate them too. I am not proud of the fare I have dined on. Man has forced this upon me as well. I am watching from near the entrance to my cave when a single rider approaches the tent city. He is dressed much like a nomad, including the coarse tunic and the knee-high felt boots, but his face is hairless. At first I think he is a boy. A small party from the camp rides out to meet him. They greet each other as friends but I note there is a subtle difference in their languages. Still, they invite him to proceed to their camp and the four horsemen ride in together. The event sparks my curiosity but I have to wait for darkness to fall. No matter. Probably all I will miss is the tending to the horses and an elaborate meal— not elaborate with food, but with formality and speeches. Man is so often preoccupied with ritual. There is a sliver of moon low in the eastern sky when I enter their camp. As I suspected, the stranger is in the tent of the elders, the political nucleus of the camp. I can hear the odd dialect of the stranger's voice amid the other voices in the tent. They are having a heated discussion in the language of the nomads. It involves family connections: 'Elka has been our responsibility for fourteen winters . . .' 'She cannot survive our way of life, it is not fair to the girl—' 'You speak of fairness, God cast that die fourteen years ago when He made her blind and crippled . . .' 'Surely someone among you—' 'There is no one, and Elka's parents unburden themselves, her father is not well, she is past the marrying age . . .' There is silence, then: 'Is she fertile?' 'Who can say? And if she is, no one wants to pass on the crookedness . . .' There is movement nearby in the dark. I realize my cheeks are wet—I fear I have been weeping aloud and will be discovered. It is not for my own safety I am concerned. I am afraid for theirs. My instinct for self-preservation is too strong for me to control. The sound is only young people sneaking around under cover of night—a boy and a girl going to steal kisses in the dark. I focus on the voices again: '. . . three days hence then, we will prepare for her arrival . . .' While returning to my cave I think about the woman-child. Snow is in the air and stings my wet face. I sit in the glow of my weak fire and imagine her deformities: 'blind' the stranger said, 'the crookedness' he said. Suddenly I am drowning in a maelstrom of bitter emotions—rage, despair, jealousy. . . . In my mind's eye I see my own promised-one, carefully selected by my father. She is there, lying on his table, completed. Then I watch her being butchered, the rending of her lovely skin, the quick dismemberment, the final—and superfluous—beheading. Death and the female form. They are forever paired in my mind, like freakish twins joined at the heart. I think too of murdering my stepmother. There was more astonishment in her eyes— beautiful green eyes with flecks of gold—than of terror as I strangled the life out of her. And there is the other female, the one who appears in my dreams. A mere girl really. I can sense her anguish and confusion. Also I can feel the impending doom that covers her like a mourning gown. Death will be her constant companion and she somehow knows it—in spite of the opiate of youth. I do not recall the girl's name. No, more than not recalling, I never knew it. Yet I share an intimacy with her, a mother-child kind of intimacy. Perhaps I am retrieving womb memories, the interpretations of a fetus. But I have no recollections of boyhood, any boyhood. My fit in the cave continues long into the night. At some point my fire goes out but I do not care. Dark and cold are two of my oldest friends. I wait for the arrival of Elka. I worry that the snow that fell will delay her traveling; but it is the fretting of an old woman. Only a finger's length of snow is on the ground and it has already melted from those places directly in the sun. On the third day, about mid morning, four riders enter the valley of the nomads. As they draw near I notice that one of the riders is on a brown and white pony. This must be Elka. She is completely cloaked in a bearskin. Puffs of her breath come from the portion of the bearskin which forms a hood. Elka's pony is being led by the stranger who had visited the nomads originally. I want to see the blind girl's face but it is completely obscured. I once had a friend who was blind. It was as if a skin had grown over his eyes. I wondered if Elka's blindness was of the same type. I often thought that if I'd had a surgeon's skill—as my father did—I could have removed that second skin and given my friend the gift of sight. Yet it was his blindness which allowed him to befriend me. We never had the opportunity to pursue our friendship. Man drove us apart. Milton wrote of the Fallen Angel; I fell that day. Dare I wish for a companion? A female with whom to share the rest of my days? God appeared to decide otherwise some years ago. However, I have felt justified in questioning Him. It is a cold day. The sun is bright but it feels distant. Here and there, along the stream which feeds the valley, pools of water have formed a crust of ice. The stream flows less briskly. I stand in a grove of coniferous trees and watch the trickling water. In the days that I have waited for Elka a plan has formed in my mind. Truly, it seems to have taken shape of its own accord without any voluntary thought from me. So standing there among the trees, a cold breeze blowing my hair, I consider the plan as if it is being offered by some outside agent. In a few weeks spring will come to the valley, and the nomads will trek north, as their ancestors have done for generations. I will watch for the signs of it, and when they are on the verge of leaving I will take my Elka—yes, damn them all, she is mine!—and bring her to my cave. They will not delay their departure for long. Not to search for a poor blind girl they did not want in the first place. Then the nomads will leave the valley, and I will be alone with my Elka. *Alone with my Elka:* The idea of it makes me lightheaded with joy. This is surely what is meant to be. Why else would my miserable life continue to be preserved? Who better to be the benefactor of the poor, the malformed, the wretched? So I wait. Nightly I creep into the camp, hoping to recognize her odd dialect coming from a tent, hoping to catch a glimpse of her by firelight. But again and again, I cannot find her. Is this a joke? Did I not see her ride into their camp? Was it an hallucination? Has this entire episode with the nomads been an hallucination? Perhaps I lie dying on an ice flow in the Arctic Sea, and in a few tortured hours I have imagined months of encounters with the people of the Steppes. No, it must be real. My love for Elka is real, my desire for her too. I must be patient. I must continue to stockpile provisions in my cave, so that when I bring my Elka home I will not have to leave her in search of food—not for many days. I do not like the thought of leaving her alone in the dark of the cave—though I know its blackness is insignificant compared to the blackness she has always known. Slowly spring has come. It rains almost daily. Buds are appearing on the earliest trees and bushes. Activity at the camp has changed; the nomads are preparing to leave. At last the day has come for them to tear down their tent city. I creep as close as I dare in daylight and watch as they pack their camp. Tonight they will sleep under the stars and at sun-up they will begin their long journey north. I must find where Elka will lie. There are so many men, women and children moving about. It is bedlam. I search frantically for her. Tears of frustration blur my vision. Finally I see a figure who is not running about. She is seated by a fire, the bearskin around her shoulders. Some final tents were blocking my view of her until they were taken down. I strain to see her eyes, her nose, her mouth but Elka's hair is hanging down. Here we are, on the eve of our union, and I still do not know my lover's face. My heart is racing. I notice that a thunderstorm appears to be building in the north. If it does not delay the nomads' departure, the storm could work to my benefit. I do not move. The day wanes. The nomads prepare their meals. They tend to their animals. Then they sleep next to their fires, which smolder more than burn. It must be approaching midnight when the first drops of rain fall. They are heavy and cold. The wind has come up and thunder follows lightning at a close distance. The streaks of lightning seem to be tinted red—perhaps a trick of the mountains. I should probably wait for the storm to pass but I cannot. My patience has been exhausted. I move from my hiding place; my limbs are stiff at first. I stay low to the ground—as low as a being of my stature is able. A flash of lightning momentarily brings daytime to the valley. I must be careful. My feet, wrapped in strips of leather, slip in the mud and I nearly lose my balance. I must make certain to take a circuitous route back to the cave for my footprints will be easy to track in the mud. The nomads have posted some sentries but they are huddled under tarpaulins smoking their pipes. I reach their camp and crawl on my hands and knees between packed bundles and smoldering fires. When lightning streaks across the sky, I freeze and try to resemble just another bundle. The thunder is a cannonade. I reach the group of bodies where Elka is sleeping; I can smell the musk of the wet bearskin she is wrapped in. Lightning flashes and I see her long tousled hair. I am an arm's length from my Elka! Short of breath, I reach out and gently touch her hair. Even wet, her hair feels like silk, which I have only touched once before: The gown my stepmother was wearing when I murdered her was of silk. The instant the next bolt of lightning has receded I snatch up my Elka. She weighs nothing. I carry her, bearskin and all, as a mother carries her newborn, except I keep my hand over her mouth, careful not to also cover her nose. I am touching my Elka's face! I want to see her but it is too dark and I am moving too quickly. I must keep my balance. I can feel her deformities through the animal skin. Her back is hunched. Her legs are as thin as broomsticks and they are not connected quite right to her pelvis. Elka is perfect. She is trying to scream but my hand prevents it. We are some distance from the camp when a ruddy lightning flash illuminates the valley and I hear the shouts: 'The Black Giant!' 'He's got hold of something!' I quicken my pace as best I can in the mud. At a great distance or just muffled in the rain, I hear: 'Elka—the Black Giant has Elka!' God, what are you doing to me now? I try to run but my foot slips and I go down on one knee. I recover and continue. Elka is thrashing about in terror. I want to get her to my cave—all will be well there—but I know my path must be serpentine. I sense that the nomads are following me. I did not expect this reaction. After all, Elka was unwanted by both her clans. I know where there is a depression in a grove of trees. Perhaps I can hide there until they stop searching, which will surely be soon. I make my way there, slip down the hill, and carefully lay Elka on the ground. I cover her with my arms, keeping my hand over her mouth. The trees shield us from the lightning flashes. So with the dark and my hand and the wet hair matted to her forehead, I still do not know my lover's face. She is horrified. I try to calm her—'It is all right, I will not harm you'—but I find I have not mastered the nomads' language, particularly her clan's dialect. My words must sound like the gibberish of a lunatic. The violent part of the storm has abated somewhat but it is still raining hard. The drops are loud in the tree limbs. Mist hangs in the air like vengeful spirits. Elka's heart beats furiously against my forearm. I can see torches through the trees and the nomads are calling her name. At first they are in front of me then the searchers seem to be all around. The rage of a trapped animal begins to swell in me. I realize that Elka is not struggling as she had been; perhaps she is exhausted. I whisper, 'Please, do not scream,' and cautiously take my hand from her mouth. She does not. Because I cannot see her still, I touch her face. Her eyes are deep set, her nose is strangely but gently curved as if molded of clay, her jaw is set irregularly and feels thicker on one side. She is perfect and I love her desperately. The searchers continue to call her name. Some of them are close. I struggle to keep my sobbing from giving me away. I pick her up again; this time she does not fight. I carry Elka up the slippery hill and place her in the open. I kiss her hair, then return to the grove of trees. I listen as she calls to her people. They quickly locate her and begin conveying her back to camp. I watch as the torchbearers come together. All I can see are their crimson flames. They appear to merge into a single blaze. When all is quiet I make my way to the cave. I look at the piles of provisions. Then the words of the poet come to me: 'As one who in his journey bates at noon, Though bent on speed; so here the Arch-Angel paused, Betwixt the world destroyed and the world restored. . . .' By the end of summer I must find somewhere else. I will go east or west. But I cannot be in the valley when the nomads return to their wintering place.

Communion with the Dead

PAULO OVERHEARD THE NEWS that Father was ill, very ill, likely dying, while he was cleaning the dinner dishes, and it penetrated him thoroughly, like the way a Christmas sunrise can, or a direct look from a pretty girl, so that even his deepest marrow registered it. Mrs. Stevedoré brought the news, and a blackberry cobbler. She told of Father's condition while Paulo's mother arranged the ground coffee in the pot and increased the fire in the stove. The smell of virgin coffee and Father's illness became paired then in Paulo's recollection forever, he knew . . . the baying of a dog and All Saints preparations, numbing cold in the toes and fingers and. . . .

Paulo absently finished the dishes then went out and poured the dirty water on the garden plot in the yard. His mother was convinced the washwater would help to fertilize the earth; Paulo doubted that such meager bits would do anything, except attract cats to their yard to noisily fight and make love in the dead of night. He often lay sleeplessly in bed listening to their feral communion.

Paulo put away the dishes—almost dropping a saucer, his young fingers clumsy still—and smelled the coffee beginning to brew. He asked, told his mother he was going out. She surfaced from her conversation with Mrs. Stevedoré long enough to tell Paulo not to be too late, her usual farewell. Mrs. Stevedoré and Paulo's mother had been neighbors for many years but only friends since his mother joined Mrs. Stevedoré in widowhood. Their dead husbands connected the two women indissolubly. Paulo did not understand the kinship but was glad his mother had someone to talk to besides him.

The village streets were quiet, save for the wind in the trees and leaves raining down, like paper bats that have lost their gift of flight. Paulo had not taken a jacket, so as he walked he buttoned his sweater as far as he could and hoped it would be enough. The moon was low and only a quarter waxed—"Uncle Felix," the elders called such a moon. "Take your sweetheart for a stroll with Uncle Felix," the saying went, "and she will love you like no other."

A paper bat struck Paulo on the shoulder before wheeling to the ground. It stirred Paulo's senses and he realized he was near Angela's house. Paulo stopped in Uncle Felix's weak glow and studied Angela's. There was only light from a back room, the kitchen presumably, and it spilled lemony onto the side yard and hedge. The rest of the girl's house, upstairs too, was dark. For a moment Paulo thought he heard people talking inside, then realized it was the record-player, Mascagni, *Le Maschere*—

/ they are lying beneath the hedge on their stomachs the opera is playing the handkerchief that lies on the ground between them is covered in the red berries that grow on the hedge her eyes are as brown as her legs that show beneath the plain white skirt raised unusually high when they scooted under the poking branches feet first he is in disbelief at what she has just told him that her parents have arranged a marriage to a boy whose father owns an olive business the boy's name is the same as his is that not funny the olive business will be the son's one day he is in disbelief still he cannot help but sneak looks at the back of her thighs he puts a berry in his mouth and lets it lie beneath his tongue before she makes him spit the inedible berry to the ground even without chewing it has a bitter taste /

There was someone coming along the street. Paulo did not want to meet anyone so he backed into Mr. DeAngelo's dark yard and stood next to the black trunk of Mr. DeAngelo's apple tree (the fruit was almost lemon-yellow, and delicious, he recalled). Paulo felt the knots of rotten apples through the soles of his shoes. None of Uncle Felix's light reached him; he was completely invisible, as corporeal as a shadow. Paulo could tell by the walker's gait it was Angela, her stride long and light, still girlish. He used to worry that Angela's accident—the whole village called it her "accident"—would alter her girlishness but these many months had passed and Angela's movement was the same as before. Just nothing else.

She came into view in Uncle Felix's semilight, and she was carrying something on her arm, a wicker basket. No doubt she had taken food to Father's, a loaf of bread or a shepherd's pie. Angela was in her long crocheted cloak, its hood up. Only her bare calves and sandals showed beneath the dyed wool. It was not so chill out tonight, not yet, but Paulo thought that Angela overdressed since her accident. Maybe the extra clothing made her feel protected, like a locust's outer skeleton; or maybe she felt hidden by the clothes, away from everyone's prying, sympathetic eyes.

Paulo wanted to speak to Angela—but he hesitated, not wanting to startle her—and she slipped silently through her side yard, past the hedge, and Paulo heard the back door shut. He stood for a time under Mr. DeAngelo's apple tree watching Angela's empty yard and listening to impulsive Mascagni. The music seemed sadder than Paulo remembered.

He stirred himself and continued down the street toward Father's, a way he had traveled so many times before. Everyone in the village had. Strange that tonight it was so deserted, just he and Angela, and Uncle Felix, and the leaves falling like paper bats. Paulo turned the final corner and even at this distance could tell there were people in Father's yard, some standing while others sat on Father's stone benches. There was a birdbath to match, and a worn steppingstone that had not been used for its true purpose in years. Paulo could not see these details in the barely moonlit yard; he simply knew them, the way a child knows his mother's hand and the curve of her lap and breast.

The thought of meeting the watchers in Father's yard—the butcher and the baker and the tailor, so to speak—seemed too much for Paulo. He did not wish to talk to them, to be respectful, could not say why he had come. The truth was he did not know why. Before the watchers noticed him, Paulo angled into Mrs. Romero's yard, through the space in the fence where a board had been missing since before Paulo was born, and expertly took the serpentine route to the back of Father's house, avoiding the broken stone in Mr. Villani's walk and lifting Mr. Spagiano's gate latch, up and a hair to the left, so that it swung as silently as a lamb's tail. Finally Paulo was at the wall surrounding Father's garden. He found the stones that protruded slightly for hand- and footholds and began the modest ascent. The stones were strange—shallower and closer together—then Paulo realized it was he: it had been some time since he had entered Father's garden in this way and he had grown. His hands and feet were larger, his legs longer.

The stones were smooth and cold, like reptilian skin.

He was at the top of the wall, perching there for a moment, as a cat might. Uncle Felix gave the stones a bluish cast. Paulo confidently reached down with his long leg to find the stone that allowed you to cut the descent in half and drop gently to the ground. He shifted his weight but somehow missed the stone entirely and fell, hitting the ground hard, jarring himself, even losing his wind for a time. But he quickly discovered he was all right and got himself up. He was standing in lush grass and just in front of him was the stone path that wound through the flowerbeds and shrubs and old trees. Even in its autumnal dormancy, Paulo could tell the garden had grown a little wild. Perhaps Father had become too weak to tend it and had no boys to help him.

The out-of-control garden made Paulo think of the long poem by the blind Englishman that they had read in school winter term. In the shadows and Uncle's cerulean light, it was easy to imagine demons and seraphs lurking. Paulo advanced along the stone path until he could clearly see Father's second-floor bedroom window, where a faint light—candlelight, perhaps, or the light of Extreme Unction—illuminated the white sheer, giving it a ghostly appearance. Paulo stopped near the statue of Jerome Emiliani and put his hand on the saint's cold shoulder. He always liked Jerome Emiliani's placid alabaster features as the saint appeared to watch over Father's house, and Paulo wished he could see them now in the darkened yard.

He thought of Angela, and *Le Maschere* continued to play in his head, and he thought of another night at Angela's, when Angela's father would not allow Paulo to see her. Paulo strained to hear what was happening beyond the closed bedroom door—there should be sound, sobbing at least, the dulcet voice of Dr. Verdi—but there was nothing, silence, silence heavier than sobs. . . . A fluttering in the black tree behind him made Paulo think of demons and seraphs again. He gripped Jerome Emiliani's stone shoulder more tightly. And he stood there for some time looking at Father's diaphanous window, not thinking for a change . . . just being. The scent of something wild and oversweet drifted in the black garden. Though almost unpleasant, Paulo breathed it in greedily, until his head nearly ached.

"You are here to wish Father well." The voice came from the dark shrubbery. Paulo was startled but, more, embarrassed to be found there, of being observed without knowing it. "Father appreciates your visit, I am certain."

Paulo peered over his shoulder into the garden but could discern only a dark shape, part of it human, maybe, another part hedge or hanging vines. "I am Paulo . . . I was on the altar with Father." His voice faltered a bit with his quickened heartbeat.

"Yes, I know you, Paulo. How have you been, you and your mother?"

"My mother is fine, thank you." Paulo wanted to know to whom the voice belonged; the man had to realize he was nearly invisible in the dark yard. The voice was inconsistent, at first sounding older, then younger, then. . . .

"And you? How have you been, my boy?" The voice would not let Paulo off.

Paulo stared at the darkness again, his hand still clinging to the statue. "I—" There was something about the voice that would not allow Paulo to lie, yet he did not care to confess the truth, that he often felt miserable and lonely and other things to which he could not attach a name. Paulo stood dumb in the black garden, his knuckles turning white gripping Jerome Emiliani's white shoulder.

The moment was interrupted when the rear door of Father's house was unlatched and opened slowly. Paulo stepped into the dark shrubbery, not opposite the voice exactly but not close either. In Uncle's bluelight, Paulo watched the baker, Mr. Ravitini, come onto the stone patio then roll and light a cigarette. The match's brief flare showed Mr. Ravitini's bulbous nose and round cheeks, his features seeming puffed up by his yeast. The baker stepped to the edge of the patio and appeared to look directly at Jerome Emiliani then at Paulo, but Paulo knew he was indiscernible. He waited wondering if the voice would speak to Mr. Ravitini. Paulo's imagination began to get the better of him. He suspected the garden was filled with strange visitors, all standing silently in the blackness, some watching the baker, others Paulo. He believed he heard their breathing, even felt the hairs on their hands as they brushed against his fingers, so close were they to him. Mr. Ravitini's cigarette must have been half smoked when Paulo could wait no longer, and he ran to the garden wall. Mr. Ravitini, startled, called out, "Whaa—who's there?" Paulo went directly to the usual place but could not locate the familiar stone; instead there was a rough patch where the protruding stone had been chiseled off. He did not panic however. There was fear in the baker's voice. He did not care to investigate; he just wanted the intruder to leave. Paulo's fingers and toes discovered alternate niches and he deftly pulled his young body to the top of the wall, where Mr. Ravitini must have seen the figure of him for an instant in the bluelight before Paulo vanished.

Paulo hurried from Father's yard, not running though. He chose shortcuts by which he could avoid Father's street altogether. He doubted the baker would report the disturbance to the other watchers but Paulo did not want to risk being seen. The exertion had caused him to break a sweat and now the breeze felt cold on his skin. Paulo shivered.

He came again to Angela's house and again paused. He listened closely for the record-player—the wind had risen—so perhaps he heard the music, or perhaps the opera was only in his mind. He thought of another evening at Angela's. Angela's grandfather had drunk too much wine at dinner and was becoming boisterous. There were dots of tomato sauce in his white mustache. He told a story about stealing apples when he was a boy. When the old man began, the story was supposed to have a moral but when he mentioned that his brother was his co-conspirator, it reminded him that his brother died in the war—of dysentery for the love of God!—and the old man lost his train of thought and did not finish the apple-stealing story. Suddenly the grandfather was aware Mascagni was playing and he hummed along, filled with melancholy at first, then snapping back to his boisterousness: "I was there the night the great Pietro opened *Le Maschere*, at Verona, January nineteen-o-one. It had been raining a cold rain all day then God said let there be moonlight for Mascagni on opening night. I was with the other peons in the back of course . . . but the music. . . ." The old man gripped his chest and hummed again with the record, or with the tune in his brain. "Do you know what the fools did? I will tell you, they hissed Pietro's opera—like a pack of asinine cats. *Hissed!*" The grandfather was indignant still, half a century later. "I could not believe what was happening. 'Shut up!' I said to the filthy cats near me. 'Shut up! Stop hissing the great one's music, you fools!' That is precisely what I said to them." The old man was quiet for a moment, self-satisfied. "Now, pish, they all *love* Mascagni . . . the *genius* of *Le Maschere* . . . the filthy cats probably have Pietro's record in their dens, next to a framed handbill from opening night, which they had to purchase from a collector because they tore theirs up and trampled it under their filthy paws!" Angela's grandfather, his cheeks crimson, finished off his glass of wine then sat staring at his stomach, sullen. Paulo recalled that he died a few weeks later of a stroke; it was before Angela's accident—God granted the old man that, and moonlight on Pietro's opening night.

With the stronger wind, leaves rained down vigorously, swept across the street one way, then swirled and went back again, as if uncertain of their path. Paulo heard them more than saw them. Felt them hit his back, shoulder, head, swirling around his legs, like an incoming tide. When his father was alive, they went to the coast once or twice a year, camping on the beach, "just like vagabonds," his mother would say, but she loved it. Paulo was opening his front gate when he noticed the glow of a cigarette; he thought of his father, who would smoke after supper, pacing slowly about the yard, observing the moon and the heavens if the weather was good. "Hello . . ." said Paulo, nearly adding "Father" for it seemed almost possible tonight.

The visitor tossed away the cigarette. "Paulo?" said Angela. "I have been waiting, I need to talk with you."

Paulo, in disbelief, came into the yard. The figure in the dark was the right height and it was Angela's voice. Yet he imagined her an older version of herself, the timing of everyone's life out of sync. He realized he had felt this way for some time but had not been able to articulate it. Perhaps he was now an older version of himself too. He wondered briefly if it was possible to go back.

"Yes," said Paulo.

"Let us walk." Angela came forward and took his hand and led him from the yard.

Paulo glanced at his companion wanting to see her face but her hood was up and in the dark he saw no features. He had the mad notion this was not Angela at all but a stranger staging a malignant prank, or even some otherworld demon toying with his soul.

"Paulo, you are my oldest friend and I need your help," said the shadow posing as Angela.

Anger boiled up in Paulo's gut: "What of your promised one? Why not go to *him*?" Paulo's venom surprised even himself. He felt hot in spite of the fresh wind.

Angela let go of Paulo's hand, perhaps repulsed suddenly by his reptilian touch, yet continued to walk with him. "I cannot; he has released himself from the promise—I cannot blame him," she added.

Paulo did not understand immediately, then said, "The accident."

Angela's voice was now rife with poison: "It was no *accident*—why does everyone call it such!—those filthy animals knew precisely what they were doing!" The wind blew back Angela's hood, and her long hair danced in the breeze, but her face was still a mystery.

"I will stop using the word." Paulo reached for her hand, and Angela accepted his.

They continued to walk and were quiet for a moment in the

quiet night, quiet save for the wind and swirling leaves, then Angela said, "I must see Father before he dies—I must be . . . forgiven."

"You know he cannot do that any longer. . . ." More strange emotions stirred in Paulo. He stopped in the dark street and fell to his knees, overcome by them. Angela stroked his hair. "Tell me," she said gently.

The alien feelings choked Paulo's voice at first. "I miss Father . . . I miss being with him. They want me to hate him, to hate him but forgive him . . . but in truth I do not hate him at all . . . I do not hate Father at all."

"I know." Angela knelt with Paulo and enfolded him in her crocheted cloak. "I know." Paulo breathed in Angela; she was soap and smoke and thyme. For once, he loved her without the desire to possess her. His tears dampened the blouse of her dress. He felt the bones of her body and her flesh—she was thin, nearly skeletal, but of this world after all. In a moment, he helped her to stand and said, "Let us see Father; it surely is not too late." The idea of seeing Father again, really seeing him, both thrilled and terrified Paulo.

They had been making their way to him all along. Hand in hand, they took the final turns, nearly running headlong into a group coming from Father's house. "Children," said Mr. Ravitini, the baker, his voice startled again, "what are you doing out?"

"We must see Father," said Paulo, giving himself away—until then Angela and he were only anonymous adolescents in the dark street.

"Father passed on this evening. Monsignor is at the house but he is very tired. Speak with him in the morning if you must." Mr. Ravitini lit a match, shielding the flame with his puffy hand, to confirm his suspicions. "Angela and Paulo, go home now—it is late." The others with the baker said nothing: Paulo and Angela were outcasts of tragedy in the village.

"Yes, we will," agreed Paulo, leading Angela away. Angela

began to speak but Paulo cut her off—"Wait." When they were away from Mr. Ravitini and his group, Paulo ducked in between houses and found the familiar route. Soon they were at the wall surrounding Father's garden.

"What are we doing?" asked Angela.

"I am not sure." Paulo found the old stones just as Uncle Felix peeked from behind clouds and shed his bluelight upon them. "Here—" he encouraged Angela to scale the wall. He followed her and had her wait a moment at the top. Paulo found a way down then helped Angela to the ground.

They took hands again and Paulo looked for Jerome Emiliani, who glowed ethereally in the garden. They approached the saint. Paulo noticed that Father's bedroom window was black—

/ it is a terrible thing for a boy to lose his father especially so young to see him killed at that he remembers the numbing cold his fingers and toes of stone they are alone in his room a silver crucifix upon the wall the scent of beeswax in the air it is all right to cry no shame in it at all you come to me any time day or night you have always been special to me like a son his touch is warm his fingers smell clean just washed in holy water he imagines his breath smells of the body and the blood he pulls down the sheer /

Angela stood behind the statue and Paulo behind her. He noted that he was nearly a head taller now. The three of them—Jerome Emiliani, Angela and Paulo—were like graduated stepping-stones in a line. Paulo stared at Father's black window and waited for the voice from the garden. Angela's hair whipped against his neck and face, the stonewall and the garden itself unable to hold back the wind. Who knew what she was thinking? But Angela was patient.

The wind in Paulo's ears seemed to carry words, or to be

words themselves. Paulo without thinking repeated them: *Confess your sins, Angela. He shall hear you. . . .*

She hesitated but only for a moment. "I confess to Almighty God, to Blessed Mary ever Virgin, to Blessed Michael the Archangel, to Blessed John the Baptist, to the Holy Apostles Peter and Paul, and to all the angels and saints—I have sinned in thought, word and deed." She struck her birdlike breast three times.

Say. . . .

"I had life within me, within my womb, but I had it taken out of me, as if a diseased thing—" Angela's voice faltered, her cloak, still open from enfolding Paulo, blew in the wind like great wings, great wings tethered to the ground; they flapped against Paulo's legs then the base of Jerome Emiliani.

May Almighty God be merciful upon you and forgive you. . . .

"Amen," cried Angela as she steadied herself on the saint's shoulders of stone.

May the Merciful One grant us pardon, absolution and remission of our sins. . . .

"Amen," she wept again.

Take away from us, Lord, we beseech you—

"Who is there?" Paulo could not place this voice at first then he looked to Father's window and saw a dark shape beyond the casement. "Who is in the garden?"

Angela turned around to Paulo, and he smelled the salt tears in her breath. "Go," he said, "it is done." She ran from him but her cloak caught on the saint's statue. In her fear, she let it drop from her shoulders. Her white dress and white arms and legs glowed in Uncle Felix's light. She stopped and looked for Paulo. Angela seemed to hang suspended in the wind, night mist floating close to the earth waiting for dawn in order to disappear completely.

Paulo waved to her and she, perhaps comprehending or perhaps not, scampered up the wall, glancing back to him for a moment before dropping to the other side. Paulo untangled

Angela's cloak and stood waiting, resolute to be discovered, as placid and as stonecold as the saint.

Figures in Blue

FROM THE VILLAGE STREETS BELOW, the house did appear magnificent, with its towers and leaded glass and cyprium roof of verdant patina—truly baronial and hence ideally suited for the dowager baroness, Kristena von Lichtenberg—but as the young painter made his way along the upward-winding flagstone path he began to see the disrepair that had come to the house and grounds, like unwelcome dispatches from an army which is slowly but inevitably losing the war. He was lugging the leather portfolio case that held a sketchbook, charcoal pencils, and examples of his work, though only three studies of portraiture as it had never been his primary interest. He preferred bodies in motion, thus painting mainly from imagination. He believed that each single moment of, for instance, a gypsy's dance was imprinted indelibly somewhere in one's mind, like a piece in an enormous gallery, and he had only to conjure that moment with his brushes and blades . . . but the trick was locating the correct gallery salon.

At last he came to the portico and looked up at the underside of its roof, which showed the mold-colored water stains of years of leaking rain and snowmelt. Each stain was picketed by large flakes of mauve paint which shook steadily but soundlessly in a persistent breeze that couldn't be felt in the village streets below. The young painter, Esteban, had begun to perspire from the strain of carrying the portfolio case up the steep path, and he stood for a moment enjoying the cooling breeze.

Esteban had been in the village more than six months but it was only supposed to be a brief stopover, to rest and perhaps earn a few marks, before continuing his journey to the Rhine Valley, where his master and the other artists in the Sevillean colony claimed that the light was crafted by God Himself, intended only to illuminate heaven . . . however, the valley was so close to being heaven, they said, the Divine One had made an exception.

That had been the plan at least—was still the plan—but Esteban quickly found work in the village stables (he was well accustomed to horses) and he also discovered that the light here bewitched him. Instead of the ruddy golden hue of the Rhine light, as the old artists had said and as he'd observed in their masterworks, the light here was infused with indigo, as if the sky had become lonely and rode the sunlight down to earth, beam upon beam, to be among living creatures. But the fellowship made no difference and the deep blue of the light retained its air of isolation, of melancholy. It was a lugubrious illumination but it touched Esteban's soul . . . and days turned to weeks, weeks to months. . . .

He went to the twin oaken doors and reached for the brass knocker fashioned in the shape of a pointed-edged sun, so disused that filaments of cobwebs ran between the points, but he'd only touched the cold metal when the door opened freely and an envelope fell to the stone floor. He saw his name written in spidery, feminine script—*Herr Espíritu*—and he picked up the rose-tinged envelope, which he realized immediately was expensive stationery. As he opened the unsealed envelope he smelled the subtle fragrance of rose. He unfolded the letter, also of the blushing stationery, with the baroness's family seal embossed at the head, and read in the same thin, looping handwriting, *Please, come to the conservatory, Herr Espíritu, at the rear of the house—K.L.* His German was not yet fluent, especially this provincial dialect, but he believed he understood the note.

Esteban replaced the letter to the envelope and put it in his jacket's side pocket. He'd worn his olive corduroy jacket, blue cotton shirt, and coarse canvas trousers—the best clothes that he owned but still shabby for the interview, he felt. He set foot upon the entryway's parquet floor, rosewood, and thought of the heel of his left boot which had started to come loose, though it wasn't obvious at a glance.

The inside of the house was not in as severe a state of disrepair as the outside but it was clear that the baroness was without a full staff. In fact no one at all stirred at Esteban's entrance, and he detected not a soul in the house—not so much as a sleepy cat.

As he walked along the central hallway, with various rooms open to either side, Esteban realized that the same sapphire light he associated with the valley itself permeated this space as well, even though the few windows he saw were curtained—however, only by a sheer panel of simple white lace, that is to say, dingy white lace as they likely hadn't been properly taken down and laundered for years.

His eyes were becoming used to the subdued lighting, so when he finally entered the conservatory, which at first appeared entirely constructed of glass, Esteban had to squint against the relative brightness, and it took him a moment to locate the source of the greeting he heard:

Ah, there you are, Herr Espíritu—thank you so much for accepting my invitation. The baroness was seated in an ornately carved chair of crimson velvet and wood so dark it was nearly ebon. She wore a gown of Oriental blue silk and white lace. Her hair was pure white and long enough to be braided and looped back over her shoulder—a style he'd only seen maidens wearing, yet it seemed to suit her. The baroness was thin but not frail-looking. His impression was that she was tall for a woman. In addition to several pieces of furniture, the conservatory was home to numerous large-leafed plants, and the baroness in her chair was all but concealed by potted foliage. He was reminded of a Goya etching of Eden.

Yes, he said, I am pleased to oblige you.

The baroness smiled, at his awkward phrasing, he suspected, and he hoped that his tanned face was not revealing a blush. He'd had a beard of several days' growth but shaved himself clean for the interview. The gruff-looking fellow who came to Esteban's boardinghouse room, wearing a suit of clothes too small for his wide frame, said only that the baroness Kristena wished to see him about painting her portrait. Esteban had had steady work in the stables—in Seville he trained mounts for use in the bullring so tending to the village's workaday horses was nothing—but, still, time and space for his art had suffered, thus the idea of a patroness very much appealed to his ambitions. Seeing the condition of the baroness's house and grounds, however, had cooled his hopes. Nevertheless he was curious as to what she had in mind, and even a modestly paying project was better than no project at all.

Won't you have a seat; looking up pains my neck. She first motioned toward another velvet-covered chair, also ornately carved, yet not a twin to her own as its wood was lightly stained—then she brought her hand to her neck, merely touching it through her high lace collar. Esteban noted that while her face retained a youthful radiance, in spite of its many fine wrinkles, her hands were typically those of an old woman: almost skeletal in their thinness with the blue of her veins easily projecting through the rice-paper skin, and swollen knuckle joints that stood out like undersized walnuts.

Would you care for some chocolate? Though it is no longer especially hot. She nodded toward a silver serving pot on a small table within Esteban's reach, and a cup and saucer of delicate and diminutive design. Esteban had found German chocolate to be quite bland compared to the chocolate shops of Seville but his long walk had drained him a bit, so he thanked the baroness and helped himself.

She waited to speak until after he had taken a sip of the chocolate, which was more to his taste than he had anticipated. It is very good, he said, thank you. The German still felt quite alien on his tongue.

How have you been enjoying our little village, Herr Espíritu?

It is . . . restful.

She smiled, revealing straight teeth whose whiteness was only partially dulled by age. Yes, I imagine for a young man, a young Spaniard no less, our village seems quite sleepy.

Esteban flinched inwardly at the insinuation that all Spanish men were hot-blooded, that their nature rejected an introspective life, but he let the remark pass unchallenged. He drank more chocolate, becoming accustomed to its milky taste.

I believe Franz explained why I wanted to see you.

Oh yes—Esteban placed his cup and saucer on the table, undid the leather ties of his portfolio case, and removed the samples of his work, perhaps all a bit too eagerly—and he handed them to the baroness.

In truth, he said, I have not done many portraits, as you see— but I am interested in the form. (He heard the falseness in his words and the clarity of their real meaning: but I am interested in accepting your money.)

The baroness's fingers were arthritically clumsy and it took her a few moments to examine the pieces. Esteban sipped at his chocolate while watching her face closely, in particular the lines around her eyes of raven blue: the expression remained one of curiosity with no sign of judgment: she may have loved his work or despised it.

She let the art rest on her lap; the piece on top was a chalk drawing of a gypsy girl, no older than sixteen or seventeen, who has retrieved water from the village well and is observing her reflection in the pail with subtle but obvious satisfaction. Esteban was especially pleased with the drawing.

I see, said the baroness, that the reports are true: you are a young man of talent.

Thank you—wondering about the source of the baroness's information.

You seem ideally suited to render the sort of portrait I have in mind.

Esteban had been evaluating the light of the conservatory without really thinking of it but now it came to the forefront of his mind. This, he said, may be the perfect sitting-room.

The baroness appeared puzzled for a moment . . . Oh, no, Herr Espíritu, I do not plan to sit for the portrait. I hardly want to be remembered to posterity as this dried-up old woman I've become. I want you to paint me in my youth, when I was a young woman who could turn heads.

Esteban was following her words intensely but wasn't certain he'd fully understood. You want me to paint a younger version of you. . . .

Yes, quite a lot younger in fact. Perhaps not so young as this— she touched the drawing of the gypsy girl—but it is the idea. The baroness continued after a brief pause, It appears you do not always require a live model but can also work from your fancy.

My fancy? . . .

Yes, your fancy—your imagination. But mind you, I want it to be accurate. I cannot protest my vanity but it has its limits. There is no need to render me a Venus.

I understand, said Esteban. Then you have some older por-traits, some paintings or drawings, or perhaps a photograph or two, yes?

I sat for Herr de Guerre in Berlin, when I was traveling with my father the baron, but the Frenchman's solutions were appar-ently spoiled and nothing came of it. My husband the baron and I sat for a wedding portrait but before it was completed Stier entered into a disagreement with the artist and the painting was never finished—I'm quite certain the artist, who died many years ago, either destroyed the partially finished work or, more likely, reused the canvas and painted over it.

Esteban was quiet for a moment, translating, then: So there are no images from your youth, baroness?

No images at all, Herr Espíritu.

How then? . . .

The baroness raised a twig-like finger, knowing his question. She returned Esteban's work to him, and he placed it inside the case. On the table, she said, next to the golden-child orchid—and she gestured to her left.

Esteban stood and walked in the general direction until he saw a plant with brilliant yellow blooms and a table of dark walnut with legs carved in a Cornish style. The only objects on the table were a stack of four books, bound in well-worn black leather and tied as a single bundle by a red ribbon, and a statue of the Virgin Mary, held together by rusted wire as an obvious diagonal fissure ran between the Virgin's broken halves. The young painter picked up the books and returned to his chair.

My diaries, said the baroness, from the earliest years of my marriage. I was a devoted diarist then; I'm afraid I have fallen off in recent times.

Esteban held the books, which had a slightly musty odor, and examined them for a moment, confused: You want me to paint your portrait, to capture your likeness, accurately, by reading your diary entries from, sixty years ago. . . .

Quite so, Herr Espíritu, quite so.

I don't understand. . . .

Franz will visit you this evening with an advance so that you can purchase any supplies you may need. Perhaps you can come again, say, within the fortnight to share your ideas and any preliminary sketches.

Esteban thought that a breakdown in language accounted for the baroness's improbable request—that when he began examining the contents of the diaries it would all become clear. He managed to say, Of course.

Very good. There are some heavy canvas totes in the kitchen; please help yourself, for the diaries—the weather in the valley is quite unpredictable, especially this time of year.

Esteban thanked the baroness for the chocolate and excused himself with a slight bow. In Seville, the young always bowed to the aged, even regardless of their rank in society, and he hoped the custom was appropriate here as well.

In a few minutes he was back on the flagstone path, now doubly burdened for his return to the village. He thought he heard a distant growl of thunder.

FRAU BECKER, ESTEBAN'S LANDLADY, operated a tavern out of her home's small summer-kitchen. In the afternoons, when he was finished with his work in the stables, Esteban would visit the tavern for a stein of stout and a pickled egg or two. He enjoyed listening to the old men argue about politics and reminisce regarding local history, their cigars and pipestems clenched between rotting teeth as they waved their stubby-fingered hands for emphasis. The conversations, though often meaningless to him in substance, assisted Esteban in learning the language, especially some of its more colorful phrases.

After his interview with the baroness, Esteban deposited his case and the diaries in his room, traded his olive jacket for his gray everyday one, and he went to Frau Becker's summer-kitchen. He was earlier than usual, and the regulars had not yet gathered. In fact Frau Becker wasn't even about, and everyone's absence made the space seem larger. In one corner a stand for the demikeg had been built from reused barnboards, and the stand mismatched perfectly the hodgepodge of stools, chairs and benches. It was a space purely of function with no consideration of form whatsoever. It smelled permanently of tobacco smoke and spilled beer, even with opposing windows thrown open to encourage a cross draft.

Through one window Esteban heard a horse and cart approach then stop. Even without seeing it, Esteban knew it was one of the workhorses of heavy breed, a Black Forester, they called it. He heard the powerful yet gentle creature shake the bells on his collar to signal the driver he was at full-stop and would remain so until instructed otherwise. Then Frau Becker, coming from the house's back porch, greeted the driver and said something about the beer of the previous week's shipment. Esteban heard no reply from the brewer's deliveryman.

In a moment the tavern door was pushed fully open and Frau Becker was backing into the summer-kitchen lugging a demikeg supported on the other end—to Esteban's surprise—by a quite pretty young girl, broad through the shoulders in spite of her thinness and as blond as winter wheat. Esteban immediately attempted to assist them but there was nothing for him to do, except stay out of their way.

Ah, our young man of Spain, Frau Becker wheezed in greeting as she and the girl wrestled their burden to the wall near the serving stand and sat it upon the plank floor as gently as they could manage.

May I help? said Esteban, trying not to stare into the molten sapphire of the girl's eyes, but not being wholly successful.

Yes, said his landlady, a woman as stout as the beer she served and whose deep-set laughter lines about her eyes and mouth added some angularity to her otherwise perfectly round face. She was no longer handsome but her expression at most times was pleasantly merry, even when doing hard work. Yes, Spain, she continued between puffing breaths, help Fräulein Hilde with . . . the remainder of the order. . . . Her father the brewmaster will . . . expect her home before dusk.

Esteban contentedly followed the brewmaster's daughter to the cart. She was tall, perhaps even an inch or more taller than

Esteban. There was such a vivacious litheness to her body that even her loose-fitting blouse and long, patterned skirt could not conceal it.

There were a half dozen demikegs in the well-used cart, and the Black Forester was standing perfectly motionless, as if a still-life. Hilde seemed to read Esteban's thoughts:

Frau Becker receives two more.

Esteban nodded, then said: My name is not Spain, by the way—

I know—her gemstone eyes cutting him off as much as her voice—you are Esteban Espíritu, of Seville to be exact, and even though you are very good with horses your true passion is art. In fact you have only stopped here on your pilgrimage to the Rhine.

I see you know everything then.

You are famous, Señor Espíritu—we do not host many visitors, especially such . . .

Esteban hoped she would fill the space with a word for handsome or dashing . . .

. . . such exotic ones.

Hilde stepped up into the cart-bed. There is one thing I don't know, Señor, none of us do.

Esteban, please. What is that?

Why you have not moved on already.

I . . .

The Black Forester twitched his ears as if even he were interested in the response.

Hilde saved the young painter from the lingering absence of his answer by putting a demikeg on its side and rolling it to him with her foot, on which she wore a heavy shoe like any workman's. She was used to this sort of labor, as were all the villagers it seemed, and did not shrink from it.

In a few minutes they had carried the remainder of Frau Becker's order into the summer-kitchen; and Hilde had secured the other demikegs in the cart with thick leather straps. Esteban stood and watched, then waved to her as she sat in the cart-seat and shook the horse's reins to enliven him. She looked over at Esteban with her dangerous blue eyes one last time as the wheels's began to move, but she and Esteban had said nothing further.

Come inside, Spain, called Frau Becker. The first stein and pickled egg are on the house. Besides, staring after the fräulein won't magically bring her back. The landlady cackled at Esteban's embarrassment.

He took up Frau Becker on her offer, and before long the quaint tavern was humming with its regular business. A pair of old men, Otto and Heinrich, had always been friendly to Esteban but on this evening they went further and invited him to occupy a stool in their usual corner. Otto, a former carpet dyer who lived with his daughter-in-law and adult grandson, was as bald as one of Frau Becker's pickled eggs and whistled a touch when he spoke due to a gap between his front teeth. Heinrich had three strapping sons who'd taken over the operation of his dairy farm, and also its large house with their wives and numerous children, leaving Heinrich to live on his own in the overseer's cottage. It was difficult for Esteban to picture little Heinrich's strapping sons, but the aged farmer's pure white hair and beard gave him the air of a biblical patriarch, so the young Sevillean accepted the sons' description as fact.

After a while of drinking and exchanging family histories—though Esteban had mainly confirmed what they already knew of him—Otto said, So they say you visited the witch today?

The witch . . . ?

Otto, don't be a rumor-monger, said Heinrich. He means the baroness. People here tell tales.

Yes, we had an interview.

Otto smiled. Her fellow, Franz, came to fetch you, did he?

Esteban felt a bit drunk, which didn't improve his translating skills. The very broad fellow, yes, he extended his mistress's invitation.

Otto snickered and his breath whistled between his teeth.

Esteban clearly was puzzled.

Don't mind him, said Heinrich, using his sleeve to dab beer from his snowy mustache. It is an old story: Franz, they say, became a resident of the baroness's household at the same time the old baron disappeared, well, died, in a boating accident in Switzerland—

There was no funeral, interrupted Otto, still grinning, only a private memorial.

Yes, the baron's body was never recovered, which isn't unusual in such cases.

So, said Esteban, trying to clear his head, would not the baroness require assistance after her husband's death? What is so strange about Franz entering into her employ?

Nothing, said Heinrich, nothing at all . . .

Except . . . said Otto.

Except?

Except, took up Heinrich, the suddenness of it—people seemed to recall that he arrived even before the news of the baron's demise.

So, what? said Esteban. She murdered her husband so she could bring this fat fellow into her house? Is that the gossip? He felt himself growing irritated with Otto and Heinrich, with the whole village.

Not precisely, whistled Otto. They say she and the baron argued, and she transformed him into this eunuch, Franz, and now the old baron does her bidding like a common servant.

Transformed him? Like placed him under a spell?

And that's not all—

Otto . . . cautioned his friend, though not very stridently.

Otto managed to maintain a mischievous grin while he gulped down some beer.

What? said Esteban impatiently.

Otto wiped his chin with his fingers. Well, they also say the baroness likes to transform herself into a young girl and come down to the village to, you know, spy on us . . . and what not.

It is a small village, said Esteban, would not a strange young girl showing up now and again raise some suspicions?

That is a good point, said hoary-headed Heinrich—but the gossips say she takes the form of a gypsy girl, and the gypsies are forever coming and going . . . who can keep track? But it's probably ridiculous.

A gypsy girl? Esteban stared at the old men, his head swimming—could they know about his sketches of the gypsy girl and be teasing him? He decided to play along: Now that I think of it, there was something familiar about the brewmaster's daughter, Hilde, whom I met earlier this evening.

The old men stopped drinking their beer and stared fixedly at Esteban. Otto said, The brewmaster's daughter? The brewmaster has no daughter; he is childless. . . .

Esteban looked at Heinrich but his expression remained blank . . . then both old men erupted in laughter.

We had you, didn't we, said Otto between snorts of whistling laughter. Wait until Fräulein Hilde hears the joke—she will love it; and Otto slapped Esteban on the shoulder.

Heinrich signaled Frau Becker to bring the pitcher and refill their steins.

The proprietress topped off their drinks, and the old men happily paid for Esteban's beer. The three sat for a moment listening to the din of the tavern patrons.

Then Otto said, So how did the baroness seem to you? She's not been down to the village in years, in a manner of speaking.

Esteban realized his ears were ringing. How did she seem?

Yes, you know, did she say or do anything strange?

Esteban thought of the baroness's diaries in his room. No, she was perfectly polite—nothing out of the ordinary. She merely wants me to paint her portrait, that is all.

Otto and Heinrich seemed to sense his lie but didn't press him. Esteban emptied his stein as quickly as he was able, thanked the pair for their generosity, then excused himself to his room. He did his best not to stagger from Frau Becker's crowded summer-kitchen.

Outside the cool night air instantly began to revive him. He looked for the moon and discovered that it was just rising above the baroness's house, which appeared pure black against the deeply violet sky.

IN THE PREDAWN HOUR Esteban woke and recalled a fragment of the dream which he'd been having for months, since before leaving Seville even: A young man who is like Esteban but not him stalks the Minotaur in a labyrinth constructed of wooden chutes like the inner workings of the bullrings of Seville. Not-Esteban follows the Minotaur by sniffing his terrible stench and observing the trail of his enormous droppings. The eye of the labyrinth is like a bullring itself, and the Minotaur scratches at the patches of blood-soaked dust with his two cloven hooves, sweat dripping down his muscular shoulders and back, human in form except for their brown hide and gigantic beastly power. The Minotaur senses Not-Esteban's presence and begins to turn toward him. . . .

The dream always concluded before the young man sees the Minotaur's face.

At breakfast, which was fried mush topped with a soft-boiled egg and a strip of boiled pork, Esteban inquired with Frau Becker about the small corner room upstairs that appeared unoccupied—he wanted to paint there. They agreed on a price for two months' use. He then went to the stables but not to put in a day's labor. Rather, he used the baroness's generous advance to rent a horse and wagon, and he drove to the nearest town likely to have the materials he desired—quality canvases, the finest oil paints, vials of mineral and vegetable powders, stretching frames, a rock-solid easel, brushes tipped in ermine, cloths of Egyptian cotton, mortar and pestle of polished Venetian marble, linseed oil, and spirit of turpentine—the sorts of materials used only by the most celebrated masters.

Esteban underestimated the duration of the journey, and it was long past midnight when he arrived back in the village. The moon had been obscured by clouds most of the night, rendering the roads all but invisible to Esteban, but the good horse he'd rented knew the way and had no trouble returning to his home. In fact, Esteban dozed during the final hour or two, thinking of the beautiful supplies he'd purchased, of sapphire-eyed Hilde, of Otto and Heinrich's wild stories, of Not-Esteban and the Minotaur. . . .

When he'd arrived, he unloaded the supplies as quietly as he could to Frau Becker's small parlor and returned the horse and wagon to their stable. By the time he'd properly cared for the trustworthy gelding and began to walk back to the boarding-house, the eastern sky had begun its transformation to predawn indigo. He suspected his usual waking time was only an hour away. Today however he would sleep until noon.

The village was silent, save for the awakening chatter-song of birds; and the night air was at the depth of its chill before the coming sunrise. Though still on his feet, Esteban's exhausted mind began to drift into a kind of sleep state and again to images of the Minotaur at the center of his labyrinth. . . . Esteban was startled by the rusty groan of the gears of the village well, more or less in the center of the village's tiny square. In the earliest twilight Esteban's tired eyes discerned a female form at the well, turning the obstinate wheel to bring forth the subterranean water.

The litheness of the form's movements suggested she was youthful—and even in the low, blue-infused light he could discern the raven-wing hair past her shoulders and the peasant skirt and blouse of a gypsy. Was it the girl he'd drawn before at the well? He heard water begin to flow in the sluice.

Esteban, though not fifty paces from her and standing unshielded in the center of the empty street, had the sense that he was invisible, a true spirit whose boots hadn't even left impressions in the thoroughfare's gray dust.

The gypsy girl loosened the sluice's baffle and Esteban heard the water run into her wooden pail, which hung from a peg perfectly positioned to capture every drop. Meanwhile the twilight's indigo steadily faded to a deep lavender, showing more and more plainly the girl's slender form, and Esteban gazed with abandon as if she were modeling for him by choice. He gazed as if thirsty for the girl's pristine image.

She finished collecting water, closed the sluice's baffle, and hoisted the heavy pail by its thick handle of braided rope. She walked toward Esteban, who stood transfixed and began to believe he was indeed no more than a lingering night shadow falling across the lightening street. The girl was passing so close he smelled the strange spices that clung to her dark skin . . . but as she moved beyond him, she said, Good morning, Herr Painter—so softly Esteban thought perhaps he'd imagined it.

He gathered his jacket at his throat as a sudden chill ran through him. He turned and watched the girl's departing figure: she slipped between darkened buildings and was quickly out of sight. It comforted Esteban that she was walking in the direction of the gypsy encampment which, he knew, lay to the west of the village, in an area the locals called the Swamp.

BY THE TIME ESTEBAN returned to Frau Becker's the landlady was in the kitchen preparing breakfast, and the scent of her strong Italian coffee filled the downstairs. It was enlivening to Esteban so instead of going directly to his room to sleep—a thought he'd been dwelling on for hours—he tapped on the open kitchen door, somewhat startling Frau Becker, who then prepared him a mug of coffee with thick, sweetened cream and sat him in a chair in the corner, cozily out of her way.

The landlady seemed to like the rare company and for more than an hour she chattered to him while she continued preparing her lodgers' breakfast. Urged by her pleasant questioning, Esteban told of his journey to the town where he purchased his painting supplies and what it was like—when a newlywed, Frau Becker had often visited the town with her dairy farming husband, long deceased, and she enjoyed discovering how the town had changed and even more so how it had not. While they spoke Frau Becker had prepared another coffee for *Spain* and handed him a plate with buttermilk rolls, a poached egg, a boiled potato mashed with a fork and lightly peppered, and a chunk of beef brisket left over from dinner.

When the other lodgers began to come downstairs, Esteban went to his room. He looked at the plank bed with its straw-filled mattress, taking up a full third of the room, but he no longer felt sleepy. He removed his jacket and went to the small table in the corner, near the room's only window, sat in the solitary chair and untied the ribbon around the baroness's diaries, four in all. On the cover of each black volume was written in faded gold ink *K.L.* and the years, the earliest being *1866~67.*

Esteban began glancing through the diary, trying to become accustomed to the young baroness's handwriting. He opened the rose-tinted and rose-scented letter, which also lay on the table, and compared the thin, cursive scrawl to that on the diary pages. The baroness's hand had become weaker and less fluid over time but there was no question that the letter and the diary entries were penned by the same woman.

The diary took up in the first year of baroness Kristena's marriage to Stier von Lichtenberg, and the young bride, only seventeen, often wrote of the challenges of managing the household with its many servants and groundskeepers—even a huntsman was mentioned from time to time. The baron's social engagements seemed especially stressful to the girl whose parents were older when she was conceived and preferred their little family's quiet, close-knit company. It appeared the baron was quite exacting in his desires for their parties. One of their first rows was over a dress he wanted Kristena to wear . . .

> *It makes me appear a street trollop, too tight in the bodice and open at the throat besides.*

The diary page was marred and some of the ink smeared suggesting that the girl baroness had shed tears over the ordeal. She wore the dress after all and one of the baron's guests, identified only as *J.*, had too much schnapps after dinner and drunkenly pawed Kristena throughout the evening. The baron seemed not to notice or care as long as his business ally was amused . . .

> *I was mauled like I was a common maid and he didn't so much as lift a finger or even raise an eyebrow at my distress. Just sat in the drawing room leering at J.'s daughter, a full year younger than I and stone-faced with wine, blinding herself to her father's deplorable behavior.*

The diary entries returned to the mundane for several weeks—household matters and the weather, including a description of an evening when *moonlight shone through a shoal of fog rendering it a blue shroud which seemed to wrap around the entirety of the house.* Then the mundaneness was suddenly shattered on the sixteenth of June, 1866:

> *Does he think I'm a fool!—I know who the girl is, so does the entire staff no doubt, his gypsy whore, brought into the house as a scullery maid! Just to save him the trouble of having to go to the swamp to root around in her tent*

like swine . . . and to humiliate me.

Perhaps it was the lack of sleep or the potent coffee, but Esteban felt as if he were slipping into the baroness's place, more than simply feeling sympathy for her unhappy marriage—rather, he felt her world upon his skin, tasted it upon his tongue.

Drunkenly overbearing one night, the baron tried to force himself into Kristena's bedchamber, irked by her aloofness to his concubine . . .

I would sooner die than have her filthy gypsy diseases brought into my bed. He pounded on the door cursing as if he intended to grant my wish.

It was the girl who saved her. The baroness heard her, Zoria, coaxing the baron to their bed. At first it infuriated Kristena, calling her a *wanton nymph*, but even as she was writing the entry it came to her that Zoria was attempting to lure the baron away for her, the baroness's, sake—also that she and this girl were both captives here—

A sound outside in the street, like heavy crates falling, broke Esteban's reverie and he was suddenly overcome with exhaustion. He put the baroness's scented letter in the diary to mark his place; then he rolled himself in a blanket on the bed and fell instantly asleep . . .

Not-Esteban is in the Minotaur's labyrinth, smelling his sweat, breathing in the humidity of his breath, which is the very air of the bullring's fetid passages. As he runs along, blind to a clear destination, Not-Esteban feels especially not himself. He experiences a kind of resigned pain, a familiar fear that over time has transformed into some other unnamed emotion. And even Not-Esteban's body moves in strange ways, quicker but less agile, perhaps taller yet definitely lighter. Not-Esteban puts out a hand to maintain balance, and skimming it along the rough boards of the chute a splinter penetrates the first finger—this is odd: in his dreams Esteban had never felt physical pain before. A bead of blood crimsons to the surface of the delicate-looking finger. Not-Esteban stares at the finger, intently watching as the bead drips from the wound and falls to the sandy floor. The blue muslin skirt and feminine shoes, between which the blood-drop lands, simultaneously elucidate and puzzle Not-Esteban: this dream-figure is a young woman, but who? The baroness Kristena? Zoria? The gypsy girl at the village well? Hilde, the brewmaster's daughter? The snort of the Minotaur, almost like the shout of a human voice, makes Not-Esteban look up, startled: he . . . she is in the eye of the bullring, and the beast has sensed her presence, perhaps smells the drop of blood, and he is turning his half human, half tauran head, the grotesque muscles of his back undulating beneath a sweaty sheen. Not-Esteban tries to become the Minotaur, to see with his sulfurous eyes. Instead, Not-Esteban thinks of Europa, ravaged by the bull. . . .

IT WAS NEARLY DARK when Esteban awoke. He knew he had been thinking of the young baroness throughout his daytime sleep, and over those many hours an image slowly formed of her, like a picture emerging in the photographist's chemical baths. She was a pretty but haunted figure, thin and pale, with lustrous blond hair that saved her from seeming one of those Gothic heroines from the previous century's literature.

Esteban untangled himself from his blanket then lit the oil-lamp in his room and retrieved his sketchbook and pencils. He flipped past the gypsy drawings until he came to a clean sheet. He searched the gallery of his memory for the familiar salon, the one of the Minotaur dream, and found her there: the image of the young baroness. Esteban began with the thin line of the left side of her face, wan and gaunt in his artist's eye, and continued smoothly into her neck, then skimming across to imply her clavicle, as fragile-looking as avian bones. The pencil's charcoal tip briséd to the cleft of the youthful Kristena's high bosom, surrounded by its plunging neckline, accented in delicate Portuguese lace. The tip of Esteban's pencil traced the opposite line of Kristena's neck, where loosened strands of her long hair looped and fell upon her bare shoulder. The pencil worked on the baroness's ear, though mostly obscured by her refulgent tresses.

And from this partial frame charcoal began to tease out Kristena's distressed features, the thin arch of eyebrows, the oval eyes with just the subtlest of Oriental angle, and wisps of worry as light as a cob's solitary thread; the upturned nose with its bridge's nearly invisible bump.

Finally his tip was at Kristena's lips. He took a moment to sharpen his artist's instrument, which felt heavy with possibility between his graceful fingers. Then he placed the dark point at the corner of the young baroness's mouth and began by tracing her lower lip, plump with care—he knew her mouth would be key to the portrait, not the eyes, though they were a critical element as well. His pencil lingered at her lower lip for several minutes in an effort to render it perfectly, even on this first attempt.

When he began, lamplight and the final pulse of waning daylight cast the baroness's portrait in a citric wash; but now day had fully faded and the moon had crept into the sky opposite Esteban's lone window. Though weak, the gibbous added a touch of violet spectrum to his work emphasizing the baroness's mood of frustration and melancholy. Esteban used a smudging technique with the charcoal to highlight her cheekbones and to shadow her jawline and to round the crests of her bosom.

Then an element inserted itself into the sketch as if suggested by another. Esteban began drawing a hand flat against Kristena's stomach, just below her left breast. But he only rendered the most basic outline of the hand before stopping: he could not complete it because he knew not whose hand it was, not even if it were masculine or feminine.

* * *

DARKNESS HAD FALLEN like a heavy blue curtain by the time
Esteban put away his materials, retied the diaries with the red
ribbon, and straightened his rumpled bed. He thought of going
to Frau Becker's summer-kitchen for beer but first he was drawn
to peer out his window and on the street a figure was standing in
a posture that suggested it was gazing up at his window. It was a
feminine form and for a moment Esteban presumed it was the
gypsy girl whom he'd seen at the well; however, just at that instant a horseman bearing a lantern trotted past the female form
and the quick glint of light in her hair informed Esteban it was
in fact the brewmaster's daughter, Hilde.

She seemed to raise her hand toward Esteban, who must have
been an indistinct figure himself in the boardinghouse window.
He took up his old jacket, locked his door from the hall, and
hurried downstairs to meet her. Hilde was not in sight, though.
He looked up and down the deserted street. Muffled conversations and punctuating laughter came from the summer-kitch-
en. A damp breeze blew his hair before his eyes; he had not cut
his hair since leaving Seville and it had grown past his jacket
collar. He pushed back his hair and as he did so he thought he
glimpsed a figure in a blouse and long skirt pass between buildings down the street.

Esteban rushed to overtake the figure. He followed between
the low brick buildings—one a small chapel, the other the village's post and telegraph office—and the figure had vanished
again. The path led to the stable where he worked most regularly
so it was perhaps out of habit that he continued in that direction
even though there was no sign of the girl. As he neared the large,
two-story stable, the familiar smells of straw, oats, manure and
equine sweat came to him on the chilling breeze.

When he reached the structure, he saw that one of its wide
doors was ajar and saffron lamplight spilled angularly onto the

ground. Though he did not mind being alone—he believed what his masters said, that true artists required their time of solitary contemplation—Esteban had had his fill today and felt the yearning for companionship. It seemed that one of the stable-hands or a groom was still at work—no one would leave a lamp burning unattended—so Esteban slipped through the barely open door.

Only two lamps were aglow, hanging from hooks on supporting timbers that ran along the wide central alley. To each side were occupied stalls (the horses seemed mildly unsettled), and at the midpoint of the alley crossed a narrow walkway that led to a tack-room and feed-room on one end and to an office with overnight quarters on the other.

Hello, called Esteban. Who is here?

There was no human response—the Forester to Esteban's right, the color of Frau Becker's sweetened coffee, dipped his enormous head and nickered softly at Esteban's voice.

Esteban advanced farther into the stable, becoming annoyed at the carelessness of leaving the lamps lit while stepping out for who knew what purpose. He tried to imagine which of the workers may have done it and three or four likely faces formed in his mind. He stood near the second burning lamp and watched while a serpent-shape of black smoke rose up from its glass chimney, an impurity in the oil, and it circled along the timber then vanished in the dark air of the rafters.

Espíritu

It was so quiet he thought his ears were deceiving him—that the casting of his name was only the whisper of the black smoke just before its serpent form fluttered to oblivion. Esteban peered up and down the central alley and into the stalls and up toward the railinged loft.

Espíritu

Esteban took the lamp from its hook and called, Who is there? Who is saying my name? He positioned the lamp to see farther into the nearby stalls—onyx eyes shone glossy from behind forelocks. He held the lamp higher, above his head, but the light could not penetrate the shadowed loft. He heard a subtle movement to his left that didn't strike him as quite equine, in the direction of the tack-room. Is someone there? He realized he'd only whispered the query, like a thespian on the stage. He began toward the tack-room, his lamp held before him as if an amulet. He'd only taken a few steps. . . .

Herr Espíritu

. . . from behind and above, an androgynous voice lilting toward the feminine. Come down! You should not be up there! Footsteps as light as a child's scampered along the darkened creaking loft then after a moment ceased.

This prank is not funny . . . you could hurt yourself. . . .

Nothing—only the racing pulse in his ears and the horses' gentle movements behind their stall gates.

He thought that he should climb a ladder to the loft and put an end to the game-playing but he easily convinced himself the prankster had gone elsewhere. He decided instead to look in on each of the horses to make certain all were well. He'd been to several stalls and was stroking the neck of a powerful three-year-old named Hans when he spied a figure through an open upper gate in the back of the stall: the figure was all but invisible but seemed to be seated on the whitewashed corral fence and facing the yard and the stable.

Esteban's ire toward the brewmaster's daughter was extreme as he pushed open the door near the feed-room and marched toward the girl, his lamp still in hand and swinging light along the choppy ground. What do you think you are doing? Trying to frighten me with your childish game?

Hilde seemed startled, as if she'd been quite lost in her thoughts—What are you talking about? Childish game?

Yes, game!

Hilde's voice was strange. The girl finally fell within the weak arc of lamplight and it was not the brewmaster's daughter after all but rather the gypsy girl. Esteban stood before her speechless.

What game? she repeated after a few moments. The lamplight and moonlight competed to highlight her glossy ebon hair, which she'd loosed from her usual scarf so that it fell across her shoulders.

I thought you were someone else. . . .

So it would seem, Herr Painter. She turned about and leaped down from the fence's top rail and stood facing Esteban from the other side.

Were you in the stable?

When?

Just now?

Why would I be in the stable?

Esteban's flame wavered; from the weight of the lamp he'd known the font was nearly empty. Just a moment, I have to return the lantern. He began walking toward the stable door. Halfway he turned and called back, What is your name? The lamp went out altogether.

Zoria, she said, lost from view.

Esteban felt he was the butt of another joke . . . Zoria.

He quickly replaced the useless lamp, blew out the other, then exited and secured the streetside door. By the time he reached the opposite side of the stable, however, the girl was no longer by the fence; she seemed to be nowhere at all but in the utter darkness of a night shadow she may have only been steps away.

Esteban's yearning for companionship was even more intense and he felt drawn back toward the boardinghouse, believing it was the human-hive of the summer-kitchen he desired. However, as he was nearing Frau Becker's yard he heard the merry commotion and knew it didn't suit his mood and that it had not in fact been the object of his yearning. He went straight to his room, which now felt warm and a trifle stuffy, and he retrieved his sketchbook with the charcoal of young Kristena von Lichtenberg—it was as if he'd been missing her: not the living dowager but rather this rendering of her younger self, as totally false as it may be.

He placed the drawing on the table near the glowing lamp. He examined the mysterious hand beneath Kristena's breast and experienced a weird prick of jealousy. Though he had of course drawn the featureless hand himself it seemed even more of an enigma than before.

Esteban removed his jacket, raised the sash to let in some cooling air, then sat and prepared to draw further sketches of the young baroness. He began by untying the ribbon and reading from her diaries. Images of this flaxen-haired girl materialized in his mind's eye as if they'd been part of his hidden psyche all along and the diary entries were merely conjuring them forth, from shadow into light, that is, into the somber cerulean light which infused everything here.

Esteban read and sketched, the words firing his illustrative imagination: the girl baroness waltzing, the girl baroness wearing an expression of absence, the girl baroness weeping, the girl baroness writing, the girl baroness rising, the girl baroness writhing . . . all studies in the singular—except for the hand that inserted itself into every drawing: on the baroness's shoulder, on the baroness's hand, on her arm, her breast, her thigh.

He sketched through the night. In a corner of his window he absentmindedly noted the moon's rise and decline, at times obscured by wisps of lavender clouds drifting like dragon smoke across the picture-box sky.

* * *

FROM MY WINDOW, *I watched the girl in the garden as she carefully worked the weeding-hoe between rows of beets and lettuces and endive. It hasn't been an especially warm day, but she sweated through her white blouse, and she used a flowered scarf of scarlet to tie back her long black hair, trying to cool her glistening neck. I thought of how she no doubt sweats beneath the Baron's bulk—weeding must be a much more pleasurable way to raise one's perspiration . . . I rang for the downstairs maid, three times, but she was not answering the call, so I put on my dressing-gown and slippers, resolved to retrieve my own glass of buttermilk. It was not terribly late, not yet eleven, but the house was exceedingly quiet. For reasons that were not clear, I chose a longer route to the kitchen which took me past the Baron's private chambers; and just as I was there in the hallway, Stier's door opened—but before I had time to react I saw it was she, just as surprised as I but with the added emotion of shame. We stood facing one another and it burned in her tawny cheeks as clearly as if she'd handed me a missive of heartfelt apology. They say the eyes of gypsies are hypnotic—it aids in their mischief-making—and this Zoria's certainly were, such a deeply umberous brown they were nearly black. I sensed no mischief here, not of her making at least, and when she turned away to scurry down the hall, the breaking apart of our vision was almost physically painful . . . The music-room is at the end of the east hall, a hall otherwise of guestrooms and since we never invite overnight guests, the rooms are shut up and the furniture covered. No one has occupied the music-room for years, yet this morning—I had risen especially early—when I was passing the entrance to the east hall, I heard the faint notes of the piano, almost ghostly in their airiness. I stood in place for a moment, but then there it was again—a mournful sound in the quiet, empty hall, made even more mournful by the badly out of tune instrument. I could not imagine who the pianist was—Stier did not play and had little appreciation for music anyway—and I thought again of the ghostliness of the sad melody. After hesitating a moment I proceeded down the hall, my velvet slippers light on the carpeted floor of red diamond pattern. As I drew closer to the music-room I knew the piece, the 'Lovers' Sonata' by Schlönberg, but I'd never heard it played so adagio, so melancholy. I hesitated at the door, which was half ajar. Perhaps the pianist wanted his privacy? Perhaps I could satisfy my curiosity without disturbing his playing. I carefully pushed back the door just far enough to take a single step into the room and observe the piano and its player—I was quite shocked to see the girl, Zoria, on the embroidered bench. She wore a silk robe of deepest scarlet and her face was hooded by her dark untethered hair. She was quite focused on the sheets of music and as such lost in the moment, affording me to watch her in profile for some time while the bittersweet notes fell upon the still air. On a small table near the piano was a statuette of the Virgin, blue-cloaked and beatific, the only art in the somber and colorless music-room. I quietly stepped back into the hall, not wishing to disturb the girl, nor to be discovered watching and listening so intensely . . . Another night of fitful sleeping, dreamt again of performing a duet with the girl—we are in a large concert hall, the houselights have been turned down, it seems that every seat is occupied but the audience's faces are obscured, I wonder if the Baron is in attendance, perhaps seething with jealousy, then I know he is not, and our playing takes on a lightness in the perfectly acoustical hall. . . .*

IT WAS THE COMMOTION in the hall which first woke Esteban, Frau Becker having words with someone, and Esteban was thinking he should get out of bed to see what was happening when there was pounding on his door. He rose so quickly his head swam as he surveyed the messy room for his pants— sketches lay on the table, the floor, even the foot of his bed, and the baroness's diaries were open here and there—

More knocking and a man's angry voice: Open the door, Spaniard!

Still disoriented, Esteban realized he was wearing his pants, that he'd only managed off his heavy canvas shirt before crawling into sleep. Sí, sí—I mean, yes, just a moment; and he opened the door.

An enormous blond fellow filled the door frame, blond hair, blond beard. Where is she?

I'm sorry, Spain—Frau Becker spoke from behind the flush-cheeked fellow—I asked him to wait in the parlor. . . .

Where is she? And he began surveying Esteban's disheveled room.

Frau Becker, now peeping from a small space between the fellow's meaty biceps muscle and the frame, spoke again: This is Herr Müeller, the brewmaster. . . .

Finally some clarity came to Esteban—Ah, you are looking for your daughter. . . .

Of course, what did you think, Spaniard, I'd come to invite you to drink a beer with me! Where is my Hilde?

I do not know where the fräulein is. I have not been with her.

Herr Müeller's frosty eyes darted about the tiny, unkempt room as if seeking a place where his daughter may be hiding, though obviously an impossibility. But you know where she is.

No, said Esteban, suddenly realizing it was a lie, or nearly so—he somehow did sense where Fräulein Hilde may be keeping herself—but he merely reiterated: I thought perhaps I had seen her on the street, from my window (he peered over his shoulder for a second at the window, as if to prove the veracity of his statement) but I have not spoken to her since our brief introduction at Frau Becker's.

Two days ago, offered the landlady, invisibly. Perhaps Hilde is only taking a stroll in the woods.

Dissatisfied, Herr Müeller stormed off, headstrong as a bull to locate his overdue daughter.

Frau Becker and Esteban looked at each other for a moment; then she noticed the condition of his room. Yet she merely said, The coffee is ready—I will fry you a blintz with potato and egg.

Thank you; I will be downstairs in a moment.

Esteban dressed and ate quickly, so it was only a matter of minutes after the brewmaster's visit that Esteban was on the road leading to the gypsy encampment, the whereabouts of which he knew only by reputation.

It was becoming an overcast day with a threat of rain on the azure air. A mile or more beyond the boundaries of the village the road began to slope downward, and in a few minutes a well-trod path appeared falling away from this already secondary road—the deep ruts of cart-wheels and mule hooves showed Esteban he was on the correct course. He thought of the gypsies, of Zoria in particular, carrying well water such a great distance: Shiftless, the villagers said, but there was no doubting the gypsies' heartiness. The quality of the air had changed and was suddenly tinged with a fenny dankness. But there were also the scents of cookfires and the sweat of mules, and Esteban soon came to the camp of tents and carts and flimsy movable shacks.

Besides the mules, which were tethered to posts or stumps here and there, Esteban noted molting chickens, splay-legged goats, halfbreed herding dogs, and a trio of undernourished milk cows—in fact, at first look it appeared a camp solely of animals. Shouldn't there also be music-playing monkeys, chained tigers and dancing bears? In a moment Esteban was approached by a short fellow with black mustaches, twisted at their ends, and shoulders as broad as a water yoke. He'd been carving a block of pine, and the wood and knife were still in hand.

May I help you?—his German almost as poorly accented as Esteban's.

I am looking for my friend, Zoria—calling her a friend didn't feel like a lie.

The broad little fellow studied Esteban's face suspiciously, all the while turning the handle of the knife over in his large, heavily creased palm. Esteban saw that he was carving an animal shape in the block of pine—it appeared to be a bull rearing on his hind legs, which were yet undefined in the wood. Meanwhile other gypsies had emerged from their tents and shacks and were looking at Esteban warily.

The long moment was broken by a feminine voice: Herr Painter—what are you doing here?

Esteban turned to her, still half hidden by a tent flap: Your father is looking for you, Fräulein Müeller.

The black-haired girl Zoria appeared next to Hilde in the tent's opening.

Hilde said, Did you tell him of your suspicions?

Esteban shook his head. I did not.

Zoria said, We were about to have breakfast, Herr Painter—join us. Then she spoke to her people in their own tongue and they returned to whatever they'd been doing beforehand.

The young women, both in simple blouses and flowered skirts that reached to their unshod feet, led Esteban through the ramshackle camp without speaking. He was somewhat behind and able to observe them unabashedly—he was reminded of a printed photograph and the photographist's glass-plate negative image, the girls were so similar in height and form and even gracefulness, and only varied greatly in their lightness and darkness.

They came to a part of the camp set up for dining, where two large copper pots were suspended above smoking fires, and at a third fire meat was sizzling in an enormous iron pan. There was also an odd assortment of chairs, stools, tables but also stumps and rough-hewn logs, around which here and there were a few old men and children—while a trio of thickbodied women appeared to be in charge of preparing and serving the meal.

Esteban, Hilde and Zoria seated themselves at a round table, and in a moment they were served bowls of thick porridge with, Esteban discovered, bits of meat (goat, he assumed) and a strong scent of sage. He was also given a cup of milk, still warm from the udder. The woman who served them set a fourth place, and when she brought the small pail of milk she seated herself. Her complexion was darker than Zoria's and uneven with darker still age spots from long hours working out of doors; her hair was bound in a purple scarf but Esteban noted filaments of white mixed with the ebon strands which had come loose. She was perhaps forty or forty-five, the age of his mother back in Seville.

For a time they ate in silence with their wooden spoons while around them old men and children chattered amongst themselves in the language Esteban couldn't identify.

When they were nearly finished with their food, an old woman came holding a metal coffee pot with a rag, steam rising from its spout, and she poured the richly black coffee into the cups which had held their milk. The woman at their table removed pouch and paper from a pocket of her skirt and deftly rolled a cigarette, then struck a match on the underside of the table to light it. The smoke escaped her lips as she spoke: Now we can talk—her German was perfect. It is funny, Herr Painter, but the question you keep raising around you is, Why is he here? The village folk ask it because they believed you had designs to move on months ago. The stable operators ask it because you are so gifted with horses that it seems a waste for you to be tending simple beasts of burden. And now here you are, in our home, and we find ourselves asking it too. She brought the cigarette to her lips as she finished speaking.

I did not realize, said Esteban, I was such a source of wonderment.

The woman studied him with brown eyes flecked in blue, and she didn't need to comment that his response was equivalent to no response at all.

Then he said, The light. . . .

The light?

Yes, there is something about it—I cannot say that it drew me here—

Like a moth to a flame, offered the woman.

But once I saw it . . . well, it seems to have cast a spell upon me, or something to that effect.

It is blue, the light.

Yes, yes, quite so—you see it too.

How can one not?

Sapphire-eyed Hilde spoke up: Blue is the color of sorrow.

And of fidelity, said Zoria as a counterpoint.

And of nobility, said the woman, more smoke rising from her lips.

Here, said Esteban, I am afraid it is mainly the color of sorrow.

Don't be so certain, Herr Painter—it is safe to say that blue is a complex color and not easily known.

Esteban drank the rich coffee. Then: I could ask the same of you.

The woman arched her black eyebrows in puzzlement.

Why are you here? You are nomads, yes? Why not move elsewhere, someplace where the air is less . . . oppressive?

Perhaps we are.

You are planning to move on?

No, perhaps we are moving now, even as you and I speak, but at such an incremental pace it is impossible to detect in the short term. Like a glacier.

Perhaps I too am traveling to the Rhine at the same rate. Like a glacier.

Perhaps, said the woman, and she touched her cup to Esteban's in confederation.

Large drops of rain began to fall noisily upon the table top, and everyone in the camp started to seek shelter, including the woman and the two girls. Esteban rose from the table—there was more he wanted to say, to know. . . .

He followed the woman as she was hurrying off, and he reached out and touched her shoulder.

She stopped and turned, tossing away what little was left of her cigarette and then using her hand to shield her face from the raindrops, which were falling faster now.

Esteban said, Something happened. . . .

Where? When?

At the baroness's house . . . something bad. His German was failing him in the rush of the moment.

The woman looked at him for a second or two: Something bad, Herr Painter, or something . . . complex? Then she turned and went quickly into a nearby tent. Farther away, Zoria and Hilde, holding hands, also disappeared behind a tent's flapped opening.

No one invited Esteban in to shelter from the rain. The wind also had risen. He pulled the collar of his jacket over his head, thinking, What *am* I doing here?

BY THE TIME ESTEBAN reached Frau Becker's he was soaked completely, and waves of chill cascaded through his body like electric current, which he'd once seen demonstrated in the capital. He went directly to his room, meaning to swiftly shed his wet clothes and wrap himself in blankets, but upon entering his room he saw that it had been tidied—no doubt by his landlady—and she'd even neatly pinned his sketches to the walls. The baroness's diaries were reassembled, bound together with the red ribbon, and placed on the table along with his sketchbook, pencils and sharpening stone.

I hope you don't mind, Spain.

He was standing in the open doorway to his room, and Frau Becker was behind him in the hall.

No, it is fine, said Esteban, a shiver accenting the word *fine*.

Give me your wet things and I'll dry them in the parlor. I'll also bring you hot chocolate with gingerbread—it'll ward off lung fever.

Presently, Esteban had changed into his dry clothing, and with a blanket around his shoulders he was looking at his sketches in the gray-blue light from the window. Frau Becker tapped on the door and entered with the steaming chocolate and a thick slice of gingerbread, both of which she placed on the table next to Esteban.

Then she joined him in gazing at the drawings.

There seemed to be an order to them, she said, almost like they're telling a story.

After a moment Esteban said, Did you know Baroness von Lichtenberg when she was younger?

Not really, my husband and I were on the farm until, what, twelve years ago, but I knew *of* her of course. And of the baron's accident.

His drowning.

Yes, the baron's drowning.

Esteban waited for her to elaborate, to express her skepticism, but she didn't share Heinrich and Otto's fondness for gossip, and only the landlady's tone possibly hinted at something untoward.

Drink your chocolate while it is hot, Spain, and eat the gingerbread whether you care for it or not. I have no desire to nurse a sick lodger—that's not part of our arrangement. Frau Becker smiled and left Esteban alone.

He did what he was instructed, and the food and drink did assist in warming him further. Nevertheless he went to his bed and burrowed beneath the extra blankets Frau Becker had brought him. Rain pelted his window, and in a moment he had returned to the Minotaur's labyrinth as the female figure he knew to be the young Kristena. . . .

She is following the beast's scent, treading upon the sandy floor as lightly as she is able. The passageway is in severe shadow but she resists lighting a lamp though they appear now and then on the rough-plank walls. Surprise is her ally—that and Mother Mary, whose graceful beads she holds in her palm, rubbing gently with her thumb and fingers. The motion releases a scent like lilac and it helps to mask the beast's semi-human stench. She reaches the entrance and steps quietly into the eye of the labyrinth. She hears the beast's grunts before spying him in the dim light—there in the center of his world, taking the girl, sweat rolling off his bestial shanks with every brutish thrust. As silent as fate, she goes to the beast, oblivious in his copulation, and she raises the beads above her head . . . at that moment her prayers are answered in the form of the Virgin herself, which she brings unto the beast's skull with the full force of her divinity. . . .

The day was still rainy when Esteban awoke, and immediately he began the task of completing the feminine details of the hand in his sketches. When the weather cleared, he would gather his work and begin the long climb to the baroness's lonely house, beneath a sky of piercing blue.

Melvill in the Marquesas

July 13, 1842

DRIPPING.

It is the dripping and the insensible voices which bring him
up from the depths. Darkness and heat. He tries to feel the
pitch of the sea, now as familiar as the expansion of his lungs,
but there is no movement. Becalmed, he thinks. He cautiously
sniffs the air, anticipating the stench of boiling fat. But there is a
sweetness instead: thick, oily.

He remembers.

Panic begins to surge in him, like the ocean's surf, like the
fever he has had . . . how many days? The number will not come
to him. He wants to rise, to step over the darkshape bodies, to
run outside, past the dripping cataract to the starlit ocean.

It is all impossible. He heard their cannibal voices; at least
two are awake. And Toby? He reaches out and touches the coarse
cloth of Toby's shirt and he hears the familiar sleep breathing of
his friend. Like so many nights in the belly of the *Acushnet*. The
dripping and Toby's breathing take him back for a moment: the
roll of the ocean, the stinking blubber, the footfalls above on
deck . . . and something else.

Toby moves in his sleep—perhaps he is fitful too—and Toby's
hand brushes against his side. He lightly takes hold of Toby's

arm, feels the hairs at the wristbone, the slow steady pulse. The rhythm of Toby's blood calms him. He tries to turn toward his friend, to watch his dark outline, but the pain in his leg will not allow it. Shards of agony vibrate through his leg, which has become like wood or stone. He tries to imagine dragging the swollen limb the many miles to the sea. It is impossible.

The cataract and Toby's pulse become synchronous, and Melvill achieves a kind of sleep.

It is daytime when he realizes the old man is talking to him. Melvill is the only one still lying on the floor of the hut, which is rectangular with a bamboo and thatched ceiling about fifteen feet high at its centered apex. Along the walls are baskets, earthen pots, woven mats. Toby is gone. It is unsettling again to see the fading ink on the old man's almost naked body: the bluegreen vines twisting along his still-muscular arms, the disintegrating bluegreen triangle on his forehead, the sinking ovals on his chest that make his nipples dark bull's-eyes. The old man repeats himself for perhaps the fourth time. Melvill understands only two words. "Hermes," the way they have decided to pronounce his name; and "Korykory," the young cannibal who seems to reside in the old man's hut.

Melvill tries to stand but his leg provides him no leverage. He believes he may topple when he feels Korykory lift him to a standing position on his good leg then deftly turn and hoist him onto his back. Melvill is half a head taller and his bare toes nearly drag on the floor. Korykory's wavy brown hair is shaved in arcs over each ear and tapers to a point between his shoulder blades, where the shapes of longwinged birds in flight have been tattooed.

Outside Korykory lifts him higher on his back. Men and women are calmly busy with the demands of the new day. All these many months around the islands of the south Pacific and the stark nakedness of the natives still surprises him. It seems the Typees prefer a short white cloth which hangs from their waist, or even more simply broad waxy leaves. Korykory carries him past the cataract to where the stream is calmer. Melvill is relieved to see Toby floating on his back in the clear water, his bare white chest bobbing like a seaduck among the other dark-skinned bathers. Melvill wants to call out to Toby but he does not want to do anything to provoke the Typees. Half a dozen somber warriors, with long spears and sharktooth necklaces, kneel on either side of the stream.

Korykory takes him beyond the pool of bathers about a hundred yards to a place where the stream begins to pick up speed again. Next to the stream is a patch of high green reeds. Korykory places him at the edge of the reeds and motions for him to proceed in. Melvill is confused. Korykory talks to him with patient meaningless words. Then the native wades into the reeds himself, urging Melvill along. The pliant reeds, which come to Melvill's stomach, snap back after being trod upon. Korykory squats with his back to the swift running water, and Melvill understands. Korykory stands and tries to unbutton Melvill's trousers.

He pushes his hand away, like a bothersome child's. "I'm with you."

Korykory shrugs then moves his tappa cloth aside and urinates a thick stream into the water. The islander waits at the edge of the reeds for Melvill to finish. Korykory points back to the cluster of huts and the bathers. Melvill climbs on and is carried toward the pool. His leg is throbbing from the exertion.

As he is carried along Melvill views the mountains, lavender at their peaks, that Toby and he traversed for three days. This is correct: three days. And the discomfort in his right leg began on the morning of their second day of flight from Nukuheva Bay. By nightfall the discomfort had become the debilitating pain he suffers still. So that is the number that would not come to him: four days of pain. In spite of his bad leg Melvill feels better that his head is clearer now, the fever abated somewhat.

At the bathing pool he sees Toby wrapped in a long swath of the white tappa, like a haphazardly placed toga. The old Typee woman who lives in the hut where they slept is holding the bundle of Toby's clothes and is having an animated dialogue with his friend.

"But, please, I need my clothing, at the very least my trousers." Toby is holding the toga together at the shoulder.

Korykory places Melvill down at the edge of the pool and the old woman gestures at Melvill's checked shirt and duck trousers.

"I believe the witch wants your things too, old fellow," says Toby. "They probably would prefer not to cook us in our breeches—we will be too tough no doubt."

As if she can understand the nature of their conversation, the old woman renews her efforts to explain and screws her face into a foul expression and touches her nose, meanwhile spitting out some Typee expression.

Melvill says, "I believe she is telling us she finds our sailor's smell disagreeable. Perhaps she is offering to launder out the sweat and sea salt."

"Or she intends to burn and bury everything, part and parcel, forthwith. In either case it appears we have no say in the matter."

The stony warriors have formed a loose circle around the four of them, Toby and Melvill, the old woman and Korykory. One of the warriors takes hold of Toby's bare arm and urges him away from the water's edge. Melvill pulls his shirt off over his head then sits on the grassy bank to remove the rest of his clothing. Korykory hands the wad to the old woman and he scoops up Melvill like his new bride and wades into the pool, releasing him when the stream is waist deep.

The water is cool and clean and a great relief to Melvill. The buoyancy relieves much of the pain from his swollen leg. Melvill ducks his head then allows it to bob to the calm surface. The droplets that run from his scalp and ears taste of his own salt. With the temporary relief of his leg Melvill realizes the profundity of his hunger and thirst. For three days Toby and he ate only their ration of a dry mouthful of sea biscuit—"sailor's nuts"—each noon hour. The breadfruits they believed were in abundance beyond Nukuheva Bay were not to be found in the wild mountains. They had agreed to refrain from breaking into ship's stores and risk alerting their mates of their plan to take flight.

Water was also scarce. At the end of their second day in the mountains they discovered a narrow stream. It relieved their thirst, which was terrible and close to undoing them, especially Melvill, who was burdened with fever too. But there was still no food and the biscuit was nearly gone. Also they needed shelter from the sun and periodic rains.

They knew the little stream would lead down the mountain to a settlement—but which natives: the Happars, of whom very little was known; or the Typees, whose cannibalism was infamous throughout the south Pacific? They had no choice but to follow the stream. Turning back was out of the question. The penalty for jumping ship was severe: flogging and treatment befitting a slave for the remainder of the voyage. Their shipmates would not venture into cannibal terrain, no matter what reward was offered by Captain Pease; but a band of Nukuhevas could be easily commissioned for the job. Three or four pounds of Brazilian tobacco and a modest supply of shot and powder would probably turn them out like a pack of red hounds. In the mountains several times Toby and he were startled by a wild boar in the undergrowth which they mistook for a Nukuheva ambush.

Finally, descending from the mountains, they saw a fruitful valley and its huts with steeply pitched thatch roofs. It was midday, the tropical sun high and hard. For a great length of time—Melvill was beyond keeping track of it—they stayed under cover while Toby observed the distant goings on and tried to determine Happar or Typee or some other indigenous tribe.

They choked down the last crumbs of biscuit, which seemed to push Toby into a decision. "I must know, old fellow, I must." And he rushed down into the valley. Melvill watched his friend half stagger out of the shadow of the mountain, then he attempted to follow him.

His memory beyond this point is patchy. He recalls falling and struggling up, many times. He is helped—by Toby, he first believes, then realizes it is a girl and boy, dark and naked, on either side of him. Then they are in a hut, the brown faces surrounding them. They are given fresh water (so sweet!) and a kind of citrus mush to eat. "Poeepoee." Toby is attempting to explain who they are and that they have come in peace—which must be obvious from their half-dead, unarmed condition. It is night, the only light from the bluish glow of a taper outside the hut's opening, when Toby and he come to understand that they have arrived in the valley of the Typees. Melvill is too exhausted and feverish to be panicstricken. The knowledge is like a lead weight in his brain, sinking deep as nearly all the natives exit the hut and he and Toby are left to sleep among these cannibals.

After his bath, Melvill, also in white tappa now, is taken to the hut and seated next to Toby at what seems like a place of honor. They sit on woven mats in a corner while a dozen natives eat their breakfast facing them in a semicircle. The hut is spacious, perhaps forty feet by twenty, and the interior walls reveal the simple but sturdy bamboo construction. Here and there pegs protrude from the crisscross of bamboo so that various utensils hang on the walls along with bunches of breadfruits and bananas. Melvill and Toby are each given a bowl of poeepoee plus another of coconut meat and a half coconut shell filled with a citrus juice. Eating with their fingers the tender chunks of coconut are not a problem but the poeepoee is another matter. The day before, starving, they scooped it and poured it like a stringy soup, making a mess of themselves. This morning Marheyo, the old man who is their host, tries to show them the proper technique. Using only one finger he twirls it in the bowl nearly up to the last knuckle until a thick ball of poeepoee is wrapped around; then he sticks the entire finger in his mouth and pulls it out sucked clean. Melvill discovers the technique requires practice.

The natives have begun several conversations and are paying little attention to Toby and Melvill.

Toby swirls his shell of juice before drinking it. "How's the leg holding up?" Toby has raked his reddish blond hair straight back. Like Melvill's, it is long enough to bind in a ponytail. Toby's beard is patchy while Melvill's is dark and thick.

"Not well I'm afraid. Perhaps rest will help." Melvill finishes chewing a chunk of coconut meat. "Why are we receiving service at the captain's table?"

"I can't figure it—unless they are fattening us for the feast."

Melvill had had the same thought. "All this trouble just to murder us."

"The cattleman and the butcher are not a lazy lot."

When breakfast is finished the old woman, Tinor, places all the dishes into a large wickerwork basket and takes them from the hut. Marheyo speaks earnestly to Melvill. The old man repeatedly takes hold of his own right leg, kneading the flesh.

"Yes, my limb is ill," says Melvill, lost.

Marheyo gestures to Toby that it is time to leave the hut with the other guests. The native waves his long brown fingers like he is shooing a cat. When it is just Melvill and the old man together, he speaks emphatically again and points to the mat where Melvill had slept the night before. Melvill understands to move there. Marheyo gently pushes him to a reclining position; and he walks to the hut's opening. Maybe he merely wants me to rest, thinks Melvill, already feeling sleepy. But in a minute or two Marheyo appears to be greeting someone. Melvill watches the old man's back, with its withered fish tattoos, as he speaks to the new arrival about Melvill's leg, all the while massaging his own leg.

A kind of shaman? wonders Melvill.

Marheyo steps aside to let the visitor enter. Melvill is surprised to see a young girl—fourteen or fifteen perhaps—carrying a tortoise-shell bowl. She is the most beautiful island girl Melvill has seen in an ocean filled with vibrant beautiful girls. Marheyo seems to be introducing her. He says her name "Fayaway" several times and each time the old man touches his chest: illustrating her closeness to his heart? Fayaway is thin with long umberblack hair. She appears to be free of tattooing except for two dots at the crests of her upper lip.

Melvill is up on his elbows. Fayaway kneels beside him and puts her hand on his shoulder to urge him to lie flat. There is a bracelet of small blue feathers on her wrist. She moves the tappa away exposing his swollen leg from hip to foot. His skin appears almost phosphorescent in the shaded interior of the hut. The girl gently explores the leg, moving her light fingers over his thigh and knee and shin bone. She and Marheyo speak for a moment. To explain their conversation, Marheyo takes a banana from a bunch hanging on the wall. He uses his bony fingers to show Melvill the yellow skin is smooth and unblemished, then the old man peels the skin and breaks the banana in half, exposing the tiny black seeds inside.

"Yes, there's no outward sign of my distress, no laceration, nor boil, nor prick—so the problem must be inward." He can sense the fever is beginning to overtake his reason again.

Marheyo has a parting word for Fayaway then he leaves his hut eating the banana. It is a bright day and the old man appears to be swallowed by the light.

Fayaway dips her small hands into the bowl and they come out glistening with an oily gelatin. Starting with Melvill's toes she slowly rubs the slick ointment into his skin. Frequently she glances at Melvill's face, perhaps to see if she is hurting him. Melvill is struck by the similarities between her glittering eyes and her half-erect nipples: the same size, the same rich brown. The four perfect circles dance like alien moons in the sky of his feverish mind.

As Fayaway's hands, which are now his entire reality, move past his knee Melvill cannot subdue the sexual arousal he is feeling. He hopes that it is hidden beneath the folds of cloth but senses it is not. Her hands move over his thigh with the same slow rhythm. At first the ointment was cool but now a penetrating heat has begun at his foot and ankle, and is moving up at the same pace as Fayaway's massaging fingers. When she reaches his hip she gently lifts his leg enough to coat the underside in the gelatin. When she is finished Fayaway instructs him to close his eyes by pointing to them with her slender fingers and closing her own eyes for a moment.

Melvill does as he is instructed. Soon his entire leg is engulfed in the heat. His body is totally relaxed, lifeless, except for his twitching organ, uncomfortable under the folded tappa. He wants to uncover himself to relieve the pressure but senses Fayaway is still at his side. No, not Fayaway . . . Madeline. He believes he can smell the prostitute's pungent city perfume, can feel the irregularities in the feather mattress of her New Bedford boardinghouse room. Then why not pull back the sheet? Propriety is not an issue, only price, and he has what remains of Captain Pease's advance. Eighty-four dollars minus—?

But propriety is an issue for a reason he cannot recall— only its vitalness. And there is the dripping . . . as the icy rain overflows Madeline's clogged gutter. Dripping, yes, but aboard the *Acushnet* now . . . the arousal still pulsating with the heat-rhythm of his leg. The dark figures below deck, the ominous whispering, the ubiquitous stench of the cooking whale sperm. There is the leaden weight of threat on his chest—worse than fear because fear is fleeting. This threat lingers, like a cancer, and there is no escape at sea. . . .

Strong hands are upon him and Melvill strikes out. Once,

twice. But his arms are restrained as he is lifted. He wants to shout out but he cannot recall to whom. He finds his captor's face. Korykory. The Typee carries him outside. The sunlight, although partially filtered through the tropical green canopy, is painful to his eyes. Korykory transports him to the bathing pool for the second time that day. He helps Melvill wash the ointment from his leg. In places the gelatin has turned white and cakey. Melvill attempts to hide his buoyant semierect penis.

Still floating, Melvill feels weak but the pain in his leg has subsided. Korykory points to a grove of trees and says something about Toby. Melvill thinks he understands. "Yes, take me to Toby, please." He is helped from the stream, then he covers himself in the white toga and climbs upon Korykory's back. The momentary muscular strain causes the native's tattooed birds to take a single wingstroke. When they are past the boundary of trees Melvill sees a grassy clearing in which there are several huts of varying sizes, including one that is several times larger than the average. Melvill notes that many of these huts are built on a foundation of high stone slabs. Korykory takes him directly to the largest hut, the one that dominates the clearing, and uses footholds that are notched into the stone base to carry Melvill to the entrance. Melvill is amazed at Korykory's vitality. There were strong men on the *Acushnet*, men who could do the heavy work of the sea for hours without tiring; but the strongest among them could not have carried Melvill the distance that Korykory has and then ended the trip with a vertical climb up eight feet of rock.

The front wall of the hut is recessed a few yards so that the stone base forms a portico, which is protected by the extended thatch roof of the hut.

Korykory, only slightly winded, waves his hand before the enormous hut and says, "Ti."

Melvill, balancing on his good leg and Korykory's shoulder, repeats the word and Korykory happily affirms the connection.

Korykory suddenly assumes an air of seriousness and seems to resist an impulse to step back. Melvill realizes that a Typee has come from the hut. The man is considerably older than Melvill but is made as muscularly as Korykory or any of the young warriors he has seen. He is richly decorated in tattoos, more so even than the old-man host. He puts his hand on his bare flat stomach and says, "Mehevi." He steps aside and invites Melvill into the Ti. For the short distance Melvill elects to hobble inside with Korykory's support rather than be carried. A tobacco-smoke smell reaches him immediately in the dark hut. The scent is pleasant, although distinct from the cuts of tobacco he is used to. The rich smoke seems to be impeding the adjustment of his eyes. Not quite seeing them, he can sense the dark shapes sitting or reclining on the floor. Melvill has the disconcerting feeling that these shapes are animals peering up at him, wolves and predatory cats. In the entire hut filled with bodies he hears no voices. Perhaps it is his visitation that has caused the Typees' muteness, or it is simply the way of the place.

Korykory is behind guiding him through the clusters of natives.

"Old fellow, there you are!"

Melvill, relieved, can hear the relief in Toby's voice too. Korykory helps him to a mat by his friend.

"I was afraid they'd decided you would be the appetizer and I the main course." Toby is holding a short wooden pipe.

Mehevi has sat facing them. From a basket he produces a pipe similar to Toby's. It is already stuffed with tobacco. Toby takes a small stick and puts one end into the bowl of his own pipe until the tip is glowing orange; then he uses it to set off Melvill's pipe.

Melvill inhales deeply and lets the warm smoke out of his mouth and nose. "A tad rough but a godsend nonetheless."

Toby nods. "Must be a local leaf."

Melvill notices the murmur of conversation throughout the

hut. Apparently the silence was a reaction to his arrival.

"How's the leg now, old fellow?"

"Perhaps a bit more limber but still a fount of pain. My physician is lovely, but I'm afraid I may need less primitive doctoring."

"I'm afraid we may yet become the guests of honor at a Typee feast."

Mehevi, who has been smoking silently, smiles and says, "Typee," his white teeth aglow in the shadowy Ti.

Melvill's eyes have adjusted finally so he scans the interior. There are dozens and dozens of Typees, young men and old, all sitting or reclining with their pipe; on woven mats that are either rolled into cushions or flat on the cool stone floor. They are in groups of four to six or seven, carelessly arranged. Ever since entering the Ti Melvill has been sensing dark circular objects hanging at regular intervals on the walls. With his improved vision he looks up to discover the dark shapes are human heads. The pipe nearly falls from his lips. "Toby . . . on the walls."

Toby glances up for an instant. "Yes, quite a pleasant decorating touch isn't it?"

The faces look to have the texture of smoked meat, desiccated and shrunk close to the bone. The eyes have been replaced with something white and iridescent, chipped stone or seashell. The heads glare wildly from their mounted positions. Melvill thinks perhaps they retain the shadow of their horrorstruck expression at the instant of death.

Mehevi must notice Melvill staring and he gestures toward the heads and offers an explanation. The only word that Melvill understands is "Happar," the Typees' neighboring enemies.

Melvill says to Toby, "Perhaps this Ti is one large hunting lodge and these heads the cherished trophies."

"Yes, and a men's club as well."

They spend a peaceful hour in the Ti with their pipes and the indistinct native voices. From time to time Melvill can imagine that the voices are mumbling English, the meanings just beyond his comprehension. Also, the displayed heads start to become as familiar as sconces. Even though there is no signal that Melvill can detect, all at once the Typees extinguish their pipes and begin to herd outdoors. Melvill and Toby follow suit, Melvill with Korykory's quick assistance.

The women and children have come to the grove and set up a midday meal. Korykory takes Melvill and Toby to a spot where the old couple, Marheyo and Tinor, are waiting with the meal. They sit on sheets of white tappa in the grass in the narrow shadow of the Ti. The meal is the same as breakfast except for the substitution of coconut milk for the citrus juice. Melvill is surprised at the number of Typees who are having their meal in the grove. It is an aboriginal scene, unchanged in hundreds of years, perhaps thousands. But their time is limited, speculates Melvill. He thinks of the three French men-of-war anchored in Nukuheva Bay, and of how the occupation has already changed the coastal region of the island, and of how the French will not be satisfied with only the coast and will systematically work their way inland. He thinks of how the Christian missionaries will follow the French like the scavenger sharks in the wake of the *Acushnet*.

"This certainly is superior to starvation," says Toby after sucking poeepoee from his finger, "but I keep thinking about sinking my teeth into a thick beefsteak."

"One day soon I'm certain—when we reach the Hawaiian Islands." Melvill hears the skepticism in his voice.

Melvill wants to stand when Fayaway approaches but his leg will not allow any sudden movement. The beautiful girl speaks to Marheyo and Tinor then she says something to Melvill—he guesses about his leg. Before he can find a way to respond she picks up a large bowl of boacho and offers it to him. Melvill points to his smaller bowl which contains the fruity mush. Fayaway insists that he take more.

Toby says, "I believe the doctor is prescribing a remedy, old fellow."

Melvill pours the yellowish boacho into his bowl. "Thank you."

Fayaway continues kneeling at Marheyo's side talking to the old man. In profile, with her dark hair spilling over her shoulders, she appears totally nude.

Toby runs his finger along the rim of his bowl. "Aside from the distinct possibility of ending up as sustenance, the Marquesas have their redeeming qualities."

Melvill does not comment.

When the meal is finished Tinor and Fayaway load the empty bowls into the large basket, placing the folded tappa on top. A majority of the men, including the decorated Mehevi, saunter toward the Ti. Melvill, weary, mounts Korykory's back thinking the Ti is their destination too; however Korykory begins following Marheyo, who is walking directly away from the massive hut.

"Where are we going?" Melvill watches over his shoulder as Toby stands hesitant for a moment then shrugging turns toward the Ti.

Korykory must sense the meaning of Melvill's question and offers a lengthy but fruitless Typee reply. Not bridging the gap with the old man they follow, Korykory takes a path out of the ring of huts; and Melvill discovers that beyond the grove about a third of a mile are dozens of small flat-roofed structures. Each one they pass has a totem of carved stone blocking its black opening. Many of these small huts are in disrepair and collapsing in on themselves. Several of the totems have fallen over. Another footpath to the left and they come to a hut which is under construction. Korykory unloads Melvill near a log on which he can rest then Korykory and Marheyo begin working on the bamboo-reed hut. They work without speaking, each knowing his part in the process. Korykory uses a sharp-edged stone to snap the bamboo at the proper length. The reeds are slightly larger around than a man's thumb. Marheyo skillfully lashes the bamboo together with vines to extend the second wall. The first wall stands erect supported by thick tree limbs; the wall being built is approximately a third of the first wall. Each is about six feet high, estimates Melvill. He is surprised that Korykory uses such a primitive method to size the bamboo because Melvill has noticed metal blades and tools among the Typees—evidence of some contact, if only indirectly, with sailors.

The spot where Melvill has been placed is shady and drowsiness soon begins to overtake him with the rise in his fever again. He waits quietly hoping that Korykory will finish his part and return him to Marheyo's hut, or at least the Ti. But Marheyo and Korykory work without pause and there are so many dozen bamboo reeds to be sized.

Melvill hobbles a short distance to a grassy place near the log and lies down. The grass feels cool and soft, and soon Melvill is asleep. The snapping and lashing of the bamboo enters his sleepworld to become the sounds aboard the *Acushnet*: the reeving of the sails, the banging of the tackles against the masts, the securing of supplies below deck. And there is something missing . . . some*one* missing. Melvill watches the search boats circling astern, gray boats on a gray sea, and Melvill knows the truth. He believes he knows.

When Melvill awakens Fayaway is sitting on the log watching Marheyo and Korykory work. The change in light filtered through the leafy canopy—now more yellow than white—tells Melvill it is late afternoon. Fayaway smiles down at Melvill then speaks to the silent workers. She says the name "Hermes" and she uses the word "kiki," which relates to food or eating, Melvill has learned.

Melvill tries to raise himself and finds that the pain in his leg is less acute but the stiffness is profound—truly like a piece of driftwood. He cannot bend his knee at all, barely his ankle.

Fayaway, seeing his difficulty, calls to Korykory and the two of them help Melvill to the log. Melvill notices the differences in their grip on each bare arm: Korykory's hands are callused and powerful; Fayaway's small and light, like a bird's wings.

While Melvill and Fayaway sit she is explaining something about the structure being built. Marheyo *this*, she says, and Marheyo *that*. The second, or back, wall is erect and the third wall is a quarter finished. Marheyo and Korykory are tidying up their materials, wrapping the bamboo into long palmetto leaves, balling the vines. When they are finished, Korykory readies himself to carry Melvill, who feels a pang of guilt at not being able to walk. After all, Korykory has been laboring all afternoon and now he must carry Melvill the great distance from the secluded flat-roofed huts, past the grove with the Ti, and back to the cluster of huts where Marheyo and Tinor live near the waterfall. There is nothing to do about his guilt. Marheyo and Fayaway walk in front, Korykory with Melvill behind. Fayaway, though tall for a Typee female, comes only to Marheyo's shoulder, and the old man is somewhat stooped. Their bare feet leave no trace on the hard earth.

The grove where they lunched is quiet. Melvill believes there must be dozens of men in the Ti smoking and socializing but he sees no one near its black entrance. It is as if the entire grove is sleeping—even the huts and the wildlife—or holding its breath, suspending living for a time. The quiet makes Melvill uneasy. He wants to ask, "Where is everyone?" but anticipates no response. Half dozing on Korykory's back, Melvill recalls legends of magic spells putting entire villages to sleep, of evil palls cast upon castles. Always it is an heroic act which lifts the spell. He senses no heroism in himself nor in Toby. Desperation, trepidation, primal fear—just beneath the surface.

As they approach Marheyo's hut Melvill sees Tinor and other old women bent over a large piece of white cloth working it with some sort of hand tool, like a small rolling pin. They are chattering but stop as soon as Marheyo's group draws near. Marheyo speaks briefly to his wife, or so their relationship seems to Melvill, before Korykory takes Melvill inside. Fayaway continues past Marheyo's, presumably to her family's hut.

Korykory eases Melvill down then immediately goes to a corner of the hut and lies in a fetal position. In seconds, while Melvill is still watching, Korykory is asleep. At first, in the dim light, Melvill does not recognize the things stacked on his sleeping mat but touches them and realizes they are his clothes. He is happy to get out of the makeshift toga and put on his familiar shirt and underbreeches and trousers. They are freshly laundered and have a pleasant floral scent. He leaves his shoes and stockings on the mat.

Melvill sits, thinking that is all he will do, but the drowsiness of fever quickly overcomes him and he lies down. He recalls sleeping in a strange room with his older brother. It is Christmastime and outdoors a thick blanket of snow covers the ground. Melvill hears his father's voice . . . downstairs, talking and laughing—storytelling. Melvill reaches for his old patchwork quilt but it is not cold really. His groping hand finds the white tappa and he covers himself. His father's story is a dissipating echo, like invisible dripping in a cave. He tries in vain to revive the dream of New England, to resurrect the ghost of his father. The darkness of the cave becomes real when Melvill awakens. The hut is black. He sits upright and looks at the opening. It is a rectangle of lavender twilight. Korykory is gone. Melvill struggles up and goes to the opening. No one is outside. From Marheyo's hut Melvill can see the grove with the Ti and between the blacktrunk trees is the orange glow of fire. Supper time? he wonders. Then why was I not called? And where is Toby?

Because of his leg, the Ti seems a great distance but Melvill begins to make his way. He is surprised that the ground is cool under his bare feet. He expects it to feel like baked terracotta, only minutes from the kiln. Walking is painful and he wishes he had a sturdy stick. He can detect the smell of woodsmoke now and of roasting meat. He thinks of Toby, whom he has not seen for hours. Queasiness slows his already slow pace. The light from the fire in the grove reminds him of the bellies of the cookstoves on the *Acushnet*, day and night boiling down the blubber when a kill has been made. The sickening smell of the melting fat, which permeated every space on the ship, comes to him again, adding to his nausea.

The light of the fires—the one in the grove and the recollected fire from the ship—nearly blinds him. Melvill stops, as if the twin fires have consumed his energy, his will. It is all he can do to keep from falling to the ground.

The Typees who emerge from the grove are like two shadow-warriors: black shapes against the fireglow. Melvill wants to run but cannot. He collapses when the dark figures reach him. Each taking an arm and a leg they carry him to the grove. Melvill, sick with fear, tries to shout out—for Toby, Korykory, Fayaway—but he has no voice. In the grove he sees that it is not one great fire but many fires. Their heat, combined with the sultry tropical heat, is intense. The warriors, who at least have distinct features in the firelight, carry him to one of the smaller ground-level huts adjacent to the Ti.

"Old fellow!" Toby rushes over. "I had really given you up." He helps Melvill to sit upright. They are alone in the small dark hut.

"What's happening?" Melvill's voice is a hoarse whisper.

"I can't say for certain. They've been dancing about these fires for some time—rather ceremoniously."

Melvill leans over to see out. "Is the ceremony for us, do you think?"

Toby rearranges himself so they are on either side of the hut's opening. "I can't say; but it seems likely."

"Why not get on with it then?"

"It is their religion, I suppose. You know that religious rites are not known for their swiftness."

"Toby, you must escape. I'm in no condition to flee, but you. . . ."

"My chances out there are no better, especially in the dark. There are hundreds of them. Thousands maybe. The whole damned cannibal nation has turned out for the event."

They sit in silence for a time. Outside the fires crackle and the Typees dance and chant. Melvill wonders about the decisions they have made, jumping ship and setting out for the wild country with no provisions and no weapons—totally at the mercy of who or what would find them. The whole episode makes no sense. There is no logic to any of their moves. Melvill, the gifted student, the debate society president, is awed by the rashness of his actions. He and Toby were doomed the instant they left Nukuheva Bay—running in that torrential downpour like freed schoolboys.

"I'm sorry it has come to this," says Melvill.

"It's not your fault, old fellow. We made the plans together. I knew what the possibilities were." Toby glances outside. "They're coming."

Their hands clasp on the sandy floor of the hut.

Melvill recognizes one of the trio approaching as Korykory. Another is Mehevi, the richly tattooed chieftain. The third Typee, who stays close to Mehevi's side, Melvill does not know. All three, backlit, appear to wear plumes of fire for headdress.

Korykory kneels at the hut's opening. He holds a flat piece of wood. He says something "kiki."

"They bring food," repeats Melvill.

On the wood are several strips of smoking meat.

"Yes," says Toby, releasing Melvill's hand, "but my god, what kind of meat?"

"Kiki," insists Korykory thrusting the strips toward Melvill.

Melvill's stomach is turning, partly from the fear that has been consuming him and partly from the idea of this cannibal offering. He recalls the severed heads in the Ti. "No kiki," he says weakly, shaking his head.

Korykory seems confused, almost embarrassed. He takes a piece of the meat and bites it himself. "Puarkee." He grins and chews the meat; juice trickles down his chin. "Puarkee." He holds the remainder of the meat to Melvill's lips.

Melvill, his head pounding from the tension and the fever, hesitates then opens his mouth slightly. Korykory pushes the meat past Melvill's parted lips. He fights the urge to gag as he begins to chew. The rich flavor floods his tongue and it is familiar. He swallows some of the meat. "Pork. The natives are roasting some of those wild boars. It's delicious."

Korykory, visibly happy, turns to Toby, who takes a strip of meat. He cautiously puts it in his mouth. "You're right—damned succulent too."

They come from the hut and sit near one of the fires. The Typees dance and chant and tell their incomprehensible warrior stories. The halfmoon is high when the feast finally ends.

Early Stories

The Composure of Death

HE HADN'T FANTASIZED about the dead girl; there was some small satisfaction in that. The line of mourners stretched outside the funeral home's double doors, under the bright red awning nearly to the street, then turned sharply toward the parking lot. Jon Mann had joined the line only a minute before and already a dozen more people had come behind him.

Amber had been beautiful and popular and nice, and there was no reason she should have died one week before her senior year. Her classmates, dressed in the clothes they may have worn to dances the previous school year, hugged and cried and knew not what else to do.

The August day was hot and Jon was itchy in his tie and tweed sport coat; he was one of the few visitors in a jacket. Inside the funeral home it would be cool but he guessed he had at least thirty minutes outdoors. Just ahead of him, a group of three schoolgirls consoled each other and complimented each other on their dresses: bright blue, yellow, and celery green. Jon knew them. In fact, one, Trisha Macintosh, had been in the same literature class with Amber. He didn't think they were friends per se, but it was a large class, thirty-two, and it was hard to know the students well. There was a time during her sophomore year that Jon suspected Trisha Macintosh had a crush on him—something that occurred with less frequency over the years.

Finally the girls noticed him. Trisha said, "Mr. Mann, you

cut your hair short." Trisha, small and light in the celery dress, giggled at his unfamiliar appearance.

"Yes, for the summer. How're you?"

It was taken as a rhetorical question and that is perhaps how he meant it. The line moved a few inches and the girls returned to their private version of mourning.

He thought of Amber Wright and how she was in his class: pretty and quiet in the farthest corner from his desk. She was a good student, always prepared, but not one to volunteer, and prone to short, quick (accurate) responses when called on. She was a dancer but he didn't know her when the team had last performed for the school the previous fall, so he didn't notice the brown-haired girl among the blonds and auburn reds. She was a lifeguard at the country club pool (she wrote about it once) but Jon and his wife didn't belong to the country club.

He recalled seeing her in a dress shop before prom. His wife, Lucy, was looking in vain for a black cocktail dress, and Amber was there with her boyfriend. They were having fun looking at all the dresses Amber would never wear: tight, short, slit up the side, low cut, glittering. The boyfriend was laughing but Jon imagined his secret anguish wishing that his beautiful girlfriend would wear such a dress with him, for him. Jon felt a wave of anguish of his own: those dresses were designed for women who looked like Amber, and seeing her would make a man's chest tight with lust and longing. Jon's wife gave up and they left the shop before Amber noticed her teacher among the display racks.

He reached the funeral home awning but the shade did little to cut the heat. Ahead the doors were open and somewhere inside a woman or a girl let out a piercing wail. The animal sound stopped all the quiet talk outside until it was over just as suddenly.

The newspaper account of Amber's death was vague. It was an accident on Highway Twelve. She had swerved into the oncoming lane and was hit by a man in a truck. "Dead at the scene." Jon wondered about alcohol but she didn't seem like the type—of course half of the worst users didn't seem the type. Amber died on her birthday. Seventeen, exactly half Jon Mann's age.

A group of young men came out of the funeral home in white shirts and ties; they looked like door-to-door missionaries. They were solemn and strong and went immediately to the three schoolgirls. They took turns hugging and kissing and consoling each other. The young men had returned from their colleges. Jon imagined the drama and excitement they must have felt (and sadness and fear too) packing quickly to come home for the visitation and funeral: one of their own fallen, and not to cancer or suicide, the great teenage killers.

Bryan Anderson noticed his former teacher. "Mr. Mann, how are you?" The redhead shook Jon's hand.

"Fine. How is everyone holding up?"

"It's tough." Bryan Anderson would probably become an attorney like his father, but public defense or environmental law—some area that wouldn't make him rich and influential. His four friends stepped to the side, in their own conversation.

"What happened exactly? The paper didn't really say."

"It was crazy. It was her birthday, you know, and she had been at her grandparents' for a little party. They live in Riverton. Presents, cake and ice cream, the same as every year since Amber was born practically. She was coming back to town and her grandma had given her the leftover cake. She must've reached down to get a piece while she was driving and swerved into the oncoming lane. There was nothing the driver of the delivery truck could do. He walked away without a scratch."

"That is crazy. How do they know about her reaching for the cake? Was someone else in the car?"

"No, we'd be having two funerals. The car was demolished. Jack, her boyfriend, had met her at her grandfolks' and was following her back to town in his car. They were going to meet some friends for dinner. He saw everything." Bryan shook his head. "You just don't know, do you?"

"No."

They shook hands again. "A bunch of us are getting together at O'Rourke's Café tonight at seven-thirty or so. You ought to come down."

It was an odd invitation. Bryan was feeling mature and if it was just he and his college friends that would be all right. But there would no doubt he high-school-age students too, and the appropriateness of that socializing was questionable. He thought of the schoolgirls with their grown-up dresses and their summer tans. Bryan Anderson joined his companions and they left for the parking lot. They had to stop and console another group of girls who were at the end of the line.

Jon reached the funeral home doors and saw that the line led away from the parlor where Amber lay (still out of view), into another room, and serpentined between velvet ropes before heading out again into the lobby. He thought about phoning Lucy, who could have been home from work by now. But she would not want to join him anyway. Lucy, exhausted and stressed, would go straight upstairs, remove her dress clothes, then slip into a hot bath with a romance novel. She wanted the silence and the vanilla bubbles and the faraway lives in her book.

Robert Hanson, the physics teacher at school, was in the opposite part of the line. They nodded hello but had nothing to say. Jon waited . . . observed the calmness of the funeral-home men in their green blazers and navy pants. Waited . . . tried to remember more about Amber Wright but nothing new came to him. He just saw the same images and felt the absurdness of her death. What would he say to her parents? Did she have siblings? Is there an open casket? What will she look like? How is it that her parents have not gone mad with grief?

By now Lucy would be partially draining and refilling the tub to keep the bathwater hot. Did she fantasize in there alone, about her exotic fictional lovers? No, he honestly didn't believe she did; the romance was enough for Lucy. A year or two before, Jon had tried to join her in the tub—like they had as newly-weds—but it wouldn't work. They were too big to be in there together. The water slopped over the rim onto the floor. They tried facing each other, their legs bent up and out, the faucet in Jon's shoulder; they tried in tandem, but Lucy was too crumpled and pushed her buttocks painfully into Jon's submerged lap. They gave up and he left her to bathe in peace.

In the long line there were adolescents and middle-aged adults and old people; most standing, some sitting in dark straight-back chairs. On the far side of the room, in front of the bay window (many minutes away), was a babbling stone fountain. In here, still far from the dead girl in her casket, the conversations were light. There was an occasional subdued laugh. Jon wished he had someone to talk with, just to pass the time more quickly.

Little Trisha, in her celery dress, was ahead of him, then turning the first bend in the line. It gave him a prolonged time to admire her small shapeliness, first her backside, then her profile. The summer sun had bleached her short, bobbed hair so that it was light, light brown. He liked the way it curved uniformly around her slender tanned neck. In a few minutes they would be side by side and he thought about running his finger along the smooth curve of her neck, then her firmly sculpted shoulder, and down the length of her arm to her small hand with its perfect mother-of-pearl nails.

He observed the girl discreetly—never staring, barely even focusing on her adolescent shapeliness. He knew that part of the attraction was her ebullient personality and clever mind. She was a good student, a good girl—the kind he dated in *his* high-school years.

The line brought them together and he thought she might ignore him since they had spoken outside. But Trisha was too well-mannered, probably intuiting his isolation.

"Teaching American lit again, Mr. Mann?"

"Yes, and a couple of public speaking classes, of course—my lot in life. What are you taking?"

"Your normal senior year stuff—calc, A.P. history and human phys, French four, and P.E. and a foods class—you know."

"Sounds like you'll be a busy beaver."

"Oh yeah—my folks say it keeps me out of trouble."

"Does it?"

"Most of the time." She smiled innocently (facetiously?). "Did I hear Bryan mention O'Rourke's to you?"

"Yeah, seven-thirty."

"You should come by—" It seemed that she was going to say more but didn't. The line was pulling them apart.

"I told Bryan I'd have to see what was going on. Thanks."

The serpentine line brought them together twice more but they didn't speak. In the lobby he thought about calling Lucy— to let her know what was taking so long and to bring up O'Rourke's. He imagined her ambivalence to the news about the long visitation, and her negative reaction to the idea of joining his students and former students at the café. *Why in the world would you want to do that?* Jon wouldn't know what to say.

He passed on the opportunity to call.

Outside the room where Amber lay were a number of photographs on display: Amber as a little girl at her birthday party (seven candles on the white cake), Amber in her lifeguard chair (black glasses, black suit), Amber and a friend in mouse ears at Disneyland (a Snow White character in the background), Amber and her boyfriend at prom (she in a tasteful green dress, he in a black tuxedo with green bowtie and cummerbund), Amber's dance team (all smiling in shimmering silver and black costumes).

Mourners examined the pictures, shook their heads. Tears flowed freely. Jon also felt grief and loss, yet it seemed too much over the death of a student. He was grieving something more but couldn't quite grasp it, couldn't surround it with words. Jon signed the guestbook.

In the room finally: pews filled with family and close friends; flower, flowers everywhere, from ceiling to floor, everywhere—and all their scents so powerful; her parents and a boy (brother?) receiving the visitors in line; then the white casket. Open. Amber lying as if asleep, waiting for a fairytale prince's magic kiss. She was in a faded denim jacket (no doubt her favorite).

Seeing her in the jacket reminded Jon of a required oral report she did in class. It was the most she'd said at one time. He could see her there at the podium with her notecards. But which author had she chosen to report on? Which piece of literature? Amber was intelligent and thorough, even though she was clearly hating the limelight. He remembered the essence of his critique: "Slow down, Amber—and relax. You're prepared and you have a good voice. Don't rush!" Still, he couldn't recall the subject of her report.

Mrs. Wright was hugging everyone who came to her in line. Maybe these people were all close to the family . . . or maybe the mother was exhausted from the grief and long visitation and was beyond trying to differentiate the visitors and how she should respond.

Close now, Jon saw Amber's paleness, in spite of her lifeguard's tan, and he saw a faint bruise on her chin, like a smudge someone should be able to rub away. However, death couldn't conceal the loveliness of her face, pillowed in the long brown hair.

"Hello. I'm Jon Mann, Amber's English teacher at school. I'm so sorry."

Mrs. Wright, a short woman, hugged him tightly. "Thank you for coming. I know Amber appreciates it very much." The mother let go and Jon shook Mr. Wright's hand. He was tired and gray. "Thank you. This is our son Jimmy. He'll be up there at high school next year."

"Terrific," said Jon as he shook the boy's cold hand. He saw Amber in the boy's eyes and nose.

Now Jon could walk out at a more natural pace. He noticed an elderly woman sitting in a pew wearing a dark hat and veil—the only veiled woman in the room. And he recalled the subject of Amber's oral report: Hawthorne and "The Minister's Black Veil." Jon thought of the part of the story where the minister presides at the funeral of the dead maiden, and then later when the ghost of the dead girl is seen walking beside the minister. That was Amber's favorite part, she had said.

Jon felt a pang of anxiety at the real-life foreshadowing. He fought the urge to rush from the parlor room. Outside, with the line still stretching to the parking lot, Jon loosened his tie and removed his sport coat. The sun was low, out of sight behind the appellate courthouse, but the heat was suffocating nonetheless.

He hurried around the corner to his hot car. He let the Escort idle for a minute while the air conditioning ran. He considered his options: going home to Lucy, who would be out of the tub and probably reading on their bed, in her white bathrobe (was lovemaking a possibility?); or driving to O'Rourke's Café, where Bryan Anderson and his friends and Trisha Macintosh and others would be drinking coffee and sodas and talking about life and their futures and death . . . and sensing their mortality, their vulnerability for perhaps the first time.

The Escort was headed west toward the café.

It wasn't proper to be going there, to socialize with adolescents. To see if there is a seat open next to little Trisha (maybe left open by design), to feel the warmth of her young body as the booth's cushioned seat yields them together. To follow instinctively whatever unlawful trail life would lay down for him. For them both. After all, what was the role of propriety in a world where life can end so abruptly, so unfairly? What is the purpose of good grades and the hours of physical and mental dedication? And of being punctual and kind? And faithful?

He stopped the car in O'Rourke's asphalted lot, which was three-quarters full. He knew his party was inside though he couldn't observe them in the brick building's shaded windows: white shades that reflected the light and heat, and shielded the faces of strangers and friends alike. As he was turning the car around to leave O'Rourke's lot, Jon Mann checked the rearview mirror in hopes of glimpsing someone familiar entering or exiting the small café. But the faltering daylight made it impossible to see.

Walkin' the Dog

TOM GEST CHECKS THE DOOR of Dorm C to make sure it's secure and he peers through the safety glass. The inmates seem to have settled down. Their orange jumpsuits hang from the ends of bunkbeds like emaciated spirits. There is a faint light coming from the far end of the barracks-style dormitory, from the restroom and shower area. But that is the responsibility of the guard in the surveillance station. Tom pauses for a moment to notice his own ghostly reflection in the thick glass. His dark hair is neatly trimmed, as is his beard and mustache, but there appear to be a few more filaments of white, and the creases around his eyes are deeper set. There is no doubt about it: Tom is becoming his father. He carries in his wallet a laminated black-and-white photo of his father from his fiftieth birthday party; Tom is three months away from forty-seven.

He reaches into the pocket of his green uniform pants for the watch he keeps there. His fingers have to work past the envelope which is folded in half. He regrets wanting to know the time; he had been able to put the envelope and its contents out of his mind for a while. It's just before midnight, more than six hours until his shift is finished. He puts the watch away, but in the opposite pocket, with his ChapStick and his lucky Kennedy half-dollar. He's had the fifty-cent piece for over thirty-five years. Has it brought him any luck? His transfer request was rejected again; again for being incomplete.

When Nancy calls tomorrow and eventually asks about his transfer, Tom will be able to report that the paperwork is still in the system. His fellow guards often complain about the bureaucracy of the Department of Corrections, and Tom has complained too, but now he is comforted by its tendency toward stagnation, its unflagging support of the status quo.

He feels the outline of the folded envelope in his pocket.

Tom will check the other dormitories in Building Two and make sure that it takes about an hour, then he can justify a coffee and a smoke. He will leave Little Muddy Correctional Center at six a.m. with his body and mind in tact. Again he feels the shape of the envelope in his pocket. He'll take another transfer form when he leaves the prison, to fill out later when the kids are at school.

TOM TURNS HIS JEEP into the long gravel drive which runs in a straight line past the big front yard and the brown two-story house and the man-made fish pond in back. He maneuvers around the blue Corolla fringed in rust that Nancy's daughter drives, then he parks in front of the garage, which also serves as a workshop and storage for the riding mower and other equipment. Tom can't see inside because the door is down but he thinks of how the garage is cluttered with kids' stuff—bicycles, skateboards, roller blades—and partially completed projects, particularly a pine bookcase he's been working on for over a year. Barely more than its frame is assembled.

He steps out of the Jeep and remembers all the weeds growing in the drive. He needs to spray some herbicide and put down a new layer of gravel. He knows it won't be done any time soon, probably it will never be done by him.

Yeller is whining in her kennel next to the garage. The big Lab's tail beats loudly against the metal fence.

"I hear you, girl." Tom takes a five-gallon plastic bucket from in front of the garage and fills it with water from the garage spigot. The rim of the bucket has been chewed ragged by Yeller. He carries the heavy bucket to the kennel and unlatches the gate with his free hand. Yeller has been standing at the gate but backs away on her hind legs to let Tom enter with the water. Inside the kennel is a dilapidated wooden dog house, yesterday's water bucket and a large metal food bowl, which is turned upside down and caked in mud.

While Yeller drinks noisily from the bucket, Tom observes there's about five pounds of dog shit in the kennel. Matt, Nancy's oldest son, was supposed to clean out the kennel yesterday after basketball practice—she's his dog—but he obviously neglected the chore. At least on a cool fall day the flies and the stench aren't as bad as they might be.

Tom picks up the muddy bowl then goes to the garage to wash it and fill it with dry food. He returns it to the kennel and stands there petting Yeller, his hand feeling the powerful muscles of her back, while she devours the food; the crunching is so loud it could be her teeth that are being ground to bits. Later he will take her to the pasture behind their house and let her run. For now Tom leaves Yeller to her food. It's time to check the progress of the kids getting ready for school.

Tom goes into the house through the back door, which brings him into the dining area of the lower level's great room. The dining-room table is supposed to seat eight, but right now there are so many books and backpacks and other stray debris, including a pair of basketball shoes, that there is just one spot carved out for actual dining, and it is occupied by a cereal bowl half-full with milk and a few bits of cornflakes. It could be from breakfast, or last night's snack.

The house was built in the seventies, so the concept of having the living room, kitchen and dining area essentially be one large room was ahead of its time. The realtor said the great room, with its fireplace, exposed beams and hardwood floor in the kitchen, is an important selling point. It and the four nice size bedrooms upstairs should more than compensate for the half-bath downstairs with its toilet, countertop and basin all in bright orange—"men-at-work orange," the realtor called it. The little bathroom has never appealed to Tom and Nancy, and they always intended to remodel it. Then Nancy was in graduate school and there was the mess with Nancy's second husband, the internist, over the terms of custody and support payments. Their six years in the house, and for that matter their eight years of marriage, have slipped by so quickly.

Officially the house isn't listed yet—there's no for-sale sign in the yard—but the realtor is keeping it in mind. Nancy is anxious for the house to be put on the market and to sell, so that Tom and the kids can join her in Jacksonville, where she is the nurse practitioner and licensed midwife at a rural health clinic. She wants to buy a house in Jacksonville—she's been living in a one-bedroom apartment for the past six weeks. In fact, there's a rambling Victorian that Nancy has inquired about. Glen Fork Correctional Center is twenty-two miles from Jacksonville, "but less than twenty minutes by interstate," Nancy has reminded Tom a few times.

When she calls today, she will use that phrase Tom has come to hate: suspended animation. She will say, "Any news on your transfer?" Tom will say no, it's still in the system. Then Nancy will say, "If you don't hear tomorrow, can you call Springfield? I just feel like we're in a state of suspended animation—I want to flip some switch so that our lives will start moving forward again." I know, hon, I know.

From upstairs Tom hears the dull thuds and muffled footsteps of the kids getting ready for school. He also smells the fresh coffee in the kitchen. Since starting college in the fall, Allyson has become a coffee drinker, and already she makes it better than her mom. Nancy's is either too weak or too strong, never the same twice. Allyson is Nancy's from her first husband, a documentary film producer for public television who keeps in touch and has always sent money when it's due. Tom goes to the kitchen and pours himself a cup of steaming coffee. It will probably affect his sleep but he can't resist. Besides, he doesn't seem to sleep more than three or four hours no matter how exhausted he feels.

Tom stands at the kitchen counter drinking the good hot coffee and craving a cigarette. Later he'll go on the deck for one. His smoking is no secret but he doesn't like to do it in front of the kids nonetheless.

. . . . IT WAS NEARLY MIDNIGHT when Nancy came upstairs to bed. The director of the clinic had called about ten. He apologized for the late hour of his call as he asked for Nancy. They spoke for nearly two hours; Tom had come upstairs to read in bed after listening to Nancy's excited chatter for only a few minutes. He didn't need to hear her words: It was obvious the director wanted Nancy for his nurse practitioner and midwife, and it was equally obvious she wanted the position.

Nancy was jittery when she came into the bedroom. Tom interrupted his reading, Walter Mosley's *Walkin' the Dog*, for an instant to smile at her. Nancy was in her cinnamon-orange, man's-style pajamas; she and Tom had talked about getting to bed early. Nancy's blond hair looks good with the cinnamon color, truly like gold.

Tom watched the page of his book, waiting, knowing Nancy would have to speak. She would have to tell him about the conversation, but Tom already understood the most salient facts. Nancy removed her earrings, replaced the backs, and set them one at a time in her jewelry box on the dresser. She rubbed her earlobes as if they were cold and she was trying to restore circulation.

Tom watched the page of his book.

Nancy looked at herself in the oval mirror above the dresser. "That was Glenn," she said matter-of-factly.

Glenn—no longer Mr. Jeffries.

"The position sounds very good—he's awfully generous."

Tom set the book aside, his finger marking the spot. "Nanc', you want the job."

"Yeah, yeah I do. It's just the kind of position I imagined when I went back to school." She stood looking at Tom for a moment, studying him, as if from behind a glass partition.

Nancy unbuttoned her silk pajama top and let it fall to the floor. Tom loves her perfect breasts, full and artificially symmetrical. Thanks to a lifetime of avoiding the sun, in her forties Nancy has the smooth, fair skin of a twenty-year-old. Still wearing the cinnamon pajama bottoms, she knelt on the end of the bed then moved on her hands and knees toward Tom.

She pulled back the blankets. Tom had on one of the three pairs of boxers he always slept in. Nancy kissed her husband's chest and lightly touched his nipples. Tom noticed that a hint of her perfume, applied hours before, lingered still. She kissed down his stomach toward the waistband of his boxers. He pulsated against her perfect breasts. She ran her tongue in and out of his navel.

"Nanc'?"

She paused long enough to say "yeah?" dreamily, without looking up.

"What about the kids?". . . .

ALLYSON IS THE FIRST to come downstairs; Tom recognizes her quick, light steps. She is wearing her college's sweatshirt, faded jeans and her oldest running shoes. In high school Allyson was determined to sport the latest fashions. Her bedroom was littered with magazines like *Vogue, Glamour, Seventeen* and *Allure*. Her preoccupation with her appearance bordered on an obsession, and it sometimes worried Nancy. But she was too busy with her masters program to do anything more than worry. For much of Nancy's schooling she lived on campus three or four days a week, commuting the eighty miles home for long week-ends; then she would sequester herself in some corner of the house with her laptop and her textbooks.

"Good morning, Ally-cat." Tom says it even though she doesn't respond well to her old nickname. Allyson forces herself to say "morning." She goes directly to the kitchen counter and pours herself a cup of coffee. Three months ago she drank it with milk and sugar; now she prefers it black. Allyson's honey-brown hair is pulled back into a ponytail. She's wearing a touch of eye makeup but it's hard to see because of her glasses, which have small oval frames. She is a pretty girl, though barely recogniz-able as the exuberant ten-year-old who was her mother's maid of honor. Then it was emerald taffeta and a tiara of baby's breath.

They stand drinking their coffee for a minute or two. The entire time Tom is thinking about how to engage Allyson in a positive conversation; he finally manages, "Are the boys about ready?"

She lowers her cup and speaks over the coffee's heat. "Yeah." She pauses. "You've got to talk to ass-hole Matt. He refused to help Drew with his homework last night. No big deal, just read-ing a couple of chapters out of his science book. Mr. Honor-roll could've handled it but he locked himself up in his bedroom playing video games all Goddamn night."

Allyson rarely cusses around Tom, so she must be especial-ly frustrated. Drew is a bright sixth-grader but has always had trouble reading. He's been making progress—tough words, sci-entific words, are still a struggle though. Tom thinks it's his turn to speak and opens his mouth, but Allyson cuts him off:

"As a consequence I read Drew the chapters, which took for-ty-five minutes, and I had a soc. project and a final draft for comp. to write. Talk to the ass-hole or I'm going to kill him, I swear to God." She takes a big drink of coffee.

"O.k., Ally, I'll add that to the list." He's thinking, along with Yeller's kennel and the basketball shoes on the table. "You should've woke me up. I would have dealt with young Matthew." Except Tom knows he's not pleasant when his sleep is interrupted, and the kids have been strongly discouraged from doing it. He recalls telling them once, "If you get me up, the first sentence out of your mouth better include the word fire."

He knows that Allyson isn't upset about helping Drew; it's Matt's selfishness that truly angers her. She's not a selfish person and she can't stand it in others, especially her half-brother. She and Matt used to be close, but during junior high Matt became a different person. Maybe it's as simple as his being the star of the freshman basketball team—Matt's coach is already talking about a trip to state in a year or two. Maybe it's just puberty. Or maybe it's some unfathomable tangle of being a child of divorce; of a father who has little interest in him; of a mother who has been away from home attending classes, or, now, working; of a stepfather who has had to request the graveyard shift at the prison because of his therapist's anxiety-management plan.

Tom repeats his promise—"I'll talk to Matt"—even though too much time has passed and it sounds as if he's muttering to himself, a habit his father developed later in life, some time between the prostate cancer and the dementia. Alzheimer's, they call it now.

Allyson puts her cup in the sink then goes to the stairs: "Come on, you two. I'm going to be late."

Each of the boys calls back something but Tom can't make out what they say.

Tom comes to the stairs. "Go ahead to class, Ally. I'll run the guys into town. It'll give me a chance to talk to them."

Allyson digs her keys out of her pocket and retrieves her backpack from the dining-room table. She turns before going out the back door: "I won't be around for dinner. James is taking me out."

"What's the big occasion?" Tom asks lightly.

"It's our six-month anniversary." Allyson's voice cracks at the end as she rushes out the door.

Way to go, dumb-ass. It would be six months. Allyson's first date with James Harvey was their senior prom. James is a good guy, works part-time at a pizza place and takes classes at the college. He's what Tom's father would have called a straight-shooter.

THE PASTURE BELONGS to Tom and Nancy. It once was used for cattle grazing but now the grass grows wild. They pay a local farmer to mow the two-acre field three or four times a year. Tom opens the gate for Yeller and she bounds into the pasture. Running in the grass, chasing birds and rabbits, is clearly the high point of her quiet day. She never catches anything. Perhaps, Tom thinks, she doesn't really try.

A crisp wind has stirred and Tom turns up his collar against it. Winter is coming. He lights a cigarette and walks along the white-washed fence line, keeping an eye on Yeller as she bounces through the field like a gazelle. Tom notices a prairie flower that still has its summer color. The orange petals are a stark contrast to the gray-green pasture grass. It is mid-morning. In a while he will return Yeller to her kennel, then it will be time to work on the projects he's been putting off.

Yeller's sudden barking startles Tom. She's trapped something in a patch of high grass. She jumps and yelps and dodges for it with her big Labrador head. Before Tom can start over to her, Yeller comes up with something in her jaws. At first Tom thinks all the commotion was over a stick, then he realizes Yeller has caught a long, orange-brown cornsnake. It's still writhing in Yeller's grip but a couple of quick shakes and the hapless snake goes limp. Lifeless, Yeller has no interest in it. She drops it in the grass and trots over to Tom, proud of herself, seeking his praise.

He scratches between her ears. "That's great, girl. As if today won't be heavy on carnage as it is."

He leads Yeller out of the pasture, through the yard, and back to her kennel. Tom is tempted to clean the shit out of Yeller's kennel but he'll wait. He wants to give Matt the opportunity to do the chore, to redeem himself. It was a lesson his father taught him: Given the chance, most people will do what's right . . . eventually. Besides, Tom has other projects in mind.

He goes to the back of the Jeep, which is parked just off the driveway in the yard, and opens the hatch. He gets out the bottles of weed-killer. At the hardware store he figured two bottles would do the job but he bought three just in case. After glancing at the directions, Tom breaks the safety seal on the herbicide and chooses a particularly onerous weed to spray first. He squeezes the trigger and coats its leaves. The scent of the spray is sweet, but overly so. He looks at the long driveway stretching to the road. In a month or two he will be plowing snow from it, and in the spring he'll shovel on a new layer of gravel.

That much, at least, is certain.

Unnatural Deeds

HE SAT AT A SMALL TABLE near the front window of O'Leary's, their agreed upon meeting place. Misty had suggested it because she knew the restaurant wouldn't be busy on a Wednesday evening. He had offered to pick her up at her apartment but she preferred to rendezvous at O'Leary's. His other blind dates, when he lived in Garden City, were simpler: a phone call, then he picked up the young women at their house or apartment. But this date had been more complicated, even though it too had been arranged through mutual friends, mutual co-workers really. He had been given Misty's email address, a generic Hotmail account, and they had corresponded a couple of times before agreeing to meet here. She was probably reluctant to give her address or even phone number for fear of being stalked by some nut.

It had been less than four years since his last blind date. The flowers of complexity seemed to have bloomed during that short period. In the meantime he had been seeing someone steadily, Suzanne, his fiancée for a while, but that was over.

O'Leary's was one of the few bistro-style restaurants in Hillcrest. It was known for its quiches, desserts in crepes, and gourmet coffees. The waiters and waitresses wore khakis with white cotton dress shirts and black vests, not identical but definitely uniform. This evening, the crowd was light and mostly old people; he wondered if a retirement village was nearby. He sipped at his house blend and studied the menu as if he was preparing for an exam.

He checked his reflection in the large front window: a mediocre hair day (brown, receding but far from bald still), he had put on some weight since moving to Hillcrest but his face didn't show it (maybe because of the goatee he was growing), he still wasn't sure about the necktie (blue patterned silk with an overlay of small red geometric shapes)—it was all right but he didn't want to look like a tie-wearing geek. He thought he had good taste in ties though and wanted to show it off.

He'd take the necktie off if he was certain Misty hadn't already seen him, maybe watching him right now . . . from across the street, from some other table in the restaurant, except there were no tables with solitary women . . . maybe she came with someone as a decoy in case she didn't like what she saw: a pudgy thirtysomething who is trying to grow a goatee and who wears a tie on a first date.

Maybe—

"Hi—Rex?" She was suddenly standing by the table. Misty put her hand out; he noticed the rings on her pinkie, thumb and index finger. She had shoulder-length blond hair (light but not bottle blond). She was pretty. She'd worn an orange sundress with white floral shapes, and sandals. She had on a gold ankle bracelet. She was tan but not falsely so. She hadn't come in through O'Leary's front door; maybe they had another entrance in back.

"Hello." He took her hand; it was light, soft and cool.

Misty seated herself before he had a chance to stand and help. She placed her basket-style purse on the floor. "I hope you haven't been waiting long."

"No, just got here myself." She might know I'm lying—maybe she'll attribute it to politeness.

"I was on my way out the door when my mom called. I would've let voicemail get it but I've had an aunt in the hospital and I thought it might be my mom—I was right." Misty unfolded her triangularly shaped napkin and placed it in her lap.

"I hope your aunt is okay."

"She's older; she has several things but nothing life threatening fortunately. Now she thinks she's having problems with her eyes, problems focusing." Misty inspected her silverware. She wore rings on her left hand as well, and the numerous bands glinted in spite of the low lighting.

He wondered how old Misty was. 26? 27? Their waiter came and took their orders. Misty was a regular and knew what she wanted: asparagus quiche and ice tea with mint. He ordered ham and mushroom quiche with a cup of spinach bisque and stayed with his coffee, which the waiter continually freshened. He was beginning to feel a caffeine buzz.

He kept watching Misty's hands—the odd assortment of rings, yellow gold and white gold, primarily medium-width bands with intricately inlaid patterns, the pink-tinted polish on the perfect nails, making her tanned fingers look especially long and lithe. She had pretty eyes, brown. And her teeth were straight and white and not artificially white. But it was Misty's hands, her fingers, that kept drawing his attention. The angles they formed when she held her spoon, drank from her tea glass, or the curl of them at rest on the table, like something sleeping. He thought of them nimbly pecking at the keyboard as she composed her email to him.

She asked him about his job at GlassCrafters, how long he had been a lens technician, had he done that before, when he lived in Garden City. She complimented his tie.

He asked her about her job at Ye Olde Bagel Shoppe, which was just one of her jobs, he discovered; she also worked at Phit-America (he could see that). He wondered to himself if she wanted to sleep with him—she was very nice. Probably not. For just a moment he imagined her ringed fingers stroking him, stroking him. He felt a tweak of arousal and postponed the image.

Their meal came. They had a pleasant conversation with few awkward lulls while they ate. He wanted to make her laugh but no topics arose that inspired his wit.

The waiter took their plates and said he would be back in a moment to see about dessert. When he had disappeared Misty said, "I really shouldn't but their black forest crepe is out of this world—it's vanilla ice cream, homemade, inside a warm crepe with chocolate and cherry sauce, and of course real whipped cream and a maraschino on top."

"It does sound good." He knew what it was of course; he had studied the menu.

"It's really too much for one person—will you split it with me?"

Is she testing my will power? I should say no thank you and show her the stern stuff I'm made of. Or is she fishing to see if I have any intimacy issues, or weird phobias about hygiene? She'll think I'm a cold carp if I say no. Maybe she's flirting, maybe she does want to go to bed.

"Sure, I'll give it a try."

The waiter was back and Misty ordered the dessert with two forks. While they waited Misty talked about the other crepe desserts they had and how good each was but how the black forest was her favorite. The waiter brought it on a plate that was nearly a platter and set it between them. The dessert filled the large ceramic oval.

Each took a fork and started with the nearest side. The ice cream was melting in the warm crepe and running in with the chocolate and cherry sauces. He took his first forkful of crepe; it was light and sweet (not at all like a thin pancake as he had imagined).

Misty smiled to see him enjoy the crepe. Soon they were nearing the middle of the dessert. Inevitably they would be eating from the same scoop of ice cream, the same fold of crepe, the same puddle of sauces. His arousal had returned. He was getting full but he had to share the middle portions of the dessert with her. Soon the tines of their forks were almost touching as they scooped up the last bits of crepe and globs of ice cream, all dripping with the mixture of sauces. They had achieved a perfect rhythm—it seemed mutually natural but maybe he had adjusted to synchronize with her.

When the dessert had arrived it had two maraschino cherries. Misty had eaten hers immediately but his was still there on the over-sized plate, ground zero for their explosion of rapacity. At last it was all that remained, half submerged in chocolate and cherry sauces and melted vanilla ice cream. He intended all along to let Misty have the other maraschino: a gesture of supreme generosity. And she stabbed it with her fork, still in perfect unbroken rhythm, but to his surprise she held it up to his mouth.

"I believe this is yours," she said.

He hesitated for a moment then took her offering, enjoying the sensation of his lips and tongue on the same tines hers had so frequently touched. She does want me, he thought. His erection searched for a comfortable place inside his boxers.

The waiter had brought the check with the dessert and Misty began the mental math as soon as they finished the crepe. (They agreed when arranging the date to split the check.)

He tried to think of a way to prolong their time together. Certainly inviting Misty to his apartment was too forward; maybe she would invite him to hers. Unlikely. A walk, perhaps they could just go for a walk. Lakeside Park was only a few blocks away. He had just begun to speak when the electronic trill of a cell phone sounded. He looked around to see whose it was. Misty reached into her purse and pulled out an orange flipphone. She smiled an apology to him as she said hello.

While she talked to a friend about meeting in a few minutes, Misty retrieved an orange gel-pen from her purse and wrote a dollar amount on the dinner check. She showed him the figure and he put a twenty on the table, his half plus a tip.

Misty ended her conversation. "I hate to eat and run, but a friend is working on her masters and I promised I'd go to the library with her, for moral support." She put a twenty from her wallet on top of his.

"That's very supportive of you." He made sure to conceal his disappointment. He was feeling jittery, his soul charged with sexual energy and too much caffeine. He watched Misty's hands as she applied a fresh coat of transparent lip gloss. For her girl-friend and their trip to the library? Suspicion was added to his stew of unrequited libido and generalized disappointment.

Misty picked up her purse as she rose from the table. They walked silently out of O'Leary's. He wanted to ask for a second date. His emotions were making it difficult to find the words. "I had a good time," he managed to say.

"Oh I did too." She was standing in a yellow sunbeam. It was early evening and the street and sidewalk were mostly in shad-ow. It was going to be a warm night. "I love O'Leary's—thanks so much for meeting me here." They stood in front of the restau-rant under a canopy of awkwardness.

He opened his mouth to try again but suddenly a blue Miata pulled up to the curb in front of them. The driver, a pretty girl with brown hair, smiled and waved, seemingly at both of them.

"There's my friend," said Misty as she went toward the pas-senger door. He noticed that she had a small butterfly tattoo (mostly orange and red) on the back of her right shoulder. She turned to him before ducking into the little blue sports car: "Email me."

"O.k."

"O.k." She was inside then gone. The pretty driver smiled and waved good-bye to him before they zoomed away.

Email me. Sex? Hell, he didn't even get her phone number . . . or her last name.

* * *

HE SAT DOWN at his computer because he was tired of his collection of *Playboy* and *Penthouse* magazines that he kept beneath his bed. His computer, a Gateway with a Pentium 4 processor and 17-inch flat-screen, was on a trestle table in his bedroom. He had to move a stack of bills on the keyboard.

First he went to the *Playboy* website, then to *Penthouse*. The women available to nonmembers fueled his sexual energy but he wanted something more intense. His browser led him to *Hustler.com*, from there *Busty Beauties* and *Barely Legal*. From time to time he masturbated enough to maintain his erection. He wanted to try some of the really hardcore sites—*Cheerleadersluts*, *Cumface*, and *Cornhole.com*—but he was afraid he'd pick up a virus that would erase his C drive.

He had found dozens of images by which he could have completed masturbating but they were all so contrived, like the pictures in his magazines under the bed. He yearned for something more real. He went to a search engine and simply typed in the word "women." As expected he got over a quarter of a billion hits. When he selected the subcategory "sex/erotica" it narrowed the possible sites to just under 600,000. He noticed the sub-subcategory of "voyeur" sites. When he selected it several dozen voyeur sites were listed. The idea of connecting himself to some anonymous female's life and watching her . . . shower, blow her boyfriend, cook broccoli in the nude . . . certainly appealed to his yearning for realness.

He clicked on *Susie.com*. Susie was a 27-year-old computer programmer who had set up several video cameras in her house so that paying members could keep track of her life. She was average looking, not fat but stocky with brown-blond hair. No video for nonmembers, just still pictures of Susie's life: Susie eating cornflakes in a fuzzy pink robe, Susie watching TV with her boyfriend (presumably), Susie putting on her make-up wearing only a black bra and a long khaki skirt.

This site had potential but Susie herself didn't appeal to him.

He tried another voyeur site: *Littlesis.com*. Five college-age women living in a sorority-style house. *Littlesis* promised all access for members: shower cams, bedroom cams, even underwater pool cams (an implication of skinny dipping?). It also boasted regularly scheduled lingerie parties, "fantasy confessions" from the hot tub, and body painting (one of the girls was a part-time tattoo artist). The five young women were attractive and represented a cross section of ethnicities, hair colors and body types.

Tempting but still too contrived.

His erection had lost its focus. He decided he'd just navigate back to *Playboy.com* and get his masturbation over with so that he could go to bed; but there was one more voyeur site that piqued his curiosity. *Watchmegirl.com* was six young women living in different parts of the country. The site offered "24/7" access to members but there was no mention of scheduled events. He clicked on the Midwest girl to check out her bio:

"Misty is 26. She loves outdoor activities, her cat George, and reading a good mystery. She has two jobs, including one at a health club, and hopes to save enough money to move to Hollywood and become a screenwriter."

He kept blinking at the monitor. Was it *his* Misty? It had to be. The girl in the picture had different hair, shorter and lighter blond, but the facial features were the same, the same arc in the eyebrows, the same distinct cheekbones. She was wearing a tangerine-colored blouse and holding George, an orange tabby. The hand holding George was beautiful and the fingers were accentuated by several simple rings.

He quickly retrieved his wallet and used his Visa card to become a member of *Watchmegirl* for three months; at $12.99 a month it was a $5 savings over the 30-day trial membership.

It took a few minutes for the electronic transaction to be completed but he soon found himself looking at Misty's apartment. No one was home. He checked the livingroom cam, the kitchen cam, the balcony cam, and the bedroom cam (through which one could also view part of the bathroom). It was a typical one-bedroom apartment, similar in layout to his own. Misty's was more homey though: coordinated furniture, art on the walls, knickknacks here and there, a vase with yellow flowers on the small circular kitchen table. George the cat was asleep on the loveseat in the livingroom.

The view from the bedroom cam transfixed him. The room was neatly arranged; everything was in its place. Except lying at the foot of the double bed was a black bra, one cup hanging over the edge. Misty, the Midwestern Watchmegirl, was out but she'd left a token for the visitors.

Absentmindedly he finished masturbating.

MISTY JOGS AT 7:40 in the morning she wears a white cropped top and orange running silks afterward she sits in a chair on the balcony and drinks a bottle of water she is beautifully sweaty in the morning sun Misty drinks decaffeinated coffee her 4-cup coffeemaker is programmed to start at 8:15 George sits in her lap while she eats a bowl of Raisin Bran and reads a book Misty has reading glasses she often calls George 'my pretty boy'

Monday through Thursday she works at the bagel shop 10 to 3 and Saturday 6 a.m. to 11 on Friday afternoon and two evenings a week she is at the fitness club

Misty falls asleep on her right side more or less turned away from the camera she wears a pair of boycut shorts to bed she reads for a few minutes before turning out the lamp on the bedstand usually a mystery novel but sometimes Vogue *or* Cosmo

Misty is at her computer a couple of hours a day doing email or just writing maybe a screenplay Misty doesn't seem to have a lot

of visitors she talks on the phone frequently it's often to her mother Misty rarely cooks most of her dinners are frozen ones that she microwaves Lean Cuisine or Healthy Choice

Thursday 8:03 p.m.
<trex35@iweb.net>
I really had a nice time at O'Leary's. It was a great choice you made. I keep thinking about the black forest crepe . . . another great choice! I enjoyed the conversation too. You're an interesting person. I'd like to get together again. Take care.
Rex

Friday 10:11 a.m.
<butterfly678@hotmail.com>
i enjoyed myself. you can't go wrong with olearys. thanks for sharing the crepe. i just have a second before i'm off to the club. email again soon.

Friday 6:38 p.m.
<trex35@iweb.net>
A crazy day at work. I made nearly 50 pairs of glasses in six hours. GlassCrafters lets kids come back to watch their glasses being made . . . as if seeing me through the window isn't good enough . . . and this one kid drove me nuts with a thousand questions. I don't have anything against kids. They just shouldn't let them back there when we're so swamped.
You probably have plenty of craziness at your jobs too.
Got to run. Have a great weekend.
Rex

Sunday 4:25 p.m.
<butterfly678@hotmail.com>
thanks for the email. sorry about your crazy day. the week-

end was good but i had to work a while both days. now i have to squeeze in my workout.

Sunday 5:02 p.m.
<trex35@iweb.net>
Have you been to Murphy's Steakhouse? They're supposed to have the best steaks in Hillcrest and I believe it. They also have chicken and fish of course. Would you like to go sometime this week, maybe Friday? My treat this time. Hope you had a good workout.

Tuesday 3:26 p.m.
<butterfly678@hotmail.com>
this week is kind of busy. sorry.

HE LOOKED IN ON MISTY every morning and every evening (late on Tuesday and Wednesday because he worked until nine). She fixed her meals, she laundered her clothes (apparently there were machines in her building), she watched television, she listened to CDs, she worked at her computer. Her week didn't seem particularly busy. At least there was no boyfriend who came calling, some muscle-bound twenty-year-old from the fitness club. Friday night her friend, the pretty one with the brown hair and blue Miata, came over with a bottle of wine and a video. They sat on Misty's couch and drank from rose-tinted wine glasses. There was a box of tissues between them that they used frequently. Whatever they were watching it wasn't a comedy.

He had had other women ignore his overtures but his ego gave them the benefit of the doubt. He allowed himself to believe their flimsy excuses. But this time it was clear—digitally clear—that Misty didn't want to see him again. And it wasn't because there was someone else; she just didn't find him attractive. He wished that he knew enough about computers to email her a virus, some nasty little bug that would lay waste to her hard drive. In high school he had egged the house of a girl who had dumped him; he anticipated the glow of a similar joy in his heart. He pondered his rejection and enjoyed the idea of revenge for a few moments.

No. Misty wasn't a bad person. She was untruthful, but probably out of politeness. She had no way of knowing he had found her on the Internet, that he paid money to watch her day and night. She probably has become oblivious to the cameras, as one does clocks or light fixtures or windows. They are just part of the environment, of the decor.

He felt a twinge of guilt, like he was a common peeping tom. In a moment of strength he resolved not to watch Misty anymore. The problem was that Misty was playing by the Rules of Love from an earlier age, when lies could be white. Love in the Digital Age is different. For one thing, when Big Everybody is watching, acts of kindness are as transparent as polycarbonate, and viewed from the other side become the most basic of lies, even acts of subterfuge.

He shut down his computer and went to bed early. Before turning out the light he flipped through an old issue of *Penthouse*. It felt wholesome, even nostalgic, like bobbing for apples, or running in a three-legged race, or riding through the snow in a one-horse open sleigh: an activity from a simpler past. He fondly glanced at the pictorial of three lesbians who meet at a masquerade party; he affectionately read the "Forum" letter about the couple who have sex in Times Square and climax as the glittering New Year's ball descends toward the pavement. He huddled in the warmth of long-established friendships.

He jerked off for old time's sake.

WHEN HE AWOKE (the morning sun turning his bedroom mini-blinds into a blazing white panel), it took him a moment to pinpoint his sense of loss. He recalled his vow to not look in on Misty, and he felt her absence.

He moped around his apartment and made himself a cup of coffee. It had only been a few days that he had been watching Misty. What had he done with his time before? He wasn't sure. He wanted to turn on his computer, to check the newest head-lines, but when he clicked on the Internet it would automatically go to *Watchmegirl* and he had no confidence in his will power. He could go to his control panel and designate a different home website but he didn't have the resolve for that either. He looked at his living room clock: Misty would be drinking water on her balcony now, wonderfully sweaty from her run. He thought of the series of clicks he would make to follow her . . . in the kitch-en to have breakfast with George . . . then the living room to watch "Good Morning America" for a few minutes . . . and final-ly the bedroom and bathroom to get ready for work. He thought of the navy shorts and the green polo, her uniform for Ye Olde Bagel Shoppe.

That's it: if he wouldn't allow himself to see her on the mon-itor, he could see her in person. Maybe face to face she would remember that she likes him. It was the remoteness of email that made her feel remote toward him. He thought of the increas-ing distance he sensed in her messages to him, as if she had in-crementally (though quickly) forgotten him and what they had shared: more than a dessert—a connection, a camaraderie, a bonding.

Ye Olde Bagel Shoppe was in the Eastgate minimall, more or less on the opposite side of town from GlassCrafters. He called his supervisor at home and told her he had an appointment and might be a few minutes late to work. He got himself ready and discovered he felt better just at the prospect of seeing Misty. He did an extra thorough job of brushing and water-picking his teeth. His goatee had come in fully but was not in need of trim-ming yet. He went about selecting a shirt and tie.

HE DECIDED THERE was nothing ye nor olde about the bagel shop; the interior reminded him of a McDonald's. The customers occupying the plastic and vinyl booths were mainly older people, perhaps having their breakfast after a lively session of mall walking. A young woman with long black hair was at the counter. Behind her, racks as high as the ceiling were filled with bagels of every flavor, texture and hue. Maybe Misty was in the back making bagels.

"Hi. Can I have a blueberry bagel and a small cup of coffee, please?" He remembered he didn't have any cash, he'd have to use his debit card. He was embarrassed to use it for such a small amount. . . . "And a dozen peanutbutter crunch in a box." He checked his watch. Misty was supposed to be at work.

The young woman got his order ready and swiped his debit card. They waited together for the transaction to go through. He noticed that she was several months pregnant.

"Is Misty around?" He tried to sound casual.

"No, she's not in today."

"Funny, I told her I'd see her this morning."

The woman considered things for a moment. "She was supposed to work but she called me late last night to trade her shifts."

"I hope everything is o.k." His mind was whirling. "It's not her aunt I hope."

"Actually I think it is. I think she took a turn for the worse."

"That's a shame." He held his box of bagels close to him.

"You aren't Rex are you?"

"Yes I am." He became hopeful: maybe Misty had mentioned him.

"I'm Carol. Ed's friend."

Ed, Ed . . . Ed from work—Carol and Ed who had set up Misty and him. "Nice to meet you." They shook hands.

"Nice to meet you." She smiled. "I guess things are working out for you two."

He smiled and let Carol fill in the blank of his silence. He wanted to say, Yes, I see her all the time. "Hey, I can't think of the name of the hospital Misty's aunt is at. Do you recall it? I really should send some flowers."

"No, but Roseview's not that big. I can't imagine there's more than one hospital."

"True. Well, thanks a lot. It was nice meeting you." He picked up his coffee and left the shop.

Roseview. He checked the atlas in his car. No interstate but mostly four-lane highway. It couldn't be more than forty-five miles away. Somewhat in disbelief, he listened to himself call work on his cell phone and tell his supervisor he wouldn't be in—"family emergency," he heard himself say vaguely—they should have Ed come in early.

He drove to Roseview as if the town itself was his goal. He listened to the radio. He switched to AM even though he never listened to AM. He quickly found National Public Radio. His father used to listen to NPR when they took family trips. The incessant talking irritated him as a boy. Now it was soothing: one clear voice, evenly modulated to be as comprehensible as possible. He thought of water trickling down his back, drop by drop from the foamy bath sponge he used then, contemporaneous to the family trips and NPR, before showers were the thing. As a teenager he developed the habit of fast showers; he hadn't taken an actual bath for years.

An orange triangular sign to his right caught his attention. He soon discovered it was a horse and buggy moving slowly on the highway's shoulder. He tried to see in the black buggy as he zoomed past but it was completely enclosed. He didn't know there were Amish or Mennonites in the area. He imagined a stern looking man with a beard holding the reins, sitting next to a woman of indeterminate age wearing gray from neck to ankle.

Then he noticed a radio tower to his left. It probably wasn't broadcasting NPR but he thought of it as doing so. He arranged himself in an awkward position so that he could momentarily view the top of the tall tower, blinking bright red in the bright sky. He thought he could see something radiating from its zenith: transparent ghosts of streaming words. Fainter than that: shadows of transparent ghosts of streaming words. Pouring down into his car's radio, through the wiring and out of the speakers. Words, words, words . . . filling his car like rising bathwater.

As he neared the Roseview exit there was a blue sign with a large white H. He hadn't considered that it would be so simple to find the hospital. Roseview was a town like any other. He passed McDonald's, Burger King, Kentucky Fried Chicken, Appleby's, a dentist's office, a school. He pulled into the visitor's lot of Crossroads Community Hospital. Its emblem was a large heart with a pair of shaking hands at its center.

He straightened his tie, a black silk one with gold floral shapes, before stepping out of his car. It was hot as he walked toward the four-story building. The hospital doors slid aside for him. He first noticed a woman with white hair sitting at a small information desk. She smiled at him. No one else was in the lobby. The air was cool and smelled faintly of antibacterial (maybe the scent was only his imagination).

He didn't know what to say to her. He didn't know the aunt's name. He didn't even know Misty's last name. He smiled back at the information lady as he walked past. There was a small gift shop to his right. A giant poster on its only window advertised FTD's *Flowers.com*. Wing-footed Mercury was rendered in gold.

A sign on a wall listed various departments, including ICU. It made sense that if Misty's aunt had taken a turn for the worse she might require intensive care. The sign directed him to the fourth floor. He stepped into the elevator and pushed the button for the top floor.

Perhaps he didn't believe Misty was really somewhere in the hospital. He had no idea what he would say to her but it didn't worry him. He still felt more like an observer and he was curious what words he might use. It was like watching a situation comedy on television and anticipating the actor's next line.

When the elevator doors opened he was there at the ICU waiting area, and Misty was only a few feet away, with an older couple and another young woman—maybe her parents and a sister or cousin. She was in profile. Her hair was pulled back with an orange band and she had on a blue tanktop (he noticed the butterfly tattoo). She had been crying but now just seemed to be talking quietly to her family. The man was on the heavy side with black hair mixed with white—"salt-and-pepper," they used to call it. The woman wore glasses on a cord, like a librarian, and had toffee-colored hair. Misty's sister or cousin was slender with red hair, but not "carrot top," more auburn.

The elevator doors began to close so out of reflex he stepped out. No one noticed him. The waiting area was small but there were several open seats. He moved toward one. There was nowhere else to go except back on the elevator or through the ICU's double door, which bore a sign saying RESTRICTED— ONE VISITOR FIRST 15 MINUTES OF EACH HOUR—AT NURSE'S DISCRETION in large red letters.

There was a *USA Today* next to the chair he chose. He quickly put the paper up to obscure his face. He watched Misty intensely as she sat with her elbows on her knees (she was wearing white shorts and the same sandals she had worn to dinner with him). He wanted to see her lovely fingers but she was clenching wads of Kleenex. She and her family weren't talking loudly but he could follow the conversation. It seemed they were discussing the aunt's house (Dotty, was that her name?) and what needed to be done because of her long hospital stay. They would cancel the newspaper, rent a post office box, a neighbor boy would be paid to maintain the yard and flowerbeds. These plans caused Misty and the other young woman to start crying again. They were not hysterical; their sobbing was disturbingly quiet. There was the sense that the aunt may never return home.

The family sat in silence for several minutes. He watched Misty and continuously reread the headline on the newspaper. It was about Microsoft stock; he had grabbed the business section.

A nurse came out of ICU and he indicated the aunt could have a visitor now. The nurse's black hair and beard were a definite contrast to his white uniform. It was agreed that Misty's mother would go in this time.

He knew he wasn't going to approach Misty. Not now, not in this setting. Maybe never, nowhere. He replaced the newspaper and went to the elevator. The doors opened and when he was inside he realized Misty had followed him. He pressed the first-floor button; she pressed B, for the basement.

He prepared to smile and say hello, to act surprised, to concoct a story about a relative in the hospital, to comment on the size of the world. As the elevator descended she glanced at him and offered a brief smile before returning her gaze to the changing numbers above the door. Misty didn't recognize him. They were two strangers temporarily sharing the same space.

He tried to say her name but the sound wouldn't form in his mouth. He parted his lips in hopes that something would come out.

The bell chimed signaling their arrival at the first floor and the doors opened. He stepped out automatically, leaving Misty to complete the descent by herself.

The white-haired woman at the information desk smiled at him. He smiled back then turned into the gift shop. Another elderly woman was behind the counter. She was perhaps the information lady's clone. She smiled at him; and he smiled back. On the counter was a computer monitor with the FTD emblem. It was a touch screen. He scrolled through the myriad choices before selecting a pretty arrangement of red, orange and yellow flowers, accented with a silk monarch butterfly. The computer screen wanted to know who was to receive the order. He still didn't have a name. Besides, he had heard somewhere that ICU patients couldn't receive flowers. He recalled that maternity was on the second floor. He used the keyboard which appeared at the bottom of the screen to type "the woman in 201." He left *From* blank. For the message he started to write "congratulations" but thought better of it. Who knew what tragedy may be underway in 201? He removed the Visa card from his wallet and entered its number and expiration date. He hesitated for just an instant before touching *Send*.

He made sure to smile first at the two old women as he left the gift shop then the lobby.

Outdoors he checked his watch. He could be to work by lunchtime, which he would offer to work through, plus he'd take the late shift, if Ed wanted, all next week. Losing his job at Glass-Crafters would serve no purpose.

Anyway, there was nothing else in the world he wanted to do.

Missing the Earth

JON MANN ROLLED OVER violently in his sleep, more half sleep. He strained against his myopia to see the alarm clock on the dresser. Just after two a.m. The noise was still there barely in his range of hearing but he could hear it—it wasn't his imagination as Lucy liked to suggest. The electric hum of television voices, a chord of theme song, a ripple of laugh track. He'd been in bed since eleven but hadn't fallen asleep, waiting for his wife to turn off the TV and come to bed. They lived in a two-story house, solidly built in the forties, but their bedroom was directly above the living room so not more than fifteen feet separated the television's speaker from his pillow, a layer of ceiling and floor and mattress between that seemed merely to mutate the sound instead of muffle it.

Four and a half hours until he had to get up to teach a class at the college.

Jon got out of bed. The room was cold because the central air had been running almost nonstop. Normally he set the thermostat so that the air-conditioner didn't run all night, but tonight he made sure it would be on more often than not. He didn't like the thought of the coming utility bill but he hoped the white noise would help him to sleep. When he had asked Lucy at 10:30 if she was about ready for bed she was distant and evasive. He was afraid it would be one of those nights.

He padded past their daughter's bedroom door then downstairs. He was wearing only his white jockey shorts; goosebumps stood up on his white skin. He was hoping he would find his wife asleep on the couch. If so, she might be persuaded to come upstairs. If she was wide awake she would be snappish. He approached her from behind. The only light in the room came from the television, an irregular strobe effect, an epileptic's nightmare. Even with his nearsightedness he could tell it was a Fred Astaire musical. *Finian's Rainbow*—Jon recognized the actor's phony brogue. Lucy was tangled in a quilt on the couch. One leg, in plaid pajama bottoms, protruded atop the quilt. He knew the pajamas were red but in the weird glow they appeared a kind of blacklight purple. Jon stepped cautiously, like he had come upon a hibernating animal. When he was close, he squinted to see if she was awake. Lucy's eyes were open. He stood by the couch rubbing his hairy stomach. He wasn't fat but he could use a regimen of sit-ups. "Not tired yet, dear?"

"The sound is barely on. I can't even hear it." Lucy was prepared. It was not a new debate.

"Maybe we should trade. I can hear it just fine upstairs." He'd gone from pleasant to sarcastic in an instant.

"I don't know how."

"It's not the noise so much—it's that the house isn't settled. I can't sleep if the house isn't settled."

"If you're tired you can sleep."

"I have to teach in the morning. I mean, in five hours."

"So go to bed. I'm not stopping you."

"Can't you come to bed? At least for a while?"

"Why? So I can listen to you snore?"

Hostility and frustration boiled in Jon's belly. Why couldn't his wife just go to bed like normal people? He walked to the kitchen and found a bottle of Tylenol PM. He swallowed three capsules standing at the sink. Then he took a couple of Tums and chewed them on his back teeth while he went upstairs. He knew he wouldn't sleep right away, if at all. He would lie in the dark contemplating the impossibility of divorce. A financial impossibility certainly, and there was Sara, asleep in her room, dreaming of cheerleading and shopping at the mall and the hottest boy band.

JON WAS GRATEFUL he was teaching Composition and Rhetoric. Most days it didn't require him to talk much, to lecture. The class was held in the PC lab, and the students were usually composing or revising on the computer, or accessing the college's databases for research. His primary interaction with them was via comments on their papers. This morning they were in the early stages of an argumentation paper. Jon had given his five students a pep talk, a verbal checklist, then let them loose on the computers. He read through their prewriting material, scribbled a few remarks, passed back the papers while doling out some words of encouragement, then had time to sit and think about his wife's insomnia. The morning passed slowly and Jon felt as lethargic as housefly on an October morning.

In the light of day, he didn't think seriously about divorce. After all, Lucy wasn't having an affair or doing drugs. She went to her job as the office manager at Benjamin's Custom Kitchens, she did her share of housework, she chauffeured Sara as needed. It was just her infatuation with television. Lucy was already pregnant with Sara when they married, so Jon attributed her television time to a difficult pregnancy that didn't allow her to be very active. But even after Sara was born and Lucy eventually returned to work, her television obsession remained.

Jon noticed one of his students, Rebecca Lenz, yawning at the computer. He said, "You look as tired as I feel."

She spoke without turning to him. "I had to close last night, or this morning I should say."

"Where is it you work?"

"The Starlight Saloon, on Harrison Street. Rebecca was little and blond, but mostly little. She had a little head on a little body, with little hands and little feet. Jon tried to imagine her hoisting a tray, laden with pitchers of beer and glass mugs, over her little blond head. Rebecca was schoolgirl cute and not much older than his own daughter, though she had to be at least twenty-one to be working at the Starlight.

"That's right. How often do you have to close?"

She swiveled around in her chair, forgetting her composition for a moment. "Usually only a couple of nights a week, but the other girl who closes is on vacation for two weeks." Rebecca yawned and put her little hand over her little mouth.

"You should go home and nap this afternoon."

"I'd love to, but I have to watch my boyfriend's little brother. I might be able to squeeze in a cat nap before I go to work."

"Well, hang in there." A pedestrian way to conclude the exchange but Jon was busy thinking: that's right, Rebecca Lenz is a cocktail waitress at the Starlight Saloon on Harrison Street, a barmaid, a serving wench. He tucked the knowledge away like a business card in his wallet, alongside the car salesman's and the mortgage broker's—people he never intended to call on but there was no harm in keeping their number.

JON TOOK OUT HIS HOUSEKEY but found it wasn't necessary; the side door was unlocked. He walked into the kitchen and set his briefcase on the counter. "Sara?" he called to his daughter. No response. He tried again. He walked into the empty living room. He called up the stairs. He started to fret. All of a father's nightmares sped through his mind. He went to Sara's room and opened the door. She was lying on her stomach on the bed watching television. The sound was muted, and she was listening to her iPod with earphones. Jon could hear the boy-band music as the noise rattled through his daughter's skull then leaked into space, like carbon monoxide, colorless and odorless and therefore all the more sinister. He imagined the lyrics were prodding Sara, programming her even, to behave in ways he wasn't prepared for yet—would never be.

He plucked off the earphones. "Dad. . . ." She squirmed to a sitting position. "What's the matter?" She paused the music.

"What have your mom and I told you to do when you're by yourself? We've said it about a thousand times."

Sara offered a sarcastic look of puzzlement. "Don't use the stove?" Her hair was pulled into pigtails. Combined with her freckles the hairstyle made her look younger than thirteen. Thirteen going on thirty-one.

"The door, the door—lock the door. Why don't we just put a neon sign out front: 'Serial killers and pedophiles right this way'?"

"Don't freak, Dad. I'm still alive aren't I?" She turned her attention to the television screen.

"What's this?"

"Springer."

"With the sound off?"

"I watch for the fur to start flying, then I turn on the sound. It's boring until then."

"Isn't there anything better on? Like *NOVA* or *Reading Rainbow*?"

Sara didn't justify the question with a verbal response. She hit the mute button and some hysterical woman's voice emitted from the TV.

Jon started to leave the room. Sara muted the sound again and said, "Almost forgot. Can I spend the night at Marcy's?"

"What's going on at Marcy's?"

"Nothin."

"Can't you do *nothin* here?"

"I do *nothin* here every night. This'll be different. Well, can I?"

It had been awhile since he and Lucy had had the house to themselves. Ideas started to fill his head like heated air rushing into a particolored balloon. "I don't see why not . . . but call your mom at work. Make sure she signs off too."

"Thanks, Dad." Sara put her earphones back on.

JON USUALLY PREPARED the meals, so it was no trouble for him to go to the market and gather the ingredients for Lucy's favorite dinner: fettuccine Alfredo with French bread and a tossed salad. He picked up a bottle of white wine, and chocolate cheesecake for dessert. He wanted to surprise Lucy; he wanted to woo her; he wanted to seduce her. He cut daisies and snapdragons from the garden in the backyard and arranged them in a glass vase on the table. Throughout the afternoon, he imagined how it would be: the dinner, the music, the wine, Lucy's surprise and pleasure, their troubles forgotten, coupling in the kitchen, the living room, on the stairs, like newlyweds again. Then falling asleep together, contented, at peace. After almost fourteen years of marriage, Jon still wanted his wife. Sometimes, though, that didn't seem to be enough.

Jon had dropped Sara at Marcy's house on the way to the market. She waved from Marcy's porch, her backpack over her shoulder. Marcy's mom wouldn't be home for a couple of hours, and that was part of the fun—for Sara and Marcy to be independent, to be emancipated from childhood for a while. They were good kids. He didn't worry about them doing anything stupid. Marcy's parents were divorced. Her mom worked at a bank; she seemed to be doing all right.

At home, Jon was restless. The meal was simple and wouldn't take long to throw together. The wine was chilling. Lucy's arrival was tricky. She didn't leave the office at the same time every day. Sometimes she was home at 5:15, some days six or later. Jon aimed for about 5:30 to 5:45. He had plenty of time to kill. He considered mowing the yard but it didn't really need it and that would make his afternoon rushed instead of too leisurely. He looked at the paper. He flipped on the TV and quickly surfed through the afternoon talk shows. On ESPN Classics, Jack Nicklaus and Arnie Palmer were battling over some long-ago golf tournament. They wore funny hats and cardigan sweaters. This would do. Jon watched them take their swings and line up their putts. After only a couple of holes, he lowered the sound and fell asleep on the couch. The respectfully subdued applause of the television gallery might as well have been waves gently lapping against a summery shore.

Jon woke with a start, feeling that he had overslept. The living room clock said 5:06. He hurried to the kitchen to begin preparing supper. He started by putting a large pot of water on the stove to boil for the pasta; then he set about preparing the cheese sauce. While that was melting and mixing, he got out the French bread and the ingredients for the tossed salad. He kept an eye on the kitchen clock, hoping that Lucy wouldn't arrive home early. At 5:35 there was no sign of her, and things were coming together. By 5:50 the meal was in order. The salad was on the table, the fettuccine sauce was ready on the stove, and the bread was warming in the oven. All Jon had to do was toss the pasta in the boiling water and open the bottle of wine. The kitchen was filled with the aroma of food lovingly prepared, and Jon's anticipation bubbled like the pasta pot on the stove. He was relieved that Lucy was a bit late: now the evening would be perfect.

At five after six Jon turned down the burner for the water and lowered the temperature in the oven so that the bread wouldn't become croutons. He watched out the front window for Lucy's car. He was growing hungry. And impatient. He thought about trying Lucy's cell but it was almost never turned on, eternally buried in the bottom of her purse, to be used only in case of emergency, more like a roadside flare than a communication device. He watched the evening news. At 6:15 it occurred to him he should check the answering machine in the small downstairs bedroom that served as a den.

When he walked into the room and saw the machine's red

light was blinking, he tasted disappointment. He played the only message: "Hey, it's me. Julie called, she's having another crisis. So I told her I'd go out with her after work. Since Sara's at Marcy's, we'll probably grab a bite so you won't have to worry about fixing anything. See you later." Julie was Lucy's neurotic friend who averaged three crises a week. It wouldn't be a quick outing. Lucy had phoned while he was at the market.

So now Jon had the perfect dinner for two, except one of them was dining out and the other suddenly wasn't hungry. He went back to the kitchen and turned off the burners and the oven. He got a beer out of the refrigerator and sat at the nicely laid table with the cut flowers in the vase and the tossed salad. He drank, and ate radishes out of the salad bowl. He thought about a couple in their old neighborhood, a few doors down from the little house where Jon and Lucy first lived after Sara was born. The man and woman were both teachers and they seemed completely in sync with each other. In the summers, Bob cut the grass and pruned the trees and tinkered in his woodshop in the garage. Sue read novels and fiddled with the little herb garden next to the front porch. As Sara grew to be a toddler she came to know the couple as one word, as "bobansue." When they would drive by their house, Sara would wave and say "Bobansue," even if only one of them was outdoors. When Sara would ride her tricycle down the sidewalk to visit the teachers, she called each of them "Bobansue." Before the Manns moved, when Sara was six, she finally understood there were two names mixed together in her word for them, but it always seemed right to Jon to refer to them as *bobansue* because they truly appeared to be one harmonious being, perfectly balanced.

As he sat at the table with his beer and his radish slices, Jon ruminated on the fact there would never be a "jonanlucy"; they would never be so in tune with each other. They would always be pulling at each other's needs, getting in each other's way, saying the wrong thing at the worst time, one wanting most what the other couldn't give. Like ballroom dancers who couldn't keep from stepping on each other's toes and clashing with each other's style.

He went to the refrigerator for another beer. He checked behind the milk bottles and in the vegetable crisper. There was none to be found, however. Jon wasn't ready to stop drinking so he found his keys and his wallet and went to the car.

In college Jon went out to bars, and when Sara was a baby he and Lucy would sometimes hire a sitter and meet other couples for a drink. That had been several years ago, though, in a different city, so Jon was no longer accustomed to it. He wasn't sure where to go. As he backed out of the driveway, he noted that it was getting dark already, that summer was winding down. Of course, he knew where some bars were located. He steered the car to those parts of town and drove by the establishments slowly, not stopping: there was no parking space, or the bar looked too seedy, or too high rent. Though he didn't articulate it to himself, he understood the real reason he didn't stop was that he didn't know a soul in those places. Lucy not coming home had stirred up a variety of emotions and among them was loneliness. Even though they lived in the same house, Jon missed his wife. He wanted to dine with her. He wanted to sleep next to her, with her. He wanted to share his thoughts with her, face to face, not with a sticky note on the refrigerator door or a message on the answering machine or relayed through Sara.

He stopped at a redlight. The cross street was Harrison and Jon thought of little Rebecca Lenz serving drinks at the Starlight, only a few blocks away. At least there he would know someone. He could have a couple of beers, exchange pleasantries with his student, leave her too big of a tip, then go home, probably more depressed than before. He turned the car onto Harrison Street.

The Starlight Saloon's sign advertised it as "A Family Place." A garish temporary sign also said it was "Karaoke Night." A small asphalted lot in front was full so Jon parked around the corner. He felt a little silly coming here and he half hoped Rebecca wasn't working after all. Nevertheless his anger about the way the evening had turned out spurred him on. He was tired of the feeling he had with Lucy, the poor connection. He was ready for a new feeling, even if it was disconnection.

Inside, the Starlight smelled of stale cigarette smoke but not too bad for a tavern. There was a hostess at the door who asked Jon if he wanted a table. About two thirds of the Starlight was set up as a restaurant, while the remaining third was for the bar area on the other side of a partition that was about head high. Jon said no thank you, he would just go to the bar. The Starlight was busy but certainly not to capacity. There were a half dozen stools available at the bar. Jon ordered a beer and glanced about for Rebecca Lenz. The bartender set Jon's glass of beer in front of him along with a bowl of popcorn. Very salty popcorn.

A television perched in the corner was showing Headline News. The volume was so low Jon couldn't hear the talking heads so he contented himself with reading the news blurbs that crawled across the bottom of the screen. Not even blurbs: blurbettes. He drank the cold beer and ate the salt-laced popcorn. There had been an earthquake near Bengal, India—more than two thousand missing and feared dead.

As Jon finished his glass of beer he thought about his college days. When he wanted to unwind—a euphemism for becoming sloppy drunk, he reminded himself—Jon ordered rum and Dr. Pepper, a variation on rum and Coke. He hadn't drunk one for almost fifteen years, so when the bartender came to refill his glass Jon ordered his old drink. The bartender said all they had was Mr. Pibb. It didn't have the same ring to it but Jon said it would do. It was sweeter than he recalled. Not only did Jon rarely drink alcohol anymore, he had cut out soda from his diet too. The rum was smooth though and its effects were almost instantaneous. He read the TV screen: the Dow had dropped 76 points at closing.

"Mr. Mann?" Rebecca Lenz was standing at his shoulder, no taller than in fact. Her hair was pulled back and she had a white rag draped over her arm. At first glance it looked like a cast. "Thought that was you."

"Hi. I thought maybe you've been pulling my leg about working here." He half turned on his stool.

It took her a moment to process. "No, I was just on supper break." Rebecca was undoubtedly trying to figure out if she was the reason her Comp. teacher had come to the Starlight. Alone. Without his wife.

Jon said, "I'm here for the karaoke."

She thought a second then laughed. "Yeah . . . sure . . . I'd better get back to work. See you later." She went to the far end of the bar to the waitress station where there was already a tray full of drinks ready for her.

Now Jon had something to do besides read Headline News. He could also discreetly watch Rebecca Lenz while she served cocktails. It was going to be a big evening. He ordered another rum and Pibb. He looked at the time in the corner of the television screen. It was almost eight o'clock. He'd been at the tavern longer than he realized.

Jon heard a microphone being bumped around, then a man's voice said, "Hello, everybody. Welcome to Karaoke Night at the Starlight Saloon. I'm DJ Dan and I'm ready to have some fun. Are you ready for some fun too?" A voice or two in the room mumbled in the affirmative. Jon imagined the disc jockey with rainbow suspenders and a handlebar mustache. "Remember, DJ Dan is the one-man band with the master plan. I've got it all, from disco to punk to Sinatra. Let's listen to Bill Haley and the Comets and 'Rock Around the Clock' while you cruise on up and check out the play catalog—over six hundred titles. Just sign your name on the yellow sheet along with the catalog number of your selection, and you're all set. Let the fun begin!" DJ Dan used a hokey echo effect on his parting remark and cued the Bill

Haley song.

Jon glanced behind from his bar stool to see if anyone bolted to the play catalog but the staging area was out of view behind the partition. Rebecca walked past him with a tray full of umbrella drinks. She noticed him noticing her and smiled at him for a brief moment. He returned his attention to his drink and the old rock song. Jon noticed the time again: by now, he'd hoped to be making love to his wife, perhaps for a second time. He drained the sweet rum drink and signaled the bartender for another. Jon felt hot and his head was beginning to swim. The noise in the bar was muffled, as if the alcohol had filled his ears.

On Headline News, there was a riot after a soccer game in Barcelona. Meanwhile, the first karaoke singer began butchering the theme from *Grease*.

"Are you meeting someone, Mr. Mann?" Rebecca Lenz was at his shoulder again.

"No, just little ole me." He made an effort not to slur.

"Thought maybe you were waiting for your designated driver." She smiled and set some empty glasses on the bar for the bartender.

"Guess I'll have to find one here." Jon felt himself slipping into a conversation he figured he'd regret.

"Don't wander off without saying good-bye." She vanished to take more orders.

Bless her little heart, thought Jon. She doesn't want her old Comp. teacher to drive off a bridge. Her pathetic old Comp. teacher. Old . . . pathetic and old. He drank his rum and Pibb.

Jon realized that a new karaoke singer was doing a remarkable job on Bette Midler's "From a Distance." The woman's voice was clear and her notes precise, even with the tavern's poor acoustics. There was something familiar about the voice, like he'd heard it on the radio . . . or the telephone. Jon crept down from his stool—his legs were slightly gelatinous—and peered over the partition. There on the karaoke stage was an attractive dark-haired woman, mid thirties, her warm eyes glittering in the spotlight. She wore a black pantsuit that revealed gentle matronly curves. But her subtle matronliness added to her allure, implying she would be a nurturing lover, a friend in and out of bed.

It was Lucy on the stage, wowing the audience with her voice. Jon recalled that his wife was a singer—both recollection and revelation. She was in a vocal jazz club in college, and she even was a soloist at a friend's wedding when they themselves were newlyweds. But at some point she stopped singing. There was no place for it in her life. How could that be? Jon wondered. How could she abandon such a gift? He marveled at the passion she brought to the song.

Jon noticed Lucy's friend Julie at a table, a margarita glass in front of her. Jon went around the partition and cautiously moved toward the stage area. With the spotlight in her eyes, he knew Lucy couldn't see her audience. Even without the spotlight, she would have been oblivious. She was in the song, existing from note to note, every one of which she hit perfectly.

Jon approached Julie from behind. Her unnaturally blond head kept time with Lucy's song. Jon was only a couple of tables away when his wife finished and then left the miniature stage, the audience clapping and whistling their appreciation. Jon clapped and whistled too. He smiled, preparing to surprise his wife. He felt giddy and disoriented, almost an out-of-body sensation.

Lucy returned quickly to her table, the adrenaline and adulation rushing her along. Jon started to raise his hand in greeting— but Lucy didn't notice him and sat in her chair. Julie squeezed her friend's arm, congratulating her. DJ Dan sang her praises. Jon was paralyzed on his rubbery legs. He expected someone to ask him to move because he was blocking the view. No one did. Perhaps, then, he *was* invisible, transparent, disembodied. A drunken ghost moving gracelessly among the quick.

"Mr. Mann." Rebecca Lenz was at his side. "I have a break now. Why don't I drive you home? This is Julio." There was a tall, thin man of Hispanic descent next to her. He was all in white, like a ghost himself. Julio and Rebecca were a desperately mismatched pair: he as dark and tall as she was fair and small. "He works in the kitchen. He's going to follow me and bring me back to work. Mr. Mann . . . ?"

Jon found his voice. "Yes, Rebecca. Thank you. That's a good idea." Another singer had taken the stage. The first notes of Elton John's "Rocket Man" pulsed in the smoky air.

Jon followed Julio and Rebecca robotically. Before leaving the Starlight, he looked back at his wife. She was in profile, sipping a drink. He tried to recall her favorite. Did she like rusty nails? Long Island iced teas? Amaretto stone sours? It wouldn't come to him. He also took a last look at the television in the bar. There was a NASA animation of some object crashing through the atmosphere, a long tail of fire stretching behind it. Jon stepped outside before he saw if the object made it to earth, or burned to nothing in the sky.

An Alabaster Moon

IT DIDN'T OCCUR TO ME at first that she was in danger. I was combing the beach for seashells (depending on the size and shape, I could get as much as $2 a shell—then a friend would slap a nickel's worth of paint on them and sell them for $10 to $20 in his stand on tourist row). I was a long way from tourist row when I saw her. It was a more remote stretch of beach, where the rich vacationed in their condos. Most of them were time-share and it was late in the season—so very few of the beach-houses were occupied. The developer paid me to do some groundskeeping and generally look after the properties. It always seemed strange to me that the rich vacated around Labor Day, like crabs scurrying after the tide, because the fall and winter are the best seasons here.

I had just found a nice shell, a banded kitten's-paw, and was admiring its worth when I noticed her, maybe 150 yards away: khaki shorts and a black swimsuit top, a straw hat and canvas beach shoes. She looked tall and thin, but she may have been quite small. Her legs were lean and muscular. She had some color but she obviously wasn't here for the sun. A blond ponytail hung down from her straw hat, and she was carrying something in her hand—maybe a camera. I thought of her as being a girl but she may have been close to forty: a youthful, beautiful forty.

She had used a series of stones, many of which are completely submerged at hightide, to reach a large rock in the bay. Waves beat at the rock; they must have been soaking her shoes and spraying her taut legs.

Perhaps she was staying at the beach-house alone; perhaps a friend was helping her to get over a messy divorce and had given her the keys for some solitude and quiet reflection. Perhaps she had come to the cape to put the finishing touches on a novel or book of poetry.

Perhaps one day around sunset I would be drinking a beer from a six-pack I had bought up the road. Out walking on the beach, maybe she would join me, and I would gather some drift-wood and make a fire. I would admire her smile and her bare shoulders in the crimson glow of the firelight. She would laugh at my stories—eighteen years of life on the beach. She would say I should write them down, they'd make a wonderful book.

Perhaps I would give her my denim shirt because I knew she was cold in spite of the nice fire. Thanks, she would say while she wrapped it around herself more like a blanket than a shirt. Perhaps I'd comment on the shapes I could see in the rising moon and she would say that she could see them too. Perhaps we would do all we could to not take those last swallows of beer; but ultimately we would. I'd help her up from the sand and she'd offer me my shirt. I would tell her to keep it, maybe I'd see her tomorrow night. All right, she would say, with a schoolgirl smile.

Perhaps I would stand for a long time watching her walk back to her beach-house holding her sandals by their straps and keeping my shirt gathered at her neck.

Perhaps she didn't know how deep the water was; perhaps she didn't understand about the undertow. Suddenly a giant wave reared up from the sea, like the hand of an angry god, and washed her from the rock. I dropped the kitten's-paw I'd been admiring and sprinted up the beach. The three shells in the mesh bag tied to my belt clinked against my leg. I called to her. I ran into the surf until it reached my waist. I felt the cold pull of the undertow.

Far out, I saw her straw hat bucking on the sea.

I needed to call for help. The nearest house was hers, so I ran until I came to the wooden steps, which I took two at a time. They led me up to her deck. There was a book spread pages down on the arm of an Adirondack chair—as if she was only leaving it for a moment. The French doors were unlocked so I let myself in. It smelled as she must have smelled: honey and jasmine and talcum powder. The living room was neat except for a folded towel on the back of the sofa and an empty coffee cup on the glass-top endtable.

Next to the cup was the base for the cordless phone but the phone itself was not there. I looked about the room. I followed the hall to the master bedroom. The bed was haphazardly made; a disheveled newspaper lay upon it, as did the telephone.

I called 911 and told them what had happened and gave them the address. As I spoke to the police dispatcher, I noticed a desk on the opposite side of the room. There was a computer on the desk, and books, and various sheets and scraps of paper; three yellow Post-It notes were adhered to the computer monitor, which was in sleep mode.

When I finished talking I put the phone down and went to the desk. They were old books, like library books, and the papers were filled with scribbled words. The lighting in the room was low and I couldn't read the papers by just glancing down at them. I touched return on the keyboard and the monitor came back to life. The screen too was full of words. My eye caught a phrase: *a beach with sand like satin.* I reached into my mesh bag and took out the nicest shell I had, an alabaster moon, then I placed it on a stack of papers.

I had to go wait for the police. I noticed that I had tracked into the house; it didn't matter—the hardwood floors were made to withstand sand and seawater. My sandal prints showed everywhere I had been. When I came to the kitchen's entryway I stopped . . . I slipped off my sandals and walked barefoot toward the refrigerator. I checked and I was leaving no prints on the floor. I opened the refrigerator; it was sparsely stocked. There was drinking water and a grape fruit, a quart of skim milk, some packages of meat wrapped in white butcher's paper—and a half drunk bottle of chardonnay that had been recorked. I even looked in the crispers to make certain: but there was no beer.

I went back to my sandals and pulled them on. I would go down to the beach and point out the spot for the police, who probably would do nothing more than stare at the sea and wait patiently for the tide to return the woman to them.

And to me.

In a Strange City

HE'D MET ALL FOUR of her high school boyfriends: the lawyer, the plumber, the restaurateur and the ad writer (the one who discovered something very near to sex with her). He was comfortable with them all. They each meant something to her still but the meaning was forever tied to the past. In fact once, before the tenth-year class reunion, he dreamed of them being four gray goats shut up in a rough wooden pin; and he and his wife watched them from a sunny hillside blanketed in wildflowers. In his dream he and his wife were holding hands and when the dream woke him in the night he was holding her hand. Nina was sleeping soundly. He lay on his side in the bedroom's half-light and watched her bare breasts heave subtly with the rhythm of her breathing. In the morning he didn't tell her about the dream.

THOUGH THE HOTEL was busy with Fourth of July travelers, it seemed empty without Nina's twin sister and brother-in-law, who stayed home because their son had had an emergency appendectomy. The boy was fine, they said by telephone, but still recovering. Even when there was no class reunion, the two couples farmed out their children to their paternal grandparents and met at the hotel for the long weekend. Nina's parents were deceased and there were no relatives in the area. So each year the city was becoming a strange city to Nina and her sister. In a sense he and his brother-in-law knew this strange city better than their wives.

NINA WANTED TO SWIM in the hotel's indoor pool in spite of being on her period. They put on swimsuits. The room was cool so he draped a towel over his shoulders. Regular exercise had kept his chest and arms in good shape, but he had to hold in his stomach to see the physique in the mirror he wanted to see. Nina changed in the bathroom because she had to insert a tampon. She came out wearing her black two-piece. It wasn't a bikini; it had an athletic-wear cut, with a high waistband that hid the cesarean scar. She was trying to tie back her hair but it was too short. Nina had had this style for some time. It seemed that being in her old city made her think of her hair as long again. She tossed the rubber band on the floor near her suitcase. Nina was still beautiful, he thought. Maternity had widened her hips slightly and her long legs weren't as muscular as when he met her their freshman year of college. But her breasts were fuller now and the nipples better defined than in those first encounters in her dorm room. Her eyes seemed to be a richer, stronger shade of brown too, like espresso, and Nina was *funnier*: being a wife and mother had improved her sense of humor. Before walking down to the pool they kissed for a moment. "I love you," he said. He had vowed to himself to stop telling Nina he loved her only before he climaxed; he'd read about the phenomenon in one of Nina's magazines. She pecked him on the cheek and gently squeezed his erection through his swimming trunks before throwing her own towel around her shoulders.

THE POOL WATER was too warm and didn't refresh them at all. They lay in the loungers at the side of the rectangular pool breathing the sultry, chlorinated air. Side by side, they locked pinkies and felt the emptiness of the hotel press in on them. If Nina's sister and brother-in-law were there, they would have been joking about their children and jobs and, since it was a reunion weekend, telling stories about their high school days they had all shared many times before.

He looked across to the far side of the pool area. "Hot tub's finally open."

Nina looked across to the wooden tub. "Go ahead. I pressed my luck to go swimming on my heaviest day. I'm going back to the room where it's at least cool."

He watched her walk away with a white towel wrapped around her like a skirt and the room key in her hand. From behind with her hair wet and the towel covering everything from waist to knee, Nina might have been the girl he made love to in college, or she might have been her twin sister, or even a stranger in the hotel.

He was ambivalent about sitting alone in the gurgling hot tub. He'd positioned himself so that a jet of water kneaded his left ribs. When a fat man with a cigar and three diamond rings on each hand said hello and lowered himself into the tub, that was enough. He waited a moment so he wouldn't appear rude, then he took his towel and headed dripping toward the room.

When he called to her, Nina opened the door and stepped back behind it, shielding herself. She was wearing only her cotton panties, which he knew held a thick feminine pad; she would have discarded the uncomfortable tampon while she was relaxing. On the hotel bed was a dry towel that Nina must have been using as an inadequate blanket. In the cool air, fresh from swimming, Nina was at the height of her sexiness. Nina helped him untie his swimsuit's drawstring. He slung the wet suit into the bathroom and spread the towel flat over the bedspread. Nina removed her underwear and lay on the bed so that her vulva was at the center of the towel. Birth-control pills had a bad effect on Nina, so they used condoms normally. The natural sensations he could enjoy only five days a month frequently occupied his thoughts during the weeks in between.

When they were finished, he quickly went to the shower and washed the menstrual gore, some of which stuck in black clots, from his penis and pubic hair and abdomen up to the navel and his thighs. It looked like he'd been attacked and injured by his wife's vagina. The pink soapy water swirled down the drain. The smell of it, which aroused him in bed, nearly sickened him in the shower.

THERE WAS NOTHING on the television that interested him, so he found a music station to his liking on the hotel's cheap clockradio. And he read about a scandal involving politicians he didn't know at all in the local newspaper he'd bought spontaneously in the lobby. Nina was in the bathroom getting ready for the reunion. The door was open and every so often a pleasant scent from some body spray or powder or cosmetic would come to him in the room's one reclining chair.

She spoke louder than necessary from the bathroom sink: "Are you sure you know how to get to the Gardener's Club?"

He kept his eyes on the meaningless newspaper story. "I think so. Don't you know?"

"I think I do but I'm not sure. My sister was always the one to know the way."

It was a long-established truth. "We'll find it all right." He tried to match the volume of her voice. "Of course we could skip the reunion and have a really nice dinner somewhere. The fifteenth isn't that significant anyway; it's not the tenth or the twentieth."

Nina poked her head out of the bathroom. "We've already paid our fifty dollars." She popped back inside. She had put on some eye makeup and a touch of blush.

"I know, I know. Don't remind me—fifty bucks!" He refolded

the newspaper and placed it on the nightstand. "Besides, you like seeing them all: the lawyer, the plumber, the restaurateur and the damn ad writer. You like seeing who's put on weight, who's lost some hair, whose wife is pregnant." He checked his own hairline in the mirror on the opposite wall. It seemed stationary and the waves of dark brown familiarly thick; but he did notice two or three new filaments glinting silver-gray as he turned his head left, then right. "You enjoy keeping tabs on them."

Nina turned on the faucet at the sink, making her words harder to understand. "Actually I can't keep track of them *all*."

"Why not? Who do you know won't be there?"

She switched on the exhaust fan and the heat lamp. It sounded like she said, "The one who's never come back. Boyfriend number-five." Nina shut the bathroom door.

Boyfriend number-five? He went and opened the door enough to see inside. "What'd you say?"

Nina was on the toilet reading a magazine she'd brought in her suitcase. "You mind? I'm trying to use the bathroom." She swatted at the door with her open magazine.

He didn't want to let it go so he shut the door and questioned her again from outside. "What do you mean, boyfriend number-five?"

She didn't respond. Maybe she didn't hear with the water and fan and heat lamp echoing in the little tiled room.

THE GARDENER'S CLUB was a genteel setting for the reunion with long linen-covered tables, an old-fashioned bandstand, an oak-parquet dance floor, and flickering candlelight. The club had a spacious courtyard where the members displayed their gardening talents. Paths wound through a plethora of flowers, vines and shrubs. In the center of the courtyard was a brilliant rose garden surrounding a tall gazebo. Inside the gazebo was a bubbling fountain of stone cherubs gazing heavenward. Unobtrusive fixtures splashed just enough light to make the courtyard navigable at night.

The club was on an obscure avenue, and it had taken a few tries before finding it. In the car he asked Nina nonchalantly about the possibility of a fifth boyfriend in high school. She claimed that he had misunderstood her words, but she was visibly irritated when he brought it up and more so when he tried to pursue it.

Could there have been a fifth? And why would she have concealed the fact? Then the question of Nina's virginity came to him again. In college she said she was a virgin but that night in her dorm room (with her sister, who was also her roommate, awkwardly sent out to watch a movie or something) he saw no signs of her purity afterwards. There was no blood on him or her. And there was supposed to be blood—wasn't there? He never asked because he didn't want to appear to doubt her and because he didn't want to admit his naïveté. He felt certain she had been with no one but him since that night. It was just before Christmas break and garish strands of lights blinked un-uniformly in other dorm windows around the snow-covered quad.

Nina's virginity didn't matter—he told her so at the time—but it seemed women were funny that way. *When* and *with whom* had an import and a mystique that most men didn't completely comprehend. He didn't comprehend it.

Was it this fifth boyfriend who had truly been with her first? Was there some love they shared that was too painful for him to recall and that's why he'd never come back?

He knew he was letting his imagination run but he wanted to ask all of these things. Nina's shortness with him wouldn't allow it. In the parking lot of the Gardener's Club, with the sun descended behind a stand of old-growth trees, he was surprised by his wife's dark beauty. She wore a knee-length black dress with see-through sleeves. The curves of her body and the rounded slope of the back of her calves in the sheer black stockings made him stare, surreptitiously, like he was staring at another woman.

In the foyer of the club greeters checked their names and made them put on "Hello, my name is" stickers. He noticed that Nina wrote her maiden name. Had she done so at the fifth and tenth reunions? He didn't recall it. He was going to somehow ask her when she spotted a high school girlfriend and hurried, smiling and shrieking, into the main dining hall.

Nina's was a large graduating class, over five hundred, and the dining hall was already becoming crowded. He went and stood near his wife while she chattered excitedly with the old friend, then another joined in, then another. Tired of standing there fiddling with his suit coat buttons and straightening his necktie, he went to the bar for a drink. He didn't feel like a beer but it was free, so he took a glass and went to look at the courtyard through tall French doors. There was just enough dusklight remaining to display the wonder of the courtyard's garden.

Maybe Nina would like to go for a walk with him in the garden before it was too dark. He went to the spot where she'd been talking, but she was no longer there. He scanned the room of strangers, but it was difficult with the low light. He walked among them for a while; Nina wasn't to be found. He took his drink to a table and sat down. He suddenly missed his brother-in-law. By now they would have been talking and laughing—sharing the common experience of being married to identical twins: a subject they never grew tired of.

WHEN WAITERS WEARING white shirts and red vests began coming into the dining hall all at once, it was a signal for everyone to be seated. As the crowd dispersed, he saw that Nina was speaking with a good-looking couple. He recognized them as the lawyer and his wife. Nina appeared to know instinctively where her husband was sitting. She led her first boyfriend and his wife directly to his table. Nina was smiling and happy. When they reached the table, she said, "I think you all have met before."

The lawyer put out his hand. "Oh yes—at five and ten if nowhere else."

He half stood and shook the lawyer's hand. "How've you been?'

"Fantastic."

Nina and the couple sat three in a row across from her husband. The lawyer and his wife *looked* fantastic—younger and more prosperous than at the tenth-year reunion in fact. Nina too seemed to grow more beautiful before his eyes. Perhaps the candlelight only showed each person's best features, hiding the blemishes and the loose skin and the thinning hair. He had to look behind to see the courtyard. Darkness had come, but he noticed that the paths were somewhat lighted. Maybe there would be an opportunity for a walk after all. He tried to catch a glimpse of himself in the French doors—to see if he also was improved by the candlelight—but there were just undefined dark shapes huddled around coruscating flames. He might have been viewing believers in the occult at a séance.

A tall man wearing an out-of-date sport coat and no tie placed a pitcher of beer at their end of the table. "We've already paid for it—might as well drink it." He carried another pitcher to his own part of the table.

Nina and her friends had no glasses for the beer, and they declined his offer to get them some. So he refilled his own glass as he watched the red-vested waiters bring out the dinner salads on impossibly large trays. He was no longer used to drinking and the alcohol, he could tell, was already affecting him. But the warm, almost-sleepy feeling was a pleasant one.

WHILE THE MEAL methodically took its course a group of four musicians set up their instruments and sound equipment on the bandstand. The musicians appeared to be about the same age as the reunion participants. He asked Nina and the lawyer if the musicians were from their class. The two turned in their chairs to watch for a moment, then agreed simultaneously that they were not. They were too young for one thing, they said. During dessert, the musicians erected a banner behind the drumset with the group's name, New Image.

After the meal, the president of the class welcomed everyone again and talked about who had traveled the farthest to attend the reunion, who had had children since the tenth and who had passed away. He thanked them all for coming; it was a larger turnout for their class than the previous two reunions. Then he instructed everyone to mingle and dance and have a good time.

Nina and the lawyer's wife went to the ladies' room together, and the lawyer drifted into a conversation with a classmate. Apparently they had been lab partners in biology. They began reminiscing about dissecting a pig. He refilled his beer glass and went to wait for his wife by the door.

The band played music from the class's high school days. The songs brought back memories of his teenage years and of *his* girlfriends. The alcohol helped him to retrieve a fondness for those skinny, giggling, immature ghosts. He wanted to really see them—not the women they were now, but as they were in their vivacious youth. It hurt him to think that Nina must have this same aching affection for her old boyfriends. Did she dream about them? Did she fantasize about their gangling, unpracticed bodies?

And what about this mysterious fifth boyfriend, the one who obviously occupied a special place in her memories? He recalled that the class president said this was the biggest turnout. Maybe old number-five had finally returned. He wanted to herd the lawyer, the plumber, the restaurateur and the ad writer into a corner; then separate out all the spouses in attendance; then all the female class members. How many men would that leave to interrogate? A hundred? A hundred-fifty? Surely he could weed him out and discover the truth about number-five's relationship with Nina.

He realized she hadn't returned. He went back to the table, but it was deserted. He emptied his glass and set it down. Where was she? Jealousy filled up inside of him like terrible heartburn. Its acidity made him queasy. He crisscrossed the dining hall and searched the perimeter. He even cut a serpentine path among the couples on the dance floor. Nina was nowhere. He didn't know his wife could be so thoughtless, so selfish. His jealousy had turned to bitter indignation.

Someone had opened a French door and several people were in the courtyard. He went to the door and looked outside. There was his beautiful wife in a group of four or five on the steps leading down into the garden. He walked up and interrupted their conversation to speak to her. "Did you find him?" His voice was gorged with accusation.

Nina was startled. "Who?"

"Old number-five. He's here isn't he?"

Nina's classmates were silent with embarrassment.

"Let's walk." She took him by the arm. At first he wouldn't yield, then he let her lead him to a path. "I can't believe you got drunk," she hissed.

"I can't believe *you*!" He kept walking but pulled his arm out of her grip.

"Keep your voice down, please."

The foliage was close on both sides. Pale blossoms peered down from descending vines. The air was heavy with sweet competing scents.

He tripped on a crack in the path and nearly fell. "Number-five is here, isn't he?"

"Of course he isn't here."

"Ah-ha! So there was a fifth boyfriend! And you denied it!"

Nina had stopped. They had come to the rose garden near

the center of the courtyard. The tall gazebo with its cherub fountain stood before them. In the poor lighting the roses looked common and plain, almost colorless.

He took hold of his wife's shoulders roughly. "Tell me all about him. I want to know the whole truth."

"Let go." There was no force in Nina's command.

"Tell me."

"Let go!" She twisted violently and flung his hands away. Nina lost her balance and leaned into a rose bush. She yelped and pulled herself away. The thorns had torn the sleeve of her dress, and three black trickles of blood appeared instantaneously.

Seeing her hurt removed all his venom. "I'm sorry." He tried to look at her arm, but she turned away from him and hurried into the gazebo. He waited a moment, trying to absorb what had happened, then he followed. Nina was sitting on the edge of the fountain holding her cut arm. The white-stone cherubs were illuminated from above and cast wide shadows on the surface of the water. She was staring at the gazebo floor. He had removed a handkerchief from his suit coat pocket. He held it out to her but she didn't take it. He sat on the fountain edge too—close but not touching her. "I'm sorry," he said again.

They sat for what seemed to him a long time. The water in the fountain dripped and bubbled, and every so often they'd hear the voices of others strolling in the courtyard. Passé songs, as quiet as elevator music, came from the dining hall. He didn't know what to say or do.

Nina's eyes were still cast down when she began to speak. "I never told you about him because I was trying not to remember. We dated the summer before college." She paused for several seconds. "I try not to remember him because I think he . . . raped me."

"You *think* he. . . ." He couldn't say the word.

"It was a long time ago. No one talked about 'date rape' but thinking back that's one way to describe it." Nina finally looked at him. "I mean, we did a lot of things. I was willing, I mean, I wanted to do them too. But I just didn't want to do *that*. He seemed to respect my decision, to respect me. But one night—after a Fourth of July party—he wouldn't stop when I said no."

He risked putting his hand on her back. "Did you tell anyone?"

"No—I was too confused. I didn't know if I should blame him. I knew his parents were out of town, and I wanted to go to his house. I wanted to undress. I wanted to do everything else we did that night. I just wasn't ready to give up that part of myself—not to him, not then." Tears began rolling down Nina's cheeks; and when she absentmindedly brushed them away, she smeared blood under each eye. She let him use the handkerchief to clean her face, then she rested her head against his shoulder. "I probably should have told you, but I felt it was partly my fault . . . I still feel at fault."

"It wasn't your fault. No is no." He understood his words had no effect, but they were important to say nonetheless.

HE DIDN'T OBJECT when Nina asked for the car keys even though he felt totally sober. He thought he might have to give her directions back to the hotel, but she guided the car out of the club's parking lot and onto the city streets without hesitation. He realized the world was a different place now that he knew the truth about Nina's fifth boyfriend. He was different. Nina too. He watched her from the passenger seat. Maybe the alcohol wasn't completely worn off. The phenomenon he'd experienced in the Gardener's Club was still in progress. Each time they passed a streetlight Nina's profile was revealed to him for a moment, and the woman he saw became more beautiful with every city block they traveled.

Fische Stories

FISCHE BOARDS THE TRAIN at the Fifth Street Station, shelter-
ing the hardcover book from the rain by tucking it inside his
overcoat. It is forty minutes to East Abbey. He is beginning to
know the route by heart: a glimpse of the gray river, buildings of
steel and plastic giving way to the hulking brick two-stories, the
stray-dog neighborhoods, the aging, ambivalent suburbs, then
finally the wonderland of estates. Fische has no trouble finding a vacant seat. The odd midday people are far fewer than the
rush-hour masses, in then out of the city. He opens the book
to his marker. It is a Kawabata novel. He reads each section as
if it is a poem, slowly, reflectively. From time to time he pauses
to turn over the images in his mind while staring at himself in
the train window, the landscape beyond occasionally intruding.
He is pale, unshaven, his hair wild from the rain. He thinks he
should present himself differently to Kate; but there is nothing
to do about it now. Besides, this is the Fische she knows.

By the time the train reaches East Abbey he is alone. It is
twelve perfectly tended blocks to Kate's house, with its brick wall
and black-iron gate, with its sculpted yard of old-growth trees,
with its turrets and arched windows. The first view of it always
makes him angry . . . sad . . . awed. He rings the bell and waits.
Answering the door in the giant's house takes some time, he
thinks. He hears her footsteps, then silence as she looks through
the peephole. She pulls back the heavy door.

"Hello, Fische." Kate is lovely and well-dressed, perhaps just arrived home from a charity tea. One time he would like to find her in sweat clothes and rubber gloves, in the middle of cleaning a bathroom. Kate has people for that now.

"Hi, Kate. Can I come in for a second?"

There is resignation in her eyes as she steps back. He follows her through the foyer to a medium-size room she calls the parlor. Fisches sits in the flowered loveseat and places the book on a richly lacquered coffeetable. Kate takes the ladder-back chair opposite him. He waits a moment for well-mannered Kate to offer him coffee or something, but she does not. She seems more agitated by his visit than usual.

Fische speaks toward the book. "The reason I came by—you know that box, the one you said you didn't need? Well, I didn't want to just toss the whole thing out, so I was going through it, and in the bottom were some legal pads with college notes, psych, I think, and sociology, and I remembered that you are thinking about going back to school, so I thought maybe you would want them." He dares to glance up for a moment to see her reaction.

A desperate smile takes over her face. "You came all the way out here—no, Fische, I don't care to have the old notes. Please, feel free to pitch them, or burn them, whatever you want." Kate stands and walks around the chair, placing her hands on its tall back. He is ashamed to see the tears welling in her eyes. "Fische, I'm sorry, you've got to stop coming out here—"

"Why, is Mikey jealous?" He is astounded at his own absurdity.

Not bothering to answer, Kate sits in the chair again. "Please listen: Michael and I are adopting a child, or at least we're trying to—it's a very complex situation."

Fische is dumbfounded.

"Our attorney tells us that during this examination period it is not unusual for the prospective couple to be watched in secret, to make sure the profile they've submitted is legitimate."

"Watched? You mean someone may be spying on you? Like a detective?"

"Yes. And Michael is afraid—I'm afraid, too—that my ex-husband coming to visit in the middle of the day, when Michael is away, might jeopardize our adoption. You can understand that, can't you?"

"This is America, Kate. People can't just go around spying on other people. It's invasion of privacy, it's uncon—"

Kate jumps up from the chair. "Fische! None of that matters. What matters is that Michael and I want to adopt this child and people may be watching us. Period." Kate goes behind her chair again. "Child or no child, you need to quit coming here, you need to move on . . . for your own good. Please, Fische."

"Thank you for the advice. However, I'm not having any trouble with moving on. For your information, things are going great at the college. There's every indication I'll get a full-time position next term. There's a publisher who's interested in my book. And on top of that, I've been seeing someone, and it's getting serious."

"That's fantastic." It's clear that Kate doesn't believe a word of it.

He gets up from the loveseat. "I have to get back. I apologize for showing some concern and risking your adoption. I hope everything works out for you." He turns to leave the parlor.

"Fische."

"Yes."

"Your book."

HE PUSHES THE BOOK-LADEN CART through the narrow aisle, glancing at the titles. He is in world history. Fische spots a title, *Commodore Perry Opens Japan,* and takes the thick volume from the shelf. The cover is noisy with age and the pages emit a pleasingly musty scent. He begins to read and in a few minutes he is slumped in a sitting position on the cold tile floor. Scenes of Far Eastern opulence bloom like a wild garden in his imagination. He is so entranced by the words, he doesn't hear the footfalls on the tiles. Suddenly, it seems, young Miranda Harper is standing there above him. Materialized. At eye level with her knees, Fisches notes the adolescent thinness of her legs.

"Mr. Fische, Mrs. Hamilton has been waiting for you to come back." Miranda's voice holds no reproach, only simple fact. "We have a loan request she wants you to locate. I'm at the desk." She holds the slip of paper.

He gets to his feet, leaving his finger in the book as a marker.

Miranda smiles. "I'm sorry, Mr. Fische. I can get the book while I'm up here."

In the six weeks of knowing her, he has not seen Miranda smile. He thinks there is a prettiness behind the patchy red acne and overlarge glasses. "No, no . . . I'll pull it. Go ahead back to the desk." He watches as she skitters away. He tries to sense her shape in the wool skirt and cotton blouse, but the fabric is too loose. Fische thinks back to their conversation. He hopes he didn't sound agitated.

He deftly finds the requested book and carries it downstairs to the information desk, where Miranda is sharpening little pencils for the periodic-guide table and card catalog. "Here you go: *Flight of the Enola Gay.*"

Miranda stops grinding the pencil and takes the offered book. "Thank you, Mr. Fische." There is respect, nearly admiration, in her voice. He heard it upstairs also.

Fische leans against the counter. "Where's the boss?"

"Her office. Requisitions, I think."

He thinks for a moment. "How's school going?"

"Fine. Love some of my classes, hate some. You know."

Fische nods. "Which ones do you love?"

"My modern foods class, and creative writing. I could write

and write all day."

"Really?" He thinks of Miranda writing and writing, the yellow pencil dancing ardently across the page, the tip of her pink tongue showing in the corner of her mouth. "That's great."

A man comes to the information desk. He holds out several slips of paper with scribbled call numbers, like an offering.

Fische says, "I'll let you get back to work."

For the rest of the evening, as Fische reshelves books, his mind leaps from image to image: Kate holding her blanket-wrapped baby, Miranda feverishly writing, Matthew Perry marching into a lustrous Japanese palace, all gold and silk. As if dreaming, the scenes meld together. Kate becomes both the explorer and the bejeweled empress; Miranda—grown up, porcelain skinned— holds the new baby. The incongruous mental pictures make him uneasy.

At closing time Fische and Miranda exit through the library's back door, which locks behind them. Their boss, as usual, is staying late. In the time that Miranda has been employed there, they have come to this point a dozen times. He has turned one direction toward his efficiency apartment on the edge of the college campus and Miranda has gone the other way to the closest bus stop.

On impulse Fische says, "If you're interested in writing, you should go to the Paris Street Coffeehouse. A lot of writers and artists call the place home."

"I've heard of it. I've been wanting to go."

"I'd be happy to take you there sometime, introduce you to some people."

"That would be great. Thanks."

He pretends to see his watch on the dark street. "I don't know when you have to be home, but I have time now—if you feel like it."

Miranda, pretty in the feeble light of a distant streetlamp, appears to weigh the invitation. "Sure. I have some time."

"Are you sure? Maybe you should phone."

"No, it's all right. Sometimes I stop at a friend's house."

They begin their walk to the coffeehouse, twelve blocks away. He feels a pang of shame, being out with this teenage girl. Yet he has done nothing wrong—merely invited a young writer to a coffeehouse where he might introduce her to some established artists. Yes, it is all right. Fische notes that the earlier rain has given the night an autumn-like crispness.

"What types of things do you like to write?" he says.

Miranda puts her hands in the pockets of a nylon windbreaker, which is out of place with her skirt and blouse. "I was writing a lot of stories. Now, though, we're studying poetry, and I love that, too."

Fische nods.

"Is it bad, do you think? Should you focus on one type of writing, just fiction or poetry?" There is notable anxiousness in her question.

"No, I think diverse writing experience is good—especially at your stage." He feels it is an appropriate time for Miranda to inquire about his writing. Surely she knows.

"That's what my creative-writing teacher at school says. He's really interesting—not like most of my teachers. You should talk with him some time."

The idea of conferring with a high-school teacher, as if equals, irritates Fische. "Uh-huh."

The city streets are strangely empty. Fische feels good about the desolation. He doesn't want to be seen with the schoolgirl, at least not by strangers. The coffeehouse is different. There he can introduce her to people he knows, carefully clarifying their connection. He thinks about the scandal at the college during the spring semester: the instructor and the female undergraduate. The college officially discouraged relationships between faculty and students. He glances at Miranda's profile. This is different. She is not a student at the college. They do not have a relationship. He is simply introducing her to local writers and artists, encouraging her interests.

Fische, beginning to feel chilled, is glad to reach their destination. "Here we are." It seems that the city is unpopulated because everyone is in the Paris Street Coffeehouse. The noise of conversation and scent of smoke reaches out to them even before they open the door.

Fische looks around inside for someone he knows well. He only sees the faces of more remote acquaintances. Miranda points to the far corner where a table for two is unoccupied, incredibly. He leads the way through the narrow aisles between overcrowded tables. Many customers are standing. They are especially congregated near the long wooden counter, to Fische's and Miranda's left as they wade to their small table. He nods to faces he recognizes. Some return the gesture. They take the unclaimed seats.

Fische leans forward. "As crowded as it is, I don't see too many people I know."

Miranda's thin eyebrows flare once to demonstrate her comprehension. The near-smile she has had since entering the coffeehouse is unwavering.

It seems they have arrived between sets of an acoustic folk band. A trio, with their six- and twelve-string guitars, step into the tiny stage area in the back of the coffeehouse, and the leader—a black-haired woman of Asian descent—speaks into the microphone. "The opening set was our 'family' portion; now we're going to perform some material that is more 'adult.' I hope no one is offended."

There is laughter from the crowd. Fische looks across the table at Miranda, who has twisted around to see the performers. Great, he thinks. Miranda turns back toward him and her expression is unchanged. Placid, contented.

They listen to a song, then another. Some of the lyrics have obscenities but nothing a teenager hasn't heard a hundred times,

Fische assures himself. At the end of the second song he leans across the table. "Would you like something to drink?" He is hoping to find someone he knows.

Miranda answers over the applause. "A latté would be great. I have some money."

"That's all right." Fische is standing.

"Thanks."

The coffeehouse is even more crowded than when they arrived. It takes him several minutes to reach the counter and order two lattés. Meanwhile he scans for familiar faces; but now he recognizes no one in the dark, smoky room. He carefully returns to the table with the hot ceramic mugs. He tries not to act surprised when he finds that Miranda has lit a cigarette. The half-empty pack is on the table.

"Here you go," he says.

Miranda blows smoke up and toward the wall. "Thank you."

He sits and is about to explain how he hasn't found anyone to introduce her to when a hand touches his shoulder. "Mr. Fische!"

It is Brenda Schnelling, the chair of the English department at the college.

"Hello—" he says, not knowing what to call her.

"How do you like the music?" Brenda Schnelling is heavy boned, blond, about fifty. Normally she wears dark suits; it is strange to see her in blue jeans and a college sweatshirt.

"It's great." He recalls hearing that she has become divorced. Involuntarily he looks at the glowing white band on her finger where the ring had been. He wonders if his own mark is so visible.

Brenda Schnelling says, "I was looking for some friends but it's hard to find anyone in this crowd."

Fische hesitates. "You're welcome to join us until your friends show."

"Well . . . if you don't mind. I *am* tired of orbiting." She turns and speaks to the group behind her who has an extra chair. Then, using the hand that isn't holding the coffee mug, she straightens the chair around. Fische half stands and tries to appear to help.

When Brenda Schnelling is seated, Fische introduces her to Miranda. "We both work part-time at the public library," he explains, "and Miranda is an aspiring writer." He hopes that Miranda looks older, smoking and drinking coffee; then, instantly recalling the scandal at the college, he hopes she doesn't look older.

Brenda Schnelling and Miranda shake hands. "What do you write?" asks the older woman.

"Stories and poems. Right now mostly poems."

Fische thinks, Please don't mention your high-school class. . . . He listens anxiously to the conversation for several minutes and realizes that a camaraderie has developed between the two. Was it because of their being female? he wonders. Brenda Schnelling is literally old enough to be Miranda's mother. Yet here they are chatting like old friends—classmates at a reunion—after only ten minutes of knowing each other.

Brenda Schnelling is giving Miranda her office number and telling her to bring her writing by some time—"Really!"—when one of her missing friends comes up from behind.

"Here you are, Bea. We were about to give you up!" The friend, a woman whom Fische does not recognize from the college, awkwardly hugs Brenda Schnelling around the shoulders. "We have a table over there." She motions nebulously over the crowd. "We've been saving you a place."

Brenda Schnelling smiles as she stands with her empty mug. "Thank you, Mr. Fische, Miranda, for taking care of me." As she pushes her chair into the table she adds to Miranda, "Do that."

"I will. Thanks."

Brenda Schnelling and her friend are absorbed into the crowd.

Fische drinks his latté, in spite of a slightly bitter taste. Miranda appears to be quite pleased, moving her head with the rhythm of the folk band, smoking cigarette after cigarette: a part of the adult coffeehouse scene. They don't bother to talk over the music. Fische holds onto a small piece of satisfaction. He has done what he promised. Miranda is introduced.

When the band finishes its set—with a song about abortion from the point of view of the fetus—Fische says, "Even though it's the weekend I have an early day tomorrow. Shall we go?"

Miranda blows smoke and puts out her cigarette. "All right."

They leave the coffeehouse and walk up Paris Street toward the nearest bus stop. A colder breeze has stirred and Fische hopes it is cleaning him of the coffeehouse smell. Buildings stand on either side like the dark walls of a canyon.

"Thank you, Mr. Fische. That was fun." Miranda seems the teenage girl again.

They come to the bus stop, where an older couple waits beneath the shingled canopy. There is no one else around.

"Here we are," says Fische. The older couple does not acknowledge them. The bus has not arrived.

"Mr. Fische, don't you live near here?"

"Yes—a few blocks that way." He waves toward the east, toward the college's campus.

"It's still early yet. You want to get some wine or something and go back to your place? I have some money."

Fische is startled. "No . . . not tonight . . . no, I don't think that'd be a good idea." He wishes for the rumbling squeak of the bus.

Miranda looks down at the poorly lighted sidewalk. "I'm sorry." She has regressed beyond adolescence now; she shows the hurt of a little girl.

"Don't be sorry. I appreciate the thought." It is true, but it doesn't brighten her mood.

Miranda looks up, avoiding Fische's eyes, and pretends to search the canyon-wall buildings for something important.

Soon the bus arrives and he watches Miranda walk through its lighted interior until she chooses a seat—on the opposite side. Then Fische walks away from the idling bus, through a cloud of diesel fumes as transparent and persistent as a dream.

IN HIS SLEEP Fische believes he hears the high winds of a storm, but realizes, awake, that it is only the train running past. And he realizes there will be no more sleep this night. He uses the bathroom and comes back to his cramped bedroom to dress: the same pants he wore to the coffeehouse but a clean T-shirt and sweater. He thinks of Miranda's invitation. Was she high on a dose of maturity and merely wanted to extend the rush a while longer? Or was it some awkward attempt at seduction?

He looks at his rumpled single bed and tries to imagine Miranda there. The picture won't materialize. Instead he sees Kate, younger but not prettier. It is not imagination, however; it is memory.

Fische walks through his dark apartment, deftly missing the stacks and stacks of books and papers and magazines. He finds his overcoat on the back of the couch. It smells badly, but it's the only heavy coat he owns. He feels the inside pocket to make sure the notepad and pen are still there. There is an all-night café on Fifth Street—college people and cops.

On his way out the door he thinks of the box of Kate's things and he considers taking it outside to throw away. But after a moment he does nothing with it.

The night is indeed cold. He turns up his coat collar and puts his hands in his pockets. He likes the feeling, after months of heat and humidity. He takes a detour through the campus and follows a lighted path between the college library and the westside dormitories. Fische notices the peeling paint on the war-built, married-student housing. Then he cuts back onto Third Street and heads in the direction of the café. On the river a barge blows its mournful horn.

A rare car passes on the street. And Fische feels the city's loneliness, like a friend's.

He sees something move on the sidewalk several yards ahead; a cat, he guesses. But then it passes briefly through a band of yellow light and Fische sees it is too big for a cat. And it does not move like a stray dog. It seems to vanish in the shadow of a hedge. He comes to the spot and is surprised by the small child standing there. The child releases a fearful sob and hurries on ahead of Fische. In better light he sees that the child, three or four, is a black-haired little girl wearing only a pair of underpants. She half runs on stubby, unsure legs.

"Wait . . . stop!"

She runs faster.

He thinks he must pick her up. But that would surely scare her—and what if someone comes by then and assumes the worst? A divorced man out in the middle of the night chasing down a virtually naked little girl. He remembers his lunatic reflection in the bathroom mirror.

Without even looking she crosses a street that is quite busy in the daytime.

"Hold on . . . please . . . stop! It's all right." A car passes behind Fische and he tries to wave it down, but the driver appears to pay no attention.

He closes the gap between the girl and him. She is beyond crying now. She moans, almost an animal sound, in desperation, in terror. She stops for an instant and looks around wildly, at Fische, at the high buildings, back at Fische, then runs on. He is within thirty feet—not running but walking unnaturally fast. The little girl has taken him away from the café and they are in a section of the city he doesn't know well at night. They are going toward the riverfront. I have to do something, Fische thinks. A block ahead another car passes and again he tries to stop it, flapping his arms, shouting. The car doesn't even slow. A barge horn sounds again on the river, which is only a blackness between the corridor of buildings; the horn is close.

The little girl slows to a walk. Fische trails her, ten feet. She continues to emit the desperate moans but they are weaker, almost below perception.

They have come to a small plaza with concrete benches surrounding a fountain with arcs of water colored by lights. Perhaps it was the sound of the water that attracted the little girl. She crawls onto a bench, which has to feel like a block of ice, and instantly falls asleep. Fische approaches her cautiously, as if she is a hibernating animal. Her sleep breathing is regular. She lies in a fetal position, shivering. Her bare skin is dark against the cement bench. Fische removes his coat and wraps it around her. She is so small—smaller than he realized—that he can double the coat over her. Even this does not seem like enough. He removes his sweater and pillows it under her head. He feels the silkiness of her hair on his fingers.

Now what? he wonders. Surely someone will come along and help him with his burden. It is only a matter of time. He looks at his watch: two, two and a half hours until daybreak. The night sky is clear. He recognizes Ursa Major and Minor dipping in the lavender blackness. Fische rubs the cold out of his arms and looks at the sleeping little girl. Then he sits on an adjacent bench to begin his patient vigil.

When the Night Is New

I MUST GIVE CREDIT where it's due: this is my brother's story, and I've heard Randy tell it in bits and pieces a dozen times—altering the details slightly depending on his mood, his depth of intoxication and, of course, his audience. Bartenders are natural storytellers, I think, even part-time bartenders. Randy was the graveyard jock, midnight to five a.m., at WGBQ Radio but Thursday through Sunday afternoons he kept bar at the Sportsman's Club in Galesburg, Illinois.

The Sportsman's was an old-fashioned tavern with a brass-trimmed oval bar surrounded by anchored stools with real leather seats. Against the walls were small square tables, and on each was a candle in a red bowl and an amber ashtray. On the walls were regal-looking paints of sports scenes: baseball, horseracing, football, golf. . . . Sports as noble ceremonies. The jukebox, which was a hulking thing between the cigarette machine and men's room, glowed purple and orange, and didn't offer a song recorded before 1965—lost of Sinatra. In fact, it was an unwritten house rule that whenever "New York, New York" was selected, everyone in the place had to sing along with Old Blue Eyes. Sweet nostalgia clouded the air like tobacco smoke.

I've never been much of a drinker but on Sundays I'd drive down to Galesburg to shoot the breeze with Randy. He's three years older and back then, when he was tending bar at the Sportsman's, he was thirty-four. It was 1985 but he'd looked the same since the Nixon administration: shaggy brown hair down over his collar, generous hunks of sideburns, a handlebar mustache, and wire-rimmed glasses with circular lenses. If it hadn't been for all that unruly hair, we probably could've passed for twins, a pointless joke we often pulled on strangers when we were growing up. During the Sportsman's period, Randy often chided me for being too clean-cut; I wore glasses, but they had trendy reddish brown frames with lenses that turned dark in the sunlight.

"A disc jockey is supposed to look like a refugee from Woodstock," I argued. "I couldn't get away with it in my profession. Junior high history teachers need to be conservative—it's expected."

He'd sort of half laugh, half grunt disapprovingly, then return his attention to tending bar. He was always under the watchful eye of the Sportsman's owner and main bartender, Wendell White, who was known to everybody as Whitey. He'd probably had the nickname since childhood but when we knew him it was particularly appropriate because his crewcut was virgin white and as thick as carpeting. His hair color must have been about the only way he'd changed since his Marine days (Whitey did tours in both Korea and Vietnam). He was leaner and more muscular than most twenty-year-olds, with a torso as solid as a side of beef, and thick simian arms. His physical condition was something of a marvel to me. Maybe Whitey was a dynamo of activity during the week but on Sundays, when I saw him, he sat on the patron side of the bar drinking glass after glass of dark beer and popping salty peanuts still in their skins. He was one of these guys who wore a short-sleeve shirt year-round, jacketless in all seasons. If a snowstorm escalated to blizzard conditions, Whitey might show up at the Sportsman's wearing a windbreaker—unzipped. A curious thing about Whitey was that he didn't seem to be very interested in sports. You'd think that a big ex-Marine who owned a bar called the Sportsman's

Club would be a regular sports junkie, but in actuality his favorite topic was the Civil War. You know they type—they can't get enough of North-South trivia. There ought to be a special term for such people, maybe "Civil War-philes," or fancier still, "bellumphiles." I never tried it but I bet if somebody blurted out "Antietam!" Whitey would respond without hesitation, "September seventeenth, eighteen-sixty-two—McClellan versus Lee—bloodiest single day of the war—over ten thousand killed—the beginning of the end for the Confederacy. . . ." Like a War-between-the-States talking encyclopedia.

(By the way, I'm not a bellumphile myself; it's just that one Sunday afternoon Whitey and his buddies were hot on the Battle of Antietam—or the Battle of Sharpsburg, the Rebs' name for it apparently. If Little Mac had done this, if The Old Man had ordered that, if the weather had been such and such . . . all afternoon.)

For Randy, Whitey's approval was important because the money Randy made at the Sportsman's was for his "getting out of town" fund. He wanted to be a jock in a big market somewhere, east or west, it didn't matter. He used to say he'd "spin polka music, if the location is right." Randy always had a resume and demo tape in the mail and when the opportunity came along, he didn't intend to be short on cash for moving expenses.

Maybe that's why I was so dutiful about driving to Galesburg on Sundays: I never knew which visit to the Sportsman's Club was going to be my last. Also, when my wife became pregnant with our first child, we agreed that we needed to get our fill of "personal freedom" time before we became parents. For her time, she chose shopping with her girlfriends on Sunday afternoons; I of course elected to visit the Sportsman's—a forty-five minute drive from Moline. You probably know my wife, Jennifer Graham. She's the co-anchor of the evening news on KWQC-TV, and she hosts "Quad-Cities Times" talk show Friday nights at nine-thirty. Jen's locally famous for being the red-headed newswoman on the leading edge of chic but tasteful fashion. Frankly, she could go with the networks in a second but Jennifer says she prefers local news. She cites the "big fish in a little pond" theory. But I think she stays put because of me. Jen knows I have no desire to move to Chicago or St. Louis or whatever metropolis such a change would send her. I'll probably never know.

Oh yeah . . . my brother's story.

I don't know if I believe in fate but the way Randy tells this story, there certainly seems to be some cosmic force at work. As Randy puts it, the Sportsman's Club had been going about its business in pretty much the same way for fifty years—untouched by changes of ownership, foreign wars, slumping economies, Democrat or Republican in the White House. Customers came in to drink their drinks, smoke their smokes, talk, laugh, cry and occasionally slip a coin in the jukebox. Then in the course of about two hours one Friday—a warm spring day in April, with Ronald Reagan in the White House—it all began to change. Randy was an hour or so from ending his shift, one to five p.m., and Whitey had already arrived to prepare for the end-of-the-workweek crowd: men and women with downtown jobs who came in to mix with the regular bunch of retirees and vets. Randy guessed that the average age of the Sportsman's patrons dropped from sixty-five to fifty-five on Friday and Saturday nights.

There were about twenty customers in the tavern that day in April, half of them at the brass-trimmed bar itself, when Mr. Oliver Hodge walked through the door and squinted in the relative darkness. His bald head reflected the red of an electric Budweiser sign in the window. Of course, Randy didn't know then who he was or why he was there, but it seemed pretty clear he wasn't a customer. He wasn't the Sportsman's type. He was too young for one thing, younger than Randy, and too . . . clean. In the Sportsman's, one had to be prepared for sticking an elbow in something moist or sharing an ashtray if need be. I'm not saying the Sportsman's Club was dirty; it's just that there wasn't a battalion of crisply dressed waitresses patrolling the premises. In fact, there wasn't one waitress—just the bartender on duty.

The stranger approached Randy, the only employee in sight. "Hello," he said stiffly. "I'm looking for the owner, Mr. White. Are you Mr. White?"

"No, he's in the storeroom," said Randy, twisting with a wave of his arm to point the way.

Mr. Hodge stood there a moment, apparently trying to determine if Randy meant for him to seek out the storeroom, but before he had decided what to do Whitey materialized out of the gloom of the back of the tavern. His bare arms were wrapped around a peach crate full of supplies. Boxes of napkins, jars of green olives, and large cans of nuts probably protruded over the top.

Randy said, "May I present Mr. White. Whitey, this is—"

"Hodge, Oliver Hodge." He began to raise his hand as a reflex but realized that Whitey's hand, which looked as large as baseball mitts spread around the corners of the crate, were occupied.

"What can I do for you?" asked Whitey as he lifted the load higher on his chest to maneuver himself behind the bar.

"I'm with the DDC, the Downtown Development Committee. Perhaps you recall receiving a letter from our group?"

According to Randy, recognition seemed to flash across Whitey's face but it was hard to tell, with his bending over to unload the crate and the dim lighting. "No, I'm sorry. I don't." Whitey thumped a box of napkins on the bar top.

"That's all right. It was probably held up in the mail." Mr. Hodge slid halfway onto a bar stool, giving his body a sort of twisted, malformed appearance. "We're working on revitalizing the downtown area—to bring back some business lost to the mall and other cities." He waited for a response but Whitey seemed engrossed in stocking the bar shelves. "We'd like to promote the downtown area as a historic district, and we've decided to begin the process with Seminary Street, and specifically this block of Seminary. It's one of the few in the downtown area that is shoulder-to-shoulder with healthy businesses. No vacant store fronts to be found. As a bonus, it's just two blocks from the Knox College campus, a Lincoln-Douglas debate site you know, and three miles from Carl Sandburg's home."

"Sounds great," said Whitey, counting boxes of straws with his index finger. "I could use the increased traffic."

"Yes, well," said Mr. Hodge, squirming on his stool, "we plan to remodel the building fronts for a common antique-looking motif, and replace the streetlights with gas-lamp replicas, and maybe re-do the sidewalks with synthetic cobblestones." Mr. Hodge blotted the sweat from his glossy forehead with a cocktail napkin. "The problem is, these improvements will not be inexpensive, so we are asking that the business owners make an investment in the project—fifty percent of the project's costs. We anticipate that owners will be able to recoup their investment via increased business within eighteen months, after which time profits could rise by as much as forty-five percent annually."

Whitey continued his inventory for a moment, then looked Mr. Hodge in the face for the first time. "You anticipate, do you?" Whitey smiled and plunked an empty shot glass on the bar top. "Your group wants historic, huh? Antique motif? Look around you, Mr. Hodge, my place isn't just historic-*looking*—it *is* history. Why should I pay to change my real historic bar to a fake historic bar? Tell me that, Mr. Hodge."

"Please understand, Mr. White, we're only talking about the exterior. The interior is fine . . . it's wonderful—I could only hope to own such an establishment. But our consultants believe that to attract customers we need a consistency of appearance. One building here, one building there, a piece of sidewalk here, a streetlamp there won't work. It would be too . . . incongruous."

Whitey's face turned scarlet beneath the glow of his crewcut. "Maybe if the city council lowered taxes on local businessmen, allowing them to do more promotion and more self-improvement, and maybe if the city stepped up its trash collection and street-cleaning efforts, more people would be attracted to downtown naturally."

Mr. Hodge's courage seemed to be bolstered by Whitey's attack. "Well, Mr. White, since you brought up the city council, I should remind you—as our letter indicated—that by recently adopted ordinance, business owners can have a special tax levied against them to help in the financing of the project—if need be—but of course we prefer voluntary cooperation."

The shot glass on the bar disappeared in Whitey's tightening grip. "You think you can force me to pay for your . . . project, just go ahead and try. I think the ACLU would be interested in that lawsuit, and the Small Business Administration and, hell, even the VA. You tell the city council that, Mr. Hodge."

Oliver Hodge slid down from the stool. "I guess I know your sentiment. I hope you reconsider, Mr. White. We'll be in touch." He was quick to leave the Sportsman's, as everyone in the place must have overheard the argument and stared after Mr. Hodge until he was gone. Somebody said they knew Hodge, that his father owned the one ritzy restaurant in town, the Blue Palms, and that Oliver was little more than a glorified, overpaid errand boy there.

Among those sitting at the bar, close to the confrontation, were the two more regular of the tavern's regulars. There was Phil, the retired barber—a sallow-skinned, twitchy sort of guy. He'd given his barber shop, which was just around the corner, to his daughter when he retired. He knew she was going to make some fundamental changes, like renaming it Phyllis's Salon, and he assumed she'd be offering the usual female services: perms, tints and trims. Phil thought she was rushing things when she added false fingernails and ear piercing to her repertoire; he was aghast to discover that it wasn't just females coming in for these procedures. Within six months, Phyllis was offering punk hairstyles and temporary tattoos. For Black customers, she was beading and braiding, and shaving in initials. According to Randy, on the day Mr. Hodge showed up Phil had been bemoaning the fact that Phyllis was going to lease his old shop and move into a bigger space at the mall. "A dog groomer is going to rent my old place," he'd been saying. "A damn dog groomer!"

On Phil's right that day was Harve, a thin gray-haired advertising man who slouched over the bar top like a vulture. He was just two years from retirement when the newspaper he sold for decided to update its advertising department with computers. Twenty-five years of cutting and pasting ads together—scissors, rulers, rubber cement—and now he'd have to learn to punch keys and crop electronic rectangles on a little screen. Harve described the situation as "a crock of crap." I guess Harve decided to retire ahead of schedule, even though it cost him some pension. You might know his son, Dal McBride, the pro bowler. In the mid eighties he was doing well—eleventh on the money list in '86—so Harve went along on the PBA tour to help Dal, who was divorced, with his three kids. Chronic tendinitis ended Dal's competitive career in 1990. He's running a pro shop in a big bowling center in St. Paul, according to Randy, who isn't sure whatever happened to Harve.

All of that was in the future, though, when Mr. Hodge threw a wet blanket on the Friday festivities at the Sportsman's. When the bald-headed man was gone, Whitey just said, "Son of a bitch," not like he was really mad, and not like he was calling Mr. Hodge that—it was just a commentary on things in general. Whitey busied himself with more preparations and in no time five o'clock was there. Randy left when his shift ended, so what happened that evening he had to hear about from Phil and Harve.

As the story goes, the usual Friday afternoon crowd assembled, and by the time the sun went down, Whitey was in fairly good humor, seeming to forget about Mr. Hodge's project.

About seven p.m. or so, a group of Knox College kids came in the Sportsman's. The Knox students usually drank at the Cherry Street Lounge, but apparently it had become too crowded, which happened a half dozen times a year. Knox kids were easy to spot: pony tails, Greenpeace shirts, ripped blue jeans, sandals or hiking boots; and these traits were unisex. That April night, maybe forced from their usual watering hole by spring break and the arrival home of hundreds of kids from other colleges, seven or eight Knox students bought a couple pitchers of beer from Whitey, squashed themselves around a corner table, and blended, more or less, into the texture of the Sportsman's crowd.

Everything was all right for a while, said Phil and Harve, until one of the Knox group wandered over to the jukebox. It took a second to determine gender but it was a girl—dark shoulder-length hair, with a loose sheep-skin vest over her t-shirt and jeans. Bess (or Beth—her name was kind of learned later from somebody—Randy usually goes with "Bess") studied the music selections for several minutes; her face and bare arms glowed with the orange and purple of the jukebox. She removed a quarter from the pocket of her vest, slid it into the machine and punched up her choice. In a moment, the beginning beats of Sinatra's "New York, New York" spread over the crowd.

Whitey, Phil and Harve began to croon simultaneously, then a second later the whole bar wanted to be a part of New York, New York. Bess had spun around to the singers. The light from the jukebox appeared to linger on her enraptured face. She must have felt like she'd been transported onto the set of some fifties musical, the kind of film to which her parents might have gone on a date. Leaning back against the jukebox, Bess began swaying to the music: the patrons bellowed, almost on key, about making a new start in old New York.

When the final notes of the song were absorbed into the smoky air, Whitey, Phil and Harve broke into warm laughter. Phil and Harve said it was a relief to see Whitey laugh. They didn't know how much the earlier encounter bothered him. "That felt good," Whitey said, almost to himself, as he finished drying a long-stem glass. He bent over to place it on a shelf but Whitey jerked straight up when "New York, New York" started again. Bess had inserted another quarter. This time when she turned around the look on her face was expectant. Whitey led into the song but it didn't feel as good.

You can imagine how it was the third and fourth times . . . yes, four times in a row. Whitey said at some point that he felt like an organ-grinder's monkey. The next night, Bess and her group came to the Sportsman's Club along with about twenty more Knox students. She selected "New York, New York" before she even sat down. Six times Whitey and the crowd sang along with Frank Sinatra. Six times.

Randy said that for thirty years, or however long the house rule had been around, three or four times a month was the average. When I drove down Sunday and Randy told me what had happened with the Knox students, I asked quietly why Whitey went along with it, why he just didn't refuse after the second or third time (Whitey was on the far side of the bar from me, out of earshot if I spoke softly). Randy said, "He told Phil and Harve he wasn't going to let some skinny college kid ruin the tradition." Whitey figured Bess and her friends would lose interest after a while and things would return to normal. If I recall correctly, that Sunday Randy didn't even mention Oliver Hodge and his committee's project. Maybe the regulars at the Sportsman's didn't take his threat seriously, or maybe the "New York, New York" thing just overshadowed it. I don't know.

Maybe Randy did mention it and I'm just forgetting. That was kind of a stressful time for me: the doctor had recently informed Jennifer that we weren't expecting our first child—we were in fact expecting our first *two*. Jennifer had already had a baby shower and received a highchair and an infant swing and a stroller, but now we were going to need *two* highchairs and *two* swings and a *double* stroller. Yeah, no one can fault me if I don't remember everything exactly right from that time.

I do recall that the Sportsman's Club became a hectic place in the days that followed. Every night more and more Knox students filled the tavern, mercilessly abandoning their old haunt by the dozens. Randy said that by the next weekend you could fire a gun in the Cherry Street Lounge without a worry. The increased traffic in the Sportsman's didn't equal increased revenue, though. The Knox bunch drove away several regulars, and on weeknights they ordered mostly nonalcoholic beverages, coffee and mineral water and soda. About every thirty minutes or so, a long-haired kid punched up "New York, New York" on the jukebox. Whitey, Phil and Harve were actually getting hoarse. By Friday, they were doing little more than mumbling Sinatra's lyrics.

To make matters worse, Whitey had also received a letter from the Downtown Development Committee that apparently cited a couple of related eminent domain cases and estimated Whitey's half of the remodeling expenses. Randy wasn't sure of the exact figure but he heard Whitey tell Harve it was "over eight grand."

I almost didn't drive down that Sunday because it was raining so fiercely but Randy had told me on the telephone about the recent events and I wanted to see the effects for myself. Plus Randy had been contacted by a radio station in Las Vegas with a contemporary Christian music format. Yes, a Christian music station in Vegas! They were going to need a new overnight jock beginning in June. The station manager had gotten Randy's name and demo tape from a friend at another station. Randy was honest—how could one not be?—and told him the position wasn't exactly what he had in mind, but if he hadn't heard from another station by May fifteenth . . . et cetera. The station manager appreciated Randy's frankness.

The Sportsman's Club was especially gloomy when I arrived

that Sunday. Rainwater dripped from my overcoat, leaving a trail on the floor as I walked toward my stool at the bar. My brother automatically grabbed a glass and went to the beer tap but I stopped him with a wave of my hand. "I think I'll have coffee. Maybe just sit the pot in my lap."

Randy placed a steaming cup in front of me.

"What's new? Where's Whitey?" I asked, wrapping my hands around the warm ceramic cup.

"Right over there, Hawkeye." Randy nodded toward the far side of the bar, where Whitey usually was on Sundays. Sure enough, there was Whitey, but I hadn't recognized him because he was wearing a gray cardigan sweater. There in the pale light from the windows, Whitey looked more like an ex-librarian than an ex-Marine. I had to strain to hear his conversation with Phil and Harve, and it didn't seem like they were discussing Civil War military strategy. I caught something about "Appomattox," and later I heard "Ford's Theatre," and later still the word "carpetbaggers" floated far enough in the stale air to reach me.

The storm had kept the Knox students away, I guess. It had kept everybody away except the five of us. I cut my visit short that afternoon and left after my second cup of coffee. It was a pretty depressing place and going back out in the rain and wind wasn't really that unattractive.

The week that followed was just as bleak—more so maybe. Supposedly on Tuesday evening, on the third rendition of what Whitey had started calling "that damn Sinatra song," he and Phil and Harve were beaten to the opening line—the one about spreading the news—by some Knox kid, but another one yelled, "Hey, the old guys are supposed to begin!" I'm not sure I believe this part of the story. Randy has only included this detail twice in the versions I've heard. In one instance, Bess was the student who started out of turn, and in another she was the one who yelled the "old guys" remark. I know if it happened at all, Randy had to learn about it secondhand.

He was, however, an eyewitness to Mr. Hodge's second visit, which came Friday at about two o'clock. He said to Randy, "I have an appointment with Mr. White. Is he available, please?"

"In the office in back." Randy had been wondering why Whitey was there so early.

Mr. Hodge's step was noticeably livelier than when he had exited the Sportsman's on his first visit. Whatever business he had with Whitey it didn't take long, only about fifteen minutes. Mr. Hodge was grinning when he passed back by the bar. He stopped and offered his hand to Randy. "You must be Mr. Graham. We'll have to talk one of these days soon. I'm very interested in keeping you on when I take over the place."

"Take over the place?" Randy steadied himself against the bar.

"Yes, Mr. White has sold me the Sportsman's, change of ownership effective June one." He looked around the room like a feudal lord surveying his lands. "Well, I've got to be going, but we'll talk soon. So long."

Whitey was still in his office an hour later when Phil came in. Before he could even sit down Randy blurted out the news, to which Phil said, "No, you're shittin me. Hodge? No way." Thirty minutes later, Harve's response was virtually the same.

But just then, Whitey came to the bar. He could tell by the silence and the looks on everyone's face that they knew. He sat on the stool to Harve's left. "My brother-in-law, my sister's husband, you know the ones that live in Pennsylvania, bought a restaurant a while back, and he's been after me to come out and manage the bar. I've gotten kind of tired of being the one to pay all the bills and worry about the taxes and hassle with the contractors," said Whitey. "It's a beautiful location, too—less than thirty miles from Gettysburg." The big ex-Marine sat there for a minute, moving his jaw like he was chewing something. He looked around the bar then pulled up the sleeve of his sweater to check his watch. "Damn Knox kids won't be here for another hour or so. Reach in the register there, Randy, and pull out a handful of quarters."

My brother flipped a white rag over his shoulder and did as he was instructed. He poured about five dollars worth of silver coins into Whitey's enormous palms. Whitey stood and shoved the wad of metal into his pocket except for one quarter, which he flipped in the air once. "There's no harm in modifying a tradition slightly." He marched over to the jukebox and peered through its glass for a few seconds. Randy said the thing reflected Whitey's image like an expensive mirror. "Ah, perfect." Whitey popped in the coin, made his choice, then removed his cardigan as he walked back toward the bar.

The opening chords of Tony Bennett's "I'll Be Seeing You" resonated through the tavern. "Listen close, gentlemen," said Whitey. "We've only got about forty-five minutes to memorize it."

Tony Bennett began singing about old familiar places. . . .

Whitey sang the first line robustly, then his baritone voice dwindled to a mumble, occasionally flaring up when he came to a word he remembered: carousel, trees, wishing.

As soon as the song ended—with the line about looking at the moon but seeing her—Whitey slipped another quarter in the jukebox. He and Harve and Phil and Randy did better this time. A dollar-fifty later Whitey felt confident the quartet knew the lyrics. It was that simple: the tradition, which had endured at least a generation, had been modified. That was one word Randy used, *modified*; in other versions of the story he's used *altered* and *adjusted* and *refined*, but he's never used *changed*.

There was nothing to do but sit back and wait for the Knox College kids to pump their parents' money into the glowing jukebox. When Randy's shift was over, he decided to stay awhile and see what happened. He said that Whitey had more zip behind the bar than Randy had ever seen. When he picked a glass off the shelf, he flipped it in the air . . . when he put an olive or a cherry in a drink, he actually tossed it in from a few inches away.

All the while, Knox students filed into the Sportsman's Club and found their favorite tables, ordered their favorite beverages. Now this is another one of those details I'm not sure I believe, because during the two weeks since the girl named Bess (or Beth) had stumbled onto the tavern's house rule, dozens of different Knox kids had chosen "New York, New York" on the jukebox—but now tonight she was back, according to Randy, sheep-skin vest and all. Like I said, I'm not sure it's true but it does give his narrative a neat cyclical structure.

Bess had learned patience in those two weeks. She drank an entire glass of beer before sauntering up to the jukebox. She confidently placed a coin in the slot and punched in the song's code. The crowd, which was mostly Knox students, actually hushed when the first notes emitted from the speakers. Bess turned toward Whitey, whom she knew only as the big bartender who always initiated the singing.

Whitey was drying the inside of a shot glass with a white rag. He smiled at her—a wide defiant grin—as Frank Sinatra's buttery voice filled the room. A couple of kids somewhere in the back belched out a word or two before they realized no one else was singing. Randy, who sat more or less in between Whitey and Bess, said that they stared at each other during the entire song. Cold, hard, calculating stares. There were maybe a hundred people in the Sportsman's but nobody uttered a sound while "New York, New York" played; nobody so much as sneaked a sip of beer.

There's another distinguishing characteristic about Knox students I didn't mention before: they're smart. Apparently in the three minutes or so that Bess and Whitey locked gazes, like prizefighters waiting for the opening bell, the young woman figured out what had happened. She immediately deposited a coin and made another selection, "Send in the Clowns" in some versions of Randy's story, "Solitaire" in others. Probably both are right. Bess spent two bucks trying to find the correct song before she gave up and returned to her table. Meanwhile Whitey polished glassware until it gleamed.

After that night things happened fast, as if the Sportsman's old house rule had been holding back the flow of time and when it was altered everything rushed forth like floodwater through a broken wall of sandbags. Randy wound up taking the job in Las Vegas at the Christian rock station and was gone by the end of May. He offered to stay until Whitey's last day, to help Phil and Harve throw a going-away party, but Whitey didn't want one. He said nobody made a big deal of it when he came to Galesburg in the late sixties—when soldiers, especially Marines, weren't very popular—so nobody needed to make a big deal of his leaving. In August Jennifer gave birth to the twins, a month early. Identical girls. She named "Baby A" Barbara, for her idol, Barbara Walters; and I named "Baby B" Wendy, for the heroine in my favorite children's story, *Peter Pan*—at least I think that's why I like the name. Until I began telling my brother's story, I'd forgotten that Whitey's real name was Wendell.

Barbara and Wendy are going to be in the fourth grade this fall. You should see them. They're little versions of their mother, red hair and emerald eyes, except that when they get upset with their father, the girls get an expression on their faces that looks just like Randy's when he's chiding me about something—like my clean-cut image.

A couple of weeks ago Randy was back to visit. The desert climate suits him; I swear he hasn't changed one bit since the day Nixon proclaimed he wasn't a crook. Randy is dating a twenty-five-year-old showgirl named Reneé, whom he met at a wedding reception at the Sands Hotel. She was a bridesmaid and she struck up a conversation with Randy when she discovered he was in radio. Apparently Reneé's already giving serious thought to her next career, knowing that she won't be able to dance forever—the knees will fail, the hips will widen . . . but that's another story.

Anyway, while Randy was back Jen went to Galesburg to do a feature on the town's annual Railroad Days, which are always the first week in June. My brother and I took the girls and rode in the back of the news van with the cameraman's equipment. While Jennifer and the camera guy went around interviewing people, Randy and the girls and I wandered among the food booths and other temporary concessions in the closed downtown streets. It was a typically hot summer day, so we decided to take Barbara and Wendy inside somewhere to cool off. We happened to be on Seminary Street, which looks great by the way, with all its pseudo-historic businesses. There's a quaint little bistro, and a rare-book shop, and a children's vintage clothing store, and a place that specializes in gourmet cooking utensils, and at the end of the block we were happy to find the Sportsman's Club. We felt funny taking nine-year-olds into a tavern but we were curious. As long as it was air-conditioned and had cold drinks, the girls wouldn't care.

At first, while our eyes were still adjusting to the dimness, the Sportsman's looked just the same. Later Randy and I talked about it, and we both thought we saw Phil and Harve sitting at the bar when we walked in. But when our pupils became sufficiently dilated, we saw it wasn't them. And we saw other things too. Instead of those regal paintings of sports scenes on the walls, there were shiny framed posters—one of Michael Jordan poised in midair over a basketball goal; one of the Oakland A's José Canseco swinging a baseball bat with his face twisted into an intense grimace; one of the Australian golfer Greg Norman lining up a putt as his white-blond hair flows from beneath his trademark panama-style hat.

Barbara and Wendy headed straight for the jukebox, probably because it was the closest thing around to a video game. It looked like the same one Randy and I remembered but the songs were all changed. The oldest title we recognized was the Beatles'

"Back in the U.S.S.R.": the Fab Four singing about Ukraine girls leaving the West behind. Metallic compact discs, of course; not the old days' black vinyl forty-five RPM records.

The girls had a wonderful time, sitting at the old brass-trimmed bar while a young woman wearing a cheap Cubs baseball jersey served them their lemonades in frosted glasses with brightly colored plastic umbrellas. They borrowed quarter after quarter from their uncle and me to play songs on the jukebox. It was an expensive visit. Songs cost two plays for seventy-five cents. At one point, Randy attempted to entertain his nieces by telling them the story of "New York, New York" and the Knox students and his working there at the Sportsman's Club then, but it was obvious the girls' interest was quickly waning. So he just cut the tale short and let them enjoy their lemonade and song selections. My brother and I watched a soccer match on the big-screen television which was squeezed into a corner; I think it was a team from Cuba versus one from Argentina.

The only way I could get my daughters to leave without a fuss was to promise to bring them back to the Sportsman's soon. We walked out into the bright summer heat and headed toward the throng in Main Street. The synthetic cobblestones were hot beneath our tennis shoes, so Randy and I agreed to piggy-back the girls. They've grown kind of big for piggy-backing, and in no time my brother and I were hunched over like a couple of prehistoric people recently descended from the trees.

Just before we turned the corner off of Seminary Street, Randy suddenly stopped. "Christ," he said, to no one in particular, "not only is John Lennon dead—the Soviet Union doesn't even exist anymore."

Barbara and Wendy were completely baffled but I understood immediately. We hoisted the girls higher on our backs and waded into the crowd to search for their mother among the mass of strangers.

Mix

HE STOPPED HIS CAR in front of the small gray house with darker gray shingles, and was relieved to see that it was in relatively good repair; better repair certainly than the equally small houses on either side—so close it seemed that neighbors reaching from opposing windows could join hands. In the yards were swirls of dirty melting snow and patches of brown grass, reminding him of desert camouflage. There were several cars parked along the narrow broken street, and a few appeared to be fixtures of the neighborhood: chunks of flaking rust, and flat or missing tires. At the end of the block a stubby corroded fire hydrant sat in a skirt of filthy snow.

He wasn't ready to go in yet, so he lighted a cigarette and turned on the radio. Rap music, heavy with bass, vibrated his dashboard speaker. Not his preference, but a news report about the rioting in Los Angeles would be on soon. There were constant reports. At the newspaper office, his computer was flooded with them: three or four updated stories an hour, around the clock.

His computer screen filled with accounts of arson, looting, armed violence, damage estimates, and lists of the dead and injured. Having never been to L.A., the details—streets, landmarks, freeways—meant little to him. But there was one name, one fatality, that he recognized: Charles Mixon. When his obit appeared on the screen to be proofread and coded, he almost didn't make the connection.

The name had nearly faded from his memory, but Charles Mixon himself had remained vivid all these years. Twenty years. The obituary gave no details of his death—just that he was survived locally by his parents, two brothers and an aunt. They all lived across the river in Moline. The body was still in California but the aunt, Mrs. Josephine Mixon, was having an open-house for friends. The address was in a bad part of town, just two blocks up the hill from the Mississippi River.

Its dark choppy water was reflected in his car's rearview mirror.

HE HADN'T SEEN Charles Mixon since 1971, Lincoln Junior High. They had three classes together: art, P.E. and wood shop. Middleton and Mixon, they were alphabetized next to each other in two of them. In art, his cousin Karen Middleton was in between. On the first day they were seated at the same circular table. Around them were the remnants of past classes—finger paintings, coat-hanger mobiles, papier-mâché sculptures. In the center of their table were jars of paint and a white plastic cup with three new brushes. The stick of each thin brush was a different color: yellow, pink and black.

Mrs. Johnson, who wore a smock that was the same shade of brown as her tied-back hair, passed out pieces of paper and told everyone to choose a brush.

"The black one's mine," said Charles Mixon, "cause it's like me." His hand snatched it from the cup. Karen chose the pink one and he was left the yellow brush.

Even though they were cousins, Karen was almost as much of a stranger to him as Charles Mixon was. She lived across town with his uncle's ex-wife. But there was a definitely family resemblance: light, wheat-colored hair; green eyes; and a band of freckles that spilled down the nose and along the cheekbones.

He was an inch or two taller but they were both slightly built.

Mrs. Johnson instructed them to paint something about themselves. "Use whatever colors you like. Pictures, words, symbols . . . whatever you want."

He was still deciding what he wanted to do when Charles announced he was finished. On his paper he had used black to paint three capital letters: MIX.

Mrs. Johnson came to their table. "That's very nice, Charles. Why don't you add some pictures, yourself or people who are important to you."

"Nope. Mix, that's who I am." He stuck his brush back in the plastic cup. Mrs. Johnson moved on to another table. Charles smiled, revealing a gap between his front teeth. Below his left eye was a crooked scar about two inches long, like a dark brown lightning bolt. "What are you staring at?" Charles said to him.

"Nothing. I'm trying to think of something to paint."

"Why don't you make a picture of your ugly, big-eared head and quit looking at me."

He chose red and painted a squiggly line on his paper, then added some more lines until he had a big squiggly TONY.

"That's original," said Charles.

"I'm not done," he lied, and hastily made three red stick people and a boxy two-dimensional car.

"I guess Sister is the painter." Charles scooted his chair closer to Karen, who had used green and light blue to paint a landscape with rolling hills, pine trees and a picket fence that stretched convincingly to infinity; in the sky, billowy clouds formed her name. "Looking good," said Charles, leaning so that his mouth was almost touching Karen's shoulder.

"Thanks," she said, still focused on her artwork.

He was glad Karen had diverted Charles's attention. His parents had taught him to respect all kinds of people, with a special emphasis on respecting black people, but television had taught him things too. On the big black-and-white Zenith, he saw images of Black Panthers, with bushy afros, impenetrable sunglasses and guns. He saw riots. He saw police wearing helmets and carrying clubs. He saw German shepherds straining to attack, until it looked like their thick leashes would snap.

Later, in school, he learned about Selma, Alabama, and Martin Luther King, and police brutality, and the Ku Klux Klan. But back then he only knew that policemen were his friends, and if they were afraid he had reason to be also.

Charles Mixon watched as Karen skillfully painted blackbirds among the clouds of her name.

EVERY DAY CHARLES wore a gray-white T-shirt, jeans and black canvas tennis shoes with scuffed rubber toes to school. In his gym bag Charles had only a pair of blue cotton shorts. It seemed everyone else's bag was stuffed with a clean shirt, shorts, sweatsocks, supporter, and a chalky stick of deodorant. When Coach Rodgers ordered the class into the steam-filled lockerroom with a shrill blow of his whistle, everyone would frantically undress and jam their school clothes into large wire baskets before pulling on their gym things. Charles simply removed his faded jeans and slipped on the blue shorts. At the end of the period, they ran naked through the U-shaped shower before getting back into their regular clothes. Charles refused to shower. The first few days Coach Rodgers tried to persuade Charles it was a good idea—"You ever had a really bad case of jock itch, Mixon?"— but after that he left him alone. There was nothing in Coach Rodgers's chubby face that indicated he was upset with Charles Mixon. Charles was a natural athlete, lean and graceful, and the coach was probably looking forward to basketball season.

After physical education, he and Charles went to wood shop, but not together. He dreaded shop class, but a vocational class was mandatory and "wood shop" sounded less hazardous than "metal shop" and "auto." Mr. Foley, whose bushy gray mustache reeked of cigarette smoke, was having the class make bookends for its first project. It only took a few days for him to fall behind the rest of the class. He was still trying to square his base pieces of wood while other students were sanding, gluing and cutting out ornamental figures on the electric jigsaw.

He wedged a base into a vise and was preparing to plane one side down to his pencil mark. The humming and grating and whining of tools filled the warm air as thickly as the sawdust.

Charles, looking from behind plastic safety glasses, came to his worktable. "Sister called me last night," he said.

He stared at the gap in Charles's teeth.

"She wants old Mix."

He wondered where Mr. Foley was; probably out back sneaking a cigarette behind the big green dumpster.

"I mean, she wants old Mix." Charles squeezed his crotch. "You're done with this, aren't you, Middy?" He took the plane and headed toward his table. About halfway, Charles stopped and turned with that grin. "Hey, who's your friend?" The question was barely audible above the din. Charles waited a moment, then went to his table; satisfied.

A feeling of intense hatred burned in his chest, but it was directed at himself . . . for standing there stupidly, for not even explaining that Karen wasn't his sister. He thought about what Charles said. Of course it was a lie. Karen paid little attention to Charles in art class. She was polite when he complimented her work, which was nearly every day, but she always seemed slightly annoyed by his intrusions—the way she was annoyed by the lack of working space at the tables, and the narrow variety of colors in the paint cabinet.

He went to the tool rack and got another plane, but that day in shop class the pattern of telling vulgar stories about "Sister" and taking tools from him was just beginning. In gym, Charles would trip him from behind and throw the ball at him while Coach Rodgers wasn't looking. After every petty theft, every humiliating attack, Charles smiled that gappy smile and asked that ridiculous question. And he remained frozen in place and mute—paralyzed by Charles's stark aggression.

One day he decided to outsmart Charles by bringing two chisels to his worktable. On cue, Charles approached him. "You've got to talk to Sister for me, Middy. She's killing old Mix, wants to suck it off four and five times in a row. I say, 'No, no, honey, you got to be full by now,' but I can't keep her out of my pants." Charles smiled and took both the chisels.

As Charles sauntered back to his area, he stood shaking, waiting for the question. Charles placed the two chisels on his table, then turned his attention to his project.

He started to relax.

Then, over the whine of the electric sander, Charles called, "Hey, Middy, who's your friend?"

He couldn't bear to look at him, to see that grin. Inside his safety glasses his eyes stung with fear and self-loathing. During those weeks, embarrassed by his cowardice, he didn't tell anyone what was going on.

ON AN UNSEASONABLY warm day in November Coach Rodgers sent the class outside to play flag football. "The fresh air will do you good. Blow the stink off you." Brown leaves somersaulted across the field. The breeze stung his arms as he fell into line along the faint out-of-bounds stripe. The class counted off, one-two-one-two, and he and Charles Mixon were on the same team.

The Ones were given the ball first, and Charles automatically assumed the role of quarterback. In their nine-person huddle Charles made assignments without hesitation. "Go out for a long one, Middy."

When the ball was hiked, he side-stepped the defender and sprinted toward the endzone. He waved his arms; no one was within twenty yards. Charles looked right at him but he threw the ball to another player for a ten-yard gain. When he returned to the huddle, he said, "Let's do it again. I was wide open."

Charles studied him for a few seconds. "You and you go long. You guys go short. You guys stay back and block. Hike the ball, Middy, and make sure they don't rush up the middle. On seven."

The huddle broke, except for him. He stood, partially stooped, in the gusty autumn wind.

Charles stopped and called to him, "You comin, Middy?"

Something deep and ugly fought to free itself from him. It finally sprang forth in a choked voice: "Mother fucker."

Charles came back to him slowly. "Middy. You call me a dirty nigger?"

He looked up . . . startled, afraid, defensive. "No. I did not." His voice quavered slightly.

Coach Rodgers, ignorant of the conflict, yelled from the sideline. "Come on, gentlemen! We don't have all day!"

He walked to the football and set himself in position. Charles said the magic number—"Seven!"—and he hiked it between his legs. He stood up to wait for the rush but the pain he felt next pitched him forward and filled his ears with silence. On his hands and knees, he saw the football wobbling on one end to his right. Charles had thrown the ball into the back of his head. Still in a crouch, he charged Charles Mixon and drilled his throbbing skull into Charles's chest. Their legs tangled and they tumbled to the hard ground.

"Who's your friend? Who's your friend?" Charles snarled until he got a fist in the ear. Charles retaliated by crushing his lip against his teeth. They clenched and rolled, then Coach Rodgers was there, blowing his whistle and dragging them to their feet.

"That's enough!" Coach Rodgers pulled them by their arms toward the school building. Inside the lockerroom, which seemed dark compared to the football field, the coach planted them on separate benches. "Shower up, then get dressed. You boys are headed to the principal's office."

He tasted blood, but just a trace, as he began to undress.

Charles just sat on his bench, motionless.

"I said shower up." Coach Rodgers's cheeks and forehead were crimson.

"Fuck you, old man," said Charles.

The coach yanked him up and clenched his grass-stained shirt. "Get to the shower, mister!" He ripped the shirt from Charles's body as he shoved him forward.

Charles caught himself on a row of wire baskets. They stared at Charles Mixon's back. It was a complex mess of brown and purple scars, and the black scabs of burn marks. Charles knew they were staring. He slowly removed his shoes and socks, then his shorts and underwear.

As he waited for Charles to finish showering, his head ached with the rhythm of his racing pulse and his lip burned, but it was the nausea—the longing to drop to his knees and vomit—that made him utterly miserable.

Coach Rodgers retrieved a shirt from the lost-and-found and placed it, folded, on Charles's bench.

They passed each other in the shower-room door but Charles wouldn't look at him. He found himself hoping Charles would ask that question again, just to hear something besides the ringing in his ears, and the dripping of the showers, and the nervous puttering of the coach. By the time he finished cleaning himself up, Charles was gone—to the principal's office presumably. Coach Rodgers pretended to forget to send him there.

Charles Mixon didn't return to Lincoln Junior High; he never saw him again. He had a vague belief that Coach Rodgers had told the authorities—whoever *they* were—about Charles and he had been moved to a better home, a safer home. But that belief took some time to develop.

Meanwhile, there were other things to cope with: art and wood shop and P.E. and school in general and being thirteen.

* * *

HE HAD CAREFULLY measured and re-measured the pencil
marks, checked and re-checked the settings on the drill press. It
took nearly the entire period to make the four holes in the two
pieces of wood that comprised the bookend. But when he tried
to insert the first screw, the pieces twisted apart at an odd angle
with just a few revolutions. He tried the other set of holes; they
too were terribly out of line. Near panic, he clamped the pieces
into a vise and tried to force the screws to go in straight. It was
futile.

Todd Benjamin had been watching his efforts. Todd—a wide,
cowboy boot kind of boy, the son of a cabinetmaker—had finished the bookend project weeks before, and was now making a
storage case for his eight-track tapes. Todd came over and took
the bookend pieces out of the vise. He held them up to the light
and aligned the screw holes.

"Hey! Numbnuts here has messed things up good!" Todd
tossed the pieces on the worktable and shook his head. Other
students stopped what they were doing and came over to see
the damage. Todd said, "I thought you'd finally get some work
done—now that that nigger's not around to take your tools anymore!" Everyone laughed.

The screwdriver still in his hand, he grabbed Todd Benjamin
and shoved him against a table. Someone's freshly lacquered
bookend tumbled onto the dusty floor. The flat-blade screwdriver was cocked back at ear-level. "Shut up! Shut up!"

Mr. Foley's hand locked around his wrist and he smelled the
sweet stench of cigarettes. "Calm, calm," said the shop teacher,
"calm. . . ."

HE CAUGHT SOMETHING about the rioting on the radio and realized he had missed the report. He crawled out of the car and
tossed the smoking cigarette onto the wet street, where it sizzled

for a moment. The air coming up from the river was damp and cold. His overcoat collar flapped against his neck as he walked up to the small gray house.

He knocked on its battered screendoor and in a moment he was greeted by a petite woman with white hair and skin the color of sand. "I'm Mrs. Mixon, Charles's aunt. Won't you come in." Shre wore a dark-blue dress with square ivory buttons.

He introduced himself and stepped inside. The livingroom was warm and neat, with green shag carpeting and heavy gold-upholstered furniture; framed needle-point adorned the walls. The scent of lemony furniture polish drifted in the air. Beyond the livingroom was a smaller diningroom, where several visitors were standing around talking. On the diningroom table was a white cake, partially served, and a photograph of a handsome young man. His face was a bit fuller but there was the jagged little scar and the familiar gap in his smile.

"Were you a friend of Charles's, Mr. Middleton?" asked his aunt.

He hesitated a moment. "Yes, ma'am. We went to school together."

She led him by the arm to the table, introduced him to each of the guests, then cut him a generous portion of cake. Through the window, he could see a tiny patch of western sky, and it had a distinctive reddish tinge. It was the sun beginning to sink beneath the cloud cover, of course—and not the glow of distant fires, as he first imagined.

Cougars in the Hills

THE FIVE OF THEM, husband and wife in the front seat and the three children packed in the half-seat behind, came in the old truck, a '67 or '8, down the slippery narrow road. Old quilts smelling of hounds and farm cats pressed upon the children. A Navajo blanket, once colorful now faded, formed a hooded cloak about the wife. The truck's engine rumbled steadily but its heater was spent. The husband had neither parts nor money to fix it. As if to punish himself, he refused the old army blanket and left it heaped on the icy seat between him and his wife; and he kept his coveralls half undone even though his wife had replaced the broken, gap-toothed zipper just last Sunday.

The two-lane road wound down, down, down between the dark hills. Falling rain-snow left a glaze that reflected the truck's headlights.

—How're ya doing? asked the wife, her voice partially muted by the blanket. The frozen cloud of her question hung suspended for a moment.

—All right. The husband hated to answer her, believing her only reason for asking was to help him stave off sleep, to keep herself and her children safe. He could no longer feel his feet and toes in their boots; would no longer have any finesse with the brake and clutch if he needed finesse. —All right, he repeated.

The husband had adjusted the rearview mirror so that he

could see his sleeping sons. The road behind didn't matter. No one was traveling it, would not be traveling it for days. The eldest boy, Eugene, twelve, was in the middle. Crumpled on both his shoulders were the twins, Carl and Bobby, seven. With the ridges of quilts, they formed a triangular mountain-shape in the backseat. Eugene's white-blond head was the mountain's snowy peak. The husband thought of skiing, of the virgin snow, of the crystalline pines, of sharp edges, of pathless journeys—always down down down, always faster faster faster. . . .

—Watch . . . !

The buck was there in the headlights, its great rack and underbelly whiter than the falling snow, its glassy black eye reflecting the truck's sudden approach.

The husband had nothing to do. But to hit it.

The jolt tossed the truck to the left, out of control. The right headlight was shattered. Then somehow, with still no brake applied, the truck righted itself and found the next curve, and the next. The husband had tried to see in the rearview mirror, What of the buck?, but the faces of the mountain were suddenly alert and frightened.

—It's all right, said the husband. It was just a deer. We're almost home. He thought of the great buck, injured and broken but probably still alive lying next to the road waiting to die in the new snow. Maybe, once the children were home safely, he could go back, with his Remington, and do right by the animal. . . . But there was no way; even with gravity the road was barely passable. It would be days before they could come up out of the valley. By then the buck would be taken care of, would be a coyote's meal, or a cougar's—there were still a few cougars in the hills. —It's all right, he repeated. We're about home.

The husband pulled the zipper of his coveralls up to his chin and stared hard into the streaks of white illumined by the truck's solitary beam.

Watching Close

MY UNCLE FROM CALIFORNIA spends his two weeks fixing stuff. Last summer it was the toilet and garage door, this summer it's the car and a fan in the attic. Dad can't fix anything, Mom says, that's why she asks Uncle Bob when he comes. He's glad to do it, though he does it all the time in California. Uncle Bob fixes stuff at Disneyland. He says he's good friends with Micky Mouse. I believed him when I was little.

I always help him. He says Screwdriver, just like doctors on T.V. And I slap it in his hand as hard as I can. To fix the car he says Ratchet then Pliers then some other things I don't know. It's fun helping, though it's hot in the driveway. Little rocks stick to Bob's back when he's done. He says Thanks for the help Cap. He's always called me Cap, though my name is Zack. Mom and Dad told me why but I don't remember.

When he visits he doesn't just fix stuff for us. Bob'll go to Aunt Betty's or Sarah's or my other uncle Lee's. I always get to help. Mom says to watch close so I can fix stuff too someday. She says Dad never had nobody to watch.

Two days before going back to California, Grandpa Dale calls Bob from Fort Madison. He's not really my grandpa. He's Bob's wife's dad. I don't really remember Bob's wife my Aunt Rita. I was little when she died. Grandpa Dale's air is out and his house is too hot Bob says when he hangs up. It's a long drive and it's too late to go today. I can't sleep thinking about the trip all the way to Iowa. I remember we cross a big river on a bridge that costs money. I remember sometimes the bridge opens to let big boats go through. I think it's neat but it makes Bob a little mad.

Next day finally. Bob gets me up when it's still dark. We stop for donuts before leaving town. His coffee makes a cloud on the windshield. You can sleep if you want Cap. It's a long drive he says. Maybe I will but wake me up before we get to the bridge. For a while I watch the corn. It's tall and green. Bob says it's been a good year for corn. Then I do sleep.

When I wake up we're stopped and I think Bob forgot. But it's just that the bridge is open and lots of people are waiting. Below the road I see a long boat going by. I want to get out to see better but I know Bob won't let me. It takes a long time for the boat to leave and the bridge to go back together. It's hot in the car and I think I know why Bob gets mad.

Over the water and it's brown. Not blue like pictures.

I forgot Grandpa Dale has a carport. We have a garage. It's good to get out of the car. My shirt and pants are sweaty and I hope Grandpa Dale has a sodapop. Bob tries the side door. It's locked. Dale! Let us in. I have to pee. Wait here says Bob and he goes around front. I hear the buzz inside one two three times. Bob comes back. His face looks funny. Kind of like when he was waiting for the bridge. He goes to the back of the house. I hear him calling Dale!

Then he's running to the car. He gets a wrench from the trunk. Watch out Cap. He breaks the glass in the side door and unlocks it. I follow him inside. The broken glass feels like the little rocks in the driveway. Up steps. In the kitchen. Down the hall. There's a smell like when Bob fixed the toilet cause stuff wouldn't go down anymore. I see in Dale's bedroom. Grandpa Dale is in bed. Bob's pulled back the covers. Dale's face is the color of the sheet. Gray. Bob is hitting him in the chest then blowing in his mouth. I think he's going to say Hammer or Air Hose but it's like he forgot I was there. I'm glad cause I don't want him to see me crying like a little kid.

He stops and pulls the covers over Dale's head.

Bob doesn't go back to Disneyland the next day. He stays for the funeral which I don't go to.

Keep an eye on your folks Cap until I come back Bob says to me at the airport. It's hard to hear cause of the big planes. We wait for his to go. Mom tells me to wave like I always do but I don't feel like waving. I feel like crying again but I don't know why.

Laertes Sonnet Sequence

Shroud

Your left-behind clothes still occupy closets and
clotheslines in the basement. She refuses to
donate them away, insisting that family may want
them (implying *should* want them). But it feels like
clothing oneself in Laertes' shroud, where an un-
finished thread may hang exposed, left incomplete
by clever Penelope, who wove and unwove to
keep the suitors at bay, to halt time, delay the fated.
Just as she is doing now, to stay the complete-
ness of your death, leave the final act unfulfilled,
a thread left unfixed. Clothes hang here, are folded
there, frozen, amplifying your absence more than
the framed photos on the walls, as she awaits your
sail, white on the horizon: gift of beneficent gods.

Pilgrim

I grasped your absence, the sudden
ceasing of a strong breeze,
a winter and a spring and a thickening
summer later—before the home of
a poet, long dead, who calls visitors
from afar. Small in number but devoted
to their pilgrimage and their modest
homage to his Gospel of Beauty.
It unsteadied me for a moment, like
a blind blow to the knees: You would
call no more. Your plain and quiet voice
of reason would call no more. I looked
toward the poet's home, where pilgrims
entered seeking something lingering still.

Seedlings

The old bungalow's basement was as low-
ceilinged as the catacombs, and equally
enclosed—a crypt to cause claustrophobia.
It was here you cared for your seeds throughout the dark winter: flowers to be trans-
planted to your garden in the spring, once
the fear of frost had passed. The green
stalks soon would show the promise of color.
Such care you'd given us during the years
you had no time for gardening, when there
were greater things to fear than a late frost,
like hastening your sons into a hostile world.
Marking our growth required more patience
than a cramped basement could hold.

Ingots

Entangled in the book's enthralling world, you
lay upon your bed reading a mystery, eye-
glasses angled on the end of your nose. You
beatified both the reader and the read—modeling
the peaceful joy of quiet contemplation, of vast
exploration while perfectly at rest. I watched from
the doorway, not wishing to interrupt, neither your
wonderment nor mine: witness to a sacred act.
I read my rhyming books, not yet ready for
the stories of yours but already eager to be
both sender and receiver of the page-borne magic,
a spinner of spells as well as the spellbound soul
wound in the works. You lauded my first novel
and offered ideas for sequels: ingots of gold.

Obsolescence

License plates from vehicles long gone
hung in the garage on a rusted nail—
each year a different color, the oldest encased
in cobwebs, suggesting you never took them
down to sort through memories of whatever cars
and road trips they may evoke. Whatever carefree
conversations and long pealing laughs caught
between the plates. Whatever bachelor dreams.
Whatever life was before we came along.
Perhaps your keeping the plates wasn't about
remembering but rather about declaring their
obsolescence, and that of the life you left,
like an old road left off a newly printed map,
like an old map crumpled beneath the seat.

Argonaut

The rumbling roll of the press, the saturating
smell of ink. Floors vibrated, hung pictures
quaked. It felt like being aboard a great
machine taking flight, or barreling down
a track to adventures unknown. And in my
child's view you were a captain of this
wondrous craft—you of the gray steel desk
in a room once removed from the chaos.
Your panoply: scissors, rulers, rubber cement.
You transferred your love of the place—
this thrumming world of the word—into
me more thoroughly than by transfusion.
Ink blood, skin print, circulation circulation.
Your gift of a trajectory still ascending.

Awakening

In retirement you first took up flowers.
Then later the rose arrested your attention.
Not quite an obsession but still a preoccupation,
a buzzing in your ear, like a height-of-summer
bee who hovers, hovers at the stamen.
The bloomless vines grew wild, entwining
the homemade trellis, birthing only thorns.
They reached out like amorous assailants.
Undeterred, you planned and pruned,
Prepped and pared, powdered and prayed,
sprinkled and sprayed. Long winters musing
over books borrowed from distant libraries.
Then one summer came a single white head,
blushing at the bees' overzealous coronation.

Galaxie

Long after you were gone she accused you
of infidelity, alleging an affair that seemed
surely a product of confused recollections,
slippage, years of bitter loneliness—the
ultimate abandonment: running off with
death for parts unknown, no phone calls,
no letters on cheap motel stationery,
not even an apologetic picture postcard.
But your eldest dimly recalls frightening
words followed by a scarier icy silence
due to a woman's shoe found beneath
the Galaxie's broad seat: only a hint, then
as now, of a life and a need unknown—like
an isolated planet in an uncharted system.

Symmetry

I don't recall how the tradition began, whose
idea it was, yours or mine—the quest to buy
the most misshapen Christmas tree in town,
searching lot after lot—scratchy carols piped
over the PA systems—until we located truly
the least lovable pine. We'd bring it home to
be weighed down with mismatched baubles,
further distorting its already far-from-perfect form.
But we pretended we chose it for its beauty,
its beau-ideal symmetry—and everyone's
boisterous needling was part of the annual play.
Wintry fall morning—
year closing like a sad-ending
book

Acts

You answered William's most profound question
the moment you received the prognosis: not
to be. An act of generosity in keeping with the
way you lived your life, to spare us the
travails of a lingering demise, a pointlessly pro-
tracted last act—weeks of emotional wreckage
to weigh and sift after heartwrenching hospice.
Catastrophe. In every sense, with no curtain call.
The question settled, you cast off the nighted color
for a more fitting role, Yorick, jesting with the
nurses who measured your dramatic decline
until you were insensible then done, five days,
like five acts, from diagnosis to death.
I find myself asking, Did I know you well?

Mass

You and your brother were Catholic School boys,
which meant daily mass—in the ways of the
Romans, who crucified Christ. You didn't care
for the sixties' reforms, the new rituals felt
cold and common, the Body and Blood re-
duced to mere wafer and wine. You missed the
magical Latin as Father intoned the Mystery
and you carefully incanted in enigmatic kind.
The hospital's chaplain, visiting from Africa,
recited in his high-rounded Rwandan lilt:
last rites for you and the cancer in your brain,
for the mass that had colonized every organ,
like a crusading religion on the march, hell-
bent on spreading the Word everywhere.

Dignity

The gray suit was pricey, three pieces of fine wool,
more expensive than any apparel you wore in
life. Polyesters and permapress for decades, even
a pocket protector—costume of the advertising man.
Small-town newspaper, far cry from NYC ad-men.
But this suit, purchased and tailored in your
retirement, went straight from store to closet,
to be kept in its garment bag until needed:
That most solemn of occasions, part of the program
so conscientiously pre-planned. Private service, modest
casket, no pomp, no pathos, no eulogy. A cold day for
early autumn, austere, bitter winter in the biting wind.
The final image: metaphor for a life lived in quiet dignity . . .
husband, father, friend, son, brother in impeccable gray.

Ted Morrissey's novel excerpts, stories, poems, critical articles, reviews, and translations have appeared in more than one hundred publications. His award-winning novels include *Crowsong for the Stricken*, *Mrs Saville*, and *The Artist Spoke*. Retired from full-time teaching, he is a lecturer in Lindenwood University's MFA in Writing program and continues to work as a librarian. A Ph.D. in English studies, his scholarly interests tend to be divided between the work of William H. Gass and the Old English poem *Beowulf*. He and his wife live near Springfield, Illinois, with their rescue dogs and about a thousand books. Visit tedmorrissey.com and his various social media accounts.